ICARUS

CHRIS TURNER

Cover Art: Battlemage

Published by Innersky Books
www.innersky.ca

ISBN-13: 978-1-927117-99-6

CONTENTS

1 : Maps   5

2 : Icarus   7

3 : Historical   247
Note

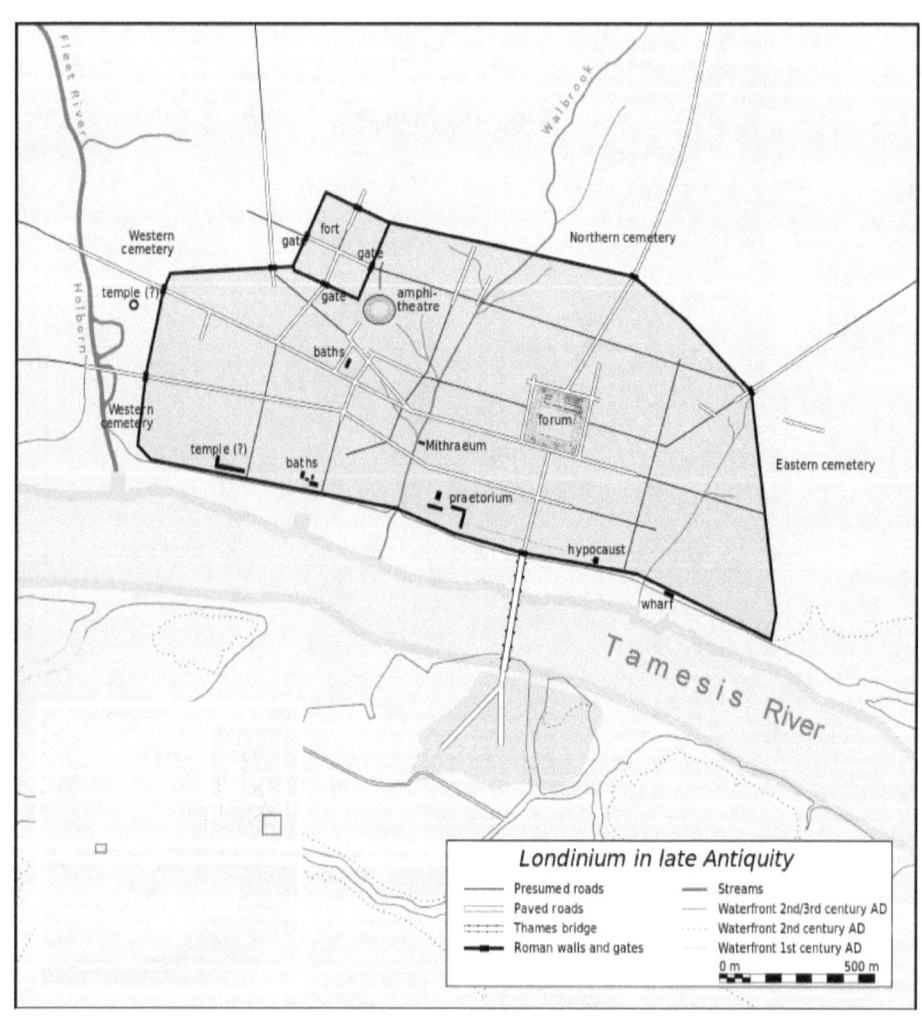

Londinium in late Antiquity

Western cemetery

fort

gate

gate

gate

Northern cemetery

temple (?)

Holborn

amphi-theatre

baths

Western cemetery

forum

temple (?)

baths

Mithraeum

praetorium

hypocaust

wharf

Eastern cemetery

Fleet River

Walbrook

Tamesis River

Londinium in late Antiquity

— Presumed roads
  Paved roads
  Thames bridge
— Roman walls and gates

— Streams
  Waterfront 2nd/3rd century AD
  Waterfront 2nd century AD
  Waterfront 1st century AD

0 m   500 m

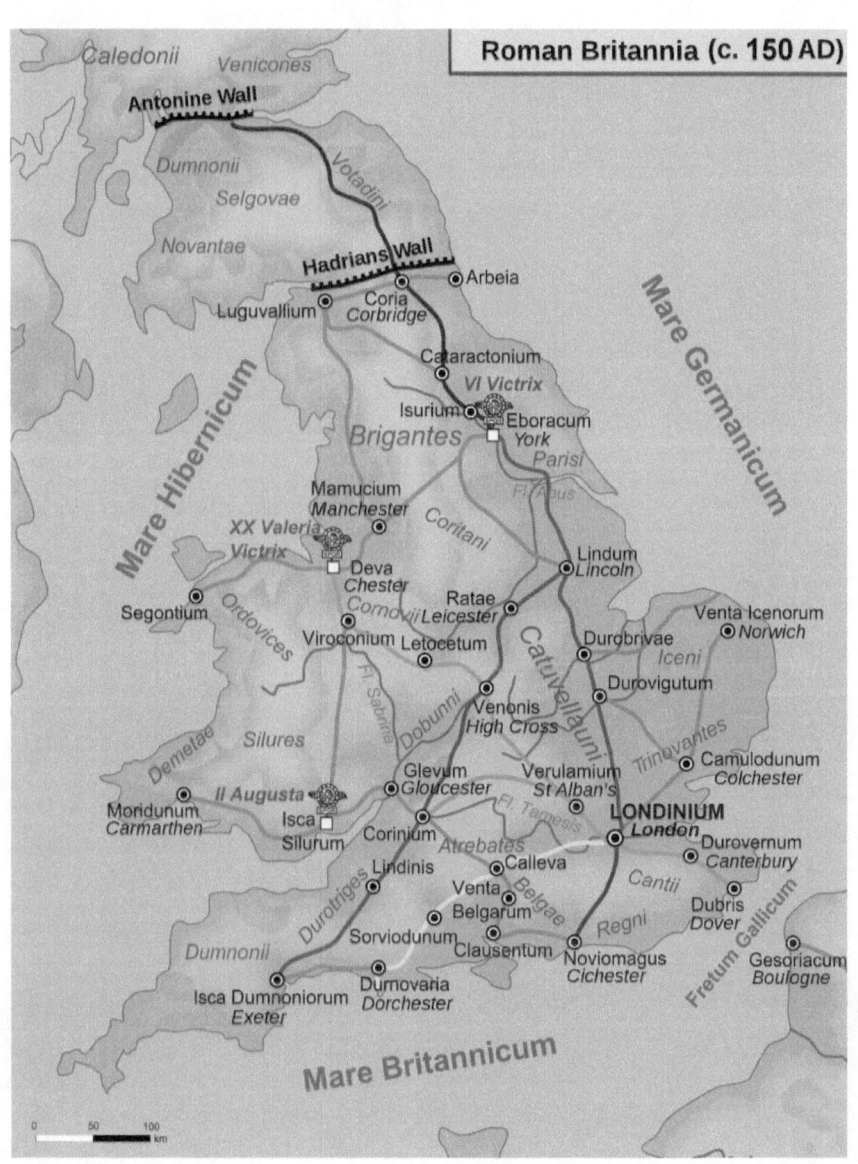

Roman Britannia (c. 150 AD)

CHRIS TURNER

6

ICARUS

Man, when perfected, is the best of animals, but when separated from law and justice, he is the worst of all.
—Aristotle

Chapter 1

Because he flew too close to the sun...Icarus, a youth who not only didn't follow orders, but also misused his father's magic. He fell into the sea and drowned. I was determined not to be such an Icarus. *Yet is fate something that a mortal man can dodge?*

Such questions became ever more difficult to answer.

Our little quintet had perfected the art of combat with our clubs. A heavier weapon than a gladius, good for bone bashing, skull clipping, killing if necessary. All the more crucial to catch every strike and counter it with something extra.

We pulled leather hoods about our heads, fitted animal masks on our faces. We attached stunted devil wings crafted of wood and red cloth to our shoulders, to stir superstitious fear, as if we could fly like Hermes into the sky should anyone try to catch us. The *Devil Clubs* they called us.

Soldiers became our worst enemy. We despised them; they hated us. They weren't used to fighting against clubs of rough-cut oak, so we had an advantage—somewhat, before they could swarm us in numbers. The club had a slightly longer reach so we could repel the *skugs*, the defenders of Londinium—if we were fast.

Londinium, a rough provincial town in Roman Britannia, waxed ever full of unpleasant surprises generated by brigands and drunken soldiers drifting from the popular taverns. Lawless no less than the prefects who turned a blind eye to the soldiers' antics. The Via Valia down which we trudged remained lit only by a single torch above a seedy brothel far down the way. Apartments above the shops remained dark as tombs, not a peep intruding upon our space. The occupants had learned to shutter their windows and block out the cries of an unfortunate victim walking the street in the dead of night. The clink of spear, the slither of sword, the thwack of a mallet on flesh—all numbered as common sounds in these parts, violence spawned in the moment.

A muffled shriek shattered the silence of the night. "Mercy to the House of Mexor Salvius Veditio!" cried a voice.

I peered ahead to see three figures hurling a bundled body up in the air. From the desperate tone and the name shrilled at this late hour I guessed it could only be one of my father's slaves, Denetio, wrapped in that blanket. Tonight he'd become victim of three drunken soldiers giving an innocent slave the old 'upsey-downsey'. Grab a freedman or slave, roll him up in a thick blanket and toss him in the air till he was frightened half to death, begging for mercy like a baby. The old game of *sagatio*. Such an innocent hardly knew whether his aggressors would let him fall on the stones and crack his skull open or let him live. Tonight, it seemed they had wrapped the damp wool too tightly and he could hardly breathe.

They'd gone a step too far.

We charged them, our clubs spinning and howls spilling from our lips. They turned in surprise at the sound amplified by our masks, almost dropping their quarry on the way down. Thrusting Denetio aside like a bale of straw, they moved in with swords. Our comrade Marcellus hopped around in a circle and hollered—he'd drunk a little too much to be very effective. But Regalis, Feberiax, Oren and I had not, and we set on them with a vengeance in an area where the street widened into a square. We batted them with our clubs; we kicked with our hobnailed boots. Five on three, unfair odds, but when was this world ever fair?

A blade slipped off my trusty club. I whipped around and lashed out with my boot, whirled again and brought the wood down on the soldier's left shoulder. He cried out, clutching his arm. Regalis ducked under a thrust and cracked the second soldier in the thigh. Feberiax and Oren baited and badgered the third man, showing little mercy. To and fro they darted in rhythmic dance.

My opponent began to get spooked. He cursed, unused to the ferocious and uncanny way I handled that club, a painted, masked devil in black and red. I parried his flashing blade, struck out at the padded leather around his ribs. He grunted and swore but let his guard down. Dracian—bless my brother's soul—had trained us well.

"You're taking the blow too high on the wood, little brother. Going to mash your fingers. Here, let me show you." In my mind's eye, Drace stepped behind me, grasped my club and hand in his, worked with me while Regalis, my sparring partner, came at me like the wind. My lanky, sinewy brother moved faster.

Whoosh. A quick in-step, a pull back with body and momentum, and our combined blow grazed Regalis on the hip, knocking him aside. My brother's leg lifted up to send him on his way to the turf.

Such a move I never forgot...

My bearded opponent's blade missed by a hair but his fist thwacked me hard across the mouth, bringing my reverie to an end. I shook out the daze and twirled back like a dancer. I swung out with a glancing blow which sent him leaping back with a howl.

"Such theatrics, Ick. For the love of Hades, get it over with!" Marcellus crowded close, club on the rise. His lean-muscled frame arched in. Down his weapon crashed upon the soldier's back.

The grog-breathed soldier took a sudden dive and fell motionless.

Shaking my head, I wiped my bloodied lip. I lifted myself from my senseless victim. Muttering curses, I scrambled over to disentangle Denetio from the blanket. He looked a sorry mess, staring wildly and gibbering like a child. He thanked me through his tears and I warned him to silence as we sped off into the night down the urine-scented alley, leaving three moaning soldiers twitching on the rain-damp paves. They'd think twice about doing the old upsey-downsey with any slaves of ours.

I thought my ruggies would razz me about my lapse in concentration. Did they think me losing my edge? They were as shaken as me, keen to get out of that place. One bit of carelessness and it would be all over for our *skundering*. Perhaps that's what ate at my gut. My number one pastime over. Finished.

Drace's tragic demise taught us not to rough up the soldiers too much. A dead soldier was a much bigger deal than some head-bashing and a few graffiti scrawls on a merchant's stall. Ten to one these three'd tuck tail and take their losses rather than complain to their superiors, and lose face at how they got sacked by a few kids:

"How'd you get that bruise on your face, soldier?"

"Nasty spill, centurion. That'll teach me for getting soused at the tavern."
"Well, see that it doesn't happen again."

The flashbacks of Drace worried me. More and more I'd been having them of late. As if something in my inner core struggled to tell me something. But, young and headstrong, taller than most, all hundred and eighty pounds of me came with a chip on my shoulder as long as a fort's shadow.

A dog barked; another snarled. One of the mastiff breed, the hunting hounds of the Britons. I shivered. That couldn't be good.

A torch winked on in an upper story to my left. A deep-throated hound barked farther down the street, sporadic growls, followed by men's voices, echoing up the murky streets.

Auscles and his muscle men of the town watch would be out patrolling this quarter since it fringed the domain of the well-to-do.

Still we prowled the streets of Londinium like wolves, looking for more trouble. Known about town more formally as *The Clubs of Londinium*, some called us the *Vandal Hoods*. Marcellus, Regalis, Feberiax, Oren and I, just the five of us. We used to be seven, now two had passed. I, the youngest of the lot, was no less keen or able. The governor, Quintus Pompeius Falco, had been the newest recruit to clean up this town. Decreed by Emperor Hadrian to make Londinium more presentable to merchants, provincial visitors and the citizenry at large in a five year plan. Good luck with that, Falco.

Depraved youngsters they called us, *'nequissimi adulescentuli'*, nothing but glorified hellraisers and vandals. I think of us more as equalizers. With our clubs, masks and our devil's garb, we appeared invincible, a force to be reckoned with. We enhanced this image by hacking at and vandalizing temples. The baddest boys in Londinium! No one could name us. Tradesmen's and statesmen's sons by day, holy terrors and ghosts by nightfall, thumbing our noses at the establishment.

I tugged at the beak on my eagle's mask. My peers had similar masks to hide their identity: a Celtic horned bull for Feberiax, grey ape for Marcellus, an owl for Oren, a hell-hound for Regalis. Sweat poured down my cheeks; some pooled where the mask rested on the bridge of my nose. My hot breath reflected off the painted wood, bathing my cheeks in a thicker sheen of sweat. From the two knot-holes of the mask, I looked out upon the scene of Via Valia, that narrow corridor of street and sidewalk, snaking between multi-storied apartments that wound down into darkness toward the stinking port.

My nose lay crooked from so many fights. Hadn't set right after the last two hits. Made me look a bit peculiar, earning such nicknames as crooksnout and flatface. The slight curve of nose, oddly, added to my mystique, if the sly comments of the slave girls in my father's household were to be believed.

I'd fallen behind again, with Denetio, our Briton slave, in tow.

Regalis called over his shoulder. "Snap out of it, Eagle. What's up with you?"

I shook my head. The wine combined with the flashbacks were playing havoc on my brain. Or maybe it wasn't, and maybe the universe was sending me another signal. Something deep inside.

With a vigorous shake of my head, I grunted a few careless words and waved off Regalis. Denetio I sent on his way back to my father's villa. He alone of our household off Via Decus knew of my secret identity. I told him not to utter a word to my father of our escapades. We set off to scale the east wall and over to the cemetery to train, then indulge in more revelries. The night was still young...

* * *

We Romans kept our places of burial outside the city. We did not lay our dead to rest too far distant from the living, careful not to offend the spirits. Just on the other side of the wall to prevent any hauntings. Crouching by the interior city rampart, I retrieved the grapple hook and hempen rope concealed under a moldering sack in a niche where the stone had crumbled. I swung it over the top edge and we scaled the wall, plunging out over the dry ditch. We followed a faint trail that led off into the shadows bounded by low shrubs and thickets toward the Eastern Cemetery.

We'd picked a place on the wall least noticeable, a place between the north-east gate and the river. Though we resided miles from the garrison abreast the west gate, caution still guided our movements. Who knew when a patrol might decide to scout the perimeter.

In this cemetery we practiced our battlecraft under the dim light of torches set on the architrave of the Medecias's family vault. If ever we heard voices or footfall coming our way, we snuffed out our lamps and beetled away to hide in the shadows. When the sounds dimmed, we resumed our sport. Our fame had reached ears far and wide, but we had to be careful with patrols looking for us. We threaded our way back to our refuge warily, staggered our training schedule to avoid any set pattern.

We sparred with each other like enemies. This I remember from a young age, crouching there with my club, breathing ragged gasps, our silhouettes stretched like giants across the grassy yard flanking the stone pathways. We promised deviltry of every kind, an eviler kind still. Maybe we got energy from those dead souls buried there under the ground. We blocked and we struck; we lunged at each other fast and loose amongst the low tombstones, in and out, huffing like stallions, feinting, drawing each other out with curses and laughs until one of us was awarded a hit and gained a point. We tallied such points and our fierce competition kept us sharp. We wore a layered nest of leather padding under our regular garb. We complemented it with old helmets that Drace and Oren had dug out of the ground on some night errand, from places where soldiers he knew had been buried. For our added protection, we donned such gear in case one of us should get a little too spry or eager, like Marcellus was wont.

My brother's words came clear and true in my ear. *"A sword is for stabbing and slashing. A club is better for beating and a quick close-quarter brawl. An intimidator. Like the early inhabitants of Britannia had. When they used to smash in the head of their neighbor, they knew their business."* He'd shown me his dog-eared grin with that slick cowl of black hair swept over his high forehead, and I would grin back at him, worshipping him as if Mars himself. Me, a naive boy, who had yet to get his ass kicked.

But club or fist, or hobnailed boot, we had something going. Our own style of roughing-up and pommeling. Pounce and beat in a surprise attack. Hit an enemy and melt back into the shadows. Take out the knees, do the braining after, if they weren't already crying for mercy. A chest hit would do, but knee, neck and head were better targets.

And so, there we gathered, hunched in the dark like night toads in the cemetery, with almost a post-coital low now that the thrill was over, even though the pickings had been slim that night.

"The reality is," said Marcellus, "Drace is dead. So is Aurelius. Now we have to pick a new leader." He heaved a theatrical sigh, leaning back against one of the weathered grave markers. "Unless you want the Clubs of Londinium to die?" He flashed me a pointed look.

"The hell I do." My fists bunched at the mention of Drace's death. I rose to my feet.

"Good, then let's pick one. Me or you."

The words hung hollowly in the air, as if it were pure blasphemy to suggest that any other ruggie except Drace could lead us.

Regalis, ever faithful to my cause, held up a thumb and nodded in my direction. Feberiax made a sign for Marcellus.

All eyes turned to Oren, the surly Thracian. He frowned, shifting nervously in the damp grass. "I'd say both of you."

"What kind of answer is that?" Marcellus cried. "You're wishy-washy, Oren." He glared, as if expecting the Thracian to change his vote.

"It's the best you'll get." Oren sneered. "Take it or leave it. I don't want to be the one to split up the band. I can always bid for Icarus."

"We both lead then," said Marcellus, sounding somewhat put out. "Up, you stinking laggards. Time for us to do some more training."

"No mercy to soldiers," I spat. "None. They did Drace wrong. We train as if it's an all-out war." I'd never forgotten the promise I'd made to Drace. That I'd avenge his death. That I'd keep up the tradition of what he'd started.

"War to the bastards," echoed Marcellus. He picked up on the energy of my violent stirrings and roused the others. I could see his grin grow as if he were the cherub Cupid, and he'd won the day. Crafty Marcellus, deflecting the awkwardness of the vote.

"We confirm it in blood," he said. We each drew a knife's edge across our forearm and touched our crimson wounds to another. It signified we were blood brothers, brothers of The Devil Clubs.

Oren was the stoutest of us all, a square-jowled hawk-eyed brute at sixteen, a mix of Thracian and northern barbarian, maybe Dacian, prematurely balding even at his young age. A shock of short red brown hair covered the top of his head down to his squirrel-like ears. Feberiax, tallest of our gang, thin, lean and fast, a born ballbuster with his smug, two-toothed grin, rose three inches over Oren. A confirmed thug with long sandy hair like his parents, pure Britons to the core. Marcellus boasted a stringy mop of black hair, sparkling green-eyes. Easily the slyest and most outspoken of us, a natural leader, but a bit too crazy for my tastes. A rogue who'd earned the resentment of all of us at one time or other. Regalis, with his charming good looks, the sanest and most level-headed of us, remained perhaps my best friend, his father Roman, his mother a Celt from Corinium.

I, on the other hand, dark-eyed and flaxen-haired, an odd combination. My father had bedded a tall barbarian from one of the windswept lands, one of the ice maidens from the places north of Gallia, and produced me. I stood proud of my heritage, being a somewhat mongrel breed, but a good breed, good blood, better than pure Roman. Why my father had come back to collect me, I didn't know. A whim? No matter. I'd found my place here. All of us boasted good physical condition. We could run all night, we could swing clubs and bash heads even after several rounds of wenching and our bellies full of ale.

Lo and behold, when we drew straws for who would spar with whom, 'twas me paired with Feberiax, Oren with Marcellus and Regalis to sit out the first round and fight the winner.

"Well, a sore irony that is," Marcellus said in a resigned voice. "Ready your club, Oren. Seems as if we have a bone to pick." We set aside our totemic masks and donned our old crusted helms and extra padding.

Out of the corner of my eye I watched Oren's fight while I parried Feberiax's advances, earning some hits to the thigh and growing bruises when my attention wandered.

Marcellus's swing went a little too close to the mark and heavy-clipped Oren's padded shoulder.

"Mad bastard! Get away," croaked Oren. "That was uncalled for."

"Sorry, there, Orey. Don't get ornery. Just a little play gone wild. A little slip happens from time to time."

"And maybe I should swing closer to your neck too? Seems you sat back in that last fight with our soldier friends and let Icarus take most of the heat."

Marcellus shrugged. He gave a sour smile. "All in a night's fun, Orey. Don't get sore."

While Oren grumbled and griped, they circled each other again. He took up his club in a firm fist and Marcellus crouched and moved on the balls of his feet, ever more confident, chirping at Oren once again for the last sour remark that had lost him some face. Oren slammed in for two hits of his own, prompting Marcellus to hold up a hand in defeat. "Okay, enough, I've had too much ale. You win, Oren."

"What?" hissed Oren. "This from the one who's been pestering us to spar, spar, spar? You filthy hypocrite." He laughed. "Think I'll vote for Icarus then."

"The hell you will!" growled Marcellus. He charged forward and they were at it again. So they gnashed and rolled on the ground, scrapping like dogs until each lost their clubs, leaving the rest of us in stitches. Oren and Marcellus finally called it a draw, both of them huffing and puffing, sweating and cursing.

We practiced for another hour before we all lay exhausted on the grass under the flicker of our torches. The land sloped down from the distant cobbled street and the vault house hid their glow from any passing eyes. I opened a wine amphora I'd brought from my father's stores and deposited in the cooler ground earlier. "A little refresher for our efforts."

The rebelliousness in our adolescent hearts I equated to the unrest that still festered among the native Britons here in the hinterland, the westernmost point of the empire. *Pax Romana* weighed on us like a stone, the imperial policy governing the provinces—the defiant Queen Boudicca and her Iceni tribe and King Caratacus and his Catuvellaunians, now distant memories. Like them, we entertained a desire to take a bite at the establishment, like a rat on the hide of dead cat. A worse threat, of course, the bully-boy savages gnawing their way south from Pictland, the barren highlands, raiding across the northern frontier, rather than the rebellious, freedom-seeking Celts in this rainy land of Britannia who prayed to their pagan gods for the departure of the Roman conquerors.

I snuffed out the light with these pieces of trivia floating in my brain, and amidst the sputtering of oil and wafts of blue smoke, we lay down to catch a few winks before the dawn's breaking light.

Chapter 2

In my restless sleep, a strange music came to my ears...whether in dream or waking I could not tell, nor whether a woman sang that song, so fey drifted her voice.

My eyes fluttered open. I grew increasingly amazed for the melody persisted:

Ni Canir Ferçadlw Ab Fustos Illis Weuntg,
Voxbis Aqeron Illis Weuntg!

One wish to stir the heart of desire,
Then Maig's spell setting wood to fire!

To my astonishment, a flicker of flame came to life in the dark spaces between the gravestones—a torch of sorts, illuminating a fair, but mud-smeared face. The owner, a slender figure, feet playing upon the dewed grass and stone grave markers, approached in the pale moonlight. The pommel of her torch, a bulb of wicker, held several red stones that rattled when she moved.

The other ruggies stirred and crouched, blinking at the apparition. A rustle ensued among our group as hands groped for clubs.

Oren bent to light our torch and the figure stopped short, a dozen feet from where we huddled.

She held herself erect and stared in curiosity at us rather than fear. Rags and furs clung to her slim figure; a stoat hide, head and all, ringed about her shoulders. Her eyes blazed a fiery blue and were much beguiling. I circled to the side and saw her raven hair hung in wavy curls down to the small of her back and would trail longer if not for the adornments fastened therein.

Marcellus huffed a soft sound, rising to his feet. "Well, if it isn't a fancy piece of ass calling at our den. Don't you know this is a private club?"

Feberiax gave a growl of appreciation. "Looking fair enough, Marcy. We could have ourselves some sport before cockcrow."

"Aye, Feb, we could." He sauntered forward, patting his club with a palm, nodding at her wolf's hide figure. He halted, sniffing at the air. "Ouch. On second thought, Feb, this morsel seems tainted. Smells like— well, I'd rather not say." He turned his nose away.

"Back, you animals!" she cried, her eyes glinting and torch rising in a clenched hand.

Indeed I smelled her foul reek: unwashed body, sweat and fur and something sourer still. Regalis gaped at my side, blinking, wiping the sleep from his eyes.

Oren leaned on Feberiax's shoulder, yawning.

"Whence came you?" I demanded, thinking it odd to see anyone in the cemetery after midnight.

"Caerdyg."

"Never heard of it," grunted Regalis.

"No doubt. 'Tis the old name of a Celtic village on the way to your Roman town Durovernum."

"And what business have you here?" inquired Marcellus.

"I could ask you the same thing."

Oren laughed. "A feisty one, Marcy. I don't know about you, but I might get over her stink." He made motions to step closer, but she raised the staff and spat.

"Back to your ale trough like pigs at the swill. Take an innocent woman by force, would you?"

"Now you were the one who said that, not us," quipped Marcellus.

"And what are you but a bunch of petty vandals and rogues?"

"You know, you're tossing some very insulting words for an innocent girlie," he warned. "One ragged female against the five of us? Seems a bit farfetched. What do you say, Feb? Shall we have some sport with this one?" And he, Oren and Feberiax circled the woman, drawing ever closer.

Her eyes grew baleful; she drew herself up to her full height, as a giant might face off with a taller foe still.

"Settle down, Marcy," I cautioned. "Are you that drunk?"

"Relax, Ick. You're far too sentimental. Just going to spar with her a bit."

The others ignored me. I readied my club to jump in if things got messy. She shook the menacing torch with the colored stones and its rattlesnake echo careened about the tombstones. Feberiax slipped on the damp grass and fell hard on his ass. Marcellus's club seemed to jerk out of his hand and whack him on the side of the head. He swung about. "What's this? Some hocus-pocus?"

The rattling sound entranced our ears. Oren surged in to grab her about the waist, tossing aside his club, but she flung him off and thrust out her weapon, landing a thud on his side. He scrambled for his club in time to deflect her next strike. They sparred as two gladiators might, jousting and stabbing. Crack! She spoke a word. The tip of his club twinkled in flame. His eyes rounded in alarm. He threw his weapon down as if it were an ensorcelled thing. "Rotten witch. What sorcery is this?"

We gazed at the fallen club, but the light had winked out; one would never know that it had ever been on fire. No smell of smoke, no char marks. But her torch-and-red-stoned staff still burned as brightly as ever and her calm and steady eyes gazed at us without blinking.

"Tricks, my ruggies, tricks!" cried Marcellus. "Only foul deceptions to fool our minds!"

But the three of them—Marcellus, Oren and Feberiax—made no further move on her. Regalis and I were the only ones who had stayed our ground and didn't end up looking like fools.

Oren sheepishly retrieved his club, checking it for any damage or magical tampering.

So, a crazy old druidess in the cemetery. A strange bird who held a magic stick in her hands, the tops of her hair tied in bits of bone and baked mud, her hide smelling less rosy than the hogs in the yard.

Her voice rose stern and ominous. "This land is sacred, wrested from us Celts by you Romans. It used to house our dead who once rested in peace with the gods. Now you defile it, playing with your hickory sticks on our hallowed land, letting rude sounds slip from your lips, blaspheming the spirits of the dead and the ancient gods."

Sniggers came from Oren and Feberiax. Regalis and I stared in surprise at this enigma.

"Disrespectful rabble. How long will it take you to learn the evils of your ways?" She peered around our group. When her eyes settled on me, the look chilled my blood. "Sure as rain you'll be taken away in chains. Pleasant bashings to you. I hope you all die happily."

"Be gone with you, woman," bellowed Marcellus. "Take your smelly hide and witch sticks with you." He lobbed a clod of earth at her.

Feberiax started forward. He jerked back at the last minute. "Boo!" he cried.

She spat like an alley cat and took a swipe with nails as long as any badger.

Regalis and I murmured dark words. Oren and Marcellus stooped to take great swigs from their clay bowls and belched. Oren, in his adolescent clumsiness, trod on Marcellus's foot. Then they began scrapping again.

She shook her head in disgust and turned and walked away.

The Romans hated the druids and chased them out of every town they conquered. Likely that's what had befallen her, chased from Londinium. As much as she horrified me, this brazen mystic with her mud-caked face, barn-dung scent, and weird creeping around cemeteries late at night, I felt a certain sympathy for her. Where would she go? What would she live on?

While the others grumbled and sneered and lay back to rest, I went to relieve myself. In an odd moment, a strange compulsion came over me. I took a sampling of our best wine and hurried after her.

Within six paces, I halted and uttered a breathless word. "Drink."

She paused in mid step. She snatched at the bowl and raised it to her lips. "At least an old druidess will not go thirsty tonight."

I kept my distance, wary of her tricks. Any fool could see she was not without means. It paid to tread carefully around that which one did not understand. Curiosity got the better of me. "Why come here?"

She took a breath, as if reluctant to answer. "One of my ancestors was buried in that barrow hill over there—" she pointed a slender finger to a moonlit mound "—the mistress of our lineage, Glorifeliax. Her spirit—a restless spirit wanders far. I come thrice a year to this place to try to ease her way. Never thought to stumble on others here in the middle of the night."

"Nor did we. You've not explained why your ancestor's denied access to your spirit world."

She paused, a scowl tainting her face. "There was once a Celtic chieftain who desired her. Borealis was his name. She defied him, being a powerful priestess of the Cult of Morrigan. He wanted her for her magic—to aid in his conquests of the rivaling tribes. He chained her to a post in his yard, until she would repent, become his willing slave, and pray for his victories, have his children. She would not give him any of these and she died in captivity. The chief wept, as Glorifeliax was fair and more stirring than any, but the damage had been done. She had cursed his name while she was alive, and the names of all his children and their offspring."

"You're full of evil tales, woman," I grumbled. Despite my expression, a cold shiver ran up my arm.

"'Twas you who asked."

"You say you come from Caerdyg." I frowned. "What manner of place is that?"

"A village where all the clans come to sing and dance in the forest glade at night. We sow wheat, raise sheep and hogs, also make wool, the finest in the land. We feast on the spoils of the hunt, the stag, the boar, and we dance around our hearty fires, high and true, roaring towers they are, singing our old songs that none but us can remember. We wear mistletoe and oak twigs in our hair and give offerings to the wood spirits and the horned gods. Caerdyg is a place where the maids are fair as dawn, and the young men are proud of their land and go with their kindred on the hunt and seek new adventures. 'Tis a place you'll not likely know, young hood. A merry place, made less merry by the marching feet of your helmed soldiers."

I made a curt sound. "Certainly a place more wholesome than the dockside taverns of Londinium. But maybe a bit too pure for my tastes." I turned back to join the others.

"Wait," she called, studying my face. "Want your bowl back? What's your name?"

"Icarus."

"A bully boy, yes, that much is evident. But rare, not like the others. You're the most thoughtful of the lot. You'll be needing some magical guidance in the near future, prayers at least—but I fear you'll face the worst. Were I a priestess, I'd make a charm for you, something to tether your soul so you don't fly into the sun. But alas, that I am not. Best to quit this rough gang of yours, devote yourself to good service. Perhaps you can redeem yourself."

I gusted a laugh. "That's a funny thought, woman. One I'll save for a rainy day."

"Listen to me, boy! Maig has more years on you than you think. Not much will you get past her, but by the blood of Bel, you're on a road to trouble. I've seen much of this world. Our land raped by invaders who build monstrosities of stone and wood and carve limestone pathways through the glens to every settlement, disturbing the natural order. Men who chase us from our glades and our brooks and our fields and kill our leaders and burn our shrines and defile our gods and groves. We suffer, we endure. It's happened in times before, it will happen in times to come."

I shrugged and sighed. "'Tis an evil world where progress has no patience."

"Pah. I'd like to scrub that tongue of yours with wire brush dipped in lye."

Her eyes flicked over me in morose reflection. She looked at her worn boots. "Yet, one day these invaders, whose same blood runs in your veins and who call themselves our protectors, will leave this rain-misted island. A worse enemy will lurk, more ruthless than any we've seen to date. They'll rape our forests and maids and bathe our hides in pools of our own blood. We'll cry for our old enemies, the Romans, but they'll have long gone." She spat out a wad of brown stuff then licked her fleshy lips before loosing a long breath. "In the fanes and the bloody gizzards of owls I've seen it, and the offal of the white wolves of the north."

I shivered. "A grim prediction, woman. A cold day in Hades it'll be if Rome falls. We'll rule till the end of time."

"Will you now?" Her harsh chittering laugh grated in my ear. "Enjoy these easy days while you may, Icarus. Still time for you to mend your ways."

I rounded on her. "What do you see for me, sorceress?" A shrill note entered my voice. The power of her presence had infected me and her words had started to rattle.

"Best you don't know, boy." Downing the rest of the wine, she passed back my bowl.

I saw in her gaze the passing of time and an ineffable sadness crawling across her proud features. It spoke of griefs of generations. This Maig, a youthful-looking woman, puzzled me, and yet I saw her true age flash before me as if she were a much older woman.

The image vanished with her wayward laugh. Just a trick of the torchlight. She wandered off, singing the haunting melody I'd heard on her way up. *Ni Canir Ferçadlw Ab Fustos Illis Weuntg...* The bittersweet tune echoed among the tombstones, a refrain I thought must be that of a person deranged to risk walking the lands alone at night, witch or not.

Chapter 3

The encounter with the druidess was but a fading memory as I staggered back to my father's villa at sunrise, my mask and wings stuffed in a sack at my hip. Denetio let me in, his brows raised at my disheveled look. Stiff and sore, I pushed past him down the marble entranceway and through the main hall to the back of the house, quietly unlatching the door to my room. I lifted a tile under the bed by the window and stashed my eagle's mask there and small devil wings. A secure place existed under the floor, in a locked trunk. I lay there in my bed feeling sour from the night's activities, the alcohol seeping in my veins, the ever-present memories of Drace's demise.

Drace never believed in beat-downs for the sake of senseless killing. We only drew blood when the situation demanded it, like those who'd tried to extort my father, or who'd raised weapons against us. We kept to a strict policy, but now more with a payback motive—a kind of tax imposed on the city of Londinium and the soldiers who'd brought about Drace's death. Foolhardy, looking back at it all, but we were young. Me, fifteen going on sixteen. Piss and vinegar days for all of us and we did some devastatingly idiotic things. But the rough-and-tumble strengthened us for the days to come, which would hit hard and heavy. Amazing we hadn't been caught in the act of our violent pranks and deviltry thus far.

Plagued with ever sadder recollections of my brother, my head had barely touched my down pillow when a familiar voice snapped out at me. I squinted in the pale light. The sun had barely risen an hour, sending glimmers through my window.

"Out late again, Icarus? I won't even begin to ask what you've been doing."

I muffled a curse and grunted through half-closed lids. To add a disparaging remark to my father's quip would accomplish nothing, so I held my tongue.

"There's a pile of work to be done today, so get your hide up and move those amphorae of wine and crates of figs out to the wagon."

I groaned and hid my face under my pillow. "Can't you get Setrius to do that? Why do we have slaves?"

"They're busy with other tasks. With the Mithras celebration on tomorrow, the market and taverns will be full. Don't forget your class with Dionos this afternoon."

I loosed a defeated breath. "How can I forget? Triangles and polygons don't interest me, Father."

"And who do they interest?" he growled. "But I'll be damned if my son isn't going to learn something."

No use arguing with him. He wouldn't budge. Paterfamilias. It was one of the greater evils of life, obeying my father's rule, attending those wretched sessions. But if I humored the old man, he gave me certain license in other areas, so I juggled the pros and cons with careful deliberation. Certain perks availed themselves, including the toothsome Metella, the animal trader's daughter. One thing was for certain, I could gaze at her cleavage for hours. My friends told me private tutoring remained a thing of privilege in these days and I should be grateful.

I sat up and donned a fresh woolen tunic and my sheep's wool cloak, dragging myself to the triclinium where Denetio busied himself piling bread, olives and other foodstuffs on the table.

Mexor, my father, gave a low whistle. "You both look battered. If I didn't know better, I'd say you both are in on some scheme."

Denetio cast me a nervous glance and pressed his lips together. His shaky hands did nothing in our favor. I shot him a warning glance of my own as I reached for some grapes. Denetio poured mulled wine rather clumsily from the urn. My father, a big man, grabbed a handful of nuts and dates and plopped them in his mouth. His steel grey eyes raked me as his muscular shoulders dropped with an exhaled breath. A dark, low Roman cut with forelock lay pasted over his brow. Denetio, a fawn compared to my bear of a father, disappeared off to fetch more wine. Though I towered an inch over Mexor already and for the most part had his looks, my fair hair came from my mother. My crooked, flattened nose was a product of my own doing, broken too many times to remember.

I hunched and blinked. Rubbing my eyes, I stifled a yawn.

My father stepped out and approached the household shrine in the corner of the atrium, murmuring his customary prayer. He set a piece of bread soaked in olive oil into the candle flame as an offering.

My father was a deeply superstitious man who observed his faith without fail. Regulated his routine to clockwork. Whereas I despised the gods, and thought it all hocus-pocus, we had many a heated argument between us. Still, the protector gods would keep him and his business safe today.

He caught my look of amusement upon returning. "Your irreverence will catch up with you, Icarus," he grumbled. "I see potential in you, but you take no interest in practical affairs."

He frowned at my smirk. "Grin and smirk all you want, boy, but a few years from now you'll be put to work. Sixteen years old and a chip on your shoulder the size of a galley's prow. Nothing but sour ale and cheap wine in those veins of yours."

I grinned, proud of the fact.

He gave his head a resigned shake. I saw beneath the cynicism a smile creased his worn, seamed face. A smile I was to recall in later years with some fondness, though I liked it less now. Whenever he smiled after a dressing down, I knew something more unpleasant was brewing.

"Come on, follow me." I trooped after him as he stepped over to one of the store rooms on the street-side.

"Look," he rumbled, pointing to two amphorae, a wooden crate and some large grain sacks. "These are the finest wines from Gallia and Italia. Olive oil, dates and figs from Hispania. Grapes from Rome, as far as Antioch. Artichokes from Macedonia. Exotic spices from Judaea, imported from the far east, by camel. Fine grains, pomegranates and oranges from Mauretania. You don't know how lucky you are." He poured his hands through the sacks of grain, stuff I'd never seen before. They looked like barley and amaranth but weren't. "I sell and trade to the rich and not-so-rich of Londinium, not for my own amusement, but to promote good commerce."

A thought danced at the edge of my imagination. "Perhaps I'll go to one of those places someday...Might be better than hobgobbling around this provincial town."

My father gave a sharp laugh. "I doubt it with that nonexistent work ethic of yours. It takes denarii and means to travel to such places."

The hope died in me as soon as it came. I shrugged. "Well, so be it, I won't then. But I shan't become a merchant like you."

He grunted. "Your choice, Icarus, but you're a damned fool if you don't. I've paved the way. No easier way to amass coins in this day and age."

I disagreed with him on that point, considering the coins Marcellus and I'd swept our greedy fingers over in opulent villas. A small urn of silver at the last one came to mind. I stifled a grin, my mouth curling at the corners. A lot of cheap ale and whores to be had from those spoils. But I didn't let on to my father of my nefarious pastimes. The old man would've had a seizure had he known the extent of our debauchery.

As if divining something of my thoughts, he narrowed his brows. "I imagine what you and your cronies are up to is more interesting than studying the craft of an architect or engineer. That good head of yours goes to waste with those ruffians."

I shrugged, blowing air past my lips. "Always a matter of opinion, Father."

"Don't 'Father' me." He sighed. "Here," he said with more lightness, "I've already recorded these sacks. Get Zeno to help you get them down to the wagons out back. Vesparian brought them to me earlier today as advance samples. They check out and I'm taking them to market. Our supply ship's come in with more goods than I can handle. I'll need you again later this afternoon."

After loading the cart and setting the donkeys and driver off, I went back to my room to sleep for a few more hours.

Waking up around high noon, I felt little refreshed, burdened with a furry tongue and raspy throat. Denetio was off to the market to fetch food for us tonight while Zeno, our sun-bronzed Macedonian cook, buzzed about the copper pots. After relieving myself, I glugged down an urn of water, took some bread and goat cheese, and got ready for that dreaded class.

Walking down the crowded main streets of Londinium, the day in full swing, I caught the gathering thrum of the crowds and the cries of busy folk mingled with bleating animals and clucking fowl. The market drew a restless breed of hucksters and peddlers and showmen trying to make their fortune in the designated capital of our province. The narrow streets around the forum teemed with folk: vendors trying to sell goods, from fried fish to cheap ornaments of amber, to fortune tellers with glazed eyes, crowned with pointed caps pretending to be magi. It always amused me, their necks circled in beads and hair dyed with garish colors and tied in long braids. Snake-charmers with old wizened faces played flutes, lured banded snakes, coral and green, from their woven baskets. Sword-swallowers with fire on their blades blew out puffs of blue smoke. Men performed tricks with ferocious beasts like black bears and snag-toothed badgers. One even put his arm inside a bear's mouth, had him gnaw on it. The beast must have been trained to go gently, but its snarls and clawings at the air convinced me enough and had me stopping to gawk and stare. I had to give that act a commendation, and threw in my two sesterces to the upturned hat. I had a healthy respect for bears, for anything that large and furry.

At the upper west end of town, Pius's father, Balthius, hosted our peer-group tutoring session. Five of us attended the class, the cost being substantially less to my father than one-on-one lessons at home. Dionos, our tutor, an erudite Greek slave of the house of Balthius, treated us well. His master owned and operated a pottery manufacturing business and exported to various ports in Gallia, Hispania and Italia. We alternated houses but today Balthius's villa hosted our class. Two days hence it would be at Horatio's house, closer to the river. Horatio's father, Tracias, managed part of the tax collection service reporting to the Quaestor of Londinium himself. Horatio, mouse-faced with his golden curls, oiled and trimmed, scented with heady perfume, had a fin of a nose always upturned as if above the rest of us, or set in an attitude of sublime inquiry much beyond everyone else's. Julius and Metella, brother and sister, came from a well-to-do family invested in the animal trade.

Metella, my love interest with her flaxen curls and fine, aristocratic features, proved a more intriguing study than any teachings of Pythagoras this day. Or any other, featuring dry theories on the geometry of triangles and distance. The short, bright-eyed Greek slave Dionos, with his olive-colored cheeks and small, triangular beard, remained indifferent to our preferences; he just put us through a rigorous curriculum spanning all the subjects. We were more than literate in Greek. I could read both Latin and Greek, whereas most couldn't. But I couldn't get inspired. Not that I lacked brains, for I surely had them, and I could grasp the concepts easily, but I grew ever wayward and bored. Running with the wolves aligned more with my passion, and this data gathering and the dull promise of a bureaucrat's life or becoming a merchant didn't cut it. The privileged life I had been born into dictated a combined military and political career. But to Hades if I was going to embark on that path. My father hoped I'd clean up my act, for he hadn't a formal education and wished he had one.

First came a question-answer exercise on Plato's philosophies of ethics and metaphysics.

"Icarus, you seem sleepy," said Dionos. "What do you think about the idea of the afterlife and whether a soul or god could exist without an earthly body?"

I paused, making such a smirk and todo about any god wanting to rove around like a ghost and give up the fleshy pleasures must be a daft one indeed, that Pius's ears burned and Horatio snorted and rolled his eyes.

Dionos sighed and chided me. Looking on sternly, he took a time out to give some in-depth explanation. "If you recall, Plato, in his writings on the Theory of Forms, suggests that the world of ideas is the only constant and that the perceived world through our senses is deceptive and changeable." He paused. "So you don't believe in the afterlife or gods?" I didn't fail to catch the sly twist to his lip.

I replied with mock caution. "If I were to say 'Jupiter strike me down now, because I'm a heretic and I think you're nothing more than a marble statue staged in the forum', is that a good enough answer?"

"Very clever, Icarus, but the problem with that logic is that maybe Jupiter will strike you down tomorrow, or next week or three years from now. How will you know? It's not for mortals to know the penalties of heresy."

"And maybe Jupiter will never strike me down," I countered.

"Circular arguments gain no ground."

"How can we even say anything about the afterlife or the whims of the gods, if such gods don't even exist?"

"Too abstract to qualify?" Our tutor's eyes narrowed. "Is that what you're implying?"

I chuckled. "Why put words in my mouth, Dionos?"

That got a rise out Metella. She gave me a curious glance and clicked her tongue. I flashed her a cheeky smile, not a winning one, for she turned away seeing the effort I had in keeping my eyes on her face rather than other prominent parts of her anatomy.

She flicked back her curls.

Dionos raised an eyebrow. "I don't think it's just you who is confused on this point, Icarus. Many minds greater than ours have pondered questions as these for centuries. For the benefit of others, let me explain. Plato stated that our world is incomplete, in a constant state of flux, thus requiring a higher spiritual realm, one stable and unchanging, to glue it together."

I clicked my tongue. "Beliefs only, Dionos. Maxims, that don't amount to much. Where's the proof?"

Derisive murmurs came from Horatio and Julius.

Dionos broke out in a broad grin. "What do you think, Horatio?"

"I think we're fools to think we can understand Plato or even critique him, let alone top him."

"That answer sounds good, but it's defeatist. And you, Metella?"

She responded in shy fashion, "I think Icarus has a point, but he's closing off possibilities, discarding the likelihood of a higher power or powers that govern the universe."

"Well put." Dionos cleared his throat.

Horatio mooned his eyes and uttered a rude comment. "I have no time for daydreamers or critics."

I gazed critically upon his thin, gangly frame and decided to teach little Horatio a lesson in manners next time I bumped into him on the street.

The time would come sooner than later.

The final lessons of the day came to an end, an overview of Roman history from the republic transitioning to empire. We scratched the names of emperors down with our wooden styli in the wax tablets on our laps. My head swam with names from Tiberius to Trajan, from Nero to Domitian.

Dionos's voice droned on, reminding us of our place in the scheme of things. "Britannia, your homeland, was merely an accident of ambition. Claudius, emperor fresh on the throne after the assassination of Caligula, needed to prove himself. What better way than to win a glorious military victory?" He gave us a wry inspection. "So began the invasion of Britannia, nearly a century ago. Our island, always an attractive target for Rome because of its mines and slaves and agricultural wealth, became ripe pickings. Claudius defeated the Catuvellauni clan, its king, Caratacus, and set up the provincial capital here in Londinium."

Wearing a deadpan look, he added, "All of this is fair game on next week's quiz."

Dionos didn't pause to listen to our groans. "That's all for today. We meet in two days. The topics will include Euclidian geometry, astronomy and a study of the remarkable inventions of Archimedes. Perhaps too, the geography of Asia Minor and the lands to the east." He paused, tugging at his small beard. "Oh, and let's not forget a closer look at the Punic wars when Hannibal had marched his elephants across the mountains from Hispania to Italia only to be trounced by Scipio. Then there's a revisiting of Spartacus's slave revolt and his seventy thousand conscripts who held out against the army in the region around Capua. I have many more things to say about those battles."

As we filed out of the peristyle, I gave Metella a suggestive wink. She did a nervous little dart of eyes while toying with her flaxen curls. Jupiter, she was cute. "I like what you said back there," she said. "I don't necessarily agree with it all—too reactionary and rebellious for me, but it makes me think that, well…I'm taken by the Christian belief in one god, believe it or not, though I was born and raised on Minerva and Apollo like all the rest."

I smiled, gave her an appreciative nod, wondering how long it would take me to peel those clothes off her and become more familiar with her gods. Horatio, the pesky little sod, pushed his nose in to intercept, uttering a mousy little squeak in that voice of his. "Metella, walk with me?" he said. "I'm heading down to the pier." He turned his back to me. It was a smooth move, if not a trifle bold, considering who he played up against. Her face fell, flashing me another nervous glance. I turned away with a snort. "Okay," she said.

Dionos seemed to make a mental note of the interplay. I could read the wry mirth underneath his impassive face. I growled as Horatio fell in lock step with her, as a slave girl discreetly followed the pair, carrying their tablets.

"All Plato's and Socrates's wisdom pales compared to the complexity of the female," he said.

"What mystery?" I jeered. "They're predictable, no different than men."

Dionos chuckled. "Perhaps. But much prettier than men. I can't help but wonder if that's more profound than it sounds. Plato himself would approve. Are you up for a friendly game of Battalia, Icarus?"

I shrugged. Let Horatio think he had scored his little victory. If the girl fell for that puffed-up excuse of vanity, let him have her. "Sure, why not? I have some time to kill." I raised an eyebrow. "Aren't we two for two?"

"Something like that." Dionos brightened, pulled out his carrying case under the marble table: a wooden board with chips and wooden pieces which he unpacked with quick fingers and I sensed a boyish excitement in his movements. Dionos, it seemed, didn't get to let his guard down much.

He spread the board on the table and dispersed the pieces. It sported an intricately-carved map of Britannia, the narrow channel, and Gallia. We distributed our tokens across the board and studied our strategies, rolling dice to simulate battles: carven pieces, rose and grey, represented galleys and infantry. The goal was to see who could command Britannia, employing strategies not dissimilar to Claudius's landing eighty some years ago. Dionos played the Celts while I played the Roman forces.

Dionos had come to enjoy my unconventional and stubborn views. During these games, he looked forward to fencing with me, debating, engaging in rhetoric, as was the traditional ways of the Greeks. He delighted in pushing my limits, rattling me, cajoling me into probing deeper, seeing if he could crack that stubborn pride of mine, one that refused to recognize higher learning as the end all of human aspiration. I think he let me score points off him deliberately so that I wouldn't get too discouraged. He never gave up on any student, and as much as I resented a lot of the philosophy he taught, I admired the man, his quick mind, breadth of knowledge.

Even I was not arrogant enough to think I had any tactical advantage on our tutor. An hour later, I gave a heavy sigh and swept the pieces off the board. "You win, Dionos. You're ruthless."

He gave me a consoling pat on the back. "You relied too heavily on your naval forces, Icarus, you know that. Look how they got depleted from storms."

It was true. Rolling the die to see what weather would prevail, I bit my tongue as my ships foundered in foul weather, leaving my land forces exposed to attack. Not dissimilar to what Caesar had faced while fighting the Britons and their blade-wheeled chariots and fierce war hounds a hundred years before Claudius's beaching.

Losing badly, my mind wandered to Metella. Her flushed cheeks and her slinking steps, stuck in my mind, her body in full bloom of ripe adolescence. I departed Balthius's villa more restless than when I had arrived.

Chapter 4

I retraced my steps back to the forum to watch my father's wine shop as I'd promised. I caught the glint of sunlight off burnished helms, greaves, swords and shields as a group of soldiers led by a horsehair-plumed centurion came marching in from the north gate with quick steps and on toward the watchtower. The high-walled garrison stood somber and strong and housed the guardhouse and defense of the main entrance. The fighting men were likely coming from one of the northern ports at Camulodunum or even farther up. They'd take their leave here and be sent elsewhere. The governor Quintus Falco rotated soldiers about the province regularly. For now, the city'd host them here at the *castra* outside the city walls. More chance for night games with new soldiers, I suppose. Or potential disaster.

I scanned the ten-foot high stone wall that surrounded the northern precincts of the city. Three manned gates, north, west, and north-west connected the city to all parts elsewhere while the bridge to the south ran out over the river. I walked east from Pius's residence past the baths and the amphitheater and on to the Via Forum that connected to the market.

The bustling forum loomed dead center ahead. Passing under the soaring arch and massive ionic pillars twice a man's breadth, I leapt aside to let a cart laden with clay pots clatter by. "Stupid bastard!" I waved a fist at the reckless ruff-beard who'd almost run me down. My feet ached to give chase and deal him a proper drubbing, but the two soldiers peering my way made me think twice.

A cornucopia of nationalities and social classes flooded the market—Celts, Romans, Gauls, Greeks, Hispano-Romans. A medley of tradespeople, moneylenders, soldiers, artisans, hawkers, and priests advocating the boons of each god—Jupiter, Apollo, Minerva, Mars—with the Cult of Mithras high amongst them. Even temples to dark Celtic gods resided, to appease the Britons, with, of course, a Roman name tacked on the end of them, like Rhiannon-Proserpina, Lugh-Apollo or Mabon-Bacchus or even Andraste-Minerva.

Women pushed by with hair piled up in coils; slaves, thin, fat, old, young, of every race and culture, with sandaled feet running about gathering goods; merchants bartering wares, watching with hawk-eyes; farmers with stubble beard; soldiers thumbing blades; toothless children wandering in groups; endless sheep, carts, donkeys and mules; noise, confusion and a hundred odors, from animal hide to goose dung to burning incense to fried fish, sweat and exotic perfume. This was Londinium's forum and we were proud of it.

As I walked down the main way, a figure caught my attention. A particularly loud and effusive bigshot, some money lender and banker, pontificating to his associate. Large and portly, with a bald pate and some curly fringes, and his fingers stuck full of rings. I recognized him at once—Gaius Pluvius Maxus—a kingpin who controlled the major holdings and investments around Londinium, also areas of Gallia and Hispania. He had rubbed my father the wrong way some years back, almost foreclosing on his loans. My father had managed to squeak out of it, just barely. It was the reason Drace had started *The Clubs*. To fight back at extortionists like this fat pig. Now matters had gotten out of hand…

I cast him a chill glare as he passed. He didn't see me, nor would he have known me from anybody else in that teeming crowd. These types of men I despised most, those we lashed out against in our nocturnal rages, we feral dogs of the night, snapping at our exploiters' hides.

I pushed through the throng and reached my father's shop, grinning at the crimson graffiti we'd scrawled on the walls not two days ago. His slave was still scrubbing it off, with my father himself standing by in foul humor when I approached. "Hail, Father. How goes sales today?"

"Been fair enough. You're late."

"Dionos had our heads spinning with the escapades of Spartacus and Hannibal."

"Well, glad the Greek's earning his denarii," he said. "Maybe teach you a few lessons on the consequences of defiance."

I appreciated that my father could land a good joke from time to time.

I settled into the routine, sorting some amphorae and making sure I'd committed all the types of wine for sale to memory. A huge amphora out front sat filled to the brim with choice red wine, and clay cups laid on the counter under an awning. Leaning over the counter, I readied my pitch for any customers. The provincials we sold the cheaper wine to could be detected by their coarse garb: stained woolens and workmen's cloaks. For the ones in finer silks and soft woolen togas, I reserved our specialty wines, aged and imported from Italia and vineyards more distant. I knew the sales pitch. Our shop stretched far back, the bottom front of it classic brick with a sliding wooden door, the top half open, but that would be barricaded and locked with wooden shutters during the night to prevent petty theft.

I swung about and saw none other than Feberiax and Marcellus marching up to our stall, wearing grins as wide as drunken sailors.

I gritted my teeth. I told those rogues not to come by when my father was around. The less he knew of the crowd I ran with, the better.

"Hey, Ick. What's up?" crowed Marcellus. "You into some *skundering* later on?"

Why drop our codeword for hellraising? Idiot. Only made things worse. "Bad time to swing by," I hissed at him, pointing to my father who gathered ledgers in the back.

"Sorry," Marcellus said, purring a note of apology. Feberiax gave an insolent smirk.

Me and my ruggies. Strutting around unmasked by day as if we owned the world. Bashing heads, vandalizing, snatching a pretty piece at one of the whorehouses for some fleshy pleasures by night. When in adolescence, there's little time for morals. It's a playground—building sand towers in the air, all kites, hoops and rolling balls for the young mischief maker. With corruption, violence, the stench of poverty on the rise, and rich getting richer and poor getting poorer, there's not much scope to imagine any other world. Some born into slavery, others born free, full citizens. A crapshoot. Why was I born in this family? Why were they born in that family?

As the two sauntered off, scuffing their feet and flashing me smug looks, my father seemed to sense my rebellious musings.

"Watch it, Icarus. You think I'm just a sleepy old man. I know you and those ne'er-do-wells are up to no good in the streets at night." He held up a hand. "I know you're not going to listen to me." He heaved a sigh. "If you weren't my son, I'd turn you in myself. I do not want to break your spirit, but you've got to settle down." That crooked smile I'd remember forever, where the pink scar peaked, as if he'd been held at knifepoint. He'd had wounds in his days. Plenty of them. "I was a shit disturber myself," he said. "Just be careful it doesn't get you bludgeoned."

I grinned. So the old man was not such a lame duck after all. Once when he got to drinking his expensive wine, I overheard him talking about his years of pirating, those days when he engaged in the sea trade business. Before he had settled in Londinium seven years back, after he'd been in Noviomagus for a few years. Who knows how many half brothers and sisters I had, and would never meet. I could get to like a life like that, if the boots were on my feet.

I thought to trip him up as I jogged his memory of his exploits, see if I got a different story this time. "Why didn't you stay in Rome?"

He grunted. "I'd seen a lot of the Mediterranean world, and done a lot of sailing and scouting about, looking for goods to ship. Landed in Gallia, in Gesoriacum, saw hard times—and drinking. I'd already fathered you and couldn't convince Wyvurre to come with me. Needless to say, it was unbecoming for a Roman merchant to marry a prostitute. Trajan was field testing a new imperial policy at the time, encouraging 'settlers', so to speak, to start up a business in one of the provinces. Giving everyone a thousand denarii. A minimum five year term. I considered Hispania and Britannia. I chose Britannia. And here I am."

I shook my head. "It's warmer in Hispania."

He laughed at that. "Certain debts needed to be paid. Londinium was safer, as it was not as well-established as Italica."

"You've got a sound business now."

"And you've got too much of your mother in you," he said. "Ah, she was a wild one. Wish she was here with me."

A trace of my old resentment rose, my regret for not having a mother. "You've only got yourself to blame."

"Don't forget who's paterfamilias here," he grumbled. "Watch the shop. I'll be gone for a few hours, so be on the alert for crooks and scammers. There's enough of them roaming about this market. For Mercury's sake, record everything you sell."

I saluted and watched him stride off to complete his errands: many of them bill-keeping and visiting various suppliers who could ship wines and produce to other parts of the province.

I was glad to be free of my father's company. After my nighttime activities, I was about at my limit for today.

The afternoon was a busy one, teems of people moving about with baskets and carts, grabbing this and that item and bartering for others. A man tried to get me down to two denarii for some fine wine but I smiled and told him to come back later when my father was about. A warm scent of animal hide and dung, the sweat of humans. The sounds of hawkers filled the air. The sun came out in fits and clouds hovered, threatening to douse us with rain again. I sold generous quantities of wine and figs and kept proper ledgers on this late summer day, although it was work as dull as hammering tin. When Mexor returned, he muttered his gruff thanks.

With my family duties finished, I headed up the east hill, zigzagging along back alleys in no special order, looking for places for me and my band to hit at nighttime. Much safer to scout by day in the cobbled streets than the narrow alleys flanked by darkened shops, apartments and taverns. I enjoyed a certain sense of irony knowing that I myself was one of those skulkers who ruled the streets at night. I kept away from the north gates and the soldiers posted there. I couldn't stand the sight of any of them; Drace's unjust death still clung to my memory like a bur.

Most of the other gangs were all political or rebel Celts. Dumb sods. I could give a rat's ass what petty, puppet governor the Romans put up to rule us in this provincial town. They'd all die in pools of blood anyway when the Celts had enough sense to band together and slit their Roman throats. Just a matter of time. How long could they keep those painted, naked hordes from storming down from the north? The Picts they called them. Talk of a wall echoed about to keep them out. I laughed, but I was young and too cocky to grasp the obvious. War knew no favorites. I heard tales of brutal slaughter and skirmishes on the borders up there that made one's blood congeal.

From a high point at the end of Via Peligra, I caught a glimpse of the Tamesis river, a broad ribbon of dark ultramarine that contrasted with the rare sunlight this misty land bestowed on its waterlogged citizens. A steady stream of barges poured up and down the river, transporting kiln-fired bricks and chiseled blocks for roads and buildings. And upriver from the seaside floated cargo craft carrying wines, pottery, olives, figs, and amphorae of oil and crates of fish. And of course—soldiers.

Our nocturnal haunts included the northern section of the city and I swept down to the seedier areas of the natural stone port. We'd rove in a broad oval during our night raves, lessening our chances of getting caught. The cemetery, thankfully, resided outside the city walls. It was our place of refuge, and lay diagonally opposite the fort where the soldiers lodged.

As I was making my way further east toward the temple of Mithras, I bumped into some old 'friends': Raicus and his brood of three young toughies. The rival gang had caused us some trouble in the past. Now they sauntered up to me with an earnest curiosity and brazen delight.

"Icky, Icky! Fancy meeting you here. Shame about your brother," Raicus bantered. "Drace was a good man."

I growled, the mention of my brother's name always a sore point, like a stab to my heart—especially from this lowlife sack of shit who called himself a member of 'The Painted Grouses'.

"You'll get your blood money, Raicus. Not right away."

"Have it your way then." He made a signal to his mates. They came in to encircle me. Dressed in their light brown leather, hair braided, they were a menacing lot. Celts, all of them, with billy clubs and knives at their belts. I'd made a note to Marcellus and the others that we'd need to clean up this riffraff soon enough. How close we'd come to nipping their asses that dark, rainy night off Via Flaxis, but the cowards had fled and made it to the guardhouse before we could pull them back into the shadows and beat their brains in.

"Hate to play it the brutish way, Ick, but business is business. Either you fork over the two hundred denarii for our silence or we bust up your arm now and go to the prefect with names of 'The Clubs', not necessarily in that order."

I gave an explosive curse. "No centurion'll believe you, Raicus. You thugs are no better than us. The soldiers'll laugh you out of town."

"Maybe, maybe not. But do you want to take that chance? To have the suspicion of the law hanging over you?"

His black-toothed comrade gave a mocking grunt. "Word's out that the prefect's itching to lay fingers on the pranksters doing the defiling around town and the busting of heads. You wouldn't believe the lark we've had pulling pranks like yours. Posing as you. Marking up walls, scribbling all sorts of filth, breaking into law-abiding citizens' lodgings, sometimes having our way with the master's wife." They all laughed. "Don't imagine it's giving your lot a good name."

I stepped back, my legs braced, keeping my cool, as Drace had taught me. I looked for an opening. A quick fist to someone's jaw, a knee to the groin. The one on the left looked tentative, the way his eyes kept darting to my fist clutching something black and hard. I lacked my club, but I carried a lighter version of it on me, a 'beater-stick', eight inches long and two inches wide. Plus I had my fists, which were deadlier weapons than anything those cockerels were expecting.

The bully beside him feinted left and came in on my right, huffing out a breath. I knocked him aside and the knife fell out of his hand. My strong leg shot up to graze his right thigh. He lurched back, cursing, shaking his sprained wrist where my beater had come down on his forearm, hard.

Raicus uttered a weary sigh. "Going to go about it the hard way, Ick? Suit yourself." He moved in like an adder, his narrow, pinched face grinning. I ducked his ironwood club aimed for my skull, as his other friend's club caught my ribs, knocking the breath out of me. His glinting knife angled close to my ear. I twisted, blocked with my forearm, and hammered out with my beater-stick, prompting a yell when the thug sagged back, wincing. The sound of voices echoed from up the street. I glanced around. Raicus hissed out a warning, then drew his toughies to his side.

"You scum bastard, saved this time by the hair of your ass. Lucky for you it's daylight. There're some witnesses about."

"Yeah, saved by my ass," I grunted, wiping my bloody lip. "Crawl back to your kennels where you belong, you mangy dogs."

"Just a couple of slave girls, Rake. Why turn tail?" murmured blacktooth. "Let's crack this puppy and be off."

"No time, Janus. More coming." Rake motioned and pulled his blacktoothed bully back.

To further the irony, I looked over my shoulder, hunched, massaging my ribs, and caught a glimpse of Horatio and four of his mates strutting down the street toward me. Metella was not with him. No doubt it had not taken her long to find out what an incurable bore the tax collector's son was. While I shook out my stinging limbs, watched the lowlifes skitter off, sandals clapping on stone, I murmured a dry curse, clenched my muscles as the blood got moving again. Part of me just wanted to get the blazes out of here. This strange day was getting stranger by the minute.

Horatio enjoyed the sight of me nursing my rib. He frowned in mock puzzlement. "What's the matter, Ick? Getting high off some street urine?"

His mates laughed.

My black mood was getting no lighter. I pulled Horatio aside and whispered dangerously in his ear, "I don't appreciate your loudmouth cracks, Whore-ass, especially when I'm in pain."

"My heart bleeds. I'll say what I please." He thrust himself away and gave me a shove. "Might even court Metella formally, cozy up to her father, thought you'd like to know."

That was about enough and my knee came up into his thigh and my fist on his back as he sagged. Horatio crumpled on the paves, gasping for air, cupping his leg. I scrutinized him like a curious cat that's cornered a frightened mouse. His nearest oil-haired friend jumped to his rescue, and I caught his flying fist on the edge of my arm as my other fist plowed into the fleshy part of his chest, just below the spleen. He gave a painful cry. Ouch, that must have hurt. He staggered and up came my beat stick, clocking him in the shoulder. Down he went. His two other friends stood there motionless like whipped chickens. Then they got enough sense to gather up their groaning comrades while I stepped over the huddle of bodies and strode off. Needless to say, those mambies'll give me wide berth next time, and no smirks or jeers'd be coming too soon during astronomy or philosophy class.

* * *

Mexor came home late, no doubt caught up in his business affairs. His life, hectic at best, remained strictly regimented and his precious moments in high demand. I could hear his heavy tread echoing in the atrium with its marble floors and the mosaic of Hercules slaying the nine-headed Hydra. Our compluvium, open to the sky, showed a grey overcast and drizzle as it let in fresh air and rainwater. The kitchen was alive with sounds of industry as Zeno worked his wonders and Denetio set plates, bowls of fruit and fresh bread fetched from the market today, on the small dining room table. My father's predictable patterns were no less this evening. After giving general instructions to the slaves for the tasks of the morrow, he stepped into his tablinum to file certain ledgers from the business of the day.

It was a quiet and subdued meal tonight. We reclined on our cushioned couches in silence, munching our slow-roasted mutton and looking anywhere but at each other. Stuffed veal, partridge eggs with olives, goat cheese and figs on the side. My father was in one of his moods. Something was bothering him, I could tell, judging by his stony look and I guessed it had to do with me.

Downing a healthy swig of red wine, he motioned Denetio for more and quaffed down the rest. He set down his bowl with a loud thud. "Heard you roughed up Horatio and one of his friends today."

I took a long time finishing my own mouthful of veal. "Those pests had it coming, Father."

He loosed a sigh. "I told you to lay off the violence. I don't fault you for sticking up for yourself, Icarus, but I think you have to think a little before you go bashing heads. You're worse than Drace—and that delinquent friend of his, Aurelius, and look at where it got the two of them, in a deep grave."

The mention of Drace got my hackles up and I growled, lurching to my feet.

"Sit down, you puppy!" my father warned. "Finish your meal. I'm not done with you yet."

I sat down, glowering, but wary.

"That boy, Horatio, comes from a long line of patrician old boys in Londinium, and on the mother's side, silversmiths. Word is he wouldn't have revealed what happened on the street today, his pride injured so. But his father got it out of him that it was you who beat him silly and it looks bad on me."

I shrugged. "A few knocks is hardly 'beat silly'. It's a messed up world out there, Father. Always going to be problems. Let a snob like that get away with too many insults and it looks bad. You should know that, man of the world."

"Watch your tongue, you little bastard."

"Nothing but a bunch of hens out there, these so-called 'men' of our society. They don't have anything better to do than gossip behind peoples' backs and demand such and such in defense of their little boys' bad behavior."

He sighed. "Ball busting's hardly gossip. Perhaps you're right, but this bellicose attitude will earn you no friends in this city or any other."

I shrugged off the speech and yawned. "I'm not in this life for 'friends', Father, especially mamby-pambies like Horatio and his old man."

"Then you'll go down, Icarus. Down hard. See it now, and don't delude yourself. These people you despise are your neighbors and part of the status quo. Part of the social makeup of this community, whether you like it or not."

How I disliked the name Icarus. He'd given me the nickname in jest when I was but a few months old. Too much drink and he didn't notice I'd climbed up on a crate and held my arms out like an eagle as if to swoop down and fly across the ocean. I landed on my chest and started to bawl. So, I heard. He'd laughed, fine gentleman my father was, and had my name changed from Domitius to 'Icarus'.

"Is this lecture over?"

"It is. And I just hope I don't wake up to find you dead like your brother." He rose from his couch and lumbered off, having drunk more than his share of wine. I listened to the echo of his fading footsteps.

His words rankled me. I couldn't yet determine the exact reason. Not like we hadn't had our share of abrasive discussions before. Nor did I particularly care for the reasons. Nothing that a few nocturnal beat downs couldn't solve. I grinned, stretched my arms and cracked my knuckles. Training tonight would be harsh. My turn to lead the sparring, and I'd not go easy on Oren, Feberiax or Marcellus, who I thought were slacking of late. My lips curled upward. Nighttime was always my favorite.

Chapter 5

I stood at the foot of the east wall, the midnight moon glowering down at me from behind a wispy cloud. I was about to scale the wall when the scuff of a boot and moving shadow gave me a start. I raised my club. False alarm. Only Marcellus and the others lurking about.

"What are you doing?" I hissed.

"A change of plans," said Marcellus, his face masked. "I'm in favor of striking out earlier tonight. Mix up our schedule. Keep any interested parties from guessing our patterns."

I grunted my objections but they seemed to hold no weight. The rain had stopped, the streets were dead. Tonight was 'graffiti' night, a change of pace from our usual masked mischief and spur-of-the-moment head-bashing.

We stalked on toward the port and it didn't take long to select a target: Usekes's smithy down by the old market, a place neither spacious nor adorned as our central forum, rife with the smell of urine, dog shit and decay. Dressed in our animal costumes, we quickly chalked up the limestone façade of his shop with all kinds of cruderies and symbols of our creed. Why, because we could, and the night, restless with danger, carried strange energies in the air. Oren, not a bad hand at artist, scribbled some gonads and skulls, and I scripted the letters underneath, big looping scrawl, bold and angry, like our rebellious hearts, the ones becoming more like beasts.

We moved on to the butcher's stall down the way and hadn't got half way into it, when from the shadows came a rustle and a hoarse shout. I edged back. Another shadow hovered behind the first. A burly shape moved in fast. "Get away from there, you worthless, bird-beaked brats!"

Veronus, owner of the meat-chopping shop, blocked my escape. I couldn't flee into the back alley without engaging him and his friend.

His companion, a hulking, snarling brute, looked much like one of those bearded giants from Germania.

"Teach them, Bruthal!" Veronus cried.

"Gladly," I heard his ox-faced slave grumble as he blocked my path, thumbing his knife as he lumbered toward me.

Fresh back from the pubs, Veronus, a chunky man himself, gripped a big stick. What hunch of deviltry had brought him here?

I turned to race around him but Bruthal, quick and ready, lashed out in the shadows, wearing that fat sinister, violent smile. Regalis and Oren were hard put to club him, being on the other side of me who hunched monkey in the middle.

While Marcellus and Feberiax faced off with Veronus, Regalis, Oren and I squeezed round in a tight circle to fend off the bruiser. All three of us came at him at once. He got in a few good hits, clubbing me on the arm, stinging me to the bone. I cried out a pantomime of curses while Oren took a grazing swipe at him behind the ear, drew blood, almost knocked him senseless.

A thud came to my left: the lubberly form of Veronus skidding sideways, clubbed by Marcellus. Feberiax finished him off, hoofing him in the gut.

I heard the splinter of bone as my club made contact with Bruthal's arm, yet the giant still clutched that cursed knife, damn him. I think the break only served to anger him all the more. He gave a hoarse growl and knuckled me in the side of the head. Stars swam. Jupiter's sluts! How could I be so careless? I spun sideways, the stars turning to prickles of pain as more danced about my eyes and I fought the dizziness and nausea. A knife tip whisked by my ear. I felt a crimson line drip down my cheek. Regalis bunted me away from the charging hulk, a move which saved my life, steering me away in the right direction before the muscled shape could make hatchwork of my ribs. Marcellus edged in at the last moment as he always seemed to do, and lay into my opponent. The brute sagged with a soft groan. We were all shaking and pumped with adrenalin, gazing at the senseless body on the cobbles and Veronus who lay groaning at his slave's side in his own spit and blood. Marcellus stood grinning over the spoils, like a scavenging jackal.

We made our getaway, but just by the skin of our teeth—the town watch came clattering down the filthy street after us. The familiar thrill of pursuit burned in our blood. We skittered off down the dim-lit ways, through various back alleys and raced toward the east wall and the grapple which would grant us safety over it onward to the cemetery where we could all hide. I heard Marcellus's hyena-like laugh still behind me, a chittering echo in the darkness. Puffing with the effort of running, waging my private war with dizziness, I thrust off the aches of battle, cursing the evening's work. We were too fast for the watchmen; we split up. Regalis, Oren and I took the grapple route, Marcellus and Feberiax headed farther up where a companion grapple was stashed. The backup plan we'd cooked up for just such an emergency.

Two sets of fleeing boots and our crazy, echoing zigzagging remained enough to confuse the guards.

* * *

We met up at the cemetery, all of us slumped on the dewed grass, panting behind an old marble mausoleum in the moonlit darkness.

Marcellus rolled over and play-punched Feberiax on the arm. "Liking it, Feb?" Feberiax gave a laughing snort.

"Some fun, splitting a few heads," Marcellus croaked.

Something about it seemed not so amusing this time as I massaged the cut on my cheek. "I thought we agreed not to take on shopkeepers?" I growled.

He turned and patted me on the shoulder. "Well, aren't you the mamma's boy? Only two of them and five of us. What does that say about yourself, Ick? What would your big brother say? Rest his soul. This Veronus was one rude bastard who insulted us. He provoked a fight. What were we supposed to do? Just let him off?"

He'd phrased it in such a way that any argument'd only make me look a weakling in front of my peers. Marcellus was shrewd that way.

The two of us had always clashed. Even before the leadership went sour and we were in this wretched situation. Split right down the middle. Co-leaders of a pack, but not really—more like tops spinning off in different directions. Study a pack of wild dogs and see how many co-leaders there are. None. Only one alpha dog can survive.

"Drace always said, practice makes perfect, didn't he?" Marcellus went on. "Keeps us fresh—on our toes. Right, ruggies?"

Feberiax gave a grumbling chuckle. "A bit of the old bounce and bash and thrill of the unknown'll never hurt anyone, Marcy. Keeps a night thug sharp."

"Next time," I said with a rasp of sullen disapproval, "you take on the crazy brute." I glared at Feberiax while mumbling curses at Marcellus.

"Don't be a baby," Marcellus scoffed. "A few cuts'll mend. Maybe you're getting slow, Icarus, a little soft under the cover."

"Maybe I almost got beat down by Raicus and his slugs today. Knocked me in the ribs. So yeah, I'm a little angrier, off my game, can happen to anyone."

Marcellus scowled. "We have to do something about those worms. Never liked Raicus."

"Who does?" grumbled Oren.

"And what'll we do?" scoffed Feberiax. "The Grouses are never around. When you want to beat on them at least. We don't even know where their hideaway is."

"Rumor has it, their crib is that outbuilding by the baths," said Regalis. "Some tunnels go underneath to the heating pipes. We could try there."

"So what are we waiting for?" Feberiax grinned, rising as if he were going to take them on himself. Marcellus laughed and grabbed his leg.

"Hold up!" I cried. "That's a dumb plan. What of the town watch? They're going to be prowling around these streets all night, now that we've alerted and riled them up."

"He's right," Regalis said.

"I wish Drace were still here." Oren picked up a clump of grass and gave it an idle toss.

Marcellus snuffled out a contemptuous growl. "Suck it up. He isn't. Enough of this prissy talk."

"So what do we do?" mused Feberiax. "Twiddle our thumbs? If it's not safe to hop the wall—"

"We train." I strove to control my impatience. "But under moonlight only, no torches. Let's tighten up our moves. Improve our game. That was sloppy work back there. Drace would've clubbed our ears for that. He'd have us working twice as hard to burn off our clumsiness and redeem ourselves. Two hours a night minimum, remember? Now we're lucky to get in a few hours every second day. It's a disgrace. Come on, grab your helms."

Regalis gave a chirping laugh. "You heard the man. Let's draw straws and see who spars with whom."

"Forget it," Marcellus croaked. "I'll take Feb here. You three can go yank your cranks as much as you like. Do whatever you want."

"As you like," I said coldly. I strode over to the thick bush where we hid our gear and donned my helm and pads and started clubbing with Regalis.

* * *

The echo of Drace's name had brought a flood of memories that I neither wanted nor needed. Drace's essence shadowed me, every move I made, his spirit dancing at the edge of my mind, a restless shade hovering over my shoulder. I didn't like the feeling, but at the same time I felt comfort that he hadn't gone away completely. I suspected his beleaguered spirit, snatched away too suddenly from life, wandered in the ethers. That if I'd look over my shoulder, he'd be there, as some disembodied ghost. As Regalis and Oren sparred, I sat out this round and the clashing sounds brought him to me. Teaching me my moves, his club gripped like a sledge. Taking the heat, covering for me when I was out late and drunk, shielding me from our father's wrath. Recalling how he got me my first lay, sneaking Uella, Miscelia and two others out to the cemetery on my fourteenth birthday. What a place to lose your virginity. Juno's wrath! Regalis, Marcellus and I got the royal treatment, even though I counted as the only birthday boy.

Snatches of conversations, lessons learned, pride wounded, pride restored, the thrill of fight and the terror of chase, all the nighttime tricks and risks.

My throat choked up. Stepping in to spar with Regalis, I came down hard on him, in a series of strikes pushing him far back against the nearby tombstones.

"Hey, watch it," he cried. "Just practice, isn't it?"

"Sorry, I got distracted."

"I noticed," Regalis grunted. "What's eating you? You're like a walking corpse, Ick. A ghoul ready to bite heads off."

I shook my head, only shrugging. "Nothing."

"It's not nothing."

Oren griped, "He's sore because he nearly got busted up by Rake today."

"That's right, Oren. How'd you get so smart?" I sneered.

"Leave him alone," said Regalis. "You wouldn't have fared much better."

Marcellus stepped in. "You and me are up next, Regalis, so watch your lip."

While Oren and he bantered, I watched them engage, lulled by the thuds of wood and the crik-crik symphony of night crickets and yet, the hollow pit grew in my stomach as I saw Drace there in those phantom movements. The comical sparring we'd done before that fateful night passed like worn clothes, yet fresh in mind as if it were yesterday. Drace blocking a kick and sending stubble-chinned Feberiax on his ass. Oren lunging in, but miscalculating and getting the worse of a ringing clang to his helm. Marcellus got a grip on his arm and twisted, then a knee came up hard against his thigh and Drace limped for a few seconds, before that cat's grin vanished and he blocked Marcellus's next strike.

"Tricky, tricky, Marcellus. Not bad, but how about this—" Marcellus's eyes grew wide as Drace, two inches taller and his senior in speed, ducked under a whistling blow, catching him in the ribs and bringing Marcellus down heavy on his knees.

He turned to me. "And you, little brother? What's on your mind?"

I threw caution to the wind and got a piece of my club glancing off his helm. But his foot tripped me as my momentum carried me too close. I fell rolling on the ground and his boot heel landed on the small of my back, spearing me like a fish.

So we were all sore and crawling there, groaning, while Drace shook his shaggy head of hair and smiled his crooked smile, leaning on his club. "Up, ladies, we've got another half hour to go."

"No, Drace," said Oren. "You licked us good. Let us rest." Groans.

"What, no joy? Up, you dirt-lickers." He kicked Aurelius in the gut. "You shouldn't have eaten that mutton so early on before coming to practice." He made a wincing grimace as Aurelius puked up his guts, fouling the crisp night air.

It went on like a dance, a choreographed mime, with grunts and sound effects, twists and turns. Drace saw to the endless surprises. The mastermind behind it all.

He had us practice in the dark alleys that night where they narrowed and made our elbow-to-elbow sparring intense. More like a real-life situation that we might face, set upon by rough boys or town watchman, or some drunken mercenaries doddering out from the whorehouses, with their cocks longer and limper than when they entered.

Wearing our masks, we roamed the streets in high spirits. Drace strode at our fore; invincible we walked with him—masters of the night.

No real plan though, just some boyhood vandalism—maybe breaking into a villa and messing the place up, defiling a shrine, scrawling graffiti on some walls, marring a fresco. Usually we targeted extortionists, like the thugs who offered my father shop protection for a price, or the moneylender who'd tried to squeeze him out of his business. Sometimes vendors who'd overcharged us in the market. Sometimes we miscalculated and the owners of the villas had not gone to bed yet and we had to rough them up if they raised a fuss. But usually we timed it right when only slaves fluttered about and no guard dog lurked in the shadows. They cowered in terror, thought us nightmare horrors from Hades. We only snatched the odd thing we fancied, maybe a silver or gold ornament, not wanting to be laden down with anything too cumbersome while we made our getaway. Londinium with all its colors and rancid smells, waxed a trifle stale and we grew bored.

But that all changed after the tragedy.

A recent rain had left the streets greasy, with a stench of urine, rotten vegetables and general filth. All of us, hiked up on sour ale and drunker than sailors, skulked around the nighted streets. We ran into three armed soldiers, likely mercenaries who'd stumbled out of the portside bordello after having sated themselves with cheap wine and ladies of the evening.

They looked like dog-eared, down-and-out swords for hire, garbed with the leather breastplates of soldiers. But they wielded curious axes at their belts, thick with runes carved in them, alongside a smaller version of the soldier's gladius.

One of our party, I think Oren, got too close and bumped shoulders with the nearest in his stumbling haste to get by, prompting a curse from the shorter, broad-shouldered thug.

"Good evening, gents," Drace called. "Nice evening for some fun."

"Tis," answered one in a barbarous accent, the most homely of the lot. He had a crooked jaw, cracked nose, fat cheeks and dishwater eyes. He stepped forth. "And you pups look as if you can only laugh at the craft of real men." He fixed us a look square in the eye, grinning at his mates.

"Come back some day when you've hair on your peckers. Or when you're man enough to show your faces instead of wearing masks."

That got some sniggers from the other two, who wiped their lips and clapped each other on the back.

Dracian smiled. "You men seem a little too witty for this late hour."

"Oi, boy. And you too much of a wiseass. Get your butt home and work your flesh there, not in the street."

Marcellus slurred his speech, pushing past me and Regalis. "Put a dress on you and your mate and you'd be tall enough for my ruggie. He'd take you to bed and teach you a few things about love. Isn't that right, Drace?" he howled with laughter.

"Careful there, rogue," hissed the soldier, drawing his short sword. "There be blood spilled tonight." He weaved and looked ready to fall if he were hit too hard. "A tongue like that'll get you mashed up."

I saw the tenuous gleam of iron axehead at his waist under the faint moonlight, and I grinned, knowing some play was in hand, for Drace was not one to back down from a soldier's taunt. I could see the ease in his tall frame as he rested his hand on the grip of his club.

"Easy, soldier. We're all friends here."

"Hades we are, friend! Take your jolly boys and your masks and move along. I can't stand the sight of you." I could see the hint of gray in his short cropped hair. None of them wore their helms, but only those strange axes at their thick leather belts.

Dracian's brows rose. Pausing, he blinked in the dim light. I could almost read his mind, his weighing of odds at seven against three and an easy fight against drunkards. "Perhaps that's a boast to get an old man like you bruised up."

Marcellus danced around the three soldiers making exaggerated faces and lewd postures that only irked them the more. Stupid Marcellus, always the ass, acting out to impress my brother. I watched to see what Drace'd do, ready to jump in at any signal he'd give.

In a fit of fury, the soldier stepped in to give Marcellus a good whipping. Grabbing him by the hair which was longer than most, he pulled him down to his knee to crack him across the back, but my brother drove in, faster than a snake, and caught the downward strike with his club and body-checked the man flying backward. The soldier landed face first in a mud puddle the size of a doormat.

That got him plenty pissed, and he scrambled up with a seething curse. The second brute lunged forward, and caught Drace in the ribs just under the armpit. I sprang into the scrum to protect Drace, but howled as a blade raked my left arm. Marcellus and Regalis, mad as bulls, doubled over the second soldier before he could swing his axe a second time. Oren and I took the other while Dracian covered us. I saw blood leaking from Drace's open wound.

Aurelius, the drunken fool, walked straight into a strike which laid open his throat. Down he went in a gurgling, choking heap. I gave a wail of dismay. I could hardly believe one of our ruggies was down, another wounded, seeing all this from the corner of my eye. Time slowed to a dead halt. All sounds blurred as in a hallucinatory dream. I hacked, split the head of the man who'd sliced Aurelius. Drace, staggering, gave a choked grunt. I fought my way to him.

With blood all around us, those three got the stinking beating of their lives. They crouched like lepers, clubs crashing all over them while they lay in pulped ruin. Panting and cursing, Regalis grabbed me and pulled me away from that grisly scene and our dead comrade. Not before I ripped off Aurelius's mask. I refused to believe he was gone. Someone at the bordello had sounded the alarm. Shouts and the thud of tramping feet soon rang all around us, echoing from down the street, heading our way.

"Get going, you fool," spat Regalis at me. He hauled me away with the mask in my hands.

I hated to leave Aurelius there, but Regalis hissed in my ear and he tugged me along like a master his errant dog. It's the lowest thing I ever did, the cowardliest, and will never do it again, so I swear.

"Run!" Regalis's groggy breath brought me to my senses. I still remember that wild chaotic look in Marcellus's eyes, as he loped along.

I never forgave the sod for riling up those pigs like he did. We ran amidst the clatter of boots of the West Watch hot at our heels.

Like rats we scuttled through every escape-way and shadowed nook we knew in that big, smelly city. We got away—but just—the six of us.

Yet a new code was in order. A grimmer one. Payback our first intent, and we'd take it out on the soldiers who'd spilled the blood of our own. I'd drawn a silent pact with myself to kill more of those whoring, soldier-mercenary bastards if any opportunity presented itself. Good that we'd killed all three of them so they couldn't identify us.

My father'd been livid when he heard of the death of Aurelius and the slain soldiers. I had to wake him in the middle of the night—and what a torrent of abuse came from his maw—while I babbled some story of getting cut down by soldiers, and us clubbing the others to death in the streets.

My father's face, grey as death, sagged. He swallowed hard, knowing it was no lie I spoke, seeing the bloody mark on my left arm and Drace's ghastly expression as he leaned against the atrium wall, trying to grin his way out of a grievous situation. My father dragged the two of us to the kitchen and cleaned and dressed our wounds, pouring raw vinegar on them that had me wailing. Drace remained silent but hunched on the verge of passing out, yet he too got his share of doctoring and chastening.

I sobered up quickly. Buckets of cold water splashed on my naked body. The vilest medicines and herbs imaginable my father jammed down our throats, cursing us. But he knew, rather than implicate us, to keep this crime away from the police and destroy evidence that we were part of a gang involved in the deaths of the mercenaries and Aurelius.

But such a tongue-lashing and a caning I'd never forget. I took it without complaint for I felt as guilty as any, chastened by Drace's condition.

When men from the prefect'd rapped on our door and had questioned our household, my father kept his voice low and lied that we had been here all night. No, he didn't know who Aurelius ran with at night. Maybe just some street thugs he'd met?

"Where were your sons again?"

"Here."

The inspector sighed and pulled something from his belt. "This piece of animal mask was discovered at the scene of the murders." He held up a wood chip, the shape of a boar's ear. My heart did a little lurch. Jupiter's harlots! Aurelius's mask must have cracked when it fell to the cobbles.

"There's suspicion this boy Aurelius was part of the gang 'The Clubs', and I understand he was a friend of your sons."

"I can assure you they were here."

The inspector stared without comment.

"I'm sure this is some misunderstanding," my father protested. "Here's some fine wine for your trouble, Prefect. Falernian wine—aged fifteen years."

The inspector studied Drace then my bandaged arm, turned to gaze at my father, stroking his chin with a sea of warring thoughts. The others couldn't look at me edgewise without a suspicious scowl growing on their bearded faces.

"Very well, Mexor. Have your slave deliver two amphorae of Falernian to my villa within the week."

My father gave a crisp nod. "It will be done."

I gave a sigh of relief.

"In the meantime," the inspector grumbled, "be sure that your boys stay out of trouble. We're keeping an eye on you and your household." They turned on their heels and left.

I don't know what filth the soldier had on his blade when he pricked Drace, but it did him in bad. He caught a merciless fever, broke out in blisters and red striations and became delirious for four days. Despite the best *medici* we could bring in, there came no change in my brother's condition. My face grew pale with worry seeing my brother laid up like that, twitching and sweating. A horrible feeling grew in my guts that he'd die. Memory is an awful thing; it plays tricks on the mind. Floods it with nostalgia not totally reliable. All the bad moments seem to slip away, then all the good moments are three times better, brighter, but gone never to be visited again. I sat at his bedside for hours, bathing his fevered brow, reminding him of his prowess in street scraps, reliving the encounter, agonizing over how I could have, should have taken the blow. I didn't even have the comfort of my brother exonerating me of blame as he tossed and turned and mumbled gibberish until he ceased even that.

My father took the death of Dracian badly. Me, stumbling around in a daze…anger and confusion welling up in my heart with no place to go, as if I'd lost my right arm and leg, and all sense of reason.

If I could kill ten times over the one who dished that smarmy blow…What ifs, hads, had I nots. Only the stuff of myth that those grieving tell themselves to ease the pain.

The images faded. A haze of grey mist grew around my tearing eyes.

"Ick, Ick!" Regalis shook me. "You're up next. Wow, you just blanked out again."

"What? Oh, of course," I lurched to my feet, somewhat woozy of head and hefted my club. The wood felt like a hundred pounds. The entire weight of sickness and loss lay embedded in that crown-bashing weapon.

"What's wrong with you?" Oren muttered. "That fight with the butcher's brute spooked you, I see."

"Must have jarred some screws loose," called Marcellus in derision, across the way.

"We called your name and snapped our fingers in front of your nose," Regalis went on. "You just zoned out and went somewhere else."

I gave a slow nod and stared at him for a long time. "Sometimes we just don't know, Regalis. When the grains of sand run low. I think we should count our days while we have them."

I doffed my helm and padding, let them drop to the grass and walked slowly back toward the city wall.

Chapter 6

It was well into the soldiers' third watch that a silver moon rode low in the sky, ready to set behind a bank of tattered cloud. A musky damp hovered in the air, bringing with it the smells of dead fish from the river. We set out for the forum from our tombstone haven after a good stiff club practice, maybe to prowl about the richer section of town, raid a villa or two of our enemies, mess up the courtyard, urinate in the fountains, perhaps score us some coins from a fancy man's house if he was away and light on guards. Marcellus and I led, he in jauntier spirits than I, tossing jests with Feberiax. My muscles felt well primed from our club-cracking.

Marcellus smiled a cat's grin. "I don't know about you, ruggies, but I'm feeling a little itch in the loins. All this running about at night marking up walls and fouling temples has worked up a sweat."

"You and me both, Marcy," Oren quipped, easily the homeliest of the lot.

"Only bitch gonna take you is one of those dogs out in the butcher's yard," crowed Feberiax.

"Shut up, Feb."

"Let's try 'The Romp' down past the Mithraeum then," suggested Regalis. "It's just a skip and jog away. All our rods are feeling a bit restless."

Feberiax waved a hand. "Forget that smarmy joint. My brother got roughed up there last week. The pocked-faced guard whacked him pretty good."

"You don't say?"

"Griax conked out on some wench's lap, more than half sloshed. The bitch let the time ride out and the owner charged him double. Of course, he couldn't pay. One of the guards damn near broke his nose while the other watched, as a lesson for neglecting to bring enough coin to a 'proper' establishment."

"What?" stormed Marcellus. "That's downright criminal. Why didn't you tell us?"

"Slipped my mind."

"That's not a proper way to treat customers," Marcellus grumbled. "I'm a bit peeved."

"I'm thinking we should have a little chat with the owners of the establishment," I said.

"The idea's not a bad one," said Feberiax, cracking his knuckles. "We're in the neighborhood."

"What about our masks?" I pointed out.

"What of them?" jeered Marcellus. "Those girls of the night might go in for a bit of the weird, don't you think?" He laughed, tweaked his ape mask on the pug nose, then made a rude gesture with his hand. I could see the devil's gleam through the eye slits, with the opium running in his veins.

"Suit yourself, Marcy. One place is as good as any. I could use a little release myself. "Haven't been able to pluck Metella's flower yet. Though I taught dear Horatio a lesson about manners. She'll be—"

"Let us know when you do," said Oren with a ribald laugh.

"How many heavies are in there?" asked Regalis.

"Two," Feberiax said.

"Nothing that we can't handle." I hefted my club.

"Especially with the element of surprise," added Regalis.

"After you." I gave a mock bow. Regalis gave a gracious nod. We trouped up the near-deserted street like lords, our wings and masks bobbing in the odd, flickering torchlight. Only a few dim shapes, restless shadows in the night wandered around the port. A few drunks and sleepy soldiers. The smell of foul sewage drifted up from the Tamesis. Nothing we weren't used to.

"Remember, no mention of our names," hissed Marcellus. "From now on we're Owl, Hound, Ape, Eagle and Bull."

"That goes without saying." Feberiax rapped knuckles on the heavy oak door. A sign hung over the lintel, 'The Bowlegged Romp' with a fresco of a naked lady bent over and a man behind holding her ass, the smell of candlewax, incense and something sourer pervading the immediate area. Four barred windows hung overhead. I heard a faint titter and a moan drift from the darkness above.

We propped up our clubs at the side of the building, kept our masks on, while doing our best to appear innocent. Five slightly tipsy young men, returning from a dress-up party.

A scrape of metal came from within. A short and dark-haired slave opened the door, blinking at us and our grotesque masks in evident surprise. "Good evening, gentlemen."

"Hi ho to you, sir!" Marcellus said with his head cocked on a jaunty angle. "And a fine evening it is."

I pushed my beak in the half open door, looking left and right with hungry expectation. A high-ceiling hall presented itself with pillared walls and candle-lit ambience stretching behind.

"How many in your company?" asked the slave.

"I think there's five in our lot, if I have my numbers correct." I slurred in an overloud voice, pretending intoxication.

"That can be arranged, sir," the slave said, toying nervously at the door. "It's a little late."

"No matter, chief," Marcellus grunted, snatching up his club and pushing past him. "We're ripe and ready. Never too late for the old in-out." Oren laughed at that joke and pulled the slave along.

"Hey, you need to leave the clubs behind," the slave warned.

Regalis piped up from behind. "We just came from a play. We're actors. I'm Uncle Romulus and that's Remus." He pointed to me, grinning beneath my mask. "We're here to celebrate our mate's birthday."

"Yeah, birthday," put in Oren.

Feberiax slid the thick iron bar across the door behind us.

"That won't be necessary," the slave objected.

Marcellus swatted him on. "No worries, chief. This'll be a private party tonight. We'll keep your girls going well into dawn, if we've a mind to."

The slave, a curious sort with a sad, oval face, gave a cautious smile and followed up with a scowl. "What's your budget, sirs?"

"Sky's the limit," called Marcellus. "Give us your best wenches."

"Very well then, an exclusive. This way, sirs." The slave motioned us inside and called over the master of the house, a plump man dressed in silk fineries, with dark, oiled curls. He came idling out of a room with a hanging curtain of strung beads, holding a cup of wine in his left hand. He nodded to us with personable grace and snapped his fingers at two scuttling shapes in the shadows. "Alissa, Jorey! Bring the others."

The two slave girls, dregs likely, slunk off to chambers deeper within, a sinuous sway to their hips, a supple movement to my eye.

I heard a tinkle of water deeper within. Clear liquid flowed over a candle-lit naked marble nymph holding arms to the sky alongside several other lewd companion statues. Various large-leaved potted plants, ferns and fig trees ranged about the interior, designed to give the impression of freshness. The marble floor appeared freshly swept, but the air smelled of sweat and the stink of rank ale.

The hour was late and a husky watchman came shuffling out of the shadows. He seemed slightly drunk, lifting his bulk off a low bench. A long spear leaned up against a pillar at his side and his hand moved to it, then to his mouth to stifle a yawn. A gladius bobbed in a scabbard at his belt. His face, lined with fatigue, showed age, and his hair looked tousled as if he'd had a toss with one of the wenches in the back. Wouldn't have doubted it. Couldn't blame the wretch for his sport with so much temptation about. Maybe the master of the house had been taking a few winks?

Feberiax gave the guard an evil look and I watched his meaty fingers tighten on his club. He had mentioned two guards. Where was the second? A worry pricked my gut. Maybe business slowed at this hour and the owner had let him off early?

A high end place, this henhouse. Still, I expected better security. Five of us ruggies could take care of most of what they had; surely we should be able to take care of a pack of whores? Always had our trusty feet to flee if something went awry. We were young, fast and far too bold.

I quelled my concerns. Things would unfold as they would. I hoped Marcellus would not try something stupid and put us at risk.

Soon a parade of bare lovely flesh came sauntering toward us out of the candle-lit gloom. Bronzed Hispanians, slender Britons, fair-haired Gauls, and some statuesque northern beauties who could have been of the same stock as my birth mother.

A tall obsidian Nubian laced a finger along our ears as she passed, earning the appreciation of Regalis who had murmured a few choice hints. The master of the house obviously prided himself on the quality of his courtesans, judging by the size of his smile.

"Welcome, gentlemen. I'm Durdax, your host. No doubt there's someone for everyone. See for yourself! Olive-oiled Grecians, dazzling

Celts, buxom Britons, invigorating Italians, big-hipped Gauls, sensuous Samarians." He lifted his palms in an expansive gesture. "I'm sure you'll find our selection to your satisfaction." Gauging our reactions with a beady eye, he smiled again as our eager eyes roved over the alabaster and bronzed flesh that had been used so many times to defy count by men high and low. "Vena's thigh clutch is not paralleled in this part of the world. While Laral's love touch is superior as are the caresses of Lutretia here who'll have you melting on the floor."

"Excellent, excellent," Marcellus muttered, "we look forward to sampling these delights, Durdo."

The owner nodded, glancing nervously at the well-notched clubs we could no longer conceal. He seemed less and less enthused at the weaponry that the door slave had let us in with. The watchman, a grim-faced man with pocked face, approached and growled oaths. "You'll have to leave those billy clubs at the door." He turned to the slave. "Sagris, you dolt, why did you let them in?"

The slave stammered, squirming. "They pushed in before I could stop them, Remor. They—"

"Shut it. Never mind. I'll take those weapons now—"

Marcellus pulled his club away from the guard's reaching fingers. "Relax, chief. They're just props. Part of our costumes."

"What do I care of your props?" He scowled and looked to the master of the house who gave a small nod of acceptance. "Very well. But no tricks."

Fool! Did the lout actually think he'd be a match for us? I suppressed my laughter.

The owner intoned in a stern voice, "Ten denarii for the first half hour, fifteen denarii for the next. A maximum of one hour. An extra five, as it's an exclusive," he said, glancing back at the barred door.

"We know all about your famous rates," Feberiax sneered.

"The ale is free," the owner declared. "Take your cups and dip into that amphora by the fountain."

"No, sir," Feberiax protested. "Not for me." He held his hands up in an attitude of mock contempt. "I wouldn't want to pass out and have to pay the next half hour round."

The man's eyebrow rose, as if thinking that a queer thing to say. We all laughed at the irony of his strange reaction.

"As you wish," the owner said with more crispness than intended. He snapped his fingers.

One by one the women slunk forward like cats in heat. A pack of them, of different races, sizes, configurations and promise of potentials, roused various primal interests in us. In various states of undress, the most obvious being a diaphanous gown of silk that exposed cleavage and thatch to impressive display and maximum advantage. Sleek thighs, pleasing swell of rump and hips, smooth curve of breast, arc of buttock. Along with the parade of flesh I caught the scent of aromatic myrrh in the air and the hint of rosemary—perhaps to mask the less pleasant odors of the trade. I saw Feberiax lick his lips, Marcellus grin with a wolfish pleasure, Regalis tug at his Roman aristocratic nose and stubble. Oren's eyes seemed to bulge like a toad's in the heat of spring. As for myself, well, I couldn't say as I did much but stand there and gawp, speculating on the earthly pleasures of this troupe to come this fine evening. No man who was a real man could help but feel a tremor in his pants, or remain oblivious to these mistresses of the night's allure, considering that for the next few hours we could have them all to ourselves.

I looked to Marcellus, and he gave an acquiescent nod. So we forewent our immediate pleasures to settle business.

While the management was distracted, we all acted at once.

I slapped the cup of wine out of the owner's hand, and pushed him against the wall, knocking the breath out of him.

"Wha—what do you want?" he cried. Oren took down the slave who was closest and Marcellus and Feberiax sent the guard reeling to his knees.

Except Feberiax went a step further. He snapped one of the guard's fingers, while Marcellus held the struggling man, then broke another finger. "That's for Griax."

The man howled, spewing threats. "Who in flaming Hades is Griax?" He kicked and gnashed, but only got his head dunked in the fountain.

The women tried to flee but I blocked their path, my club raised. There was nowhere to hide.

Regalis tore off Durdax's toga, heaving him half naked on the mosaicked tiles and hissing through his teeth. He tossed remnants to Marcellus, some to me while I bound the owner's ankles and wrists then tossed the rest to Oren to hogtie the slave.

While some of the women stood frozen in dismay, others whined in confusion. After binding and gagging the chief watchman, we selected the choicest vixens and had our play, for the ruggies sported restless hearts—as did I.

We were quick and thorough and took our turns in pairs in the back rooms while three of us kept watch in case any skulker loitered about ready to crack our tender heads.

So passed some of our more fervid moments, as I recall.

Marcellus went first, taking the feistiest Briton with the wide hips and lazy red lips and fox-brown hair. Regalis seemed somewhat fixed on the Nubian. All the while the owner of the house moaned and rolled on the ground and the guard nursed his swollen hand. I was next up; so was Oren. He chose the Italian girl. A hard choice but I took one of the northern breed, knowing that if either of us had the strength afterward, we could go back for seconds, in which case I'd go for the Gaul.

I kicked open the door to the nearest, small rectangular cubicle with a low cot to the side. It had a definite sag to it with woolen, threadbare blanket to match. Despite the open window facing the back alley, the air held the rank stench of sweat and sex.

A good night awaited us. I had chosen the young, sandy-haired northerner with the long legs and killer thighs, because the flaxen hair reminded me of my heritage. Let's just say, she was no disappointment. She knew how to move and make the right noises at the right times; quite a vixen and quite an art—those slender fingers climbing up the small of my back like feathers and up the muscular line of my shoulders and then down to grip my butt cheeks.

The ripe warmth of her underneath me soothed my nerves. It did wonders on my corded thews, and the animal heat rose to dispel much angst of the past days.

I donned my devil's robe, adjusted my sweaty bird mask and came back in time to hear Durdax pleading with Marcellus and Feberiax.

"What more do you want, masters? Ladies of the night? I can give you two apiece free of charge. Ladies from Judaea, courtesans from Armenia scented with myrrh and jasmine. The finest exotic merchandise from Aegyptus and Mesopotamia and beyond, and these from Thracia, Numidia, Lycia!"

"We've already had that," pointed out Feberiax, motioning to the females huddled about.

Our host frothed foam at the mouth. "This is a lofty cut above the rest. I won't have hooliganery in my halls. A respected, decent business, it is."

"Hooliganery." Marcellus shook his head with a hiss of contempt. He nudged Feberiax in the ribs. "Hear that? Seems our host is some smarmy wordsmith. And seems to neglect the fact that he makes his earnings off the sweaty ass of slave labor."

"That he does," laughed Feberiax. "Good point, Ape." One of the girls slinking deeper in the corner caught his eye. "Wait, I'll take this one here for next round."

The owner's eyes lit up at a glance at the slender, copper-haired woman. "A fine choice. I'll give you her for free every Friday."

A quick movement alerted Oren to mischief. He stumbled forth to slap Durdax's slave down. The man was creeping along the floor toward the exit. Oren twined the slave's legs tighter and thrust him sprawling forward. Only muffled grunts issued from his gibbering maw, but these persisted with enough insolence that Oren took offence and dragged him by the hair. The slave's eyes bulged and he squirmed and buffeted, only to get biffed in the head.

"Careful Owl, you might crack this one's skull," gibed Feberiax.

The slave muffled out some threats before Oren stuffed some more foul garments in his mouth, displeased with the workings of the last gag. "An ornery slave you have here, Durdax." He turned to the master of the house, spread-eagled on the floor. "What kind of a business you running here?"

"One that'll have the sky falling on your heads," he croaked, chest heaving. "In blood."

Feberiax clicked his tongue, gave his head a sad shake. "Seems the pussymaster here hasn't understood the nature of the situation."

Marcellus sighed and stepped over to bitchslap him. While Feberiax and Marcellus went around and smashed all the potted plants and set our guard deeper in the fountain to cool his heels, I gazed around the dim-ochre shadows, wondering if any other surprises could trip us up. There may have been other pieces of ass the 'pussymaster' had neglected to show us. Might be worth a look-see about.

I moved to investigate but Marcellus called us to attention. "Well, what do you say, ruggies? Methinks some more late night sport in the henhouse awaits. Shall we try for second rounds?"

"I think that's a jolly arrangement," said Oren.

Hear, hears came from our group to the tune of bawdy cheers.

Marcellus nodded with an exaggerated enthusiasm. "But first! Let us attend some other important business. Gather the pretties up, ruggies."

We arranged them in a line one by one by the fountain, and I checked that there were no more hiding about the hall.

Marcellus stood with his mask half askew and his tousled black hair peeking from the edges. "Now, which one of you sluts shafted Griax?" He stared about to the stir of movement and restless grunts. "No answer? Cat got your tongue? Bull... describe this deceitful minx who brought woe to Griax."

"Well, Ape," said Feberiax, "she was big and red with a mean glint to her eye and a wide hip."

"Oho! Well! That's an incriminating detail for sure." His eyes fastened on the tall whore who was making efforts to slip behind the others. "Since you're the only gigantic redhead here, I'll assume it was you, slut."

"Stay back," she cried. She backpedaled, hissing, showed her teeth like a cat. "No way I'm going in with you."

Feberiax yawned. "Think I'll take the skinny one beside her while you take the big horse, knock some sense into her toothsome hide for me."

"Good play, Bull. I like your way of thinking."

The big redhead edged against the wall, pushing her hands out in protest. But Marcellus grabbed her by the wrist and pulled her into the back room with a feral insistence, heedless of her insults and protests. A look of fear and loathing blazed in her eyes. I never heard a woman speak with such a foul tongue.

We heard a dull smack and some sobbing. Followed by some more meaty slapping.

To the sounds of Feberiax's heaves and grunts, Regalis, Oren and I chided the moaning guard to silence.

An old man burst out of a back room, partly naked. Maybe he'd been napping in there or pleasuring himself. Disturbed at last by our tumult.

"Beat it, gramps," I said. "This is a private party tonight." I grabbed him by the scruff of the neck and hauled him to the door, pulled back the bar and thrust him out on the street, bare-assed. We got a good laugh out of that. Not the smartest thing to do, considering the old man could run to the watch. But who's going to believe a naked codger babbling something about losing his underwear to some masked marauders at the whorehouse? Marauders with bird and fox masks clamped on their faces? It was a lark. Pretty sure a naked man running about the streets would make his first priority to get his ass home, though what he was going to tell his household would have been an interesting story in lies and creative tale-weaving.

While I took second watch, I noticed the owner kept eyeing the farthest door down the hall. When I looked back at him, he averted his gaze which furthered my suspicion.

I stumped over and tried the door. Locked. I banged on it. "Anyone in there?" All too quiet. I took my club to it. Splintered the wood. Inside crouched a medium-sized man with salt-and-pepper hair on the other side of the cot, with a young woman. Coward. The sod was hiding there fully dressed, knowing that something peculiar was up, perhaps hoping to ride out the incident.

Darting sideways, the man made a grab for his blade. I shot forward, clubbed his arm and he dropped it with a livid curse.

"Out with you," I ordered. "Both of you." I wondered how he had a sword, considering they had a strict no-weapons' policy in this establishment. Maybe he was a 'special' guest.

"What have we here?" Marcellus cooed, sliding in, curious as a cat. "Oh, a little surprise?" He snapped his fingers. "Your name?"

"Rubor."

"Well, Rubor, this is how it's going to go down—"

"I'm just an extra," the girl cried. "Don't hurt me. I just came today."

"Shh," Marcellus said, finger to lip.

"Relax, it's not beat-up-on-woman day," I said, "—at least for some." I drew her out of her kitty corner with a tender hand. Neptune, she was pretty. I motioned to the man with my club. "Snap it up, old boy, if you care to keep your balls."

Marcellus quipped, "These old codgers like them young." His eyes roved with raw approval over the girl. When the man made another grab for his blade, Marcellus kicked the weapon away with a whistling laugh, and dragged him staggering out while Oren ripped off his toga. Shaking and cursing, he glared at us as if trying to recognize us under our ridiculous masks.

"That's a fine sword." Oren hefted the blade, testing its balance.

"Keep it, Owl—as a memento," said Marcellus. "Matter of fact, anything my ruggies see here they want, they get."

I guffawed. "If I were to take anything, it'd be this fawn-haired beauty."

"So take her, Eagle, what are you waiting for?"

I rubbed my chin. It was a crazy thought…why not? Looking at the woman, I was almost sorry I'd wasted myself on the flaxen-haired wench before I'd seen this lithe beauty tucked in the shadows with that old bastard.

She came out in the light. Fresh as a lily, unlike the other sad used pieces of flesh in that place. She wore a diaphanous gown and copper torc that matched the color of her shoulder-length hair.

I could see the dark pool of shadow in those greenish-emerald eyes, the irises reflecting rings of light. Coupled with an innocent sway of hips, all created that kind of fatalistic magic which stirs a man to foolish deeds. It was rare I got so besotted on first sight, and part of me resented it, but not enough to staunch the thud of my heart and the quiver in my loins.

"Tell you what," Marcellus offered, tying the last loop round the man's wrists while he studied us and our clubs with glowering distaste in the half glow of the clay lamps. "You do us a nice little dance, swinging your naked butt about for these pretty girls to witness—they never get a show—and we might let you go without some broken fingers." Marcellus whirled about in a mini flourish to appeal to the women.

A stunned pause followed. Then a few hee-hawed while some gave throaty growls, warming to Marcellus's prancing antics. Hoping to stay on his good side, they murmured approval. It was like a surreal Greek play and we were characters moving in an impromptu script. Marcellus snuck in another generous lick of opium from the leaf in his pocket.

The man growled, a statesman I guessed now, judging from the fine clothes we'd ripped off him. "It'll be a sore day in Hades before I do any such thing."

Marcellus shrugged. "Your call. Hound, Bull. Hold him."

Feberiax, easily the man's size and half more, grabbed his bound wrists and lifted them.

Marcellus reached a casual hand for the man's fingers. The bone-cracking pressure built and the man's face curled in a grimace. "Okay, you shit little bastards."

"Nice and slow. Dance for us."

We clapped in unison with the stomping of our feet. The women began to sing a bawdy tune. *"Last one in, last one out, is a dirty rotten lout."* Marcellus gave them some of his stash of poppy oil to keep them amused. They gobbled it up like hens at the trough. Though the young one I held back seemed frozen in terror at these antics. She seemed quite different than the rest. I kept thinking how good it would have been to have her underneath me versus the other one, as fine as she was. Maybe there was still time.

While the other ruggies had their sport with the furious codger doing his routine to the claps and jeers, I got to studying her and something came over me.

"Ramp it up. Faster, faster!" called Marcellus, marching around slapping hands on thighs and bobbing his head up and down in time with the beat. He was really liking this stooge show, or losing it.

"Come on, ladies!" he bantered. "Move those feet, clap those hands. Wiggle those titties. You're holding out on me!"

Even the meekest who had started out with reluctant motions tapped their feet now, for once seeing the tables turned on their hosts.

"Clap and sing along with me!" Marcellus roared. He danced with a frenzy and hoofed the watchman in the gut in time with the beat.

We clapped and hollered. The girls joined in. What a lark! Hadn't had this much fun in an age, since, well…before Drace had died. Marcellus was a genius at generating laughs and getting people to opt into his crazy schemes. The girl at my side found no amusement in it at all. Her eyes pinched shut in terror.

"Relax, girl," I laughed, slapping her on the back. "Just a little fun here. Ape is a bit of a nut. But just ignore him. Let him burn off his steam, then he's as docile as a kitten."

"What's that, little ruggie?" Marcellus said, hand to ear. "Some mention of my name?"

"No, Ape, just remarking on your fine form. Keep it up." I shot up a thumb.

He chuckled and went on, hooting and shaking his head like a wet dog. I hissed at the girl. "Something to brighten your day. Unless you'd rather go back in there and hike up your dress and lie on your back for our grey dancing weasel?"

Her small frame shuddered.

I grinned. More and more I liked the look of this fawn. Fresh. Clean. Wholesome. Not like those other sluts. The opium was getting to my brain.

I began to wonder if she'd ever done the act with the old man. I pondered the possibility.

My instincts warned me something was askew.

In all our fussing about and focus on the main entertainment, we'd failed to notice our slave boy tearing at his bonds with his teeth. Now he'd managed to loosen his ankles and was making a quick dash for the door.

"Sagris! Call the watch!" the owner cried.

I leaped out, tripped the slave and sent him reeling on his face. I picked him up by the neck and hauled him back. He kicked and fought so I had to menace him with my club.

"Fool!"

Marcellus shook his head. "Aye, that was a stupid move, boy."

Nothing could be truer and it only served to enrage our resident nutcase Marcellus whose mood up till now had been genial. Now he began to take out his wrath on our host until he howled and cursed.

"For that wise trick, you're owing us double, Durdax."

"You young hoodlums won't—"

"Won't what?"

The outburst was met with grim laughs and slaps from us ruggies, loaded on wine and pleasure. Marcellus grabbed the owner's small finger and bent it until some cartilage began to give.

"Oops, smarts, doesn't it?" quipped Marcellus. "And now for gift giving. You, my fine bastard, have inconvenienced a certain friend of ours to the tune of what—twenty five denarii?—and that does not go without recompense. Ah, ah, no objections." He waved a finger. "Bull, you stake your claim first."

"Well, for starts, I'll take Griax's fee back. Plus triple expenses in damages."

"Done." Marcellus grabbed the owner and whispered something nasty in his ear. With alacrity, Durdax allowed himself to be led over to the strongbox down the hall in the beaded-off office. After some slaps and jinglings of keys, Marcellus rifled through the coffers and returned, stuffing a reasonable facsimile of fifty denarii in Feberiax's greasy hands.

"Owl?"

Oren put a finger to his hound-jowled mask and mused, "I think I'll take some gold myself. No, wait! I'll take this fine jewel on the master's finger. It's an emerald, isn't it?—there's a girl I fancy who might like the gift. Hound, you up for some coin?"

Regalis shook his head. "I'll go for this fine sword of the gentleman's. I'm thinking our host can repay our generous dancer. What do you think?"

"A fine choice," commended Marcellus. "And you?" he peered at me with an ape-like inquiry, quite apt given his mask.

"I was about to ask you the same question."

Marcellus bobbed with mirth. "My humble self is sated—with a triple shot of these fine ladies of the evening and the sights and sounds of the happiness of my ruggies!"

I grinned but gave an incredulous grunt. "Aren't you a little sloshed for such magnanimity?"

"True. Thank you for pointing that out, Eagle. I know what you want, my ruggie. That pretty girl, at your side. For some odd reason you seem to be saving her for something. Well, she's yours. Take her as a slave. I'm sure Durdax, our kind host, won't mind."

The owner, sprawled on the floor, blinked in exasperation and sputtered out a hoarse protest. "That's not possible," he blubbered. "Fortuna's worth three hundred denarii. I paid in full for her at the slave markets just yesterday—"

I silenced him with a club whistling an inch from his nose. "I think you can afford it. Judging from the posh looks of this place, you can afford triple. Marble statues, fountains, the finest porcelain and well, a private bath and gardens to boot. It's a high class place you have, as you say."

"No, take coins, if you're going to—"

Marcellus snarled and stamped his foot near the man's head. "If my ruggie wants something, he gets it!"

The man tried to struggle to his feet. The girl at my side stood rigid, as if afraid what would happen should she fall into the hands of that vindictive slave-master.

"Tell you what," urged Feberiax, "you either give her to him, or we break every one of your fingers, slow, like this..." On cue from Marcellus, he stepped over, grabbed Durdax's hand and twisted until our host sagged in a blur of agony. The proprietor gasped in pain as we heard a small bone crack. "Alright, already. Take the girl and be damned!"

"That's better."

My black heart soared at the prospect of acquiring this fair nymph for my personal own. Her exceptional sultriness and innocence so juxtaposed made the others seem almost sordid. Her delicate features, sensuous mouth, oiled and perfumed skin, and the gleaming swell of wide hips, every exotic inch of her—it was like a madness came over me, no doubt spawned by the night's drama, not unlike that which was to overcome me not too long after. But then again, I was young and naturally obsessed. Running with a pack of wolves. Drunk, high, on top of the world and with an excess of sex energy, and vandalistic fervor, inexperienced—and stupid. But all this little mattered in the moment.

Yet something told me this prize must be drawn up as a legitimate transaction. I had a bad feeling that, unless the score was settled, these rogues would come after me. It was crazy, but it had been a crazy night.

"I'll pay you forty denarii for this young beauty, fair and square, Durdax, to make this legitimate."

"Forty is not enough!" blurted the proprietor. "This woman—"

Marcellus clicked his tongue. "Eagle, you're going soft on this worm. It saddens me."

I held up my hand. "My mind's made up. I'll pay for her two days from now. Meet my slave at the market, by the old port. No tricks. No members of the watch. You bring any muscle, I walk."

Our host's lip quivered.

"In return, we won't trash this place—at least any more than it is now." I swung my club in dangerous proximity to an expensive vase poised on a pedestal.

His mouth twisted, and I could see the anger and pain in his sweaty face, how he'd plan to doublecross me once he could identify me without my mask. Get his revenge for his cracked fingers.

But I'd already figured that part out too and though Regalis and Marcellus shook their head at my naivety, I was adamant.

Marcellus sneered. "If you're going to be such a pussy, Eagle, I'll take her myself—for free."

"The hell you will," I growled.

"Oh?" He'd flipped back into one of those evil, mercurial moods. He turned and grabbed the young woman and roughly fondled her breasts, his hand moving toward her crotch. "Yes, she'll do fine, Eagle. Nice choice."

She squirmed away in distress and slapped him.

"Hands off." I shoved Marcellus away and raised my club. A tense expectancy settled over our company. Marcellus raised his club and we squared off, ready to go at it.

Regalis stepped between us and pushed us away from each other. "Stop it, you idiots! You're not going to fight over a piece of ass and get your heads bashed in and us captured. We can't hang here forever. You're both too damn mule-headed."

Marcellus shook out his shoulders. "Perhaps, Hound. But I'm just trying to make a point—Eagle's being an ass."

"Let it go," Feberiax sneered. "If he wants the girl, let him have her. The night's still young. There's more debauchery to go."

We snorted our agreement.

In our ears rang the master's sniveling cries. "Mark my words, she'll come running back to Durdax, you dumb hoodlums!"

Leaving Durdax, guard and slave to fend for themselves, we trooped out into the night. We parted ways, my mates happy at their fortunes this evening. I took Fortuna by the arm. We hurried along, the day near breaking as we trudged alone in the streets.

She wore only a light shawl around her shoulders over the nearly see-through dress to stave off the night chill. I could see she was shivering. I offered her my devil cloak. She shook her head in fatigue.

"You're not like the other night girls," I murmured.

"Is that why you made extra special efforts to snatch me up?" Her voice broke. "I thought he was going to kill us. I—I just got here. Came in on a ship. Where are you taking me?"

Shipped her from somewhere. Some prize, this beautiful young feline.

"From where did you come?"

"Gallia."

I nodded as if nothing could be more normal. That lovely innocence struck me again. Such a rare, natural beauty. A classical profile of legendary Helen of Mycenae, but even more striking.

Her expression grew frightened. "What if someone sees me, drags me back there?"

"You'll stay in my father's villa. You won't be going out."

She cringed at that. "What, so he can take advantage of me every night too?"

"Relax, it's not like that."

"But that's no life! Holed up in your villa forever—"

"And this is?" I jeered, motioning my hand back to the seedy brothel.

"Caged up back there on your back all day and night, with ugly, old lank-tooths like that grey weasel?"

She shivered and wrinkled her nose. The night air was chill. I offered my cloak to her again and she took it with a grateful nod. I could tell she was new to this game. It had just been pure luck that I'd snatched her up.

"He'll kill you when you try to pay him. Don't you see?"

"Relax." I waved it off. "It won't be me who pays him. I'll hire somebody. I've already figured that out."

"What?" she snorted. "Like—"

"Be still. This is no time for chit-chat." My mind was still stewing on Marcellus. I didn't know how far I could trust him. This leadership game was getting out of hand. Going to be the end of us all.

"Durdax'll come back for me."

"Once he takes the money and the deal is signed, he'll forget all about you. Relax."

She hissed, as if it made her less desirable.

"Sorry to blunt your pride, but slave girls are expendable."

"Where will you get the money?"

"These little escapades of ours have their perks."

"Breaking into people's businesses and homes?" I raised an eyebrow. She scoffed. "I've come from a war-torn town in Gallia, burned and looted by invaders, now reduced to the likes of a kept woman in a Roman house. What worse things can happen to me?"

"You could be dead." Her defiant tone surprised me. And yet, something more lurked there. A challenge. Then it hit me. She'd never really adjusted to being a slave, only thrust into this new world of servitude and hadn't grasped the reality.

I shrugged, still eyeing that trim package and all the fun to come. The hard part would be convincing Mexor to let me keep her. But I had an angle on that too.

"Why don't you take off that ridiculous mask?" she asked.

"All in due time. Besides, I like it on."

"Afraid to show who you are? Are you hiding some defect?"

I blinked, as if this delicate, curvy woman knew anything about brain-busting and the trials of the street and the fine line we walked. I pulled off my mask and tucked it in a bag I kept in my pocket.

"Shush. We're coming closer to my house. I don't want to wake my father."

It was getting close to dawn so I tapped lightly on the door. My secret code, two raps, a space, followed by a final rap. Denetio let us in.

His brows rose at the sight of the young woman, her flushed cheeks and wild, inscrutable eyes.

"A new friend?" he inquired drolly.

"Kind of like that." Our silent communication was sacrosanct.

As much as I wished it, there would be no more pleasures of the flesh tonight and I resisted the urge to make it otherwise. Fortuna was not some jaded prostitute to be used and abused. I'd rather earn her trust than be that to her. I instructed Denetio to get her cleaned up and find a place for her in the slaves' quarters upstairs.

Denetio took her by the hand and led her up the stairs.

I breathed a sigh of relief when I closed the door to my room.

My body was dead tired from running about, still vibrating from the bashing of heads and whoring, but the sight of the slender girl's figure made my muscles taut with expectation. That excitement had not died. A sexual thrill rippled through my body. I thrust off my soiled woolen cloak and tunic and eased down onto my bed, imagining her willing body next to mine. The dreams and half lucid fancy merged into a fantasy of fleshy pleasures. After a time, I drifted off.

Some time later, I awoke to a swish of movement. A dream? Instinctively I jerked up, reaching for my club.

A lithe figure crouched beside my bed and put a finger to my lips. "Sh". Quick as a fox, she slipped under the covers with me.

For a while we lay there, our breaths playing on each other's cheeks as the warmth of our bodies adjusted to each other.

"I appreciate you taking me from that place," she murmured. "I lay there upstairs in that clean, comfy cot, thinking about the events of the evening. A terrible life it would have been—wasting away in the brothel like the other women. I feel so lost and alone in this new land. So far, you've only shown me kindness—you've been a gentleman."

I mumbled my agreement.

"I'll have you know that old man didn't have his way with me. He paid Durdax good money for a young flower. I was to be his first paying client. You came—at an opportune time."

"I just realized," she added, "I don't even know your real name."

"It's Icarus."

She thought that over. "Icarus? Like the boy who flew too close to the sun?"

"Something like that," I grunted. "You never told me what happened to your family."

She tensed, swallowed hard.

"You don't have to talk about it, Fortuna, if you don't want to. I'm not—"

"No, it's good to talk about it." She closed her eyes and sucked in a deep breath. She rubbed her temples and sighed. "Our village was on the border of Gallia and Germania. Always uprisings and rebellions. My mother wanted out of that place, but my father's business depended on the lucrative trade of furs there. One day a large band of raiders came from north over the earthworks. Defense was weak in our village, especially when the river flooded, as it often did. They plundered us. I hid. They were ready to set up rule, seeing no resistance. But news reached the nearest garrison and the Romans soon came. They were merciless.

"Soldiers. Mercenaries! I remembered axes in the night, blood, screams—" she recoiled, forced back a tear. Her fingers curled in knots. "My father caught the edge of a Roman blade, then my mother was hauled away by grasping hands. I don't know where she was taken, only that I was taken too somewhere else, to a palisade along with a bunch of other villagers. The next days passed in a miserable blur.

I looked away. "I'm sorry." My eyes flicked back to her, catching a glimpse of her pain, and shuddering at the weight of it.

"They made us all slaves. Both Gauls and Germans. Made examples of us all, thinking we had colluded with the enemy." She brushed away a warm tear and showed a fierce face. "Hold me, please."

I held her for a long time. I clasped her and ran my fingers soothingly along her slender shoulders and back until I thought that she might not ever be able to open up to me without the memory of savagery lurking behind that damp brow of hers.

Then her warm arms encircled me; our lips met for the first time. I ran my tongue along her upper lip. Her lips received mine with moist approval, then they probed mine in more than just idle curiosity. Our fingers explored each other's taut bodies. I could sense her hesitation. A glow of passion for her kindled my loins and worked its way upward to my heart.

"Love me, Icarus." Her voice broke in a tremulous gasp. "Make the pain go away."

As much as I would have liked to ease into this gently, it was just not possible with a woman as lush and desirable as Fortuna. I shucked off her fresh light gown and suddenly our loins met for the first time.

The next few hours passed in a blur of dizzy pleasures, each one superseding the last. My blood flamed. Choosing this rare jewel of Gallic womanliness only confirmed my natural instincts. Her fiery sensuality and sinuous movements took both of us to a crescendo.

Then dropped back, only to build again, driving me out of my mind. With her in my arms I had a sudden inexhaustible energy, elevated to the status of the gods: Apollo, Mars, even Jupiter himself. And her a willing Diana. An eternity stretched before us as if we could last forever in this union. Then the wave crested and I plummeted down from the clouds of Olympus in the sweaty heat of abandon. We lay twined, deities no more, but just warm skin on skin, Fortuna's sleek curves pasted to mine in a natural-fitting cocoon, her breath fanning on my throat, her auburn locks whisked across my chest, her throat cooing drowsy, sleepy little husky love sounds. My response, a faint murmur, the gentle language of sated lovers. Our breaths gentled as we lay as one.

Chapter 7

At first I hid Fortuna in my own room. She cooperated by not making much noise or causing suspicion, until one day my father caught her rustling about the back where he kept our most expensive wines.

"Who in Hades are you?" he growled at her.

"I'm—I'm Fortuna—"

"Who?"

His grumbling voice had me stumbling out of my room. "I bought her."

"What? Are you crazy? You bought her?"

I shrugged. "That's what I said."

"Where?"

"Never mind where."

He did a double take and appraised her from head to toe, his sharp eyes lingering long on certain parts of her anatomy. He paused as she stood there in haughty pose and I'm guessing she was much used to these types of glassy stares after her trials in getting to Londinium.

My father showed his teeth. "You want to play me, Icarus? Okay, well, you get to pay for her keep."

A crafty smile edged over my lips, recalling the wealth only a club's reach away in the villas of certain citizens. "Not a problem."

"Is it really? What can she do? Besides the obvious?"

"Lots of things." I turned to her. "Well?"

She beamed. "I can sew, sing. I can cook—"

"We already have a cook."

I shrugged. "She can work around the villa. And she's good with her hands."

"No doubt," my father snorted.

"I mean, she can clean, look presentable—"

"I can make pottery and darn clothes," she spoke up, bright-eyed.

"Right, Zeno can use her as kitchen help," I said.

"We've already been through that."

"But she has lots of other skills—"

My father shook his head in disapproval. Then he sighed. "Well, if it keeps you off the streets, Icarus, then I'll reconsider. But somehow I don't think anything will cure those restless habits of yours." He frowned. "But maybe a fine-looking girl like her can."

Fortuna grinned as she took me by the arm and herded me back to my room. I cast a hopeless glance back at my father who shook his head, snuffling a low sound from his aquiline nose. But I knew my father, and I knew in that stony look he secretly approved of my purchase.

* * *

There was something satisfying about going out and being lord of the city, immune to authority, defacing temples, knocking heads of those who defied us, then coming back to curl up to a beautiful woman's warmth. Fortuna was like a red hot magnet of sexual energy, a fire that kindled my soul, and between her and the night prowlings I felt as if I were exploring a vast field of violence, power, sex and self-empowerment.

I'd put Metella on the backburner and grew increasingly distracted during tutor sessions. Plato and Socrates might as well have been geographers for all I cared. Asia Minor could have been part of Germania.

Some looting of the upper villas had gained us some coin, and I used it to pay off the promissory note I'd pledged Durdax.

One bright afternoon, I donned my leather hood, covered my face with charred ashes, and approached a young slave with moony eyes and darting feet in leather sandals. I grabbed his arm. "Here, boy, you want to make a few sesterces?"

He shied away in alarm, gaping. At first he licked his lips, but I laughed. "No need to be afraid." The boy's wide eyes grew with an enthusiastic nod.

"What's your name?"

"Fabio." With a bit of shy tilt to his chin, he blinked.

"Well, Fabio, I want you to run over to *The Romp* down the way, and give the owner this money." I planted a small sac of forty denarii in his palm and his eyes popped at the telltale jingle. "Tell them it's for the 'sale of a certain slave girl'.'"

"But that's a bad place," he protested in a thin voice.

I waved a hand. "What isn't in this world, Fabio? There are bad places and people everywhere. Go on, if you want your coins otherwise I'll find somebody else." I thrust two denarii in his other hand for his trouble.

He was quick to take both and sped off to do his deed.

I waited, watching him down the street. When I saw the door of the brothel open and the gruff exchange between slave and doorman and the money change hands, I sauntered off, doffing my hood and using my own spit to wipe off the ash. I imagined the conversation that ensued:

"What did the man look like?"

"A grey man with a hood, sir."

"Did he say anything?"

"No, just gave me the money."

It was a good laugh. The money was expendable—coins, my ruggies and I had lifted from one of the rich houses when the masters were away. That same day I hired a slave to deliver a sealed letter personally to Durdax, claiming delivery of the forty denarii. That way, if the doorman decided to get greedy and pocket the coins, he'd get a proper bashing from his master. One could never be too trusting of slaves.

* * *

A halcyon series of days passed, in a blur of drizzle and biting rain, clubs swinging during night forays and a spate of sexy, steamy encounters. My flashbacks to Drace, the memory of his death, diminished. Fortuna, the sexy minx, had gotten under my skin. Possibly even an addiction. Perhaps my father had got that right about her. Whether it would keep me from my pastimes—I doubted it. Though of late Marcellus's insolent bravado had started to wear.

Strenuous night-prowlings and extensive training in the cemetery led to overindulgence in rot-gut wine which had my brain reeling, leaving my tongue furred and my stomach sour. Stumbling back to my father's villa, I vaguely recalled Regalis proposing a change of pace, that we all go out in the country, do some fishing to let off some steam. It promised to be the one sunny day all year in this land of continual rain and mist. Despite my grogginess, I snuck into the back of my father's house and rummaged through the wine cellar. As I grabbed an amphora of wine for my ruggies from the deep shadows, Fortuna's voice froze me in place. "Going somewhere?" she huffed, putting on a sour face and challenging pout.

She'd been nagging me to take her somewhere, complaining about being cooped up all the time in the villa but for the odd venture to the market with our slave, Iuventus, to shop for fish and vegetables. Disguised of course with a hooded dress.

"You could say that."

"Take me with you—wherever that is."

I shook my head, knowing it was not a good day for taking chances. "Just a pleasure trip. Me and the ruggies. They won't like it."

"How do you know that?" she persisted. "I never get out of this place." Her voice had that whiny, brittle quality. "You keep me here like a stuffed—"

"Like what? Would you like me to take you back to the whorehouse?" I pointed out the horrors of that option, keeping my temper in check.

"No, but I can't be kept here like a pea hen all day." She thrust out a hip, leveled me an icy challenge. Arms akimbo, she peered at me through half closed lids. Even her coquettish pleas landed too heavily on my hung over brain.

"Alright, Fortuna, okay," I said, trying to get her to stop harping. "I'll discuss it with the others, see if they agree. If they do, you can come along."

"Hurray!" She brushed back her lustrous hair and flashed me one of her provocative smiles. They'd always make me melt. "See that you don't break your promise."

I grumbled. I had her don a slave's rain hood and tie her auburn hair back so none showed. No doubt Durdax or his watchman would have slaves out looking for her. It would be a year or more I figured, before I could ever hope to take her out in the public eye without disguise.

The two of us along with Denetio took my father's wagon out and steered our donkey toward the forum.

The others waited beside the sprawling shadow of the entrance arch, grumbling at our late arrival. "Ick, you trying to blow us off?" Oren gaped. "Oi, what do we have here? Fortuna! You're looking mighty pretty today."

"Thank you." She nodded with an impish grin. At first they resented her intrusion on their private time together with all its confidences and rude talk. Feberiax jerked an arm. "Fishing's not a girlish pastime," he pointed out with a low grumble.

Marcellus, finger to lip, chewed a nail. "Aw, let her come—provided she doesn't take offence at our coarse banter and antics?"

Of course, she would forgive such behavior and Marcellus, much entranced by her lithe figure, grinned a wolf's grin, appraising her healthy skin and fresh complexion amongst other things, this veritable Venus.

Nothing other than what I expected from horny old Marcellus, the sly bastard. Despite his so-called indifference, he'd always craved a taste of my woman's flesh.

"Stay close to me," I said. "Keep your hood up." I dismissed Denetio who'd been intended to accompany her back to the villa if the ruggies disapproved of her coming.

We piled into the large, two-wheeled wagon and headed out as a group, with our clubs tucked under a blanket at our feet. I slouched in the driver's bench, half passed out in the sun while Regalis took the reins and dumped Feberiax in the back with his fishing gear, poles and lures. Oren had summoned slaves to rustle up some bait—fresh grubs they'd picked outside the city walls early in the morning.

Fortuna remained in high spirits, excited about the venture. We passed under the towering west gate, ignoring the unsmiling soldiers as we passed. She seemed more animated than usual, and I caught Marcellus ogling her again with no apparent effort to conceal the fact. Fortuna did not help, her sly winks and little head tosses, and feigned pats at her perfumed hair. They only fueled his lust for her, to the point of embarrassment. These flirtations had me feeling greener under the gills than I already was despite the soothing warmth of the sunlight and the rhythmic movement of the wagon.

We clattered down the cobbled road, the air fresh, the passersby numerous: horse traders from Calleva, soldiers and ox-cart baggage trains from Veralumium, Celts on foot with sacks over their shoulders and knives at their belts, dressed in leather jerkins and calfskin boots, ready to try their fortunes in the city with the coming of the festival of Bacchus.

The sun shone in a cloudless blue sky, unlike the foggy haze that afflicted Londinium most of the time. On a cue from Regalis, I snapped the reins and clicked my tongue, urging the donkey up a dirt track north of the main road along the banks of the Fleetus River, a small tributary of the Tamesis a mile from the city wall. Magpies and crows flitted in high treetops. The wind rustled through the broad leaves of tall yew and sprawling willows. I tethered the donkey to munch on the grass out of sight in case some ruffians tried to steal our wagon.

Marcellus chanced to move in close when Fortuna was bending over by the cart, and she brushed against him, causing him to catch her in his arms. His hand fell to her left breast and the other quickly followed over to her rump.

"Careful there," I growled, jerking Fortuna back. I cast her a sharp, warning look upon seeing an impudent gleam in those emerald eyes of hers. She raised her brows, gave a husky laugh and moved on toward the waterside with a jaunty step.

"You've got yourself a real minx there," Regalis muttered. "Don't envy you, Ick. She'll lead you a merry chase."

Marcellus shrugged and followed, yelling after Oren. "Hey, Orey, pass me one of those rods and a handful of grubs. Going to catch us some fine trout today."

Such games I was not in the mood for. My head hammered over every little sound and movement, and was much too bone-weary from the evening's activities and those of the night before. My stomach felt sour as if I were on the verge of heaving.

I loosed a miserable sigh, turned my back on them and looked for some place to curl up in the shade and sleep. It was one of those days, when everything seems to go wrong and one wishes to have just stayed in bed.

Over my shoulder I caught a glimpse of my ruggies: plunked in the shade of a willow tree in a comfortable spot on the bank. They cast their lures for whatever might avail itself and joked and told stories. The quiet stillness of the country and the heat of the high sun lulled me to further lethargy. I tossed aside my club and curled up in the grass like a bug. At this distance I could enjoy the sight of my proud beauty and the sparkling water and rustling leaves. Yet I thought to spy Marcellus examining her behind my back, his color rising, lips freshly licked and gleaming at her fine figure. No doubt he regretted what he'd missed in not snagging a prize like that for his own. Either way, I sunk deeper into the cushioning grass and nodded off.

I woke to a dream, my head foggy, the sun too bright for my tastes. Regalis snored fast asleep at my side, perhaps as knackered as me, bored with fishing. Two fat glossy trout lay at his side tails up in one of the amphorae empty of wine. Feberiax and Oren lounged down at the waterside.

I snatched at my club, stumbled down with haste to the grassy shore, feeling a sickness growing in the pit of my stomach.

"Where's Fortuna?" I demanded.

Feberiax shrugged. "Think she's back there with Marcellus." My heart sank. I noticed Marcellus nowhere in sight.

"Where?" I growled.

Oren jerked a thumb back in the bushes, a copse toward the road.

The blood pounded in my brain. I could hear rustling sounds and grunts and a cry and slap on flesh as I scrambled closer. I broke out of the trees and saw Fortuna with her back to the ground, all in rumpled disarray, with Marcellus reared up overtop, nearly naked, keeping her down.

My fellow ruggie, friendly Marcellus, the proper bastard. I charged him with rage in my heart. His ears pricked at the sound of my pounding feet. He jumped up, hurrying to adjust his clothing to cover his privates. Fortuna looked away as I swore, a murderous heat upon me, her face flushed.

"No harm, old sport," said Marcellus, "Fortuna's a whore. Naturally, I didn't see any problem enjoying her, seeing as we are ruggies after all. We both won her fair and square back at the wonkerhouse. Knew you'd not hesitate to share."

"Keep on talking, Marcy." I crept toward him, my club gripped in a white-knuckled fist. The insolence of the lout. It set me off and I readied my club to strike and he grabbed up his, chest bare, as we went at it.

He had me at a disadvantage, being mostly sober and me still recovering from too much drink.

The other ruggies stumbled up from the stream to watch, hearing thwacking sounds too loud to be coincidence. This time neither of us had helm or protective padding to cover us. The cracks of wood on wood echoed through the trees. Fortuna screamed. She held her head in her hands while tears sprang to her eyes. Regalis held her back. Black with rage, I caught Marcellus's weapon somewhere high up on the end of my club and flicked it off. I lunged in as Drace had taught me and caught his thigh with my kneebone. He gave a sharp yelp as my elbow also clipped his jaw, bloodying his lip. He pushed me away with a sullen curse then swung with murderous speed. My quick ducking saved my skull. The corded muscle on my right shoulder rippled as I swung on the counterattack. Marcellus backed up, the crafty rat, blocked, wood smashing on wood. The lurid echo rebounded across the water, but was lost in the rustle of wind sighing through the trees. I twisted about. I swung again, this blow grazing his upper left arm. He licked his lips with a grimace. "Not bad, for a drunken bastard, Ick. Oh, I can understand your rage. I would be too, but good luck besting me."

We circled each other, poised like pack animals. The last remark goaded me into a stupid move and as I lunged in for a crippling strike, he crouched and cracked me across the shoulders and sent me sprawling.

Fortuna's gasp came readily to my ears. I could sense my ruggies' apprehension, but I'd suffered worse, and was up on my feet in a flash, springing like a hare. My club caught his blow square on—a hit that would have emptied my gut and knocked me senseless. Instead, we stood deadlocked, glaring eye to eye, our clubs pressed at each other's chests in a tight cross. We shoved each other back and I swore. Marcellus grinned and spoke jesting words with each feint and swing as if he were claiming superiority over me. This intimidation would not work on me—at least for too long. A childish adolescent dance ensued between two foes equally matched, none about to yield. One slip and one of our brains would spill on the grass. A primal male clash as old as time—on the defense of a woman's honor and a man's pride. The ugliness had been brewing for too long between us, and the day of reckoning had come. I tensed, ready to end this one way or another.

The disturbance had alerted some traffic coming down the river road. A cartman and his workhands came racing down toward us. I turned in contempt, wanting to end this fight without distractions.

"Break it up, you young hooligans," one shouted. "Be off with you now."

The others bulled in and shoved us apart, knocking us to the ground while Feberiax assured the bumpkins it was just a friendly bout of rivalry. Hardly any laughing matter, considering we could have killed each other.

Feberiax hunched close to me and hissed, "Enough, you imbeciles. Let's not get the locals riled up and on to the fact that we're *The Clubs*."

The farmers drifted back to their wagon, seeing the matter brought under control, muttering curses among themselves about drunken young fools. Marcellus and I brushed ourselves off and Fortuna had pulled her hood up to conceal her features. She held her eyes downcast.

"Apologize," I growled at Marcellus.

"For what? Offering my manly services to your whore?"

I lunged at him, but Regalis and Feberiax held me back. "Stop it, you idiots," cried Regalis.

Marcellus smirked. Fortuna came over and slapped him hard across the face. At the sight of his cheeky grin, she tried to kick him in the balls, but he stepped back with ease. "Oh, temper, temper, vixen. Makes the disgruntled fishwife seem as if she wants more sport."

"Enough already," warned Feberiax.

Maybe it was all for show. I couldn't know and would likely never know. Fortuna was a tricky, complex woman. One thing for sure, I'd never know all her secrets.

"No more outings for you," I griped at her and motioned her toward the wagon.

"Isn't her fault. She's just a natural born vamp," quipped Marcellus.

"Let's go. This place is getting dull," I said with disgust on my tongue, refusing to take the bait. "One thing's for sure, you'll walk back to town."

Marcellus made no comment, his face curled in an offensive grin. He stared back at us, blinking, nursing his bruises.

In awkward haste Regalis loaded his gear and fish into the wagon and clambered aboard. The others hitched up the donkey and followed suit. On the ride back, a cold silence fell upon us, eager to put the day's doings behind us. At last Feberiax and Oren started chatting about the weather, the fine season for skundering and hell-raising, and oh, that was a right fight, their brains juiced up on the wine I'd brought. Through it all, I bit my tongue. I'd drunk nothing in the last while for obvious reasons. Regalis wisely held his tongue about his prediction that Fortuna would be trouble.

The copper disc of the sun sank lower in the sky when I left them all off at the Flavian arch. Fortuna and I rode in silence and pushed our way through the dwindling crowd.

After a time I turned to her. "That little show back there was uncalled for," I growled.

"What show?"

"You serious? Seems as if you got a kick out of egging comrade Marcellus on. That's a dangerous game."

"I was just doing it to get you jealous. You seem to take everything so seriously—and me for granted. I just wanted to show you that I'm a little more than cheap comfort during the late night hours."

"And look at what it did, you stupid woman! One step closer to splitting up *The Clubs*."

Her head hung low. "I'm sorry. It was a stupid thing to do." I saw her chest heave and her lower lip tremble.

I sighed and struggled to control my anger. Many thoughts warred with each other, each one making it hard for me to forgive her brashness. At last, I curled my arm around her left shoulder. It felt tense and rigid. "Forget it, Fortuna. If I could count the times I've done dumb things, you'd look like a saint in comparison."

She brightened and put her hand in mine.

"Come on. Let's get back," I said. "There's a warm bed waiting for us."

She laughed, made a husky sound at the back of her throat. "One thing I do know, Ick, your sex play makes me forget my tragic past." She snuggled into my chest and I gave a wry grunt. Maybe the day could be salvaged...

* * *

Hot weather and muggy grey skies settled over Londinium most of the summer, keeping us short of temper. Jostling my way through the dense crowd after tending my father's shop, I chanced upon our young slave Iuventus at the fish market, accompanying Fortuna on a food-gathering mission. Wicker basket tucked beneath her arm, she chatted amiably with the fish monger, a voluble, red-cheeked man, choosing her river trout with care. She was all hooded up nicely. I nodded at her baggy folds, loose enough to disguise her suggestive curves, I knew only too well in the heated hours of the night. The sight of her stirred my voracious carnal appetite. She'd always been keen for more despite my lengthy demands.

"Good day, Iuventus, Fortuna," I greeted them.

"Ick! What brings you to the forum?" Her rosy features brightened at the sight of me, her eyes traveling from my wide shoulders to the slim line of my hips.

"Oh, out and about. Thought to burn off a little steam after tending Mexor's shop. Clean my head of cobwebs from the last binges."

She sniffed. "Seems to be a regular pastime of yours, all that gadding about and guzzling of wine."

"Speaking of which, why don't we stroll about, see if there's something you'd like in one of the shops? There're some nice necklaces down at Julio's, I hear."

She shrugged. "Why not?"

I motioned to Iuventus. "You can go now. I'll take the lady back to the villa." The boy flashed me a grin and departed.

We elbowed our way through the crowd to the end of the forum, past the heady incense and the temple of Bacchus and away from the food vendors and butcher stalls where some of the higher end booths stood. In broad daylight I felt it doubtful Durdax or any of his ruffians would be lurking about to cause us any trouble.

The market bustled with traffic, noise and confusion with its miasma of scents, spices, exotic cooking, animal hides, sweat and dung. Hawkers dressed in garish tunics roved everywhere, touting wares, everything from beauty tonics to leather hides.

We found a small shop with an awning that seated four couples on stools at the back. An attendant in a slave's tunic poured wine for us with a lavish hand and we ordered some fresh eel. Fortuna took dainty bites of her fried eel dipped in olive oil, and stared from her hazel eyes at me under her hood in dreamy fashion.

A figure plunked on a stool next to me and grabbed a piece of my fish, plopping it in his mouth. "Mmm. Tasty."

My heart went cold. I turned. *Raicus!* Suddenly I lost all appetite. Smiling like a sewer rat, his companion took a seat beside Fortuna, the lowlife I knew as Janus.

"Pretty little slave you have here," Raicus quipped. "Shame if anything happened to her on the way back from the market."

"And your head would be rolling off the end of my club."

"How endearing," he jeered. "A little sensitive under the skin, Ick? Just ribbing you. No need to get uppity. Who'd want to harm a pretty piece like her?"

I turned my back on the rascal and they left, whistling and swapping coarse jokes while elbowing their way through the crowd.

"Friends of yours?" Fortuna demanded.

I shrugged. "You could call them that. Between Raicus and Marcellus, it's a tossup whether I'm in need of any more 'friends' at the moment."

A sizeable Celt sat next to us, a carpenter by the look of him. Wood shavings dusted his thick woolen cloak. He sported long braided hair and a down-to-earth manner easy for us to strike up a casual conversation with him. "Don't mind the antics of those hooligans. I saw them pestering a leather vendor not long ago. Almost had him calling the watch. You have a very pretty woman, my friend. Why hide her under that ungainly hood?"

I tilted my head sideways to get a better look at him.

He rolled his mooncalf eyes. Fortuna blushed. I thanked him for his compliment, though I wished he wouldn't look at her so closely. I toasted him with a fresh cup of wine and he laughed and began launching into a spiel about politics, religion and the way of the world, all the subjects I least liked. I catered to his banter and added a few salient points of my own. He seemed impressed at my worldly knowledge, and my being so young at that. After a while, he drifted on to look for some new tools much needed in his shop. Fortuna peered at me slantwise under half quizzical lids, noting the natural way I could talk to anyone, fit in with any rogue or citizen. I could tell her pretty head was pondering both my good name and station in life, despite my dubious pastimes.

"You needn't be what you are, Ick. You've a good home, a good father. Why go about those nightly bashings? I fear you'll kill—"

"And if I didn't," I blurted with more sharpness than intended, "would you be where you are today?"

She opened her mouth then her lip quivered and clamped—I waved her off. "From now on, Fortuna, you'll go to the market accompanied by two slaves, one at least as capable as Denetio. I don't trust rats like Raicus there." I sighed. "Come on, let's finish our wine. You wanted to get out, so let's do it. We'll take a walk down to the Mithraeum or someplace and visit more of the lovely sights and smells of Londinium."

She flashed me a startled look and I laughed. "Don't look at me as if I'm some executioner. I can be intense sometimes."

"No wonder…with friends like that."

Chapter 8

Despite my lack of appreciation for tutoring, it had served me well. Dionos had made me think about the world and the patterns of civilized behavior. I realized no matter how diverse the cultures were, they all seemed to develop in similar fashion. History, politics, economics, language, religion...all were parts of the same whole. Drace had gibed me about being smarter than others my own age, being too smart for my own good, and I disagreed with him. It had saved my sorry hide more than once in the rotgarden of Londinium's back alleys even though my hot-headed nature alone should have been the death of me ten times over.

Drace'd introduced me to *The Clubs* at the age of nine. For better or worse, I had gotten used to that life, and learned quickly. The ways of roughness, intimidation, violence and fearlessness...all were part of my fabric. Keeping face and punishing weakness and infidelity, at the same time rewarding bravery and loyalty—they were part of my internal code. Drace'd not died with a club in his hand as he'd hoped, but instead had lain on his back with fever and infection wasting away his body. His absence still cut deep, left me knotted in misery, especially knowing he didn't deserve that death. My only solace lay in the fact that those drunken bastards who'd seeded his demise had met their fate in the sheerest of agony. Those, my first kills. No doubt there would be more.

We limited our nocturnal violence for a period during the annual electioneering. Too many hired sign-writers out and about with their big buckets of black and red paint either to vilify or glorify a candidate. After that, everything was fair game.

Another half year passed and we continued to practice our craft, becoming stronger, faster and more ruthless. Relations had degraded between Marcellus and me though we kept our tenuous co-leadership intact. But the chasm widened between the pair of Marcellus and Feberiax, and me and the rest of our gang. Even the most dimwitted witness could have observed that.

In a few months Mexor would pull me out of the tutor group and set me to work at the end of autumn. I would miss Dionos's company and our competitive Batallia games, and his not-so-subtle jabs at my armor of pride and growing atheism.

Fortuna and I had deepened our relations, though we fought over the most foolish things with many a difference of opinion. Never easy living in close quarters with a woman. As the master's son, I could have had my own space, but the comfort of Fortuna's warm body at all hours of the night is something a man can get used to, and difficult to give up. She'd cast her spell on me early on in the game, with her iron-in-the-fire sexual magnetism. Was I a fool to deny it?

    * * *

In the public baths off Via Campia, Regalis and I stopped to soak and relax one grey day in fall. Pure luxury to wash the grit and rawness of Londinium off our skins. Echoes of men's voices and laughter tinkled off the steaming stone of the caldarium. I recognized that voice! Gaius Pluvius Maxus. The same who'd extorted my father. I resented that bastard more than any other who ran this city. He and a business associate, some exporter of goods, and a tax collector stepped out of the hot room to lie on a wooden bench while slaves scraped their skin with iron strigils before rubbing in perfumed oils. Pluvius, white as a gull, showed a barrel-shaped torso as wide as a bloated sow. With an impatient hand he snatched the towel from the slave's grip to wipe his ugly hide and cast the towel back at him along with a lascivious glance.

I caught snatches of their conversation. "Don't worry, Iulius, I have certain debts to collect which will help us in this little partnership. Some newfound ones too, of enemies who wish to defame my good name."

"Very good, Pluvius. Certain parties are getting anxious about developments and trade agreements in Gallia."

A snort came from Pluvius, followed by a comradely slap of skin. "You worry too much, Iulius. Relax! Look at your chum Baeus here—cool as a cucumber. The deal will go through and our chests will be lined with gold."

Regalis and I ducked back. We didn't want to be seen or accused of eavesdropping, when such men had assumed they were alone. As much as I despised these hypocrites, I also felt a sliver of anxiety in getting on their bad side or drawing attention to myself. All too much a familiar habit.

Another shape, a tall ghostlike figure, floated in beside him. His eerie slave. "Pluvius, it is getting late. Best we be going. Many errands yet await."

"Xetriam, you are right. Iulius, Baeus—we meet on the morrow."

* * *

We went on to bigger and more dangerous forays—or perhaps, capers of stupidity. Some instinct in me knew we were going to get caught, or have our skulls busted, but like moths drawn to the flame, we persisted. Despite the rivalry and growing antagonism between Marcellus and me, our group survived. Each night gave us more confidence, and a sense of invulnerability. The feeling of power became a most addictive narcotic.

Tonight, mischief lurked in the air. We shambled down past the docks on the lookout for some trouble to get our rocks off. Maybe mark up Hermes' temple tonight, if we had the balls for it. The goddesses, Minerva, Juno, Venus, we left alone, although once we added some lewdness to Venus's loins that got some shocking comments the next day.

After doing our business, Marcellus called us back to our cemetery hideaway. An especially chill wind ruffled our cloaks and a thin moon hung in the September sky. Marcellus'd procured us some poppy oil, imported from Cyprus somewhere, from one of the many trade ships that hit Londinium. A rare treat, this raw oil soaked on palm leaves, and we washed it down with healthy swigs of my father's wine, somewhere straight from the vineyards of Italia.

Now Marcellus stood before us under the torchlight propped on the Medecias vault, the ruddy flame illuminating him in hazy light. His eyes were slightly wild, and I knew something was up before he opened his mouth.

"I have a serious matter to put to you, ruggies. Seems as if a certain moneylender has declared a lien against my uncle Vaegitius's estate in Calleva. He called in the loan last Friday and Vaegitius is now beside himself, landless and slated to become his creditor's slave if he can't pay up the interest accrued."

"How much are we talking?" asked Feberiax.

"You don't want to know. As you recall, he's in the metallurgy business with holdings along the Tamesis river. Once thriving, but now his prospects have dried up. He's up to his ears in debt—a compulsive gambler. Dumb sod. He's lost that property, and he'll be a very poor and destitute man soon. This could go badly for my father too. He has investments linked to his brother's business. The obscene interest has to be paid to bail him out of this mess."

"Who is this asshole lender?" asked Oren. Rumbles and nods of disgust came from all of us.

"Gaius Pluvius Maxus."

I gasped. "That fat weaselly bastard again? Jupiter's wrath!"

"None other. Suffice it to say, we'll need to act. Any ideas?"

"That seems obvious," grunted Feberiax. "We go in and bust the bastard up. Threaten to break more of his precious bones if he doesn't toss out your uncle's loan and give Vaegitius back his property."

Marcellus grinned. He slapped Feberiax on the back. "See that's what I like about you, Feb. No messing around. All gut and brawn."

"What a minute—"

Regalis grabbed my arm and sucked in a breath. "The banker's well known about town," he said. "It won't be easy."

"Who says it will?" Marcellus rose. "All in favor, raise their hands."

I shifted and murmured a dark curse in my throat.

"What's wrong, Ick?"

I grunted a noncommittal sound.

"Didn't your old man almost come to foreclosure at the hand of this Pluvius snake?"

"He did."

"Well, what are you waiting for?"

"Nothing. Just have a funny feeling about it. Bumped into the man down at the baths not long ago with Regalis. He seems as if he's not alone—teamed up with partners."

"So?"

Regalis jumped in. "He's got some serious money, Marcy. We can expect that Pluvius's going to have his villa protected with guards, slaves and likely dogs."

"No matter. We're *The Clubs!*" Marcellus waved a fist. "Ballbusters. Killers. Equalizers. We'll break through this smarmy louse's skin of protection."

"We can try." I shrugged. "But if anything looks to go sour—"

"Atta boy, Ick! An exercise in extreme skundering. That's what this is all about."

I grunted in exasperation. Had Marcellus even heard a word I said?

He bent his neck and took another lick at the palm leaf doused with dark poppy oil. The pupils of his eyes swam in opaque dreaminess.

Outvoted then.

So we planned to break into the moneylender's villa and work our deviltry. Acting on not much of a plan, to just wing it. Full of dark bravado, like the dark hearts we were. Dressed in bestial costumes and masks, clubs gripped in fists. Each of us zoned out on magic poppy, that magic stuff drifting over the sea from exotic lands to the east, shipped in on galleys like my father's own wine shipments.

My lips curled like those of the shaggy, crop-eared mastiffs of the Britons. This venture bothered me for a few reasons. First: a bad feeling brewed in my gut about our chances. Second: Marcellus's lack of planning. The image of the greasy moneylender brought up a ghost of a memory—of how the same goat-faced scoundrel had almost ruined my father years ago. I remembered how he had called on him at his wine shop, sneered, saying that if he didn't pay up on the morrow, his case would be tried before the magistrate and his properties seized. With the further indignity of becoming Pluvius's slave if the properties did not cover the amount owing. What gall! The old hatred welled up in me and I gripped my club with a vengeful fire.

I didn't understand the complexity of the financial world yet or have a complete picture of the evils of banking, but something in my heart knew it was blacker than black. This leech of a man embodied the pinnacle of all that I hated about our moneyed society. When the gales had swept through the channel and destroyed my father's cargoes, Mexor knew it better than anybody. He had recovered slowly but barely, and I still remember my father's look of shock and despair in those moments when Pluvius had called in his loans with the ultimatum.

I once saw a stuffed marmot in the front window of a taxidermist's shop off Via Macedonia, with its hanging teeth, frozen in a feral snarl, black eyes blazing, that reminded me of that overweight predator.

A shiver of rage ran up my spine. Memories of Pluvius swaggering down the street as if he owned it, amassing his silver and gold as if he were some senator or Caesar.

I bridled my rage and we skulked on. To the upper part of town, the well-to-do area. The kind with the shady gardens and quieter, enclosed areas—the multi-storied villas fronted with elegant frescoed facades, and further back, fancy shrubbery and tinkling fountains stocked with goldfish.

Pluvius's residence looked well-guarded and it held an eerie foreboding and danger. A single torch burned over the front door of heavy wood, likely barred from inside with an iron bar. The master's seal was carved into the wall, aside an eagle on a crown and an odd bearded figure below. Some disconcerting tribute to Mithras with looping horns? To attempt the front door was foolhardy, but other entrances existed. Pluvius's residence seemed larger than most with its own inner court. Our hope of entry lay around the other side, in that inner court at the back.

There would be dogs of course, there always were. But we came prepared.

With a dramatic flourish, Feberiax hurled his chunk of tainted meat over the wall and we waited as upon a skitter of quick feet, the snuffling grew. There came a spate of snapping teeth and fierce licking and gobbling which brought much mirthful movement to Feberiax's bull-like mask. In the absence of sound, I had a suspicion our slavering Cerberus was down.

We waited several more minutes in the darkened street until no sound came our way. Marcellus readied our grapple and we threw it over the wall. It gave a tiny clink. The next part became the most dangerous. If a night watchman came by and saw the supine dog or heard the clink, we had better be ready to run.

Marcellus gave it a tug, hooked it on the outer rim. Nothing.

One by one we hauled ourselves up the rope and lowered ourselves down the other side to drop down amongst the hedgerows, counting our breaths.

We passed two unconscious dogs. Sprawled on the flagstones in ungainly heaps, they looked dead. Shaggy mastiffs with low backs and muscled jaws. Sometimes such poisoned animals would die, depending on how much ratkiller they had wolfed down in their gluttonous haste.

We threaded our way along the dogwood hedgerows like errant ghosts, our hearts beating with the thrill of an adventure, already jacked up on the wine and the special something Marcellus had fixed us with.

The light grew as we neared the side of the villa. The place looked well-kept and had a sinister look to it. Thick ropes of ivy crawled up the face, and certain bizarre statues set in the places that showed bare. Two small windows appeared on the upper levels. A single door showed dimly at ground level, past which, fifty feet away, burned a guttering torch. So far no sign of guards. But that could mean nothing.

Oren paused in midstep, whispering hoarsely, "Remind me why we're taking this risk, Feb?"

Feberiax made a brisk gesture. "To shake down the banker who's been giving Marcellus's uncle problems. Because a friend of a friend is in trouble and we help out our own."

"It's the code of *The Clubs*," Regalis hissed.

"Then let's be at it, without jawing about it," said Marcellus.

My face twisted in a sour leer. I had no interest in scouting out the place. It felt evil. I didn't like the look of the perverse Mithraic statuary out front either. It had an unkempt, eastern look to it, if such were possible. The Mithraic figure, that heroic patron god of soldiers, looked to have bestial horns on its helmed crown and a wild look of ecstasy in the eyes. More so, I disliked being trumped by Marcellus's rule. Such an arrogant son of a bitch. He seemed to read my thoughts and murmured, "Crack a few skulls, Icky. That's all." His face had that wide-spread grin showing white wolf's teeth. "We'll shake up the old moneybags. Make him think twice about policies and gouging the innocent." He patted my back.

I shook off his hand, remembering the incident with Fortuna and many others since.

Marcellus chortled. "Relax, Ick. You're tense as a tiger. I'm sure Uncle Vaegitius'll be happy about what we're doing for him."

"Sure he will, Marcy, sure he will." I grunted.

We forced our way through the side entrance without much trouble. The door, only equipped with a light latch, bent easily to our shoulders. We crept down the service hall, ignoring the mosaicked floors and wall frescoes and marble statues. No watchman patrolled these shadowed interiors.

To our luck, a flickering light shone off the atrium in a sizeable study. Pluvius Maxus, the bloated whale, sat at his escritoire, stamping a waxen seal on a document. My lips curled in a grin. To his left a quill of ink and papyrus. I pulled out the rough cloth concealed on my person in relish. The tumult that would inevitably ensue—well, the slaves must not hear. We snuck up deadly as wolves, as he pored over and adjusted figures in his waxed tablets. Readying my club, I leaped, hooked my arm around his neck and stuffed the dirty cloth in his mouth. The others pounced. He snuffled and roared while Oren held it in place and the others yanked him to his feet.

Regalis motioned to a room aside the study into which Feberiax and Marcellus dragged the struggling moneylender without ado. The darkened space, clearly some high-ceilinged chamber, ran a dozen feet. Oren grabbed a torch from the wall and we shut the door to the private room to avoid alerting wary household slaves.

Frescoes featuring dolphins and nymphs adorned the walls, but other, weirder figures, more Mithraic in construction, in blue, white and orange pigments with faces with horns, ornamented the far wall, which did not seem congruous with the other images, or what would decorate a rich banker's estate. A small door, only shoulder height, loomed off to the right. I frowned, saw the banker's eyes dart wildly toward it. So did Marcellus. "Hiding something in there, chief?" he demanded.

Pluvius licked his lips, looking away. Marcellus nodded. Oren stepped over and jerked open the door.

Immediately an indescribable stench assailed our nostrils.

"Pyew!"cried Oren.

Rotten meat? Offal?

"What in Jupiter's—" Marcellus wrinkled his nose. Feberiax gave a gasping croak. In mutual contempt, the two dragged the moneylender toward the door and shoved him in the threshold of the dark opening where he fought with a vengeance.

"You first, Pluvy," Marcellus grunted. They kicked him down in.

Our breaths stopped short as our eyes adjusted to the murk. There below, Pluvius lay at the bottom of a small stairway of a secret crypt, struggling to lift his fat bulk up from the damp floor. We ducked and stepped down into a large rectangular chamber where our eyes grew wide. Our brains attempted to make sense of the stitched nightmare of those putrid surroundings. Oren plunged the torch closer to the scene at the side wall. We all gasped.

Entrails coated the rough plaster: bowels, organs, fur, hide, grinning teeth, skulls. I could make out several pigs' heads affixed to that grisly façade, and many animal parts strewn at the back—a goat's head, hooves cloven at the ankle, broken beast limbs, perhaps those of a bull, lying in rancid heaps. All in a blood-choked gutter that ran to the side and down to the far end. A crimson-caked altar lay off to the side. Instead of the wholesome protector deities of the traditional Roman household—the Lares and Penates—this man had forged some ghastly shrine that flirted with demons and demiurges.

"Mother of Mithras," crowed Regalis. "What in Jove is this foul den you make as your shrine?" His voice lifted in revulsion.

On the main wall at the back, a fierce carven face of some half human beast jutted, the head, chillingly bull-like and Mithraic, as tall as any of us.

"Looks like the back end of an abattoir," muttered Feberiax, gaping at the piles of offal.

While Oren lit some of the lamps on the wall, Marcellus loosened Pluvius's gag, warning him not to call out or alert the slaves, or it would go the worse for him.

I gave a choked cry of objection.

"It's the end of you," Pluvius gasped when his gag came loose. His face curled in a rabid sneer.

"Come now, Pluvius," said Marcellus. "Let's not be too dramatic. Grandstanding bores us."

"You'll pay in pools of blood, you fools—filthy hoodlums! Release me!"

"Now, now, that's no way to talk to your betters," chided Marcellus. Feberiax and Oren laughed. But with some visible lack of cheer.

I did not like the snarling look on the moneylender's face either or the triumph writ there. "What's there to be smug about, old man? I asked. "Looks as if you're in a bad way right now."

"Yeah, what have you been doing, Pluvius?" accused Oren. "Running your own private butcher shop here?"

"I say we bust up this swine and be gone," grumbled Regalis, wiping his hands. "This place gives me the creeps." His dark eyes flashed about the temple, on a blasphemous idol of Mithras, the head tipped upside down caked with offal and the blood and skulls and reek of years of defilement.

"I've no objection," I growled.

"Look here," said Feberiax, wandering over to the carven bull head with its jutting fangs. "Seems as if our moneybags has gone in for devil worship."

"Do not speak of things you do not know," Pluvius hissed.

"What don't we know, old man," said Marcellus.

"You don't know the power of the old gods—Of *Orcus*."

"Who?" said Regalis, screwing up his face in contemptuous wrath.

We bound his wrists and ankles, so he could not flee. I'd have to stuff that cloth back down his throat again soon enough. But in the meantime, while Marcellus circled around him in curiosity, Feberiax and I stood ready to menace him with our clubs.

"Frightened now?" Marcellus barked. Sprawled on his haunches, Pluvius fought at his bonds.

"Don't struggle, old man. Save your strength. We only want to talk. A friendly discussion. A certain friend of ours, Lucius Vaegitius Vicus, is being squeezed very unkindly. We'd like you to withdraw your liens and allow the gentleman some time to gather up his finances. Better yet, drop the whole debt altogether. Makes things simpler that way, then we don't have to rough you up."

The fat man stared at him wild-eyed. "Who are you miserable hoodlums?"

"There's that word again. Never mind who we are. Consider yourself lucky to have both your legs right now—you're prey and we're hunters and for once the tables are turned on your stinking hide. Think of us as your 'friendly neighborhood watch' calling you to task on some nasty business. Not imposing anything on you, Pluvius. Just trying to improve the neighborhood, beef up the morality of Londinium. Seems a bit sordid these days with all the moneylenders squeezing law-abiding citizens dry."

The stink of Pluvius and this place nauseated me, the yeasty reek of his foul hide mixed with the waft of the blood-caked dungeon. I'd enough savviness to understand such serpentish personalities as him, and how this world worked. Scum like him had gotten to their positions of power by money-juggling and exorbitant percentages used to boost their status to get whatever they wanted. I did not resent him for his wealth. Wealth was fine. But it irked me that he went too far and knew it. Couldn't do his own policing, but hired an army of minions. I'd like to see him beat down his debtors with his own bare hands. He'd end up a pile of broken bones, spitting blood. Take away the man's bodyguards and slaves and his tall stone walls, and men like Pluvius Maxus were nothing more than sniveling weaklings.

He snarled like a trapped animal. "I know who you are. Those savage ruffians who go about defacing public temples and honest vendors' stalls. I don't know how you got in here but—"

"Aren't you the clever one?" chided Marcellus. "Give him a gift for his trouble, Feberiax."

Feberiax hoofed him in the gut while Oren smacked him in the ribs.

An oof of wind came from Pluvius Maxus's gut. He huffed out a groaning curse deep from his massive torso. "Rotten scum! Slime lickers!" He coughed out a wad of blood. "You think you can badger me into complying with your extortion schemes and blackmail? Never. What is it you want? Gold? I could give you bags of it, but I'll not be bullied. If you think you'll intimidate me with your black bats and toy masks—you're deluded. You think I don't have friends in powerful places? What do you think they'll do to you when they catch you? Dead or alive, who do you think runs this city?"

"An avaricious pig, perhaps," I jested, muttering into my mask.

Marcellus huffed out a long breath. "Not going to play nice with us? Even after we treated you with such politeness, Pluvy?"

Feberiax struck with a sound blow on the fleshy part of his diaphragm and he rolled in pain. I stepped in and clouted him on the kidney side, enough to deliver him a sharp pain and a good bruise. Pluvius Maxus would be walking stiffly for a few days if not longer. I spoke more dark words under my breath. "That's for squeezing another acquaintance of ours too." I recalled how the pig had nearly reduced my father to slavery when five of his best merchant ships had foundered in a storm in the channel.

He growled in desperation and as I crouched to deliver another blow, his flailing arms bound at the wrist shot up and clipped the edge of my mask. The carven wood clattered to the floor and rolled at my feet. For a second I stared aghast and Pluvius's and my eyes met.

"You! I recognize you. That son of the wine merchant. Mexor Salvius Veditio."

I reached for my mask, cursing, fumbling at it to put it back on.

He gargled out blood in triumph. "Infamous member of *The Clubs of Londinium*. So! I never forget a face."

"Woohoo!" Marcellus cried, capering about, enjoying the moment. "I think you just signed your death warrant, old man."

"Hades take you!" Pluvius spat. "You'll burn. In buckets of blood—like those rams on Orcus's altar."

"Neptune's balls, Ick," grunted Regalis, "that was a daft thing to do. Now we'll have to kill him."

"Fine by me," I croaked, stepping in, club lifted.

A rustle came at the door. Like a breath of wind, a magical fire. Our heads turned in unison.

A tall shape emerged, floating on air it seemed. He moved less like a man than the outline of a specter, backlit against the faint torchlight behind. The familiarity brought an eerie deja-vu prickling my skin. That figure—the same back at the baths some time ago—made me flesh crawl. We are given certain extrasensory faculties at birth. Some can be honed through use, others will fade into obscurity when we are oblivious to them or fail to cultivate their advantages. Everything in my being told me this man was evil, an incarnation of filth and darkness. Eyes that could peer through a man's soul and blast it to eternity. What did Pluvius have on this will-o'-the-wisp to keep him under his thumb? A shudder ran up my back.

"My lord, Pluvius," the shape spoke in a thick, barbarous accent. "This seems an awkward arrangement. Are you well?"

"What does it look like, you arrogant fool? What do I pay you for? Deal with these pups. Kill them all."

He nodded with vigor. "Yes, yes, but first I must give them fair treatment, if not warning."

I stared in awe. The man stood weaponless, we outnumbered him five to one, yet he seemed quite confident he could fulfill his master's boast. He looked like some ghoul, all built of swarthy skin and sharp angles and bony facets; a high-boned head and tailored goatee, trimmed to perfection like some dangling icicle. Agate eyes that never blinked, but bored holes in my skin. Something felt wrong about his presence as if he could suck one's energy through his nostrils if he liked, or pin one with a piercing glance.

"I would ask you to release my master. It will go kinder for you then."

Marcellus snorted out a choked laugh. "And who are you, sir stick man? Some upstart sodomite of this fat toad?"

Faster than a snake, the man grabbed a chalice on the altar and hurled the vile liquid in my eyes before I could raise my club.

I staggered back, cringing in pain. The liquid stung. Gurgling in anguish, I swiped off the foul ichor and recoiled at how it burned my skin and my lips. I coughed and spat out the vile liquid. Its merest drops had a metallic, putrid taste like fermented oil but more fetid still, like the stagnant blood of long dead animals. The rankness made my knees wobble and my ruggies peered at me in horror. I could only imagine the vile stuff was the siphoned life-juice of some of those butchered animals lying in the corners of this foul crypt.

"Abris, Vereunt. Unteris," the ghoul chanted in a distorted voice. The incantation, more ancient than Greek, gave way to a string of twisted syllables. They hit me square in the solar plexus. I doubled over. My blood felt on fire. I retched dry heaves.

Marcellus surged forward, his club on the rise. "Get that rotten creepster," he cried, and Feberiax and Oren lurched in with wood swinging to beat the man down, but he tossed some powder and I remember a foul green smoke engulfing us in a cloud. As I hunched there groaning, I heard curses, shuffling feet, a chorus of shouts, a gloating, triumphant cry from Pluvius Maxus. "Ah, see, it has already begun," he shrieked. His sick laugh faded in my ear, his leering face a hazy blemish on my sight as we hacked and swatted in futile unison as the scene billowed with thick green smoke.

Cold fingers wrapped about my throat, choking me. The magician? I thrashed with my club and its end met bone and skull, and soft flesh yielded as I heard a willowy form fall in the gathering cloud. Hoarse shouts drifted out from the haze. The clatter of boots, my ruggies making a run for the exit.

I heard another cackle of sinister laughter. Pluvius's. "No, it won't be the prefects who castrate you, young hoods, or a sudden, quick knife in your backs. No, a painful end—in the blackest of black cubbyholes. Cursed by gods too terrible to name. Crying for mercy like weasels in sawtooth traps!"

I coughed, jerked back, gasped, as a searing pain gripped my insides. I nearly doubled over again, and Pluvius Maxus's mouth opened wide in a sick grin. "You'll all burn in Hades! Floating down the river Styx in pools of your own crimson piss."

I hopped after my ruggies, though my guts heaved.

The master's slaves with clubs of their own came whacking down on us out of that swirling haze. I felt a stick smash on my thigh. Howling, I swatted out, felt good wood connect with solid flesh and then heard a choked cry.

We scrambled for safety, back up the stair we'd descended; Marcellus beat in the head of another attacker. Regalis dragged my doubled-over form along. "Got to get out of here now!" He spurred me on, pulling me to my feet while I spasmed with agony.

Across the marble floor we staggered, the antechamber leading to that lunatic carousel of evil. The vengeful cries of Pluvius Maxus echoed in our ears. "You'll all burn! Burn, I say!"

We clambered for the garden wall, past the shaggy hounds that lay still with their pale tongues lolling.

Marcellus grabbed the grapple from behind a manicured shrub. He tossed it over the wall's edge. Up the rope we shimmied, Marcellus first, while Feberiax stood braced to beat off the guards. Regalis shuttled me up the swaying rope. Oren came next, then Feberiax, bless his courageous hide: he took a hurled flowerpot high on the shoulder, prompting a bellow and curse, but it didn't stop him. He pulled up the rope and threw the grapple down to us. Crouching at the summit, he evaded another pot, quick to lower himself down the other side of the wall. Fingers gripped on the capstones, he released himself to drop down to street level. He limped on for a while, grunting through his bull's mask, shouldering me along. We fled up the street, stumbling off into the night.

Chapter 9

We tore off our masks and raced off to different quarters. Regalis tucked his arm around me as guide and support on our circuitous southern zigzag toward the Mithraeum. Catching wind of the ghastly state of me, he rasped, "We'll need miracles to pull out of this mess."

"You think?" My red rimmed eyes glared at him. My hands shook. I had a bad case of the chills. "I'm useless to defend myself in this state."

He caught me from falling, his lips pressed grimly together. "We'll take care of you, Ick." In panting breaths, we stumbled the rest of the way down a darkened alley. He offered to hide me at his family house, but I brushed him off. I told him to lie low. I had to warn my father. We split up, me staggering up Via Decus, mumbling that I'd contact him.

Either way I looked at it, I was a dead man. Half expecting the prefect and his men to come clomping down the road banging on my father's door. I felt sick to my stomach knowing that ruin was edging in so quickly.

Bracing myself for the worst, I rapped on the door, the three knock secret code I'd arranged with Denetio. He answered, blinking in the gloom , face pinched at the haggard, hunched look of me. I almost fell at his feet, splattered with reeking blood and a feverish sweat on my brow.

"What's happened to you?" he croaked, reaching to grab me.

"Never mind." I tottered in, coughing. "Wake my f-father."

"That's not advisable. Are you drunk—"

"Wake him!" I snarled.

Denetio ran off while I doubled over, feeling ready to retch. I counted the seconds, waiting for the room to stop swaying. Taking a deep breath, I gritted my teeth, feeling as if I had a snake in my belly that took bites out of each wall of my gut. I gulped down some of the poppy oil on the leaf I still had left in my pocket. Hoping it would curb the pain. It didn't. I heard the echo of brisk voices and my father's ponderous tread approaching like the toll of a death bell, echoing off the marble paves of the atrium.

I took three stumbling steps out of the vestibule and my father looked at me in teeth-bared surprise.

"Thieving, whoring and drinking again, Icarus? What have you done? Tell me!"

I groaned and collapsed on the marble tiles. He hauled me up to eye level, blinking now with concern. "What happened to you?"

I jabbered out some words, I don't know what. About some moneylender with some creepo priest and how he'd juiced me up on a poison of fermented blood.

My father's thin lip twisted in a sneer. "What are you babbling about? What did you do, break into a house while intoxicated and they chased you?" He shook me and raised my head to fix me an ominous glare. He'd hit too close to the mark and I couldn't bend the truth. Half dazed from searing pain in my gut, I remained sullen, glared away, bent over from the effect of the priest's venom, ready to spew all over.

"Who's this moneylender?"

I hesitated. This was no time to lie. "Pluvius Maxus."

My father seemed to sway on his feet and go a shade paler.

"Pluto's fires! What a thing to have to tell your father. Could you have picked a worse enemy?" He rambled prayers under his breath, lips working with wrath. "Do you even know who this man is?"

"Course I know." I mumbled unintelligible curses while Denetio looked away.

"Did he know who you were? Did he recognize you, tie you to me?"

I looked away with shame. "That's why I came back here to warn you."

He swore, licked his lips, understanding the implications now. "What did you do to him?"

I closed my eyes. "Roughed him up a bit, that's all."

"How bad?"

"Just a few love taps, nothing more, Father. He'll recover."

I could see the gears working in his head, poring over options. The old memories of the lands and commerce he'd almost lost seemed to invoke a grimace of pain.

He gusted out a wretched sigh and wiped my cheek of dried blood with his sleeve. Despite his anger and my unquestionable cock-up, I couldn't help but be moved at his deep concern for me.

"Denetio, get the wagon ready," he instructed.

I blinked. "Are you sure—"

"To hell with Pluvius!" my father rumbled. "Your safety is more important. Jupiter's and Apollo's whores! You look poisoned."

With Denetio's help, he hefted me in the wagon and we took the deserted streets to the medic Gesselix's off Meridien Way. Denetio held high the torch and the horse's hooves clopped steadily ahead. I rolled in the back, upchucking, moaning, suffering dry heaves, for I could feel the fire of the priest's curse in my veins.

My world spun sideways. Vaguely I discerned a torch burning over the heavy oak door of the medic's residence and Denetio clambering out and knocking on the Aesculapian-shaped knocker four times. A thin man with round nose and hang-dog face answered, peering up at my father's grim expression. He looked at me with dispassion. "What brings you at this hour, Mexor? Only a drunken boy? I hope it's not just for that."

"More than that, Gesselix. Icarus has some affliction."

The medic frowned, but nodded, grunting and motioning Denetio to carry me into the side room, a converted space from one of the shops into an examination room. Shelves of medicaments, clay pots and bottles of sulfur yellow and other colors lined the periphery, and below that tablets of information stacked aside papyrus scrolls. He laid me on my side on a padded table and lifted my garment and prodded my ribs, chest, back and throat. I moaned and gurgled, his fingers pulling at my mouth and sticking a wooden rod down my throat, peering into my gullet with a grimacing murmur.

"What did you eat?"

"Some liquid splashed on my face, animal blood maybe. In my eyes. A foul, terrible reek, like animal guts—goats maybe."

He grimaced. "Your eyes look redder than a rabid hare's. Your breath is putrid. I've smelled hound's breath better than that."

He tried many procedures, colon pokes, gut massages, oil application, scratching at his pale cheek, mumbling, and staring off into space. He tried to induce me to vomit by making me drink a foul green paste, then came up behind me and encircled his arms round my chest and squeezed hard. But it only caused me to dry heave and incited a sharper pain in my gut.

At last he furrowed his brow and gave a heavy sigh. "Nothing I can do for him, Mexor."

"What?" my father gasped.

"Your boy's been cursed." He looked at me, blinking through his owl-like eyes. "You'd better go and see a druid or something rather than me."

"You're giving up? What do you mean?" my father wheezed.

The medic snorted. "Try old Vercinorex in the hinterland. Near Caerdung, or some place like that. These druids have balms and pastes for conditions like this—maybe strong spirits." The name Caerdung rung a bell. I remembered some reference the druidess Maig had made at the cemetery. "I can bleed him and prick him full of holes. Then give him some herbs that will make him sicker than a dog, but I doubt it'll help, except rack you up a big bill."

My father's voice trailed off. I heard a hopeless quaver in it as he shook his head.

"What I can do is give him some ointment to apply topically, a stomach relaxant, a derivative of opium and belladonna. I advise you to have him drink vinegar or cheap wine every hour and I'll send a prayer to Aesculapius."

My father grudgingly accepted the tribute to the healing god, took the slaves and paid him ten denarii before we left. Flush-faced and burning, I cringed, fire in my veins, tense as a chased animal. My father threatened to visit this Vercinorex and tell him to give me poison and end his problem. "What have you gone and done, boy?"

I let my pale tongue loll as Denetio piled me into the back of the wagon. "Me and the ruggies went down to shake him up—that's all. He was squeezing Marcellus's uncle like he squeezed you."

He sighed, lost in a concerted war to understand. "Just like Drace. Look where it got him."

My fists clenched. "His slave, some Babylonian priest with magic in his arsenal, cast a spell on me. I know it! He looked at me with such evil before he chucked that blood poison. We busted our way out before the slaves could beat us down. The venom splashed on my face. It stung my eyes and made my lips burn."

My father grimaced. "And you licked the stuff off your face? How smart was that?"

"It wasn't like that—"

"What of the other hooligans? Aren't they as sick as mud eels too?"

"Only I got sprayed."

"That's highly implausible. Either you're a poor liar or hallucinating."

I shrugged. "Luck of the draw."

Amid his grumbles and curses, I don't know if he believed my story or not. I was only worried about whether I was going to last the night, that they'd come after my father.

Reaching our villa, he turned briskly to Denetio. "Admit no one to the house under any circumstance. And you—" he glared at me "—do not go anywhere. I'll be back within the hour, after I make some inquiries."

He turned to leave, then paused. "We're going to go up to this village. To consult this druid. I'll hide you in the back storage room in the meantime, if any lawbringers show up. Chances are I can bribe any officials who come looking this way. But I can't stall them forever, if you've messed with a prominent figure like Pluvius Maxus."

I shook all over, teeth chattering. I thought to protest, but clamped my mouth shut. Denetio flung a fleecy blanket over my shoulders as we made our way to the back room.

A cold lump of despair grew in the pit of my stomach. The thought of Pluvius Maxus's mercenaries out to kill me in the dead of night sent prickles of worry through my pores. I had to get out of here. No way in hell could I implicate my father any more than I had already. It was safer if I went with my ruggies. Make it look as if I'd run away.

I took a lamp and woke up Fortuna and told her I was going away. The pale light of day filtered through the tiny window.

She rolled over, her pale eyes bleary with sleep. "When? Where?" she murmured.

"I don't know."

She jerked up, catching the scent of my foul breath. "You've done something bad, haven't you, Ick?"

I glanced away; I couldn't lie to her.

"What's wrong with you? You look as if the cat dragged you in. Half dead, and you reek." She gave me a look of impudent challenge, her nose upturned, flawless skin flushed and radiating heat.

A spasm attacked my gut and I hunched over, cheeks burning, a feverish sweat beading my brow. "Go back to bed." I turned away, heading for the study.

Her confused whimper faded behind me. Hastily, I scrawled Mexor a note on a wax tablet.

"Sorry, father. I'll contact you when I can. I cannot endanger you any more than I have—Icarus."

Waking Zeno, I told him to fetch Regalis, as Denetio'd been ordered to stay put after sending sealed messages to the others. Regalis came to collect me within an hour. I felt better getting out of here. I kept envisaging Pluvius and his minions targeting our villa. I wouldn't have even gone back except for the fact that I owed him fair warning. At least I'd manned up and told him straight to his face. That took more courage than facing the prospect of my own death.

Regalis and I took my father's wagon out back, me lying huddled under a ragged blanket behind the driver's bench. Feverish, shivering, holding my guts, I rode in silence and we picked up Oren and Feberiax down by one of the local alehouses as arranged. My ruggies, praise their hearts, accompanied me on this journey, even Feberiax when he found out I was untreatable. All except Marcellus. Recalling the last time he and I took a road trip, better that he'd opted out.

While ragged clouds scudded across the sky the four of us struck out toward the docks and the Londinium bridge. Fishermen hauled in their morning catches along the shore, gutting fish. Regalis and I weren't sure exactly where the druid's village was, but we knew it lay somewhere along the southern road. A galley hoved to from some distant port to unload silks and spices. We drove under the guardhouse, clattering across the bridge south to Caerdyg, every ridge of the knotted planks under the rolling wheels a savage assault on my head.

Over the hills we clopped into sporadic sunshine and away southward, leaving the bridge and Londinium far behind. I sat up rubbing my chest, the danger now passed. "Where is this Caerdyg?" I asked, another violent wave of nausea descending upon me.

Feberiax, who knew the roads better than any of us, lifted a finger to the hazy way ahead. "Eleven miles. We've come this way before. My grandfather has a smithy not too far from here. We had dealings with the Celts in that village in the past."

The wide stone road meandered through rolling countryside, around stands of old oaks and beech, sometimes straight on for a way through scattered villages. With many a wheat field and hay field, grazing animals, cows and sheep. Many merchants too—some less scrupulous, with shifty eyes and ragged beards, worn leathers and bronze winking at their belts. Such eyes told me they wondered what a crew of striplings were doing in a cart empty of goods so early in the morning. But they took one glance at our roguish looks, our clubs, and their hardened expressions vanished. They thought twice about accosting us in broad daylight. Soldiers and baggage trains came and went from the southern and eastern forts, carrying weapons and long hard memories from hostilities there— from places I'd heard of but never seen: Noviomagus, Corinium, Glevum and others. Some circled a long way around from the north: Lindum, Camulodunum, Eboracum, and places farther still.

Long-faced, seasoned men with few words and haggard looks invested with unpleasant tasks of keeping the frontiers stable and the Britons in line. Some soldiers gave us salutes, others crowded us off the road with surly scowls. We didn't arouse suspicion, moving dutifully off the road, giving them no cause for curiosity. Leather breastplate, belted gladius and helm marked their gear, a well-oiled machine marching in step.

By late morning, we approached a crossroads and a weathered stone marker with the name of the village Caerdyg stuck in the grasses.

Feberiax raised his chin. "There, to the east, if memory serves."

Regalis guided our wagon off onto a dirt track that led west through scattered oak, briar and some lowlands, then rose again to yew and pine. The level Roman road had ended and we felt it. The cart wheels rolled along twin ruts. A cluster of thatched huts appeared in a clearing by the woods. Wattled fences to keep in livestock. A poor village by any standard.

Off in a grove of aspen, nine standing stones rose in a small standing circle. As old and fey as this green, rainy land the Romans had invaded a hundred years back. A fire crackled in the middle and hooded figures ranged inside.

The sound of voices grew. We turned. Children's yells, the neighing of horses, grunts of oxen, and the sounds of women's sunny laughter greeted us. A hundred or so village-folk coursed about the communal glade, talking merrily, young and old, engaged in festivity. A village fair? Another blazing fire burned in the center. Red tongues licked high into the autumn sky. Venison roasted on spits and a great stew pot brought wafts of rich aroma our way.

Tree climbing competitions highlighted the day at the glade's fringe, a horse pull of some kind too featuring four powerful bays, huffing and snorting with effort, massive hoofs below shaggy fetlocks pulling wooden sledges weighted with heavy stones along a muddy track. Barrels of apples, kegs of cider stood to the side for public consumption. Children ran and jumped in the long pits of sand, the winners decorated with leafy ribbons. If I weren't so laid out, I'd hop out and join them, but such was not to pass.

A few wayfarers with haversacks and dusty cheeks caught up to our wagon and gave us queer looks, striding in for a look-see. Their eyes roved from us to the fire and the ceremonies in play. Most of them seemed in relaxed moods, mesmerized by the tower of roaring flame.

"Maybe we should have brought some offering?" mused Regalis.

Feberiax gave a snort. "They'll take Roman coin as readily as anything else."

We'd accumulated sufficient stares from those in the glade before we rolled to a halt beside the edge of the clearing. A burly laborer treaded over to us, a straw between his teeth. "Good day, friends. What brings you to our village?"

"We seek Vercinorex, the druid," I replied.

He looked at us with surprise, even pity and doubt, as he lifted a callused hand to his furred cap over a balding head. "Unless you wish a ghost haunting you, I suggest you keep on. Our druid Vercinorex is dead."

"What?"

My heart sank in despair. I leaned back, releasing a slow breath. Was it a wasted trip? "Where's Maig when you need her?"

"Maig, you say?" blurted the man.

"Who in Hades is Maig?" grumbled Oren.

Feberiax gaped. "That skinny witch from the cemetery. Remember?"

"Who else?" Regalis proclaimed, brimming with a cheeky smile.

"Magoria's her real name," said the villager. "Here, let me help you. That nag seems to be chewing her bit something awful." He adjusted our beast's bit. "There," he jerked a thumb to where the slender figure of the druidess as I remembered her, played a game with balls and sticks amid a group of children. Sensing our scrutiny, her long, raven-haired head jerked up and her keen eyes sought us out. Patting the nearest girl on the arm, she turned to glide over, as confident as the day I'd seen her in the cemetery.

"I knew you'd seek me out," she said. "Saw it in a dream." She cast us an odd, questing look, as if looking at a wagonful of ghosts. "I didn't think

I'd be seeing this many of you alive."

"Very gracious of you," grunted Feberiax.

"I don't like this wench," complained Oren.

"Neither do I like you, Roman, but we all live in a world we must share."

"Please, Maig, can you help us?" I croaked. "I mean me. I've been laden with a terrible illness."

"What he means to say is a priest set a hex on him," Feberiax grumbled, rolling his eyes.

"Indeed." She peered up at me, her eyes taking in my pale face and rumpled, vomit-stained clothes. She frowned, unable to suppress a shudder. "You look and smell like a moldy piece of cheese."

"Thanks. That helps."

Oren waved an impatient hand. "We're wasting our time."

"A sorry irony. Only time any of you gives Maig the time of day is when you want something—or need special services. Otherwise you chase her out of your towns, throw rocks at her and call her a witch." She gave a sharp exclamation then a caustic laugh that was as sour as bitter apples.

A group of men approached, wearing unfriendly looks. Each hefted sharp axes.

"Any trouble here, Maig?"

"No, Sax, everything's okay. Just some old acquaintances from Londinium."

"You don't say? Londinium? Friends?" He furrowed his brows and stepped closer to study us.

"I can handle a few young ruffians from the big city of Londinium, Sax. Otherwise I should just retire my amulets."

"Whatever you say, Maig."

Her brazen posture brimmed full of playful challenge. She clutched a rodent-skulled amulet in her quick fingers. Her beaded torch that I remembered from earlier, lay belted at her hip.

She motioned to me. "Because this one shared wine with me and exhibited some kindness, I'll see to his needs. But these others—" she swept a hand toward Oren and Feberiax "—they can stay behind. Don't trust the likes of them."

"We're better off joining the celebrations anyway," said Feberiax with a grin. "I kind of like the idea of trying some local ale after a long ride." He stretched back, fingers clasped behind his head.

Oren loosed an easy breath. "I could teach those boys how to climb," he boasted.

One of the axemen spread an arm and saluted us. "This way then, there's plenty of fun and stewed venison for everybody."

"All the better them being gone." She watched them go as they piled out, casting her casual leers. "Better entertainment over there than witnessing Maig's craft."

Regalis helped me out of the cart and I filled her in on details.

"Sorcery and blood," she huffed. "Such go hand in hand. I can tell from the look of you it's not some ordinary spell."

"Really?" Both sad and relieved was I to hear that. An acknowledgement of something I knew, but I despaired with each passing comment of hers regarding a cure.

"Come on, let's go," she murmured. "We'll go to the druid's sanctuary and get some help."

Chapter 10

We circled around the side of the glade, closer to the nine standing stones that backed onto the forest. A tall man wearing furs and antlers stood in the middle of the circle, mumbling arcane words over his fire. Others in furs and hoods stood nearby with hands thrust in their loose garbs or holding ritual objects: beaker-shaped cups, horns of bounty, jeweled daggers. Priests and priestesses, I guessed. Despite my ill condition I could not help but feel awed, if not intrigued by this primitive ceremony. So much like my father's burning of incense I could never understand, or placing offerings to Jupiter, Juno or Ceres at the temple altars in the morning forum bustle.

"Who's he?" Regalis asked, motioning to the leader.

"That's Derdimonix, our head Druid," said Maig. "He blesses our village; he's a wandering priest from up north. 'Tis he who can offer you aid—quite a deal more than can I."

We approached the circle, her leading.

The man seemed in a trance, or not to notice our coming. Lower he sank, mumbling, then dropped to his knees, a sublime look of rapture flashing in those pale, unblinking eyes. His face was dyed deep blue; thick smears lay under those eyes. A masked face, cheeks, brow, neck exposed. Antlers like the looping horns of a bull ox curled down around his cheeks, the tips almost touching his breast. The thing must have weighed a ton.

Regalis made motions to bring me inside the circle, but Maig held him back. "Fool! Do you dare interrupt our rite? The druid honors our tribe and pays tribute to the ancient god with the horns who watches over our people."

Regalis drew back, sufficiently cowed. No utterances from us broke the silence. One of the acolytes at last brought a severed head into the circle, the stag skull gripped by the antlers, its flesh still fresh and dripping. Derdimonix lifted the primal offering and chanted solemn words. His antlered face seemed to vibrate. He lowered his head as if in prayer or contemplation, then he placed the head lovingly on a stone bench beside the other priests. Raising his gaze, he burst out in glorious song, the blood from the head dripping on the trampled grass at his feet. With a mighty heave, he tossed it into the fire and the flames ate at it, crackling and hissing with the fresh blood to slake the god's thirst. The other priests moved around in a circle, chanting in monotone.

When the rite came to a close, the stag head was nothing more than a crusted heap, antlers blackened crisps. Maig came to the druid's side and spoke some words in his ear I did not understand. His head lifted and his blue face turned to us as I felt a gaze most penetrating meet ours, not cold, merely inquisitive.

"Travelers from Londinium, welcome," he intoned in a rich voice.

Maig beamed. "I will entrust you into Derdimonix's care, Icarus, for I am not a healer as much as a spirit guide and a soothsayer. Today is tribute to Cernunnos—the horned one. There'll be no working in the fields, felling timber, or selling goods. Certainly no waging war with our neighbors." She motioned, sensing my impatience. "Be penitent, as there is much that will appear strange to you."

She and Derdimonix traded more words in a language that Feberiax might have understood. The priest, in his middle years, nodded, spoke in a low baritone. "Come!" He beckoned with a claw sweep of arm.

The massive horns edging his headpiece arched around his cheeks. It made our animal masks look like playtoys in comparison. Thick furs draped down the mantle of his broad shoulders.

"Follow me!" He swung out a paw of a hand. He led us and Maig followed. We seemed to shrink in substance in his presence.

The four of us treaded a path through the woods to a mud hut, built into the side of the hill while Regalis helped me along. Smoke streamed from the crude fieldstone chimney at the side. Maig turned to me and spoke. "I'll leave you here with Derdimonix. The village young ones are in need of my company." She turned back to the smoke and festivities.

The druid thrust open the heavy oak door, beckoning us inside. He shut the portal behind him.

The mud hut was not large, an old smokehouse that had me coughing from the fumes. Regalis blinked in the blue haze. Derdimonix went around and lit torches on the wall, illuminating the heady darkness. A hearth glowed to one side, and several wooden shelves held a row of stone tablets inscribed with symbols on the lower tiers. On the upper, bowls and mortar and pestles held herbs, weeds, and elixirs.

On the brazier aside the hearth a metal pot bubbled with some liquid, wafting scented steam into the air, an earthy odor, imbued with the power of soil and the indestructible nature of stone.

"Ordinarily I ask only ten denarii for anything related to spellcraft."

Regalis gave him the coins and they disappeared in quick fingers into the folds of his rank furs.

"Remove your tunic," he instructed.

I complied, baring my chest.

"Sit," he motioned me to a stool, while Regalis watched, blinking in the gloom.

Passing fingers along my chest, he grunted as I felt his warm breath play through his mask hole and the pale lips underneath. A musky odor, not unpleasant, but certainly not my preference in this cramped chamber. His fingers, muscled and firm, dry and cold, came probing with some dexterity to them.

The horned figure pressed with his thumbs, and I drew a sharp breath, for the pressure was not light. His blue face came ever closer, gazing at me with ever impassive reflection. I felt dwarfed by his presence, that antlered shadow under the flickering candles.

He took up a wooden staff leaning in the corner and on its end was affixed a bleached white rodent skull, like Maig's, whether weasel, ferret, or squirrel I could not tell. He dipped the end in the boiling pot then in a red liquid from a topmost jar on a cobwebbed shelf, then traced strange symbols on my chest. All the time his blue cheeks wrinkled and his lips pursed with the sounds of cryptic Celtic enchantments. At one time his staff swung back and struck him in the chest in inexplicable fashion. I jerked back in surprise. If it was by an invisible force, as a well-witcher's willow bough springs toward earth near a spring, then I remained mystified. *"Craeyrvry!"* he cried.

Regalis took a step forward, clenching his club.

"Wait! Some hex dominates your soul, laddie!—shadows dog your spirit."

His words echoed the very darkest of my fears. An enemy unseen that I could not fight.

"Yet this force protects you." He swung about. "Who gave you this curse, boy?"

I shook my head, my lips loath to form the hated priest's name.

He held up his hand, sniffing the air in suspicion. A rank odor permeated our midst, such as rotting onions mixed with dead flesh.

"The only hope is exorcism," he mumbled. He raised his staff and pushed forward, mask and antlers coming dangerously close to my face.

Regalis raised a hand. "Wait, you can't—"

"Stay back!" He shouldered Regalis aside.

I wheeled around, white-eyed in dismay. The druid picked up a clay pot of some vile blue liquid. "Drink this!"

"What is it?" I croaked.

"You'd rather not know. It'll help with the pain. What's to come. This also—" He thrust me a pot filled with greenish unguent, close to putrefaction. I nearly gagged. He mixed it with some white gunk and added some water from a battered urn and told me to drink from the pot.

I did, for reasons not wholly sane—wincing at the foul taste of the mixture pasted to the roof of my mouth. But I forced myself to swallow.

"Fire will bring the spirits to the surface," he muttered. "Up, stand up, so they can flee from their noxious holes." Stoking the hearth, he threw on a gnarled log, mumbling monosyllables of incantations old as the ice sheets come down from the north. He fluttered fingers and closed his eyes, laying hands on my chest, as if he were some miracle man.

Those hands, cold now, worked feverishly, then the strong fingers, nails dark with dirt, dug into my flesh and threatened to pry it apart. Then they grew warm with uncanny heat and I began to gasp. "What are you doing?"

"Never mind what I am doing. Ask more, what is it you've become. What are you holding inside?"

Quivering in exhaustion, I watched his face labor with a tragic effort. My hands and body shook. Regalis stared back, grimacing in disbelief as he witnessed a mysterious cloud of thin smoke issue from my nose. My back arched; my bones distended from my face. I could feel a twisting and turning and writhing in my guts. A vapor, green now, drifted out of my nose like smoke rings while strange liquid drooled from my lips. A rotten egg reek permeated the air. I gasped, choking for air, but could suck none in as no words would come out.

"What—What are you doing?" Regalis croaked.

"Back!" he cried. "Do not impede my magic!"

A dry sulfuric burning stung my nose and throat. Regalis again drew his club, but the antlered druid's eyes blazed.

"Out! You pernicious black succubus," he bellowed at my distended face. "Out into the naked air—where you can be burned!"

The door burst open. Feberiax stumbled in with Maig at his heels. "I couldn't stop him!" she cried.

The druid hissed an expletive breath. "Keep him back! Watch and listen and be forewarned!"

Regalis disobeyed and staggered over to steady me. My right hand swatted out like an eagle's talon, raked stub nails across his cheek, scratching him like a rabid fox. He cried out in pain and held his cheek to stop the blood.

"Back!" the druid called. "Fools! I told you so. Shut that door!" Feberiax slammed it tight. Lifting his club, he gripped it in a white hand.

While I convulsed there, he began to chant once again and the green vapors began to pour from my nose, curling and swirling, twisting and coalescing like a primeval fog into the shape of a hideous goat face, one of those grotesque creatures whose bloody remnants adorned the crypt of Pluvius's priest not long ago. The filmy, cloudy apparition opened its pointed fangs and spat. The druid quavered. I lurched, and the druid chanted ever louder spells in his baritone voice and swatted at the ghastly cloud with his herb-doused stave. The weapon passed through the filmy mist and the smoke demon hissed like a serpent, spitting a foul fog in the druid's face, teeth bared before part of it dispersed beneath cracks under the door. Some of it swept back into my nose and I coughed and hacked and nearly doubled over, groaning with the sick weight of whatever had filtered back within me.

The druid sagged in defeat. Was his power spent?

"Agblak Morir!" He dropped in a crouch, clutching at my ankles. I feared his power was not sustainable. My legs, still rooted to the mud-packed floor, felt like a tree in the throes of Hephaestus's fire.

When the druid rose, he looked humbled, a different man than when we had started this ritual. "Go. I can't take your money." He flung back the coins I'd given him at Regalis. "I can do nothing for you. A cold day in Caerdyg when Derdimonix fails at a counterspell!" He shook his antlered head. "All I can say is, you are to remain a slave to *Gezilmüür* for the rest of your days until you can lift the curse."

"Who's Gezilmüür?" I wheezed.

"What is he talking about?" Feberiax looked right and left wild-eyed. Regalis shook his head. Feberiax waved his club. "What kind of a wizard are you to give up so easily?" He grunted in disgust, hearing no answer. "Let's quit this animal's lair. This man's a fraud, and it stinks in here."

A chill grew from one end of the hut to the other, as the horned man loomed over us, his shadow growing tall, somber and more brooding. A snarl spewed from his lips. "Go, now, before the spirits are displeased with you all and infect your souls."

Feberiax mumbled imprecations. Regalis's lips worked as he massaged his scratched and bloodied skin.

As they gathered me up, the druid called after us. "Gezilmüür will not kill you, only use you for his ends. He would commandeer your body as a vessel for his own, to see through your eyes, to slaughter the multitudes with your hands, as sacrifice to his bloody thirst, give his dark lusts more power."

In my writhing despair, I could see the druid had pearls of tears in his eyes, inching down that blue-painted face and staining it with an icy sheen. All hope died in my heart that I would ever rid myself of this canker of death. I was Icarus the doomed.

"Wait!" He dipped some broad leaves in a flagon of oil, sprinkled a medley of herbs and some putrid essence from one of the clay pots on the shelf and let the unguent seep into the leaves some more. A minute later, he curled the sopping leaves into a square. He pressed it in a tiny pewter locket that he fastened on a leather thong. He approached, but before he placed it around my neck, cringed back lest I launch into another of those clawing seizures. But the fit had passed and only a dry, stagnant feeling filled my mouth and throat, to accompany the cloud of fever hazing my brow. As a final act of compassion: his offering.

"I can give you this to stop the pain. But it's only a stopgap. It will last you for years if you use it wisely and sparingly. Don't ever let it leave your person."

I withdrew several coins and held them in my trembling palm, as if imploring him to try some other means.

He uttered a raucous laugh, ignoring my coins. "You shan't get rid of it through conventional means, lad. *Ceirnos, Idiulus voedci! Deu!*" The words spilled from his wide mouth in an alarming, cacophonous staccato. "It has crept into your blood and is an ancient magic… *the world was young when Seth and his demons crawled from the slimes and turned the snow-white raven black…*"

"Whores of Babylon," I swore.

"Watch your tongue, lest Lugh strike you down."

Feberiax moved in to pull me away from the druid but I held up a hand. The druid did not flinch, as if Feberiax and his club were as matchsticks to battering rams compared to his powers, and I feared what the man would do if he were to conjure his full power against us.

Toying with his staff, he mumbled, "Dream of Isis, boy. Pray to Mithras, chant to Lugh. Give benedictions to Taranis, and Belenus!"

"You cast the blight of foreign gods upon me," I croaked in a hoarse whisper.

"Be afraid, boy! Drip your blood in an urn and fire it and let it sizzle and the smoke rise in rings on the eve of the full moon. This I urge you do in reverence to holy Cernunnos, the horned one." In my clammy hands he thrust a supply of a few more unguent-laced leaves contained within oilskin. "Take three drops of this with or without water when the worst fits plague you." He raised his staff. His eyes burned with an otherworldly heat, and he looked like a version of the mad gods he had named. "The seven sons of Osiris, the five moons of Min, the tower maiden, the eyeless horse, any god you can pay tribute to. Pray! Genuflect. For you will need to." And then his face sank into a deep glimmer of sadness, for he seemed genuine in his fervor.

The coins he hadn't yet taken from my trembling hand, I flung at him, so distraught was I. "Take your reward, druid, or whatever you are."

He did not reach for them. The beginnings of a snarl wormed its way to his lips. "If you were not so young and headstrong, I'd lay a curse on your enemies. But not knowing your part in this, I feel that curse might rebound upon me." Regaining his composure, he let the staff with the animal skull in his left hand drop to his side. "There is more that I see in your future, but 'tis not for me to speak, lest I make your journey all the more onerous. Let Maig be the one to tell you your fortune."

And so I kept the druid's stinking, oil-drenched leaves in the locket suspended from my neck—and pocketed the extra oilskin that Derdimonix had pressed into my fingers.

Feberiax swallowed and gave me a pat on the back. "Let's go, Ick. Nothing more to be done here." He shouldered open the door and we plunged out into the pale light, where birdsong played in the wind as it sighed through the leaves and crickets chirped in the grasses.

I had gained nothing from that tumultuous visit except the gummy prize which burned my fingers where the oil had leaked.

Nearing the village, Feberiax turned to Maig who'd been silent all this time, "Your druid seems an incompetent quack," he grumbled.

Maig offered a short barking laugh. "Perhaps because your petty Roman offerings amount to nothing in his gods' eyes—but he'll take your coins and melt them down for magical purposes perhaps. 'Tis possible Vercinorex could have done something more for you, but he passed into the spirit realm two moons ago." Her eyes, pools reflecting a faraway light, glimmered. "Derdimonix's magic is not strong enough to lift Gezilmüür's spell. But I can tell he did you some good. Your color has improved. That's a mean demon inside you. I bet it has latched onto your liver."

My voice cracked. "Do you know of any counter-spells? Exorcists?"

"Not nearby." She shook her head. "They be a hundred miles upriver and you couldn't reach them within twelve moons."

I slumped. We gathered up Oren, deep in song and quaffing flagons of mead with a group of new friends: woodcutters and smiths. Yet I didn't fail to notice both Feberiax's and Regalis's wary looks after witnessing those ghastly green puffs streaming from my nose. As we made our way down the rugged track, leaving the curling smoke and raucous cries behind, Maig's intense stare remained directed at me, her open palm tipped up in reflective salute.

Chapter 11

As the wagon clacked closer to Londinium, my heart grew ever heavy. Discovery and imprisonment, and possibly an accursed death did nothing to soothe my frayed nerves. Easy to take what coins I had and flee this place: to some remote destination, who knows where, take on a new identity. But that would leave me vulnerable to other hazards, with no friends and no means. They'd hunt me down if they could. *Don't fool yourself, Ick. You'd be no better off. Nowhere to hide.* I had only gratitude for what the druid had attempted, but I was torn between running or facing my demon and the sinking pit in my stomach. Hard to accept that my uncertain future in Londinium and the drastic change in my body was real. Nor did I like the growing wariness in Feberiax's eyes, clouded with violent apprehension, loaded with the memory of that green demon stuff streaming from my nostrils.

"You can stay at my place," Regalis offered.

Interrupted of my dark reverie, I grunted my thanks, reaching to Oren's shoulder to signal the wagon to a halt. A sudden urge struck me to put my flight from Londinium in motion and never look back. But I paused. A crossroads: one road leading to Gallia, the other to Londinium, and the terrible unknown. If I took the route to Gallia, I'd have to trudge deep into barbarian territory. Anywhere Roman rule prevailed, I'd run the risk of discovery. No, I thought the road to Londinium would be the better one. One last time I looked back over my shoulder up the darkening road. A coward I was not. Neither upon my father's name nor my brother's memory would I tarnish them with cowardice.

Rounding the wooded curve in the road, we approached the gateway to the great stone bridge over the Tamesis, looming like a Gallic torc. I lay down on the floor and covered my shivering hide with the dusty blanket.

The day had grown to that eerie pre-gloaming reflection descending over the water. Swans, ducks and geese, waded and flapped. Galleys and the odd barge moved in the grey-dark water with sluggish ease toward port. Others lay moored on the Londinium side, as ant-size men loaded and unloaded goods.

If I could salvage anything from this mess I would try.

Regalis's father, a middle-man and dealer of native pottery and comestibles, conducted business up north, enabling Regalis to refit the extra storeroom for my use, now empty of wares behind the master's study and close to the well-equipped kitchen and latrine. The modest villa lay off Via Henia north of Via Decumanus far enough away from the soldier-heavy gate. Though the atrium failed to catch the eye, several tasteful and colorful frescoes of hunting scenes graced its walls and a substantial shrine set in one corner, not dissimilar to my father's lararium. Despite the presence of four household slaves, Regalis snuck me in food.

I slept in fits and starts, gradually gaining strength from the druid's liquid concoction. The sludge went down thick and sour and my skin tingled at only one tiny dollop of the soothing balm. I lathered it daily upon my chest per the druid's instructions. I awoke from a nightmare in the gloom of Regalis's spare storeroom, soaked with sweat. My head still pounded to the dream-like rap of the prefect's fist on my father's door. Fear roiled my guts at the prospect of returning to my father's villa and risk implicating him. Regalis became my eyes and ears. Better that the one named Icarus just disappear for a while. I groaned. Maybe permanently? No, I would not consider that option yet.

A rash of recent violent offenses had broken out over Londinium. Defacings of public property, break-ins, aggressive attacks on passers-by, with the characteristic signature of our gang. Copycat crimes but with a difference. I hated to grant the Grouses the craftiness of their smear campaign.

Unlike them, we weren't murderers, excluding the stubborn watchman who'd fought back and tried to be a hero, or the odd idiotic, drunken soldier who would defy us, like those three bastards who offed Drace.

Graffiti coated shopkeepers' stalls with our sign—*The Clubs*. Random killings with theft. A young prostitute slain not far from her place of business. The trademark logo with *'Clubs'* crossed in blood across her naked chest. That sleazy murder had gone too far. It angered and chilled all of us, including Marcellus. A black mood had descended over me, seeing our name tarnished forever by our enemies, our free reign of play over Londinium finished for good, not to mention bounties on our heads. I sensed something more sinister lurking than typical gang rivalry. A crawling sensation crept in my blood, that Pluvius's priest's hand was in this.

Later that day Regalis hastened to my father's villa to inform him of my whereabouts. He returned with his face set grim.

"They haven't put out a formal manhunt for you—though there were inquiries."

"Who?"

"The town watch."

"Odd. Pluvius must be biding his time."

Marcellus got word to Regalis of an emergency meeting at the cemetery that night. Now the fourth since my return. I decided to attend and come out of hiding. The copycat crimes had fired my ruggies to wrath and I was glad that they shared my feeling that something needed to be done.

Backs to the Medecias vault, we dimmed our lamp and spoke in hushed murmurs. No ball-busting practice tonight, though all of us itched to bash down The Grouses.

I hadn't seen Marcellus in days. From his silent, cold treatment it became evident the rift between us had only grown. I could sense the feral, survivalist energy radiating from his inner being, as if I were tainted goods and that I'd give up their identities to save my own skin. He looked away in casual, dismissive arrogance, as if I already were a lesser member of the pack.

"I've been elected leader of *The Clubs* in your absence, Ick," he droned on in a lazy voice. "You're a liability. We've been trying to hunt down the Grouses, but Raicus and his clods seem to have eluded us like slippery eels."

"Good for you, Marcellus. Deciding all this behind my back like a cockroach."

"The vote was two to one. Feb and Oren in favor, Reg against."

My throat burned and I lurched forward, quivering in anger. "I challenge this unwarranted vote of yours. You know I'd never betray you to the watch, or reveal any of your identities. Any one of you."

"Bullshit," Marcellus sneered. "They'd squeeze you and twist your nuts hard enough that you'd be squawking like a river duck." He glared and rallied Feberiax and Oren. "They'll beat it out of you, Icky. Your problem makes it our problem."

"So what do we do?" demanded Feberiax.

"We've got to kill this fat Pluvius swine and his dark magician, like we should have originally."

Oren snorted through his nose. "And pigs will fly, Marcy. How do you expect us to do that? Pluvius will protect himself. His villa will be full of muscle, locked down like a fortress, himself hunkered down tight."

"Not necessarily," said Regalis. "Pluvius'd never expect us to be stupid enough to come after him at this late hour. He'll hunker down, not give up his daily pleasures."

"Either way," grunted Feberiax, "I'm not going back to that devil crypt."

Oren growled, "Me neither."

"Fine lot of blood-brothers you are," chided Regalis. "Icky's in trouble, and you hamsters'll sit back and let him sink. Is this *the Clubs* I signed up for?"

"Quit your yapping," snorted Marcellus. "It's boring and grates on my ears."

"Forget it," I mumbled. I thrust out a hand. "What about our other problem? Raicus and his goons?"

Marcellus gave an evil grin. "Those cursed Grouses. We'll make it look as if Raicus and his gang did the killing."

"Seems as if we have to teach these amateurs a lesson," said Feberiax.

"Yeah, some morality pointers in street etiquette," quipped Oren.

I turned my back and moved toward the city wall. Feberiax, our surly Celt, gave a sour laugh.

I couldn't stay here. Dismal vote aside, I knew after hearing those cynical words of my ruggies, I had to take matters into my own hands. Apart from Regalis, none of them would help me.

Regalis seemed to be on board and fell into step behind me. After we'd hopped the wall and trudged up Via Ostia, he took me aside. "I'm with you, thick or thin, Ick," he said.

"I know, Reg, you're the only one I can count on."

My mind was crystal clear. I told him my plan. His eyes clouded in surprise, but he nodded with grim acceptance, knowing that I'd do the same for him.

The next day we staked out Pluvius Maxus's villa, making doubly sure to stay concealed far up the street, disguised in our hoods and skin-camo made of ash and paste, with our clubs close at hand. A suicide mission perhaps. But desperation knew no limits. I needed to get this demon fire out of my veins. This smear campaign of our name could not be allowed to continue. Nor did I have confidence in Marcellus's bluster. I'd have to force the priest's hand to reverse the spell.

On the third day of our stalking, we'd come to recognize the banker's patterns. They varied little, as Regalis had predicted. Slinking up the cobbled street, I could hear his killer dogs roving in the vine-covered colonnade beyond that courtyard wall. There'd be more of the flesh-biters roving about. The garden was for now out of bounds.

From our concealed position, we watched Pluvius totter out of his residence at half past six, clearly in pain and agitated. He hollered at his slave to ease him into his sedan chair with care. Four slaves gripped the wooden handles and carried him in his private enclosure of curtained maroon while another four accompanied him, many looking like hired muscle, as if Pluvius'd emptied his household.

A daring plan surfaced in my mind—a swift, unlawful entry to his villa next time that door opened. Pluvius'd be gone for two hours at least—physical therapy and massage with the medic Solenius as part of his daily, bath-time ritual. My mouth curled in a vengeful smile. Time to discover more about this magician and some clue as to my unfortunate affliction. I hoped the vulture of a priest was still there. I'd wrest an antidote from his black heart and scrawny hide.

Licking some of the opium off the bay leaf Regalis had obtained from Marcellus, I hoped it'd help out in the sequence of events to come.

At that moment, a solitary figure sauntered out of the villa. A slant-eyed rogue with thin face, mousy mouth and a ruthless sneer. I recognized him well—Raicus! What in the devil was he doing here? But of course. Part of the crew Pluvius had put up to defame us and get rid of our gang. Why hadn't Pluvius reported to the prefect immediately? A shiver ran up my spine. Something more ruthless and insidious hid in the works. From now on, dirty games would be playing out.

The gang leader pushed past Pluvius's slave as he came hurrying up to the front door with a basket of fresh food. A twist now to my desperate plan. I hissed, "Regalis, let's waylay the sod, force our way in. I know the priest's in there. I can feel it in my bones. He's weaving his vile spells."

Regalis nodded. Grinning at the chance to break some bones, he murmured, "Desperate and a longshot, Ick, but I'm in."

I clapped him on the back.

Running at full tilt from our place of hiding, we knocked the slave inside the vestibule before the door closed. The slave fell backward onto the mosaic floor. I got him onto his belly and stuffed his mouth with a dirty swab pulled from my pocket. With practiced ease, Regalis handled the door slave in much the same manner before he could squawk and alert others. With gags around their mouths, we ripped off their tunics, stripping them down to their underwear and used it as cords to tie sections around their wrists, arms looped around their backs. Regalis and I strong-armed a slave each, frog-marching them through the atrium and past the master's study, twisting their arms with painful pressure whenever they resisted.

Without any other slaves in sight, we made it to the back of the villa where a familiar door loomed. We breathed sighs of relief. So far, so good.

Kicking open the door, I shuttled them into the antechamber we'd stumbled across that ill-starred night. Those pale, odd frescoes of nymphs and dolphins jumped out at me from the wall, no less that small door that led to the crypt of Hades. I felt a chill creep over my skin. I bet my career as a thug that Xetriam, the priest, practiced evil behind that blood-caked door. We readied ourselves to yank it open when the door jerked open of its own accord. A familiar figure glided through, wearing an enigmatic smile.

"Ah, the juvenile rapscallions." It was as if the priest had emerged from some foul, ecstatic trance, his eyes were glowing so eerily and mooned upward in their sockets. Whatever gods or hellish dimensions he traveled to, I daren't guess.

"I'd almost given up wondering when you were going to show up again. So rash and disillusioned the last time, I figured it wouldn't be long before you'd try again."

"Shut up, priest. Back in there," I threatened him, shuttling the slave forward then brandishing my club. The priest's blithe self-assurance irritated me, but I knew it must be an act. We had the upper hand, didn't we? He gazed at me with curiosity, as if recalling my face under the shadow of the hood. "You look remarkably well—Icarus, isn't it? Looks as if you've been healing your wounds from the last break and enter."

"Shut up," I growled, shoving the cringing slave into the priest, knocking both down the half stairs. With a grim look, Regalis followed suit and pushed his slave down into the windowless, sunken room. We strode down together, clubs in hand. Candles burned from niches on the walls, illuminating the same hideous demonic faces in the cheap brick and plaster. The obscene goat heads in the sacrificial gutter lay tilted up in mockery.

The priest leered at us. A pungent wash of reek followed in the wake of his thin, lanky body. His simple white priest's smock was smeared with dirt, offal and fresh blood. His lean, eastern face with its sunken cheeks and hollowed eyes stared back at us with cryptic significance like some evil essence of dark soulcraft. In one hand, he clutched a strange-lit incense burner emitting a bittersweet medley of aromatic herbs. In another, a disturbing figurine whose facial features appeared half crafted. Even in the half light, the palm-sized idol seemed to glow with an unnatural translucence, perhaps invested with a striking likeness of someone I knew, but couldn't quite place.

"I'm in the middle of a new spell. Come." He beckoned both of us with a welcoming hand, swarthy with elongated bony fingers.

Growling with warranted mistrust, I thrust the gagged and bound slave boy before me, ignoring the wretch's muffled shrieks. I pushed in past him, forced Xetriam deeper into the repulsive room.

"No tricks, priest."

"What need I of tricks? Your paltry club won't help you here. Leave poor Vulio and Elmio alone." He pouted in jest. "They're just children, simpletons at best."

"Move!" Regalis snorted, prodding the priest deeper into the confines toward the altar.

Xetriam bowed in sly contempt. "After you."

I bunted the wide-eyed slave before the altar, sucking in my breath at the gagging stench. The chamber was as before except for a carven scorpion effigy lurking on a pedestal underneath the hideous Mithraic head protruding from the wall—some new devil or ancillary token, I guessed. The priest made a grab for a figurine doused in blood standing upright on the altar. The torso, stuck full of needles or pins, looked alarmingly like me.

Xetriam's skeletal fingers squeezed it and I fell over, pain flooding through my torso. He jabbed another needle in it.

I howled, clutching at my abdomen. The world spun in dizzy waves. I writhed on the floor as the agony burned my solar plexus. Regalis lurched forward and clubbed the man hard in the knees, bringing him down. The priest reached again, one hand clawing at his knees, spewing forth fervid phrases, but Regalis kicked the figurine away from his reaching clutch and loomed over him with his club. The priest crawled toward the clay bowl on the altar sitting amidst clay lamps, blocks of wood and animal parts while I huddled there gasping, struggling to my knees.

The idol had landed not far from me. Breathing hoarse rasps, I clutched it in my hands and studied it with trembling fingers. A shiver of revulsion rippled through my body. The face, intricately carved of wood by a master hand, was one wrought by an artisan of many talents. Holes had been gouged in its torso and limbs with precision, plugged with metal needles so it looked like a grotesque sea urchin.

Xetriam choked out a gasp. "I studied your face when you unveiled yourself and carved it myself. The magic is more potent now that the effigy to Orcus hovers over us with his ever-reaching shadow."

Regalis flourished his club. "Let's kill this madman and be gone."

I rose to my feet and held up a hand. "Remember, Hound, I'm the one suffering from this malaise. If we kill him, we destroy any chance of my cure and I remain slave to *Gezilmüür* or whoever or whatever it is." I turned to the twitching priest. "Now, you filthy dog. Give us some answers."

I pulled all the needles out of the figurine one by one and ground it under my boot. Xetriam flinched, but made no attempt to stop me. Guarded by Regalis, the slaves cowered in a corner, shivering at what their master's priest had done. The mere sight of us and the grinning priest infused them with horror.

"I can prepare an unction which will reverse the curse," he said, "if I choose. My life—in return."

"I say we torture this dog and then we let him beg for his life," snapped Regalis.

I patted my club against my other hand. "Hound, you're too polite. Ever wonder what it's like to walk with two legs mangled and twisted in a dozen places, priest? Plenty of time to torture you before Pluvius returns."

A flicker of fear flashed in his sunken eyes for the first time. Perhaps he'd underestimated my propensity for violence. I advanced with club ready to pound him to a pulp.

"Wait!" He held up a hand. "I'll make you a special potion to give you extra strength. Magical powers. Vital as a wolf. You'll feel the vitality of

Hercules."

"That's unadulterated bullshit," I spat.

"Why would I lie?" he protested. "By the gods of Osiris and Orcus, I swear it."

"How long will it take?"

"A half hour, no more."

"What if he tries another trick?" Regalis warned.

"Ten minutes you have," I grunted. "Get to it."

The slaves' fear rose to a new level, each perhaps reflecting on what the new circumstances meant for their own chances of survival.

I looked at the wide ritual bowl with suspicion. Jupiter smash it to a thousand pieces! I'd heard of such curse bowls, inscribed with arcs of script and imbued with the power to commit horrible agonies and tragedies upon an enemy of choice. But never had I seen one up close in real life—and I liked this one less than any of my imagination.

"I still think it's a smarmy trick," Regalis blurted. "You can't trust him."

"Then our clubs smashing his skull will be his last memory." I worried my lip, a dozen thoughts creeping through my mind. I focused on the misery and anxiety this scapegrace of a priest had put me through: A filthy demon growing inside me. An everlasting curse that not even the village druids could counter. I could kill the unnatural bastard right now and go back for Pluvius Maxus.

Regalis frowned at my dark look. "You'll have to kill them all, Ick. Slaves, priest, master and his eight bodyguards."

I grunted. I couldn't easily kill innocent slaves without my conscience waking me in the dead of night, but I decided to call the priest's bluff. "I'll kill all of you if I have to," I snarled, waving my stout wood in their direction. "Get over there, priest—away from your potions." I swung my club and he slunk back like a timid deer.

With hands upheld, his eyes roved left and right. "I have another solution. I'll convince Pluvius to spare you, along with the promised antidote. It'll give you first dibs on a—"

"How?" I barked.

"I've my ways," he said deviously. "Pluvius thinks he's the master, but nothing could be further from the truth. He's afraid of me. Long ago, I discovered his weakness—a penchant for young boys, such as these slaves. At any moment I can ruin him in the eyes of the public. I can also put a visceral curse on his fat hide that'll bring him before me on his knees begging for mercy. That jar, for example, you see on the altar—I have another hidden under this floor with bits and samples of his nails and his hair suspended in a magical fluid. I can wreak unimaginable sufferings with them." He gave an evil chuckle. It rang off the blood-smeared stone like a death knell.

Regalis spat in disgust. "You're sick, priest, you know that? What filthy hole did that Pluvius pig dig you out of?"

He laughed, a raucous, bird-like caw. "Pluvius bought me off an Assyrian lord. For a hefty price. I became his magician—and his entertainer."

"I could give a roomful of Juno's tits for your history lesson, priest."

He eyed me with loathing. Pausing, he licked his lips. "In return spare me, and I'll protect you."

"So help me, priest," I grumbled, "if you double-cross me, I'll torture you with my bare hands then kill you five times over."

His swarthy face crinkled in a feral smirk. "I don't doubt you'll try."

Regalis patted his club. "While you're at it, priest, tell Pluvius to retire those boyish juvies of his. *The Clubs* are going to bash Raicus's and his gang's heads in when we catch up with them."

He gave a curt nod and went to work. Securing his curse bowl, he doused his hands in a pan of blood and added mixtures of liquids and pinches of vile things, dried plants like thistles and various animal parts to the wretched bowl, letting his eyes drift backward in their sockets, mumbling incantations in a garbled tongue while the slaves hunched wild-eyed, pulling at their bonds.

I shivered in that decrepit room. All too dank and dark here, damp with corruption, infected with a cloying reek of rotted blood. And, there in that horrid curse bowl of his, with its endless symbols and hieroglyphs, half filled with blood, the priest swirled his bony finger, all the while chanting arcane phrases in a tongue I'd no knowledge of, nor ever wanted to.

Xetriam seemed altogether too smug while he prepared that concoction. At one time he reached for a smaller figurine hidden under a blood-soaked rag. I knocked it from his hand, twisted his arm behind his back, until I heard him squeal like a pig before the bone was ready to snap. I released the wretch, knowing it would serve no purpose to break his fingers while he prepared my antidote.

That grotesque sanctuary with its animal innards, goat heads and hideous Mithraic effigy disgusted me. Especially the bull head with its twisted horns protruding from the blood-smeared walls.

I saw another oddity in the largest of the clay bowls that I hadn't before—five more figurines lined up in that basin, smeared in owls' guts or goats' brains or something and painted with barbaric symbols. Four stood with pins through their midsections; an uncanny realism lurked in their blank, staring faces and naked bodies. Young men, like us—but not. A curious, haunting familiarity radiated about them which set the hackles up on the back of my neck. I shuddered at who they might be. Carved with intricate attention to detail? The facial features and proportions of the body perfect?

I debated destroying them all under my boot heel, but I held back the impulse, feeling another spider chill worse than the last come over me. An otherworldly energy emanated from those ghoulish figurines, suggesting that I'd be tainted if I handled them. I'd already curled my fingers around one, and that brief touch had felt grisly enough to make my stomach turn.

"There, it's done," he rasped at last. "Three mouthfuls and you'll be cured of your curse." He held the curse bowl toward me like an offering of a poisoned apple.

I showed him my teeth. "You drink it first, priest."

His brows shot up. "I've no need for such a libation."

Regalis wheeled in, thrust up his club, and Xetriam snarled an oath and downed a generous swig. I looked at him as he wiped his mouth and licked his lips while wearing a cryptic smile. I jerked forward, pried open his mouth and saw the goat blood stain on his tongue.

He glared at me. "Now your turn, ferret, unless you wish the burning in your blood to stay forever?"

I took one swig and almost gagged.

"What the hell did you put in there, priest, horse piss?"

"You only wish it was that, boy. Drink!" He gave a maniacal cry, flinging up his hands.

I felt woozy on my feet. Regalis hunched forward to support me.

"Ick, you okay?"

I flung off his arm. "Does it look like I'm okay?"

I'd only swallowed a bit before I spat out the stuff and a massive grin grew on the priest's pinched face. I didn't like what I saw. My fist bunched, eager to wipe that smirk off. With effort I gathered my composure.

"That's not enough, little thug. Drink up, the whole thing. This is your victory over death!" He gave a triumphant howl. "Over pain beyond your wildest imaginations." The ecstatic trill in his voice grew to a crescendo which gave me little confidence. "You'll need three more such potions, each on the eve of the upcoming new moon."

I took two more swigs. The fiery tingling in my veins died. I began to feel more whole again. Strange. Had the priest made good on his word?

"If this is some foul trick, priest, bet that we'll be back and with no mercy."

His ashen eyes rose to gaze at the ghastly effigy. Mithras now reinforced and tainted by the scorpion effigy below and its resident priest armed with a look of worship and ecstatic adoration. "In the bygone days of my ancestors we worshiped the scorpion in lands older than Alexandria. The sting of the divine scorpion reduces all unbelievers to shattered bone and gobs of flesh."

Regalis gave a low mutter. "I don't like leaving this fiend alive."

I flourished my club in reckless anger. "Nor I, Hound, but I gave my promise and if he betrays us, he'll soon wish he were dead."

"Suppose he kills us with some hideous spell?" Regalis protested. "Like with these pierced dolls."

I ground my teeth. I could see no way to prevent it. Risk abounded either way. Pluvius could be back any minute. We were running out of time. I pulled my true friend away from the altar, though I could sense his fingers twitching to put an end to that miserable excuse for a human being.

Shouldering our way out the door, we moved like weasels through the hall, past the darkening shadows, startling another golden-haired slave on some mysterious household errand. He cast us a tawny-eyed look but the household must have become used to seeing strange folk coming and going, given the slave's lack of concern. No sooner had we stepped out into the street, when we gulped grateful breaths of air and rejoiced in the sanctuary of natural light. I wondered at the wisdom of leaving the priestly wretch alive, but I took solace in knowing that if there was anybody who could right the wrong done to me, it would be him. I'd seen the look of reserve on his swarthy face when he saw me first in my devil mask. And now if I could read his thoughts—he knew I'd be back for his head should he double-cross me.

Chapter 12

Regalis and I snuck to my father's villa, feeling more confident than ever after our victory over Xetriam. I rapped my knuckles on the door, our secret knock, but Denetio did not answer. There stretched a long pause. My heart gave an arrhythmic flutter. The door jerked open and Zeno, our cook, peered out, his face grim.

"Master Icarus! You're alive." He hissed a note of censure. His round pudgy features quickly changed to concern as he dragged me in and shut the door.

"Where's Father?" I demanded.

"Gone."

The patter of feet echoed up the marble hall. A lithe, willowy shape skittered out of the shadows. Fortuna. Her fine, chestnut-colored hair was tied back in a clasp. She gasped at the sight of me. "Icarus! I heard your name and couldn't believe it. I knew you'd come back. I've been so worried." She hurried over to press her warm body against mine and I held her close, drinking in her soft contours, not realizing how much I had missed her. Her body had filled out, likely from having a secure place to live removed of the stress of living a whore's life. Her Gallic beauty never ceased to amaze me, ruby cheeks flushed with a shine of vitality, this slender nymph with the thin, aristocratic nose and delicate features.

"Some rough men, heavily-armed," she breathed, "they were agents of Pluvius Maxus who came seeking your father. Told him he owed their master money, that Pluvius was going to impound his ships."

"Where did they take him?" A cold sweat broke out on my palms.

"The docks," grumbled Zeno, "down by the loading wharf. Denetio followed them, sent a messenger back. They left not a half hour ago."

"Bastards! Pluvius Maxus's dogs." I didn't want Fortuna to be caught anywhere in the middle of this. I pushed her back toward Zeno and told her to stay put.

She surged toward me with grief. "That night girl—was it you who k-killed her?"

I growled at her in disgust. "Are you mad, woman? Saturn's curses! Don't you know me yet?"

"No one really knows you, Icarus. What are you going to do?"

I shook my head. Frustration mounted in my brain. Regalis reached for my arm and I whispered a dark warning in his ear.

"I don't know yet, Fortuna. Zeno, stay with her. Don't answer the door at any cost, only at my secret knock—like this." I demonstrated. Regalis flashed me a doubtful look. I summoned the nimble, dark-haired slave Iuventus to inform Oren and Feberiax to meet us at the docks. "Tell them to bring their gear." The boy shuttled off.

Down Via Decus Regalis and I raced toward the flickering yellow glow of brands at the riverside wharf. The sun had long set. Now the moon's glow had painted the rain-dampened cobbles a dull copper sheen. Torches flared from the light posts and from seedy taverns across the cobbled way.

I caught sight of a broad-shouldered figure, none other than my father. Several figures milled around him. The echo of angry voices resonated. One of Mexor's commissioned trade galleys lay docked nearby, her thick hawsers tied to bollards and the gangplank to the cargo hold lying crosswise. Boxes and crates littered the loading area, some ripped open and crushed. I gasped. Dates and figs lay scattered everywhere and wine amphorae smashed. My father's stricken look told me all. I could see him gesticulating—in vain, while three others surrounded Denetio. A scribe or lawyer or somesuch waved a tablet in front of my father's nose. Mexor tore it from his grasp, and I watched in satisfaction as he ground it under his sandal's heel. But the burly man beside the scribe grabbed his arm. Another elbowed him in the gut. I was on the run as Mexor doubled over and they wrestled him to the ground. The rising altercation grew to an exchange of blows with Denetio flailing with his weapon, a billy stick I'd given him in case of trouble.

I howled in rancor and surged in, club reaching to break heads. The sight of my father, his head shoved to the ground with a bruised cheek and bloody lip, sent waves of fury through me. A cut ran from Denetio's left arm where a blade had sliced him. Cursing, I leapt in. Denetio lashed out with his weapon at a husky man parrying with sword. Seven more figures surrounded them, ready to crack bones. Crazy odds, four against eight.

Two of the four presented no match for seasoned mercenaries; a household slave used to a soft domestic life with few duties and a salt-and-pepper-haired man, skilled in his prime but having enjoyed a privileged life of leisure. Regalis and I had the advantage of surprise and our rigorous training was beyond reproach, but we were youths. What in Jupiter was keeping Oren and Feberiax?

A fury came over me, courtesy of Xetriam's devil juice. An animal heat clouded my brain, clogging my veins with madness. Much of what happened, I cannot recall. I was suddenly running, then floating as if on air, sounds merging into a background thrum like the *boom boom* of a tribal drum in my ears. A glinting blade came angling down at my father's chest. I drove in, swinging my murderous club.

Crack! Wood shattered bone, landing square on the thug's spinal column between his shoulder blades. My knee jerked up, lifting into his upturned face. Twisting to catch the gladius on the wood, I heard more bone splinter and a gassy curse as my hobnailed boot caught him in the groin, then his chin. I watched the mercenary slump senseless to the wooden dock. My father looked up into the face of my devil mask, the fiend that was Icarus, swinging and kicking, hissing and smashing while Regalis clubbed at my side.

I kicked over a crate; a bellowing assailant stumbled over it. Before he could get to me, I smashed him in the teeth. Lean jowled and heavy bearded, another enforcer came swinging in with a hefty axe. It chopped into the middle of my club, notching it. I swore, pulled the wood free, then smashed the club into his right side. He toppled with a howl and the axe slipped from his hand.

My father snatched up the grim weapon. As another tripped, staggering past a crate, my father hacked at his ribs with the axe while I savaged him from the other side, seeing his eyes glaze in death. Regalis covered Denetio, contending with three crouching enemies while our slave smacked at the nearest legs. The thug hobbled off, holding his shin.

The red rage washed through me and I hurled an enemy back into the man behind him. Toppling in a puppets' heap, they looked at me in astonishment, then scrambled to their knees, as if wondering how any man could have that much fury and strength. I moved in, grinning under my mask, menacing them with heavy blows and they shrank back, realizing this job was not worth the money they'd been paid.

Cowards! The last two ran. We stumbled away from that chaotic scene, leaving the crumpled forms groaning amidst the broken crates. I felt my limbs twitching as if a mechanical force were yet driving me on like some inner beast. A killing machine, hankering for more blood. I thrust out at a devil-masked figure approaching me who caught the wood of my rising club in defense. "Whoa, slow down," Regalis shouted in my ear. "It's me, are you insane?"

I grumbled, shook my head, mumbling my apologies. I grabbed hold of my senses.

A superhuman strength had flowed through my veins just now but in a heartbeat it had dissipated with the threat gone. Hours ago Xetriam had given me a magic elixir. Now it seemed to have transformed me into a demonic killer. It was not me, Icarus, who had slain those men, but some ensorcelled fiend. I felt suddenly appalled that I had nearly killed Regalis along the way. It could have been my father. The beginnings of shame burned my ears. Would I ever be able to control this feral power?

My father hunched over, clutching at his ribs. I patted his shoulder and he placed a hand on mine to steady himself. "Icarus," he wheezed.

Regalis helped Denetio to his feet.

Our slave and Mexor were all right. Or would be. More a close scare than anything.

"Hades take them, the bastards," Mexor spat. "That perverted clerk waved a forged tablet in front of my nose. His goons tried to confiscate my shipment. Promised to come back for more. The unmitigated gall."

He looked up at me, the club dropping to my side. "So, it's true," he muttered. "*The Clubs* of Londinium." His jaw agape, I could almost imagine him visualizing my devil's eyes blazing. I saw shock, resignation there— even fear, something I'd rarely ever glimpsed in those steel-grey eyes.

I stripped off my mask and pursing my lips, gave my father a defiant glare. "See what you want to see."

"Tell me, did you murder that woman?"

"No, it was not me. I swear it was The Grouses."

"Those lousy lowlifes." He spat on the cobbles.

"Zeno told us you were in trouble," I said. "We came down as fast as we could."

Mexor acknowledged the truth of it. "I thank you for that. Proud that you stood up for me, Icarus. For Denetio and your old father." His lower lip trembled and I could see his eyes glistening. He reached out to embrace me, his hands shaky.

I held him in my own gruff embrace before easing him away. "It's senseless to stay here."

His eyes grew desperate and fierce and a grim light came in them. "But you've killed me."

"How's that?"

"Pluvius'll put two and two together. He'll think you and your gang members ambushed and roughed them up—" he pointed to the inert forms slumped amongst the wreckage "—his men."

I growled at him. "There's no proof. We wore masks."

"They're big players. They'll figure it out."

"Not so big that they can get taken out by an old man," I grumbled, "and his slave and a pair of rowdies dressed in animal garb." I chuckled, pleased at my quip. I wiped a bloody cheek and motioned to Regalis. "Listen, Father, I've fixed things. Trust me."

He shook his head. "How? This mess is irreparable."

"The one who did this to me, Xetriam, has no love for his master Pluvius. I've made a deal with him. Sparing his hide—in return he'll control his master. He has…powers."

A small gleam of hope shone in my father's eyes. But it vanished almost as quickly. It seemed too incredible for him to believe that such could be the case so I could understand my father's doubt. We moved up the street, four hunched figures, not wanting to hang around, or answer awkward questions. The town watch would be coming soon.

We hurried off into the deepening night, as a fog drifted in off the water. The lemon glow became more ghostly than ever. Already I could hear the city gong clanging in the direction of the west gate where the fort loomed.

Feberiax and Marcellus had not arrived and I was glad to have handled this situation without them. Judging from my father's look of wariness through his hooded eyes, I knew he knew I was not his young Icarus any more. A good feeling despite the bleakness of our plight.

* * *

Regalis and I got Mexor and Denetio safely home. Turning on my heel, I was about to sweep off with Regalis when Mexor called out to me. "Don't you want to say something to Fortuna?"

I frowned, biting my lip. Yes, I'd forgotten about her in the crisis of the moment. "Regalis, wait up at your place. If I'm not there in an hour, meet me at the *other* place." Our codeword for cemetery.

He nodded and left.

I followed my father inside and made my way to the back of the villa, where I found Fortuna in my room, slumped, wringing her wrists in agony. I phrased my words carefully to her, in no mood for lengthy sermons or romantic interludes, only to say that I'd bailed Mexor out of a jam, and in the process was trying to fix a larger problem.

She flushed and brightened and leapt up. Her arms held me tight. Her radiant warmth pressed against my chest and melted away many of the knots of the weary wreck who was Icarus.

"I worry for your safety, Icarus. Something's changed in you. It's like you're battling some beast at the deepest core."

I pulled away from her, my mouth dry. At this moment the uncanny truth of her words became more than I could bear. "You're a good woman, Fortuna. Jupiter knows if I deserve you. If there's a way to fix this, I will. If not, remember the Icarus who flew too close to the sun and burned." I turned, and with reluctance, left.

I passed the study where Mexor sat, head cradled in his hands. "Take Denetio," he said dully. "The streets aren't safe."

I gave a slow nod. "And what place is, Father, with the likes of Pluvius and the stinking Grouses skulking about?"

Denetio and I moved quickly down the ill-lit streets, past the darkened shops and the shuttered apartments, saying no words to each other. My hand stayed gripped on my club and my eyes flitted from side to side. Evil lurked in these shadows tonight and I felt a shiver of disaster walking unseen. As we neared the crumbled outbuilding of the baths, a queer feeling tickled my spine; something foul was afoot. But, my mind, preoccupied with Pluvius's machinations, remained distracted, and I neglected to give the place wide berth. A lone torch burned at the intersection of two main streets from the counter of a *thermopolium*, one of the hot and cold drink establishments now shuttered up for the night. About half way to Via Marinus where Regalis lived near the baths, I heard a scuffle of feet and glimpsed several rustling shapes coming out of the darkness. Before I knew it, masked figures surrounded us, swarming in like wasps.

I turned, startled by a familiar shape, leading the pack with purple hood and long black garb. The torchlight illuminated the masked face in the sallow glow, the breeze off the river doing nothing to mask the smell of rotten garbage lying in the gutters. There was no mistaking the whites of those ferret eyes gleaming behind that rat mask and the cynical droop of mouth.

"Icarus, got a friend with you today, I see." The figure hefted his gladius loosely in a palm.

Denetio stepped in front of me, wearing a mirthless expression. "Rats abound this evening."

Raicus laughed. "Got a little bodyguard to help you? Surprised you didn't bring your other pretty slave with you." He widened his stance as four of them circled us, cutting off our escape.

I stood my ground, giving my club good play.

"Won't help." He patted the flat of his blade with meaning and leveled me a challenging stare.

"Stay back," I warned Denetio. As the slave stepped forward and flashed his billy-stick to block Raicus's jab, I reached to pull him back.

But missed. Well-meaning fool. Not heeding my warning, he stepped right in its path, ill prepared for the violence of the sword's edge.

Raicus twisted like a snake and stabbed with his compact blade. The razor-sharp edge slid off Denetio's flimsy baton and pricked a place near his neck.

He gave a choked cry and I gave a wild howl of dismay as Denetio sank to his knees. His stick thudded on the cobbles. Thick blood seeped through his fingers as he clutched at his neck, unaware that death would soon be upon him. Howling in despair, I surged in, swinging my club in a blind fury, knocking Raicus back on his heels. The club tip only grazed his bird mask, leaving him disoriented, but his henchmen were quick to defend. But not fast enough. The first went down, holding a mashed eye. Another got my boot in his nuts. I went berserk. Swinging, whirling, twisting into their midst like Mars incarnate. Right, left, my club swung with merciless precision, fired by the dark spell laid by the priest. The demon must have lain dormant after that priest's spell, but now it burst out of its cocoon in full glory, spurred by rage and the senseless slaughter of a close friend. My wild eyes turned scarlet as blood; they saw the green mist swirling out of both nostrils, my beat-stick hammering flesh as if it were an extension of my savage self. The curse was upon me in full savagery.

Raicus' thugs jumped back and raised swords to block my strokes, so ferocious was my attack.

"Minerva's tits," cried a tall rogue of Raicus's group. "Did you see that green smoke? Who is this madman?"

"Kill him! He must be leader of *The Clubs*. I recognize his slave. Take him down. Take both of them down."

They would not be bringing me down this night. While Denetio's life drained, wood whirled in my hand. The force of three men struck in that arm, killing one of their lot, bashing in a brain, crushing a forehead, and I swung with even less mercy, if such were possible. Denetio made wounded animal sounds at my feet.

"Bel and Set! What are you?" gasped Raicus, leaping out of reach of my club. "Retreat!"

I sprayed a spitting taunt, "Go back to your moneyed she-dog, Raicus."

I rounded in and swung at them, forcing them back. I dared them to try further, but they scattered like fleas. Sucking sounds echoed to my left: Denetio lay writhing, the sickening rasp of his labored breath wheezing through a broken larynx. As the scumbags fled, I was torn between hunting those cowards down and splitting their heads or helping Denetio. I couldn't leave him alone there. I ripped a strip off my tunic and wrapped it around his neck, knowing the damage was done. His sad, dilated eyes rolled up at me in hopeless apology. "Sch, sorry, Icar—"

His wheezing breath stopped. Beside him sprawled one of Raicus's ruffians, hand extended, still alive but barely. I slugged him hard with closed fist. I ripped the wings off his shoulders and tore the cat mask off his face with a virulent curse, then ripped the bloody grouse tail off his ass and dropped it on his chest.

I made it look like a gang slaying.

Denetio's death couldn't possibly go unpunished. A fierce anger surged in the back of my throat. Blood pulsed in my temple hot as a furnace. What could I do?

Denetio was more than just a slave. He was a friend…one who'd kept my secrets and had the courage to defend me. He didn't deserve to die like this at the hands of those predators.

My eyes, dull pits, turned to the night shadows. A monstrous rage lurked in my breast, aching for revenge, compounded by the occult hex of the perfidious priest.

Nothing would bring Denetio back. The watch would be all over this street. Things had fallen apart. I gave a roar of frustration. Crouching down, I closed Denetio's eyes.

It's said that if a body of the recent dead were not guided properly across the river Styx, the soul would wander in limbo forever. I shuddered at such a fate for my friend. Normally I did not go in for such old hags' tales, but an eerie premonition hovered over my skin, clinging like a damp rag. I felt responsible for his demise; I could not leave him sprawled there like a dead animal. Even I knew the importance of proper funeral rites.

I hooked my bloodied weapon at my waist and dragged him up the alley. I stumbled, sidestepped a fetid pool. I pulled Denetio out of a cone of flickering torchlight. A mound of garbage lay to my left. Leftover meat scraps and bits of entrails from a butcher's stall left out for the crows and dogs. I debated hiding him in behind some of those trash heaps. If I could return, I'd roll him up in a blanket...Stupid. No time. Dare I call on Regalis's help? No time for that either.

A torchlight flashed farther up the back alley. I cursed. Someone staggering from a piss pot. Jupiter's curses. A patrol could come by just as easily. With a savage grunt, I lifted Denetio up and over my shoulder in a fireman's hold and moved on down the street. My muscles strained, my calf-muscles bunched.

For the first time, I gave a prayer to Jupiter, tears welling in my eyes. I tried not to think of it too much. I'd have to safe-keep the body. Where? Should I run into any of the watch, I'd be sunk. A bitter curse rumbled in my throat. Those bastards would pay! On I staggered through the darkened streets, a hollow man. Even then something told me Regalis's place wasn't safe to hide in anymore. Those lowlifes at the docks had gotten a whiff of us there: his voice, a slip of name perhaps, a glimpse of his aquiline nose when his mask had slipped. Pluvius would be back-tracking my friends to identify and target them. I weaved my way through the slick cobbles to that place on the east wall. A dead mugginess hung in the air. No soldiers. Ordinary citizens knew enough to turn a blind eye to night time horrors. But the hour was not yet late enough to be skulking down the streets with such damning evidence on my back.

"Here, you!"

I turned with a hiss. A stout man lifted a hand out of the shadows. Luckily I had my mask on; he couldn't guess my identity.

The man's eyes bulged. Catching a glimpse of the body on my shoulders, he gave a roar. "You're one of those filthy Clubs of Londinium! Another murder on your hands! Vermin. You'll pay for your crimes!" He fled off into the night, calling for the watch.

I breathed a curse. Filthy fool! Another complication to add to the evening's cockups.

Running more desperately now, I felt Denetio's bulk starting to weigh me down. I hobbled to the east wall. I lay him down in a gentle heap. The blood had stopped flowing from his neck, leaving an ugly smear about his torn throat. I licked my lips.

Retrieving the grapple, I looped one end of the rope under his armpits and hurled the hook over the wall. The satisfying clink of metal assured me it had caught when I gave it a sharp yank. My breath came in labored gasps. I climbed the rope. Standing on the wall's summit, I gazed about in fierce desperation. Then by some effort of will, managed to hoist his corpse up foot by foot. My super strength was ebbing fast. Should a wandering soldier chance to see me now… Gently I lowered Denetio down to the other side.

Unhooking the grapple, I let the metal drop with a thud. Then I lowered myself down, belly sprawled against the wall so that only my fingers clutched the ledge before letting myself drop. I rolled, feeling the sting in my ankles, but I came staggering to my feet, hid the grapple in nearby bushes. The others would have to use the backup grapple if they came.

A fine mist had gathered, giving what little light shone from moon and distant torches, a haze-like bewitchment. I hoisted Denetio on my shoulders and stumbled on through the darkened terrain to the cemetery. The place was deserted, only crickets chirped a lugubrious dirge in the dewed grass and among the pale, lonely stones. I crept up to some bushes, hiding Denetio in the thickest part then plopped down myself in a heap not far away to wait out the night. I preferred not to be prowling about the city right now, dreading the news I'd hear in the morning. Better to lie low until the ruggies showed.

Chapter 13

Sometime later I awoke to the sound of an anguished animal, likely an unlucky hare caught in the jaws of a predator, maybe a fox.

I stared off into the night, listening to the snarls and the screams, my back to the Medecias wall. I nibbled at a bit of the bread and cheese, I'd stuffed hastily in my pocket. The hard stuff went down sour as a lump of tainted cod. The animal thrashings had ceased, the prey soon to be devoured. A feeling I shared with the rabbit. The half moon swung its slow arc in the sky, my only companion this night besides the retreating marauder and the ash-filled urns of the dead.

My head felt dizzy, like a spinning top, whirled to high pitch at the death of Denetio. Was I one of those puppet characters in Sophocles' plays, some tragic figure living a dream to be erased when the dreamer woke up?

Self-pity accomplished little. I pinched my eyes shut and blocked out the pain, hunched in the bushes. Sleep took me at last, but with my last thought only regret at not smashing Pluvius Maxus's skull when I had the chance.

In the restless hours that progressed, I began to have visions, hallucinations, any number of evil things floating around my cobwebbed mind. Devilish faces, snouts and horns, half god, half animal entities. They all stood behind people or floated over them. Yet only I could see them, as if these were dark spirits that hovered around us all the time, that suddenly became visible during times of revelation. The tingling rushed back into my limbs with full force. It got so bad that I nearly scratched my arms off, feeling as if ants were crawling up my veins.

A foot nudged me awake. I jerked up out of my stupor, hand groping for my club.

"Ick," called a familiar voice. "You're looking a little worse for wear."

Another spoke: "Yeah, like one of those grimy vagrants who come creeping around the plots."

I squinted up in the torchlight, easing my bulk to an upright position. Marcellus. Feberiax. Two others.

"How long have I been here?"

"Lay off him, Marcellus," grunted Regalis.

"No need to get sore," Marcellus huffed. "We're all in this pickle together. Sooner we deal with our problem, the faster we can rest at ease."

Concurring mutters rolled off the lips of Feberiax and Oren.

Marcellus smoothed back his thick black hair. "You'll be happy to know, Ick, we waylaid that priest-devil of yours on our nightly pilgrimage, taught him a valuable lesson."

"What?" I croaked.

"Sod shouldn't been wandering about the streets late at night, clutching that bag of wooden dolls of his. Doesn't he know Londinium's a dangerous place at night?" Laughs came from Feberiax and Oren. "We came up behind him, quiet as mice, wrapped the priest in a thick blanket, me, Feberiax, Oren, just like the soldiers do, swung him around, whipped him hard on the head."

Feberiax chimed in, "Begged for us to let him go, promising all kinds of his master's gold and secret powers from his spells."

Marcellus shook his head. "Poor fool wasn't in good shape when we opened his bag and listened to what he had to say. Afraid of something at home, seems his pig-faced master turned on him. Imagine such cowardice, a grown man afraid of his own shadow."

Feberiax grinned. "He wasn't convincing, so Marcellus gave him one too many clouts. To his credit he went out hissing and scratching. Threw some of his powders and potions at us. Scalded Oren something nasty on the arm, then he got me here in the neck—" he pulled back his tunic to reveal a burn mark like a brand above his left breast.

I sagged, feeling sicker than ever.

"Well, long story short," Marcellus sighed, "we weighted him down with some loose cobbles and threw him into the river." He rubbed his palms. "All done, Ick. Problem fixed."

My mouth quivered and I hunched like an old man.

"You don't look too happy, brother. Are you alright?"

"You stupid fools. Regalis and I broke into Pluvius's villa hours ago and roughed the priest up. Didn't he tell you? Forced him to make a deal with us. He promised to reverse the spell on me. I need three more treatments."

Marcellus scoffed. "That's a ballsy move, Ick. If you trusted the black-hearted devil, you're stupider than you look. As for Reg we just caught up with him now."

"That witchfire is still in my blood," I growled. "Like a demon worming through my veins. That bastard double-crossed me."

"Or is it because the priest is dead and it nullifies the pact?" Regalis suggested.

Marcellus gave a lazy shrug. "Who cares? It's a tough turn of fortune. Hard to be too careful when things get so muddled—"

I leapt at him, my hands clawing to get around his throat. Feberiax jumped in and pulled me off. Oren held my arms. Marcellus smoothed out his tunic and grinned at me. "Ick, we're getting off to a bad start again. The only way we win is if we work together. I know you've been dealt an unlucky hand, true, but don't splinter *The Clubs* over it. One for all and all for one, don't you remember? Let's get a grip here."

Everything in me wanted to club that smarmy bastard down. His smug dismissal of all that had been dealt me, despite his pretty speech... It was enough to make me murder the sod. I hadn't even told them about Denetio yet. As much as I hated to accept his words, some truth lay in them. Regalis could sense it too.

"Pluvius will be next, if we have to gut that sweat-bellied sow," Marcellus grumbled. "I think his unfortunate sidekick was too close to guessing who the rest of us were, judging from the harsh slurs of his before he died. He might have babbled something in his master's ear."

I stared like a sphinx. "Denetio's dead. Raicus and his goons waylaid us on the way to Reg's earlier this evening. I managed to kill a few of them, the rotten bastards, then I carried Denetio's corpse back here before the watch could stumble upon it."

Regalis's jaw dropped. "You carried his body over the wall?"

I grunted. "I used the grapple. Denetio's over there in those bushes." I thrust out a weary finger.

Feberiax and Oren scrambled over to the bush and indicated as much, stepping back, wearing scowls. "It's true," Oren said.

Marcellus rubbed his chin. "Seems as if there's a lot of dying going on tonight." His jaunty grin seemed appreciative of the complex irony of the situation. "Doesn't change our plans though."

"What plans?"

"Just what I told the others," he murmured harshly.

Regalis and I looked at each other. He gave me a sad nod.

Marcellus waved a casual hand. "First, we go in groups of two. Feb and Oren, you and Reg. Me, solo. You pairs comb the streets two abreast and if you see The Grouses, whistle for help and the others'll come and deal with the bastards."

"Right," growled Feb. "We sweep the whole city and we keep it up all night."

"Right, Feb, you understand fast. We'll flush out the rats."

"Tonight?" I croaked. "What about Denetio?"

"Denetio's dead. No use crying over spilled milk," scoffed Marcellus.

I shafted him a venomous look. "It's too risky. There're already dead Grouses on Via Componis."

"So, all the better to flush out these chicken shit bastards! We start with Via Componis."

I choked on my tongue. "Aren't you the little tyrant? Who's made you the de-facto authority?"

Oren said quietly, "We voted him in and I think we should follow Marcy's plan, Ick."

"Fine. Have it your way, Orey. But first, I have to get word to my father about Denetio's death."

"Do what you have to do, Ick," grunted Marcellus with impatience. "Time's wasting."

I looked sullenly away, knuckles white as I gripped my club. Suddenly I felt a very dangerous wave of non-conformity washing over me. Oren muttered. "As I said, I've no objections."

It seemed a plan with a chance of success, but like all of Marcellus's schemes, I had a bad feeling about it. I couldn't think of anything better now, so I held my tongue.

Regalis and I went out to Via Decus to break the news to my father. When we knocked on the household door, Zeno answered, his eyes distant. They arched in dismay when I told him about Denetio's death and where the body was hidden.

"You did what with the body?"

"Be sure to let my father know," I told him in a somber voice.

I didn't hang around to address my father. The events of the evening had left me sick at heart. Already my blood burned with too much vengeance to waste dealing with my father's wrath. Where there was a window of opportunity to avenge Denetio, I would take it. As much as I disliked Marcellus's impulsive plan, at least it was a start. The time would come to face my father later after this deed was done and I could confront Marcellus on this leadership fiasco.

Regalis and I met up with the others at the docks as we'd agreed. We worked our way west and north. Nothing in the first sweep. Three hours in, Regalis and I stopped short at the patter of feet. A black-cloaked figure with shoulder wings and an ape-like face came running up, hissing through his mask. Marcellus. "Roguery in Via Cetonus. The Temple of Mithras."

I growled in exultation. We wasted no breaths. Regalis and I hoofed it to the temple while Marcellus hustled off into the splash of darkness to fetch Oren and Feberiax.

The lone torch above the cave-like entrance of the temple highlighted a sprawl of freshly-applied graffiti in garish relief. A band of vandals had marked up the Mithraeum's exterior something awful. In red paint obscene graphics gleamed, wide, looping characters with lots of X's, O's and markings of clubs plastered the entrance. Nothing too subtle here. There'd be a shit-ton of enraged devotees on the morrow. The thick wooden door, normally boarded up for the night had been split open with an axe. I caught a glimpse of a lone, ragged figure being dragged through the gap. More cloaked and hooded figures followed, silent as wraiths, herding their quarry inside.

I gave no thought to safety. I pounded after them. Regalis caught up to me, clutching at my arm, hissing at me to wait for the others. I didn't, deaf to reason.

My first guess: an unlucky passerby had probably happened to wander by and witness the crime, then tried to slink off into the night. The Grouses'd captured him and pulled him into the temple to silence him. Why take the added risk? Why not just let him go? The beat-down, likely another murder, would be extra dressing, of course. Leave the battered body and blame in it on *The Clubs*, an extra sacrilege to spark further public outrage. All this might have been avoided had that numbskull Marcellus not killed the priest.

Time for us to beat some Grouses.

Regalis and I slipped through the butchered door wearing grim expressions. Suddenly we stepped from the damp Londinium air and the broad street to a stuffy, cavern with masterly-carved man-statues and marble altars encircling a round, central pool of still black water. Our senses adjusted to the dank geography. The space echoed to the scuffles, grunts and laughs of the invaders amid the shrieks of the victim. The smell of heady pitch filled our nostrils, courtesy of the tar-filled urns lined up against a wall. The vapors of flickering torches set within the overhangs of bedrock augmented the smell. Even at night the priests kept the temple alive and breathing, the ethereal glow of Mithras ever eternal.

Without preamble, we capitalized on our element of surprise. I laid my club into the nearest hooded thug who was putting fists and boots to the innocent. The victim curled in a ball, protecting his head from blows, his ragged beard flecked with spit and his soiled tunic torn. Upon a heavy kick, he rolled away with a broken shoulder.

In the midst of a flurry of snarling, black-garbed shapes, I was suddenly enveloped, with billy-sticks and gladii swinging all around me. The brush of hard wood thwacked my left side and stirred the devil fire within me. Of that tap I felt nothing. An all-consuming rage driven by the strength of ten men pulsed through my body. Hatred for all enemies who would do me and my ruggies harm drove me to actions I could not control. Even though my mind remained lucid throughout, I could not recall much of what happened and the terrible deeds that followed.

Oren and the others, hearing the grunts and echoes of combat, burst through the gap and lent their clubs to the fray. We fought as one— *The Clubs of Londinium*! Oh, what a beautiful synergy! The most fabulous bloodletting.

Even in our fighting glory, from years of training, we were hard pressed by those savages. Raicus had recruited more of his bully boys—or maybe Pluvius and his priest had hired them, netting them like fish. Mercenaries? There must have been two dozen of them. They were trained and strong, masked and hooded, winged and cloaked. Three were down, in pools of blood and broken bones, but we were pushed back, staggering to the edge of the pool. I felt my feet soaked in cool water. These fiends were not human. Slashing, bellowing, carving, stabbing, ensorcelled I suspected by the priest's magic via his carved voodoo dolls stuck with pins, they fought as a medley of grotesque hooded figures garbed in painted black, some with grouse tails on their behinds in crude mimicry of our devil wings.

I caught a glimpse of Regalis slipping in blood and going down. I clubbed away a shimmering blade before it pierced his breast. My elbow came up, caught the assailant's mask, cracking it open. Boot met nose and my club finished the job.

That organized filth fought like wild she-dogs. The death of their peers only drove them to increased fury, but for several moments I was invincible.

In a freak moment, I tripped over a boot. A howl of triumph came from a hooded face, but a familiar club rose—Feberiax's—to smash in the offender's face.

By sheer numbers we were pushed against the western wall, not immune to slices, smacks and cuts. Feberiax had an open gash across his left cheek, Regalis a bruised chin, me, numerous cuts and bruises and tattered clothes but I cared nothing of this. Marcellus dodged and swung, Oren fell in at his side, cursing every foul, hooded, monk-like figure who harried us.

A brute with a battleaxe faced me and swung that murderous sledge down with all his might. I blocked with my wood, twisting aside, but the middle half of my club suddenly disintegrated into a dozen pieces like kindling.

For a half second, I stood there like a dumb mute, staring at the severed stub of my trusty club. Then I chucked it at the brute's face and ducked a wild strike that would have lopped off my head.

Feberiax charged the man with a roar. He ducked under a massive sweep of the killer bronze.

Dodging around the giant, I scrambled right, then left like a playful sparring partner. He jerked aside, distracted by my monkeyshines. Regalis and Oren beat back at the others.

A spear nicked me in the thigh. The jab brought instant pain, but I ignored it, purchasing time in a frantic roll to land out of reach of the glinting battleaxe in the smoking torchlight. I followed up with a crippling kick to his groin. Feberiax's club smashed the wielder's left calf. He toppled with a groan and Marcellus shimmied in and delivered a strike that crumpled the man's forehead. A wash of blood and brains splashed upon his mask and hooded cloak.

I scooped up the massive weapon. The bronze hung heavy in my grip. Not the weapon of my choice, but the battle fever was on me and I swung it in a wide loop, keeping the howling Grouses back, cutting a bloody swath through their ranks while dodging hostiles both left and right.

Feberiax, limping, called out, blood and sweat dripping from his cheeks. Regalis, in his hell-hound's outfit, panted and pushed in; Oren sucked in deep breaths and nudged Marcellus toward the wall where Raicus and eight others blocked our exit and fought like wild beasts, with an animal fervor that could not be natural.

The temple of Mithras's floors ran red with blood that night.

On cries from a co-ringleader's booming voice, three masked figures brought jugs of oil and upended the contents on the floor. Then, Raicus—for I recognized the rat-faced scum's scratchy voice—tore down a torch from the wall and tossed it into the rivulets of fuel. Flames whooshed along the stone. Black, thick smoke hung heavily in the cavern. The fools intended to torch the place! Why? Pluvius Maxus was a supporter of Mithras, wasn't he? But maybe his devotion was to a demented and mutated version of the cult championed by his heretical priest. He could take out his wrath on accepted Mithraism while befouling *The Clubs* in the meantime. It made sense. With his priest dead, the mess would never know resolution. I would never be free of the curse.

Ringed by take-no-prisoners enemies, our backs now pushed up against another slatted, wood-barred entrance. Oren and Marcellus turned and beat their clubs against the slats while I raged with fury with the battleaxe, beating back the attackers who pressed in to take chunks out of our hides.

The wood barrier splintered but did not give. I gave a roar of anguish, twisting round to level the center piece with all the feral fire and blood rage within me I could. It caved and we fell through. The thwacks of cudgels rained on Regalis's and my heels, the last ones through. The shattered slats had given way to a tunnel wide enough for three to stumble abreast. Rough stone surrounded us. A secret entrance? We staggered on in the thick gloom backlit by Raicus's flickering flames. In the frenzy of the scuffles, grunts and thuds of wood on flesh, I heard the dim clang of the town watch.

"Die, Icarus!" Raicus crowed through his mask and purple hood. "The Clubs of Londinium come to an end tonight! What a pleasant sacrifice to

Mithras."

My heart sank, even in that beastly craze. "You'll die too, you rat-faced puke, with bits of your scalp on the edge of this blade!"

"Touching boasts," Raicus called back as we stumbled into the dimness.

"Rabbits in a trap, Icky—are you sure?" sneered Marcellus.

"It may lead to somewhere above ground." I choked on the smoke.

"And if it doesn't?"

"We die," croaked Oren.

"We fight our way back," I growled. "One last stand, Oren. We die on our terms."

Rimmed with fire at our backs, those fools continued to pursue us like pack animals. The tunnel slanted down. Many times we stumbled, through pools of stagnant water up to our ankles, fleeing from the smoke. Feberiax limped along. The mad torchlight, the echoing howls, all drove us on. Ever lower the tunnel carried us.

I caught glimpses of the rough-hewn walls and guessed this catacomb must have been built as part of the old city when Boudicca had razed it to the ground nearly a century ago.

The clop of booted feet and sloshing water echoed off the musty stone. The odd fire finger of pursuant torchlight cast monstrous shadows ahead of us. On those rough walls were etched crude tokens of Mithras's might: swords, warriors, ancient figures, doughty heads, stars and symbols, the red, frescoed pigments deepening to a ruddier tint under the backglare of the mob's torchlight.

"Hurry!" I rasped.

We ran through the tunnel like blind mice and I wondered anew with what cursed demonic power Pluvius's priest had ensorcelled Raicus's hounds to race to the cutting edge of my heavy blade.

"Go! I'll stall them off." I turned to face the predators, a vicious grin pasted on my cheeks as again they ran into the cutting edge of my bronze flesh-slayer. The first attacker fell in a wash of blood. More confronted me, weapons flailing, some dying, or taking gruesome cuts. I turned and ran after the others, knowing I could not fight that many with such a heavy weapon in close quarters without getting slaughtered. Regalis's back bobbed four feet ahead of me. The packed earth rose rapidly, elevating us from the nauseous puddles, and we ran into an echoing chamber, wholly black except for a pinpoint of light at the far end. Groping our way toward it, we stumbled and cursed, fearful of tripping and smashing our teeth on what appeared to be a smooth stone floor.

I caught a glint of what looked like street level. Then the welcome glow of a lamp. Amid the grunts of exultation of my ruggies, I plunged ahead.

There! The crumbling outbuilding by the baths. Wrought in the early days of the town's construction, it must have connected to the Mithraeum for some bizarre reason. We peered out on Via Fortis, with wide avenues, tall multi-storeyed apartments and tidy shops. My heart sank. Soldiers scoured the streets. Dozens of them. One yelled upon sight of our furtive movements and lifted a hand to halt his peers. The flickering glow of Raicus's trailing torchlight gave us away despite the vagrant shadows. The rest of the soldiers took heed and clattered toward us.

Trapped between two sets of foes, we looked to have no chance. I knew only too well that it was over for us then. I rallied the ruggies to fight. We stormed back into the crumbled bath-chamber. Facing the Grouses once more, we struck out at the painted bastards dogging our heels, and my grin was ever as feral as Xetriam's devil. Much blood flowed that moment.

Marcellus, nursing a howl in his throat, tore into the streams of figures, smiting murderous club strokes, and we fought back to back, side to side, leveling our foes. They lay stretched in heaps on the old marble floor of the outbuilding.

"Out of the rabbit hole and into the foxes' jaws!" cried Marcellus. "Wolves shall pick our bones tonight."

In the near darkness we hewed, barely able to see three feet in front of us, the stark outline of our many foes. It would have been a wholesale slaughter in that gloom had not the soldiers clambered in bearing torches which illuminated the scene to our advantage.

A bedlam of shouts, cries of pain, thuds of wood on limbs and slashes of iron into flesh filled the air. Unfortunate for us we wore those wretched masks and wielded our trusty clubs, as it was a dead giveaway. The sudden pounding of booted feet had me jerking around to see helmed men flashing blades and whirling nets. I kicked one of Raicus's henchmen into their path and he scrambled back to the tunnel, choosing that over certain capture and death.

But the soldiers had already circled around us and pressed in with gladii, pushing us away from our escape route. Sick despair crawled in my heart. Nets spidered over us, tangling our grime-darkened hides in an inescapable web, rendering useless our clubs.

The prefect Auscles was among that gang, stomping forward in triumph, as if he'd secretly masterminded the roundup. A prickly-bearded man with plumed helm, he held his stout frame erect with full Roman hauteur, gladius in hand.

Four muscled soldiers yanked Regalis and me to our feet, wresting away our weapons and masks. Oren was next, then Feberiax and Marcellus who fought like a wild man, swinging his club from left to right until he was brought down under a mass of flesh. "Look here," he cried, "these are The Clubs of Londinium." He jerked his arm toward Raicus and his netted rogues. "They assaulted us."

A beefy soldier muttered. "Yeah, right, and my mother's Emperor Nero. Get going!" He stepped in to biff Marcellus.

An officer motioned to Auscles and gestured a finger at me. "I think this hellcat is the one. He had the strength of ten."

"Put him with the others then. Quintus Falco's going to be mighty pleased today. Looks as if we got Grouses here too." Rough hands peeled off more masks. "And these brutes look like mercenaries."

As more hoods were peeled back and black masks were shucked off, shattered by wood or iron, I remembered where I'd seen one of those ghastly faces staring up at me now in death. The ghoulish figurines on Xetriam's altar. Even after death, he had dealt us a fatal blow through those ensorcelled minions.

They hauled us roughly from the outbuilding into the sallow glow of the torchlit sconces. One of the raucous soldiers called out to his mate. "I know this little weasel: leader of The Grouses. So why's he wearing the Devil Club's wings, and this ridiculous tail?"

"Who knows, maybe they both treated each other to a costume party?"

"Something for Auscles to figure out."

They had wrapped my arms with thick hemp and pulled them taut like hawsers on a galley. Regalis winced grimly at my side. But as the spell faded, my strength faded too, leaving me without supernormal defenses. The victim of a dead priest's curse, over which I had no control.

Chapter 14

Rude hands hustled us under the archway past the city walls and out onto the north-westerly road. Only the howl of a dog and the swish of wind accompanied the soldiers' clip-clop of boots on pavestones that were gilded under the coming dawn's glimmer. At spear point Auscles and his apes jabbed us through the double gates of the *castra*, the high-walled military camp, and thrust our two gangs in separate palisaded enclosures for examination and to await the final ruling.

Painful moments, slumped in the shadows, torn and bloodied, passed. I caught glimpses of Regalis, black-eyed and sullen, chains wrapped around his wrists and the others hunched in grim defiance. Any words between us came with the smack of a hobnailed boot. What seemed days later, a squad of soldiers frogmarched our haggard hides before the local military tribunal. Four of them stood before us with stern faces and a cadre of soldiers armed with spears and swords. Its leader, a bronzed, hatchet faced man, Drilius Bacchus Temporus, looked at us huddled there with savage contempt. Dressed in breastplate and greaves for added authority, he barked, "What were you doing at the Mithraeum? Who killed the baker Venostes? Who set fire to the temple? Which of you lowlifes killed the street girl at the brothel?"

On and on he questioned, the tufts of grey hair peeking from under his burnished helm, no pause in his clipped staccato. He grilled us first as a group then individually to glean all the facts and catch inconsistencies.

From my ruggies came only silent glares. All of us agreed to divulge nothing to these men beyond our assertion that we'd committed no murders...only defended our turf, salvaged what we could of our reputations. The graffiti, yes, some bold red marks scratched here and there, no big harm. A few pranks and fun about town, but the rest, the cold-blooded murders, remained the sole doings of the Grouses.

The accusation created a stir among some of the tribunes, no impressions on others. The prefect's men kept us in detention for more hours until the endless interrogations, brow beatings and fist smackings became a blur.

I watched for any opening, however small, hoping to purchase some avenue of escape, any ounce of sympathy, a possibility of bribery. But no such opportunity presented itself. I laughed at such naïve, short-lived hope. If I had my super powers, I'd crack some heads, break out of this chicken coop. But the dark power had deserted me. With it, my invincibility. To a few surprised soldiers, I was a temporary fiend fired up on a potent drug.

Auscles appeared again, face riddled with sneers. He had us thrown into a large, windowless room and chained to a wall. Running thick fingers through his thin hair, he bellowed, "Well, murderers. Welcome to Hades. Come meet your accuser." A centurion admitted a massive figure as several soldiers with spears and gladii stood on guard.

Pluvius Maxus waddled into the torchlit space, casting a gloating glance over our slumped forms. He pointed a finger at me. "That's the thief who broke into my villa and molested me, threatening violence with his club."

"Up, you," cried Auscles, jabbing steel at my ribs.

The banker swore under oath, pressing his ring in the hot wax a scribe had hastily prepared, and that sealed my fate.

"Five of them assaulted me. I don't doubt his friends over there, cowering in their filth, are his masked accomplices." Pluvius's damning figure loomed over my field of view.

Auscles firmed his lip, shoving his face close to mine. "The Mithraeum is now a charred ruin. You happy it was destroyed? Took hours to quench the flames. Two priests badly burned trying to rescue relics from the reliquary."

I spat an oath; a gob of phlegm landed on the dirty floor in Pluvius's direction. "Look to that fat pig over there. He ordered the burning of your precious temple. Nothing but a perverted cult worshipper."

Pluvius grew red in the face. "I want this cur whipped. You hear me, Prefect, whipped!"

While the prefect tried to calm Pluvius down, he motioned to his men and one smacked a fist into my face. One more new, stinging agony.

"No justice in this town," spat Marcellus. "This is why I'm proud to be part of *The Clubs*."

"No longer. You'll die for it, you little peacock." The prefect's knuckles whitened around the hilt of his sword.

Feberiax gave a blood-toothed snarl. "Shut it, Marcy. You want to rile these dogs and sink us deeper?"

"We're already sunk as deep as we can go, Feb. What are you worried about? No other place to go but down."

"You guttersnipes will writhe in agony," rasped the prefect. "I'll be the first there at your executions."

I growled a curse. "Search Pluvius's villa and you'll find your evidence. A foul shrine dedicated to a perverted Mithras, blaspheming the purity of good soldiers—men like yourselves and all folk of the Roman world."

"And for whatever reason?" tittered Pluvius. Raising his voice to an insulting bray, he fluttered his fingers. "What do you know? My priest is missing and I can only assume that it was you murderous rogues who killed him."

"Enough!" Auscles waved his sword. "Pluvius, you'll have your justice. If we can find your priest-slave, we will. Quintus Falco has reviewed the case and I see no problems with fast proceedings. These scum are not going to get off easy."

"That's good to hear, Prefect. Your efficiency has been commendable." The banker's fat hide rippled under his fancy silks.

Because the evidence was so damning, they sentenced us quickly and denied us trial. No appeals. Pluvius Maxus had set the bar high enough that no family bribes could stop his twisted manipulation of justice. The nature of the crimes—arson, sacrilege and murder— listed as too heinous. Auscles was clearly in his pocket. Marcellus cried out in a raspy voice about fair play and corrupted Roman justice but upon a brisk signal, a soldier slammed him in the mouth for his insolence.

Pluvius and his priest, instigators of our downfall, I reviled with the headiest of curses. And I blamed Marcellus too. Had the priest lived, this might have gone down much differently.

Of the nineteen men captured at the baths, a dozen lay dead, Raicus not among them. If I ever got my hands on the lout's scrawny neck, I'd crush it like a flower stalk.

Public outcry had been so vocal that the crowd demanded blood.

Wanton murders and public destruction about Londinium needed punishing. The governor Falco pushed for a public spectacle to appease the populous. Fettering our legs in chains, they took us by cart in the morning to the amphitheater to await our doom. Little mystery remained as to what that would entail. Torn apart by wild animals, bears, wolves, boars, even lions if they could be shipped from other parts of the empire. Roman justice would be swift and merciless.

The soldiers took us through a vaulted chamber of the amphitheater, down a gloomy tunnel and a dark set of stairs. They threw us into the dregs, the mysterious *hypogeum* crypt-like dungeon below the oval arena of blood sport. Nothing more than a squat, low-ceilinged hole full of spiders, mildewed rot, bounded by black stone. Separated by chain, we hunched shackled to our personal ring cemented into the wall.

The stench of body odor, shit and piss hit my nostrils. The groans and mumbles of the two dozen captives drifted to my ears, men not knowing when they would die, but that they would suffer a savage death. Gathered from far and wide, pulled in from all corners of the province, they wallowed in filth, from two-toothed farmers to mercenaries gone bad. The drip of water on stone seeped from some dank source. Rats rustled in the moldy straw and the soiled hay. Feral cats howled to get at them. My limbs, like leaden weights, seemed not part of my body. I could have been in Hades for all I knew—well along the forbidding waters of the Styx. So resigned to death I was, knowing my demonic power had deserted me and I faced an unimaginable death.

"Hope you're up for a little rough and tumble, Ick," jeered Marcellus. His face was purpled by wounds and the puffed-up flesh around his slits for eyes grossly swollen. "Bring up that devil juice of yours, would you?"

"Shut up, Marcy. In my last moments, I'd prefer not to hear your dumb quips."

Feberiax barked out a laugh. "Let's hear it, Marcy. A bit of comic relief isn't going to hurt us."

Oren and Regalis looked on in apathy, perhaps resigned to the coming fate. Raicus, shackled five men down the way, sported a piss-licking grin. The bastard's ensorcelled eyes glowed red as scarlet in the half gloom and his face, carved with a savage leer, would scare the bravest warrior. He must have been still doped up on the priest's magic. I shuddered at the spells that drove his black heart and I dipped my head down to concentrate on my own plight. A shame I would not see my father before I died.

I dozed off at some point, exhaustion taking its toll and sweeping me on to ever fouler dreams.

* * *

A hobnailed boot kicked me in the chin, waking me to horror and burning pain. A rattle of chains jingling in my ear announced my leg shackle suddenly being unhooked from the ring. A dozen guards looped and the clipped iron chains, linking us by leg shackles then bawled orders at us. "Move, you vermin!" A leather flail lashed my back. "Front of the queue for you." A thicket of spears prodded us past the score of other blinking prisoners. "You other rats get a pass today." One snatched off the druid's locket from around my neck. I clawed to get it back, but received a kick in the gut for my efforts. None too gently they hauled us forth out of the pit: my ruggies and the remainder of The Grouses. Pricked and prodded by pikes and gladii, they took us out of that stinking pit of stone up the crooked flight of stairs and into the pale light of another tunnel breasting a great arched foyer that led to the arena. A rumble issued from without.

Through an iron gate I caught a glimpse of slaves clad in tunics raking the sand in the arena. Hands worked with feverish efforts to mix the fresh golden color with the dirty brown stains, remnants of previous grisly activity. The gathered crowd shuffled up to the many high wooden seats above. Judging by the animated murmurs and the echoing bustle, I guessed we'd attracted quite a crowd today. That brought a curling leer of satisfaction to my face and bruised and tingling lip.

On either side of the archway sprawled giant lion statues with paws outstretched like sphinxes. The portcullis ratcheted up and a dozen arena guards prodded us through the gate with spears, our leg shackles rattling like a death omen. I squinted out upon a rough, open ground of sand colored like the somber hues of a typical Britannia sky. Twelve wooden posts lined the center into which our chain rings would be hammered. Ten tiers of seats rose high, filled with spectators. I wondered if my father sat among those gathered…

I guessed not.

Behind the wooden barrier encircling the arena, the governor, a fair-haired and husky man stood, tugging at the red trim on his bleached-white woolen toga. He gazed out from an enclosed viewing box shaded by a canvas awning, addressing the crowd in a voice naturally magnified by the amphitheater's shape and height.

"Icarus Veditio…Marcellus Aureus, Feberiax Duilius, Regalis Emilius, Oren Curello, Raicus Batano—" he chimed off the names of the other felons "—I've not had the pleasure of meeting your murderous hides, until now. You've raised quite a stir. The public demands that your crimes be punished. The authorities—I, Quintus Pompeius Falco, the prefect, Auscles Maranius, and magistrate Flavius Olanus—offer you a fighting chance, since you are Roman citizens and from good families. They must be ashamed at the sight of you now." He gave a brisk nod. The guards sprang to action to seize us. "Take them to the posts!"

"Death to murderers!" the crowd chanted.

Raicus grinned. He raised his arms to the spectators above. Fierce cries pounded down upon us—boos and hollers and a rain of rotten fruit and tomatoes, to the point that it sounded as if a riot would break out. A row of soldiers lined the steps leading to each tier to keep the crowd under control. No doubt Quintus Falco must avenge the bordello and baker murders. He would give the public a spectacle to see justice done. His catering to the public's thirst for vengeance would translate into plenty of votes in the upcoming elections.

Icarus, you wanted blood, now you'll get your crimson bath. So dazed was my brain that registered this unreal drama, I hardly recorded how our captors prodded us along and affixed us like butchers' cattle to the posts in the arena's center. The slave posts ran seventy feet along the long axis of the great oval. Stone mallets hammered the chains binding our left wrist into the rings jutting out from the thick planks. The amphitheater, only a wooden affair, including the *cavea*, the rising tiers of seats, ranked as nothing to what I'd heard of in Rome and the stone monstrosity there. Marcellus put up enough of a struggle during the hammering that they rapped his skull and sent him reeling.

"Not too hard, Restes," one of the soldiers called. "No fun in seeing an unconscious prisoner torn apart by a wild boar. Live prisoners will always give the better show."

"I'll be gentle with him, Nestor. Promise."

Sneers and ale-reeking guffaws filled the air. I made no comment. Only gritted my teeth and steeled myself for the grisly fangs and tusks that tear and rend. Twice I'd seen bear-baiting in the arena and murderers locked in stocks and torn apart by starving and enraged beasts. It had not been pleasant to watch. I suspected that ghoulish spectacles as these had long been a Roman favorite, instilled in our blood over the centuries.

At the last minute the guards thrust short daggers in our hands and gave us mocking salutes before backing away to the gates. The knives we clutched in our grimy hands were nothing more than kitchen utensils compared to the massive jaws, tusks and fangs of the beasts that would leap on us soon. I examined the blade, rolling it over in my fingers, studying its worn, dry, blood-caked edge. I despaired at the cruel joke in giving us these toys. It must have made the sport more interesting for the mindless crowd to watch.

My heart skittered in my chest when the last man disappeared behind the protection of the iron gate. It slammed shut with a fierce clang. We stood alone. Yanking on my chain, I saw it gave only four feet of play. Further jingling accomplished nothing. The governor's hand went down above, then a white flag fell to the blast of a trumpet.

A dull roar erupted from the crowd. The iron bars of another grate rattled up and a rustle of movement came from within—a murderous shadow.

I paled as four shaggy beasts came trotting out from the farthest end of the arena. Tongues lolling, their white teeth flashing. Not lions, but dogs! Huge mastiffs—champions of the Britons, trained from an early age. My skin oozed sour sweat. Might as well have given us lions to fight.

A fear of dogs I've always entertained, having gone on so many house burglaries and heard those raucous snarls at one time or other of some nasty breed chained inside the front door.

Straining at the limits of my chain, I quailed. It would take a fearsome force to break those links. I glanced at Regalis six feet away. Chained at the next station, he yanked at the links to the waist-high post. We hadn't much reach. We couldn't enter one another's circles or cooperate in any coordinated defense.

Insane barking grew to feverish yowls. I suspected the brutes had been half starved to heighten their savagery. Perceiving the scent of fresh meat not fifty yards away, they sprang as one, baying like hellhounds, saliva spraying from their foaming jowls, snapping incisors bared.

Little is more terrifying than having a hundred and fifty pounds of killer flesh barreling at one's body. In a few seconds such a beast can rip its fangs into a throat and have one bleeding out with no time to react. I've seen it happen on these very sands. Perhaps the greatest human fear is being mauled by a savage beast. All the legends of the Greeks talk about it, and what we Romans have borrowed, taken to bed with us every night…like the fate of the hunter Actaeon who witnessed the goddess Artemis bathing in the woods.

Regalis readied his hunched frame in a hob-kneed crouch. I could see by the wide orbs of his staring eyes that he crouched in the shadow of fear. Feberiax stood solemn as a statue, favoring his good leg. Oren let out a high-pitched yip, pulling desperately at his chain. His beefy fingers shook, perhaps shock settling in now in realization of the pure terror of it all, that the final instant was upon us. I stood appalled, still enveloped in a semi-daze that our pranks had come to this. Brutal, violent death loomed but seconds away.

Marcellus cast me a grim look as he licked his lips and gripped his dagger. Perhaps now the sod wished he hadn't killed that priest...maybe he hoped even beyond hope that my curse would kick in and bring about some miracle as he prepared for death.

The lead mastiff's slavering jaws snapped for his lower leg. It caught a piece of Marcellus's flesh, tearing into his lower shin. He gave a gut-wrenching howl. No more laughing for Marcellus as he stabbed down in a frenzy at the thing's head while the enraged hound growled and snapped.

I gripped my knife, teeth clenched, backing toward the wide post. Two came charging for me. No thought now for my ruggies, as I braced for the onslaught. The first dog threw itself full tilt at me. I leapt sideways straining the length of my chain as it slammed into the post behind me. I slashed once. Time slowed to a standstill. The beast, dazed for a moment, yipped and snarled and I stabbed it again and again on the torso. Blood spurted between the ribs near the hindquarters as its barrel form rolled back for another round. All sound fled into a seashell roar.

The dog twisted and bayed, ready to attack again despite its grievous wounds.

I got one more swing at it, the knife point catching it high on the muzzle before it fell back, knocking its peer off balance. The arc of my last stroke had only pricked its hairy hide above the foreleg on the downswing. That's all the flesh I got. The first fiend came in snapping and snarling and its muzzle bit deep in my left arm. I cried out in agony, as I swept up to protect my throat. Something snapped in me, blood and fury—and the rage of lifetimes—all became one as I slipped sideways and fell on the sand. All hundred plus pounds of the beast landed on my chest and shoulders, teeth tearing at my arm, pressing toward my jugular.

No sound, but a whishing of air. Foul dog breath hissing in my face.

In a superhuman flash of strength, I arched my back and flung the thing off me—a swirl of green fumes slipped from my nostrils like seaweed. I jerked away from that monster, a sulfurous reek in my face, rolling out of the reach of the second beast angling toward my throat. I whipped my full weight left with the force of a titan in my frenzied delirium as a rush of demon madness surged through my veins.

The chain snapped. Half crouching there, I yanked at it, pulling it away where it looped through the ring. I swung it like a lasso over my head to brain the second creature that came leaping at me. Maybe that link had been weakened already. Or maybe my father had bribed one of the guards to jerry-rig the links? The first beast, wheezing and limping from loss of blood, licked at its hindquarters. One flick of the end of the chain into its grey-black face and it rolled over and died.

A ripple of surprise swept through the crowd as that dog lay dead and the other swayed woozily. I could sense a stir among the multitude. How long had it been since anyone had killed one of those brutes in the arena? The crowd went wild. One dog dead, another dying, more would follow.

Shaking the daze from my ringing skull, I looked to my ruggies. They were faring badly. Oren struggled to fight off a snapping hound. A grey-black beast leaped for his throat. He swung too early and the massive hound got its slavering teeth around his right wrist and he fell gasping, dropping his knife.

The crowd roared. Fresh dogs came bounding from the grate. Splashed from toe to crotch with crimson, Oren howled in anguish as the beast chawed at his leg. He tried to beat the thing off, yanking tufts of fur, smashing it with his fists. The newly-released hounds bounded for Feberiax and Raicus and company. Marcellus, in his mad fight for survival, plunged knife point after knife point into matted fur, laughing like a maniac. He gouged dog flesh, eye, teeth, throat, regardless of the bites and scratches he'd racked up. Regalis ducked to avoid claws and teeth, slashing out, his chain jingling as he hewed. He scrambled back behind the pillar to give himself a few seconds of respite.

Like a drunkard, I tottered over to defend Oren who was now engulfed in writhing fur. I snapped the end of my chain on the hound's spine. Oren fell back as another menace spun about howling and limping. I cracked the chain down on its skull. In a moment's lull, I kicked over the knife to him. Leaking blood from multiple wounds, he moved weakly now, kneeing the next dog's snarling teeth away from his throat. I snatched up the knife I had dropped earlier and plunged it into the ribs of a fresh beast springing for Regalis. Smitten by battle madness, I yanked at Regalis's chain, and with my newfound strength tore the ring free from the post. He staggered off free! I pulled out the crimson blade and thrust it into his hand to replace his weapon lost somewhere in the fray. I could see his blood-dripping look of gratitude as he crouched, wincing from the pain of his bites, but ready to fight to the death.

Oren, I could do nothing for. One of the dogs had returned and finished tearing at his twitching form, but Marcellus ever a survivor, tottered onto his feet, swinging at empty air. Even he would have died had I not edged in at a crucial moment and whipped his last remaining hound's back, sending it yelping aside. It gave Marcellus the instant he needed to jam his dagger into the fiend's throat. I pulled his chain free from the post and he gave a croak of exultation. I hobbled over the ruin of dog bodies, feeling my left arm swollen and aching. My body quivered from shock. I surveyed the scene to see who remained alive.

Feberiax crouched, panting. Racked with claw marks, he slashed and kicked at the beast that harried him. The mastiff yelped and slunk off to rip at the ruined body of one of Raicus's thugs, easier prey. I yanked Feberiax's chain free from the post ring. Together we stood as four, blood-smeared survivors, armed with knives and chains to use as weapons against the monsters.

Sound and sense started returning to my ears. Most of the dogs lay dead but one big rangy mastiff still chewed at Oren's inert body. It licked its lips and shook its head to warn off others that might interrupt its feeding. Feberiax hobbled over and with a snap of chain crowned the marauder with heavy iron ring, clocking it between the eyes and it fell in a twitching heap.

The crowd stood from their seats, shouting their amazement and approval.

I tottered about, throat choked with bile. My hands, soaked with blood, gripped a length of bloody chain like a vise still shackled to my wrist. But I felt a euphoria like no other. They cheered us—Icarus, the doomed, Icarus the cursed! not destined to die at the fangs of the hell hounds. Icarus Veditio, two months shy of seventeen.

These same wretches who had cried out for our deaths, now applauded us, the underdogs. How fickle the human being is.

I walked around in a corpse-like daze, my hand upraised in acknowledgement of the wildly applauding spectators. Part of my awareness remained cognizant of the fact that danger lurked nearby. Nor had I completed one turn when a grate ratcheted open and a single armored figure came trotting out with whip flailing and sword at his hip.

The leather thongs came thrashing on my back. The attacker's guttural words urged the one remaining, blood-matted mastiff to sink its teeth in my side. I felt no pain from those whip lashes. In instinctive self-preservation I crouched and brought the chain up whirling in his face. He shrank back and it caught the animal trainer square on the right shoulder, cracking bone and leaving his sword arm dangling. Regalis and Marcellus slashed at the leaping dog while Feberiax snapped his heavy chain at its skull, dropping it like a stone.

The animal trainer swore, dropping to his knees. I crouched ready to finish him off with my fists, but Quintus Falco, sputtering in rage, signaled the arena guards. He lurched to his feet shaking a fist, having been made to look the fool. The portcullis grated up. Instead of soldiers coming to finish us off, someone had loosed another beast. I blinked in new horror. One of those giant warthogs in Britannia's thick forests. It trotted out pawing at the ground, snorting from wide nostrils and sensing fresh danger: four bloody figures swinging chains. It dug in its hooves, lowered its head and charged.

I gaped at the galloping monster thundering toward us. We scattered as pig hooves came stampeding in and it made short work of one of Raicus's twitching crew with its white upturned tusks. Quickly it wheeled about—to tear into the next victim, spilling his entrails on the sand. When it barreled at me, it stopped short, snuffling heavily, pausing as if in indecision. My ruggies backed away. Stamping its front hoofs, it grunted a challenge, as if recognizing a beastly kinship with that demonic presence that inhabited my flesh. A short, green mist effused from my nostrils. Then the sharp pungent odor alerted the beast to some inexplicable weirdness. It charged me as a primitive goat's head with twisted horns and monstrous fangs grew out of the greyish-green cloud. The pig careened recklessly, squinting in the acrid smoke. I scuttled sideways while its hurtling momentum smashed into the legs of the animal trainer behind me. He went down in a wash of red, crippled, the pig mauling him while *bestiarii* came running in from the sides to thrust spears at it. They jabbed and pricked it away from the convulsing, bloodied body.

The demon smoke swirled back into my nostrils. Wild cries tore at the air. Enraged shouts sprayed from the crowd at Falco's decision to release the beast despite our valiant resistance.

Mass confusion erupted from the arena guards. A herd of gladiators came storming out of the gate to secure us. Bedlam rocked the arena. Who had ever witnessed such a turn of fortune?

One such husky gladiator, wearing the red-plumed helm of the *lanista*, the head gladiator trainer, barked orders. Others joined in, including a rugged, hatched-faced man, his assistant, judging by the eagle emblem on his breastplate.

The crowd gave over to thunderous applause. "Clubs, Clubs, long live The Clubs!"

Fickle bastards!

The portcullis disgorged more running figures while others struggled to corner the rampant boar. The crowd roared. One minute we're public enemy # one, the next, we're their bloody heroes. Typical mob mentality. The underdog defying the odds. A hero to look up to.

Eight gladiators circled us, bearing a variety of weapons. Some bore gladii, others gripped deadly spears, tridents and nets. A gleaming blade arched for my neck. I caught the gladiator's first blow on a length of chain held taut in my other hand. I twisted the weapon free then flicked out with my chain to rake iron across his shoulder. He sagged in slow motion, his collar bone shattered.

A net came flying over my head. Another followed. Feberiax and Regalis struggled under a tangle of rope. I fought against the spidery strands, but my sudden miraculous strength had departed and my fingers, tearing at the fibers like claws, seemed useless against it. I could see the glint of the tridents coming down to spear me. I welcomed it. "Death come take me, you bastards!"

"Wait, Wait! Don't kill them!" the lanista bawled, racing toward us. "New orders—Falco's orders!"

The gladiators bore me back while a third net was flung over my head. They dragged me off toward the raised gate, like an unruly beast hauled across the sand. Snapping the chains free from the corpses, the arena guards dragged them off too. Oren's limp form was in tow, leaving a trail of crimson slime in the sand. Raicus's thugs ranged among the lot. Raicus and his sidekick, Janus, had miraculously survived. Marcellus cursed like a fishwife as he was ensnared in nets and hauled away. The crowd gave over to pandemonium. Half of them booed the soldiers and gladiators removing us from the arena; they hankered for more bloodshed. Never enough in one day to slake their grisly lust.

Quintus Falco called out to bring the assembly to order, but in the chaos there could be no order. Red-faced, he stood before his citizens in the lower-middle tiers and waved a hand to signal the cleanup brigade. A team of slaves hustled to remove the posts and the order came to start the gladiatorial games. A trumpet's blare split the air.

The soldiers and gladiators hauled us to safety behind the iron bars before the portcullis came crashing down. They dragged us through the vaulted archway while others struggled to contain the squealing warthog. I could still hear the rumble of the crowd as we entered that dim antechamber and the soldiers left us on the sand. Oren's half mauled body lay twisted beside me like a piece of chopped meat. To my horror, my fellow ruggie twitched, but barely, lungs sucking in hoarse rasps of breath. One eye remained open, the rest of him a slick, bloody mess. A bald, muscle-bound gladiator stomped over and brought a heavy hammer down on his skull. I winced as Oren was put out of his misery forever. I felt a sick knot burst in my stomach and I retched.

Wrenched free from my hempen coils, I remember being dragged down the crooked stairs, whacked and slapped too many times in efforts to jar me out of the violent trance, that dream dance with death. I roused from whatever madness I had succumbed to, while my comrades moaned on the floor at my side under the dim torchlight. I knew then that some shift had happened. The Icarus who should have died remained no longer the Icarus of before. Somehow this Icarus had transcended death. His being had elevated beyond the victim of a priest's occult curse. The dull roar of the crowd continued to filter deep below the red sands of the arena, the place where destinies could change in the blink of an eye.

Chapter 15

"I tell you, it's just not natural, Eberius," a squatting figure rasped. "Men don't fight like that. Much less a stripling."

The one in chinked mail and dinted helm shrugged. "You saw it with your own eyes, Tibor. The fiend took down the dogs and the mastiff trainer, a gladius gouger if I've ever seen one."

"It's a bloody miracle! There's deviltry walking. You saw that green face of his. With the smoke and the swirling deity? A mad Mithras, or a demented Mars."

Eberius scoffed. "You're seeing things, Tibor. I saw discolored sand kicked up in some mastiffs' faces. A lot of blood and screams in the arena."

I raised my groggy head, felt the cold press of iron chaining my leg to the dungeon wall while my ears registered crude speculations and whispers about my handiwork. The guards' faces peered down at me with loathing and fear. My ruggies lolled, hunched in similar manner chained along the damp wall. Bashed, bitten and bruised, we all sprawled like used pieces of meat, feeling holes in our hearts at the missing presence of Oren—while despising the blood-smeared face of Raicus farther down the way.

A centurion heeled himself over. "Quit your yammering, you simpletons. Falco and his cronies want to see these rogues topside. "If it were my call, I'd have them all crucified."

"After what they did in there? It'd be us crucified. The crowd loves them. You heard the uproar, centurion. Remember what happened to that people's hero and the revolt in Judaea and—"

"Shut up," the centurion said with a leer. "There's a distinct difference. Move!"

A spear point prodded me in the ribs as the chain fell from my leg and they hauled all our sorry hides up from the dingy shadows into the muted light of the vaulted tunnel that gave way to the shadowed back arches of the arena. Stiff and sore, I felt probably worse than ever—a thousand curses to Xetriam, Pluvius Maxus, and the Painted Grouses.

At arena level in an arched alcove lit by torches, the prefect stared down at us in gloomy displeasure. Anustus, the lanista, stood at his side with two other gladiators, studying us with care. Quintus Falco wasn't there, mercifully. After all, he'd given the initial order to have us all executed. What further deviance could he have in mind? We still had breath in our bodies and I wished to keep it that way.

Arena policy stated that any condemned prisoners who managed to survive the sacrificial baiting, very few indeed, became gladiators, no matter what their crime. A clever and practical way to solve the shortage of gladiators in this backwater province. From those tentative looks on the gathered men's faces, I knew that something was working in our favor. On the positive side, we'd lived another day to breath this musky air of the dungeon—but on the negative, we had little training with gladius, javelin, or dagger, despite our competence with clubs.

I gave them my smuggest look, trying not to look too beaten down.

"Well, you hound bashers," the prefect grunted. "How do you feel now after a day's work?"

"Could be better," mumbled Marcellus through mashed lips.

"The food's terrible and the company stinks," rasped Feberiax.

"Good joke, scum. There'll be few of those wisecracks in the days ahead. You're now slaves of the province. You'll fight in the arena till your deaths."

The lanista stepped closer, a plume-helmed man with breastplate, greaves and a carriage of presence that was unmistakable. He moved with a grace that belied his heavy bulk. "What he means is you're elected into the gladiator corps, children, and these are your trainers." He swept an arm to his peers: two hard-faced men in leather greaves and sandals.

The lanista's face curled in a sardonic grin. He pointed. "Septagerix there, that old Celt, will be your main slaver. As his job is to work you to the bone and upgrade your condition, he takes on all the new recruits. He'll be the kindest of the lot." He gave a brisk wave to a well-built man of older years, braided hair down to his chest with bronzed muscles and bare arms.

"While that black-tanned bastard over there from somewhere south of

Malta will be your shield trainer and point man. Basta'll whip your defenses into shape. He'll verse you in specialty weaponry, watch over you like a hawk so that you don't try any funny business. Your prison guard, in other words. Titus who's off dressing a wound will concentrate on fine-tuning your physical conditioning and endurance. Any questions?"

"When do we get paid?" croaked Marcellus.

Anustus grated out a cold laugh. "You're only alive, dimwit, because Falco knows if he kills you, he'll have a rebellion on his hands. Bad for the upcoming elections."

"Seems as if the state favors us," I spat with a sour grin.

"I wouldn't count on that, rogue," said Anustus. "The gods are as fickle as a mistress's favors. Worse than an old lady's flabby tits. Now get over there. As of now, you're officially gladiators."

"And what can you fight with?" asked Septagerix.

Marcellus chipped in with a humorless laugh, "Only clubs. It's all we know."

"Clubs?" he howled. "They'll get chopped to shit in this arena with those heavy blades. You'll learn the other weapons—nets, spears, swords. Seems your bully boy here, Icarus, took a natural shine to beast fighting. A born killer. If any of you can hold up to him, there'll be hope for you yet. Maybe you won't be dead by the end of the week."

"Ick's our hero," sighed Marcellus with a sardonic titter.

"Quiet down," the prefect warned.

Marcellus ignored the order. "Don't know about you, Feb, but I plan on avoiding Oren's fate, Pluto rest his soul."

Regalis gave a grim murmur, "I plan on staying alive, period."

"Well, that's good spirit, boys," said Anustus. "Get them cleaned up and fed, Septagerix. Ready them for the training yard. Let's see how they fare against real weapons." He tossed back his shoulder-length, dirty-blond hair, greying at the ends, as he downed a brimming cup of wine offered by a slave.

Slaves brought basins of warm water and towels to us. They cleaned us up proper and poured vinegar and cheap wine over our wounds, which were many and stung like Achilles' wrath, but took the swelling down. My left forearm throbbed with a pulse of horrible agony from that hound's bite. Marcellus swatted at the young slave who swabbed him down. A *medicus* came to see to our more serious wounds such as Feberiax's gimping leg, and applied salves and balms to our numerous cuts and abrasions. No longer did we wallow in that dripping dungeon under the arena, but we were relegated to the smallest cells in the slave quarters adjoining the amphitheater itself, a kind of low-ceilinged barracks complete with a training ground mimicking the traditional gladiator schools I'd heard about in Italia.

Oren's tragic death had come as a sudden shock to us, a cruel blow, despite Marcellus's crude remarks and tasteless quips. Feberiax took it the hardest. He and Oren had been best friends, and our Celtic ruggie's sinister, craggy features showed a mask of pent-up rage. Oren's club had saved us many times in street brawls and break-ins. Not any more. Nor could we know how much we counted on him until later.

* * *

Titus, a freedman gladiator and subordinate assistant, approached me while the others had gone on to the training grounds. "I can make something of you, devil-boy," he whispered in a conspiratorial tone. "While you last, you make money for me. A chance for you to earn your freedom too. Are you in? Though I doubt you'll last long."

I lanced him the coldest of scrutinies. Here was the brute who had delivered Oren his mercy blow.

"What's the matter? Can't talk?" The man dangled a familiar object in front of my bruised face. My silver locket hung on the end of a leather thong—the one that contained the medicinal formula given me by the druid. "All of us have dibs on you, swine. Basta thinks you'll die badly, so does Dividex. Me and Brolis, however, have bids on you, perhaps against our better judgment. Cheap bets that you'll survive the first month."

"Bully for you. Give me back my locket," I growled.

"Ha, ha, fancy that! Weepy-hearted little Septagerix and the lanista all secretly favor you. That's what tipped the scales. Don't disappoint me and die too early, worm. Fight in the games and win—or die."

He pulled the locket away when I made a grab for it. More than ever did I want my medicine back.

"This what you want?" He waved it in front of my eyes again like a bullying child, the thong with that green stuff, like a hypnotist's charm.

I gazed back at the bald, stocky ogre with growing hatred.

"What do we have in here?" He flicked open the silver and peered inside. Smelling it, he wrinkled his nose. "Ugh! Poppy oil. In for the kicks?

Fool. Not my thing."

He tossed it back to me. "Tell you what. I like your fighting style, lotus-eater. Enjoy your juju juice. Fight and live, but don't go strangling anyone with that thong."

I dug my nail gratefully into the sodden leaf in the locket and lay it under my tongue. I'd had awful shakes and green vapors coming from my nose lately and the spell-madness was not getting any better. I feared it would be the end of me.

* * *

I'd already graduated, it seemed, as a gladiator, as I was thrown into the arena the next day without prep or a decent club. Still I felt weak from multiple wounds. Had Quintus Falco another change of heart and suddenly brewed up a way to get rid of me? Without blame falling on his own head? Gesarius, one of the junior gladiators, drew the short straw and was given the duty of dispatching me. His instructions were explicit, to thrash the piss out of me. If in the process, a priest murderer were to accidentally get his throat cut, well, no one would mourn the loss.

Falco and the lanista denied me a club, despite my request. They'd tossed me a gladius and shield like the others chosen that day.

It was a grey day in September with only a half turn-out in the stands. No one was expecting me or any of *The Clubs* to be fighting. That husky young brute Gesarius, stocky and wide of shoulder, oiled of skin and knotted with sinew in arms and buttocks, circled me, studying me like a hound with curious disfavor and irritating disrespect. I stood my ground. With a wild roar he charged, driving in with his short sword. Without thinking, I crouched on the balls of my feet. The same way Drace had taught me how to contend with such attacks. *Let the swine come in. Use speed and guile to fake out such upstarts. At the last instant give it to him where he least expects it.*

And so I did. Sidestepping that murderous swing, I dropped nearly flat on my belly. Even though I ached all over, I drew Gesarius out. Funny how aches and pains fade to nothing when a killer with whirling steel comes bearing down on you. In my mind's eye flashed Oren and Denetio lying senseless in battered ruin. A foul rage came over me. Green vapor spilled from my nostrils. A murmur of surprise and interest stirred the crowd. I struck out with my blade and while in a quick roll, I caught him above the left ankle in a place where the thongs of the leather sandal didn't quite protect. He howled and limped away but was not taken down.

I tossed my shield casually aside. An audible gasp swept through the crowd. I sprang to my feet, bent in a fighter's crouch. I'd never used a shield, and I was better off without it right now. But that wretched gladius I clutched had none of the weight of the club I was used to.

When he saw me hurl aside the shield, he grinned like a lizard basking in the sun, thinking this would be an easy fight despite his leg wound.

A fatal mistake.

While the crowd cheered and laughed, thinking Icarus of *The Clubs* some comic madman with a death wish, I prepared myself for a fresh assault, reviewing my strategies.

He came in stabbing with his pig sticker, a roar on his lips. The gleaming tip of his weapon caught the haft of my gladius. I sliced across his left arm, shredding leather. His blade ripped into my padded breast. I leaned back, ducked low. As I did, my blade licked out and nearly hamstrung him on the same leg, leaving a trail of blood.

Now he was limping badly. But not defeated. Back he came slashing like a madman and I caught a few of those fancy strikes, some which gouged into my leather, some piercing deeper and drawing blood. My eyes grew red. I vaguely noted the pointed incisors sprouting on my bottom jaw. Then the savage, beast-like wrath manifesting as green smoke swirling from my nose. Maybe I was always this, a man-beast just birthing.

No—I couldn't accept such a primitive destiny. I fought on with half-lucidity, not remembering the exact sequence of events. Memory blurred, caught up as I was in the throes of Xetriam's cursed black magic. At one point, I remember sinking those teeth of mine into Gesarius's throat like a feral creature of the night. He died wrapped in my unnatural embrace, falling with a thud at my feet, his jugular spouting gobs of blood, his arms reaching like branches in a wind.

I stumbled in a half circle before falling flat on my face. The crowd roared. Now a monotonous hum numbed my ringing ears. The crowd's tumult abated. I crawled to my knees as the arena guards came to collect us, either corpses or winners. In the VIP's box, Quintus Falco showed a solemn face. He did not seem to know what to think of this new, feral fiend who plagued his playing field and who had bested him once again.

* * *

Septagerix, senior gladiator and trainer, lifted my chin in the vaulted

174

antechamber back behind in the shadows of the arches. "I've seen many a man fight and die in the pits, but never one so young. To fight with such ferocity—boy, what are you? Tibor was arguing just the other day about a green vapor or some strange miscolored sand kicked up in the wake of your match. It's as if a chimaera inhabits you. Cadmus's teeth. What possesses you!"

"Just lucky, I guess." I forbore to tell him how close he was to the truth. My head sank down onto my chest.

The curse tainted my blood. That diseased animal ichor I'd ingested weeks ago in Xetriam's lair—'twould be a scourge to haunt me for life. The rage would never go away, the raw, red rancor, gnarly as a carbuncle that robbed me of my humanity during my killing spree and would not let me die like a mortal man. In death, the priest had doomed me. What was he? Some twisted magician of an earlier age? Perhaps he hadn't realized what extraordinary power he'd cursed me with, that priest who was now fifty feet down under the black water of the Tamesis, courtesy of Marcellus.

Anger, hatred and fear, all the ancestral emotions of the primitive unconscious. They lurked just under the surface. Whenever the magic flared up in me, I became less a human and more a beast. My blood sizzled, sending me to agonies unheard of, granted me the power to bash, stab, maim and club with remarkable strength and diabolical force. To beat opponents into bloody pools of steaming pulp. To survive at all costs.

That I did—and more, to become Icarus the Terrible.

* * *

Hard and heavy the gladiatorial combats fell, with trials and gore aplenty. After that feral display, I was branded the sole mastermind of the murders perpetrated by *The Clubs of Londinium*. The amphitheater filled to overflowing to watch me, chanting 'Icarus the Terrible'. Raicus was deemed too stupid to have pulled off the murders on his own. No direct evidence linked Marcellus and the others to the deaths, including the one of his priest-slave, as I'd been the only one unmasked and recognized. Pluvius had fired their imaginations, exaggerating his account of the attack and stacked the evidence nicely against me. He had bribed officials when numbers or evidence didn't add up.

My ruggies' initiation into a gladiator's life had taken a kinder ramp. No one-on-ones with death yet. After opening ceremonies, the arena guards thrust us into the arena with a horde of scum criminals with whom we'd been chained in the dungeon. All of them turned loose on us at once, expendable meat with knives gripped in grime-knuckled fists.

I'd told the trainers to give us clubs. They'd laughed at us, and said, 'clubs are for babies', but the lanista held up a hand. "Give them clubs. A different type of combat will keep the crowd entertained." So they fetched our original clubs from the Roman camp. Just like old times. Now I had nothing personal against these men, criminals or victims as they may have been. But the wretches had nothing to lose, and hearing about our instant popularity, decided that they wanted a piece of that, especially if they could save their own skins and wipe out the 'heroes' of the day.

In they came like a horde of howling lunatics, snarling and spitting. Oh, did blood fly that afternoon. My ruggies fought like hellcats, like they did on the streets of Londinium, breaking skulls, smashing bones and crippling knees, kicking weapons out of clenched fingers, landing punches, flattening noses and dropping stinking, bearded ruffians face first in the sand. I whirled away from a foul-breathed rogue while a knife licked out and slashed my thigh. I loosed a howling grunt as it pricked through protective leather to my rib. I stomached the pain, no longer the Icarus of old, cherished by Mexor and Fortuna, but some beastly engine with only survival in mind. We fought before an audience's wild approval on this day of victory, patroned by the powers to be. Not limited to the invisible shadows of Londinium's streets and alleyways. The crowd hooted our names: *The Clubs of Londinium! The Clubs of Londinium! Icarus the Terrible!* How they cheered our names!

I couldn't quite understand it. This mob mentality. About as intelligent as a crate of rusty nails. Yet, if our intense training and the mob's cries and my dark primal flare-ups kept us alive, I was all for it.

The bets were on, and the enslaved gladiators watched behind the closed grate as their turn loomed next. I knew there'd be just as many bids against us as there were for us.

Feberiax smashed the legs out from under a howling thug. Marcellus clubbed the last of the criminals down until the wretch was a writhing worm in the sand. Falco tilted his thumb, indicating a kill. Marcellus stove the man's head in, and we looked up into the faces of our audience, knowing our trial had come to an end.

The second test we had now passed and the full rigors of training now descended upon our heads.

The rigorous and punishing daily practices that followed had us sweating in buckets. Our tortured bodies racked full of aches, pains and bruises. Ten miles of jogging a day around the arena, hurdling obstacles along the way, our golden-haired lanista bawling insults at us to move our asses. We jogged with weighted stones strapped on our backs in leather packs. We ran with heavy swords gripped in our hands; we practiced combat maneuvers in the rain, in the sun, in the wind, sparring for hours with the best of the gladiators. The training yard that adjoined the amphitheater was a combination obstacle course and fenced-in area containing several 'cages' or squared-off cubicles. Oak dummies stood within padded in thick leather rotating on a central axis powered by crude mechanical means—machines that thrust out spiked arms and knee-high blades. We had to weave in and out amongst these mannequins, jump over their elongated limbs, or duck their mallets of arms as they swung alongside our heads and torsos. We wore helms and padded leathers on limbs and chest, and mostly we trained with wooden swords. But even those instruments could inflict pain, especially when whacked and stabbed time and time again. Thirty two of us in total. All slaves. Only the lanista and his captains: Basta, Septagerix and Titus, were freedmen, but that did not prevent the other gladiators from making bets. Perhaps the only entertainment they got in this bloody line of work was wagering and collecting bets. They'd offer buckles, the special knife tucked at their waist, the extra thongs on sandals, the opium snuck in by the crooked Basta among other contraband—slaves such as we were never allowed favors or luxuries according to law.

Then early to bed on hard cots in the spartan barracks with a single covering and a flat, dead pillow. We were given regular meals of potatoes, onions, lentils and fish worked into a palatable mash. Then amphorae of cheap wine—the sourest of spirits the Roman stocks could afford. They did not stint on that. Some of the gladiators indulged too headily and woke the next morning with sour bellies and fogged heads. But it helped numb pain and give them a boost to face the day. We bathed, shat, pissed and ate together, slept two to a cell. We lived and fought at the amphitheater on the bloody sands that lay raked clean of blood after every event. One big happy family. A brotherhood of violent killers. In this way we got to know each other's personalities, but never cultivated friendships. The risk of a split second of compassion could mean death. I particularly disliked Titus

Marcus Vasus. Even Marcellus's obtuse habits were tolerable but that cynical bastard Titus with his vile simian's grin was something that never ceased to irk me. Both reminded me of our combined misfortunes. Ever a thorn in my side, Raicus was downright evil too, and I awaited my chance to slip a dagger in his guts. But I'd save that for the games when we were pitted together. For some reason the lanista had not done so, recognizing that would be the end of one of us. Our job was to fight and entertain, not to die—or at least not too soon.

Whenever Marcellus and I were paired against each other, it was bad news and we fought like tigers. Today's training was one such fight, and Marcellus wiped his split lip where my fist had connected when his shield had slipped a notch lower than it should.

"Very fine, ruggie," he rasped, "but how's this?" And he whirled in, thrusting his dagger at my groin.

I twisted and deflected the murderous swipe but the tip grazed my wrist and drew blood where the leather thongs didn't quite reach.

"Alright you, ruffians," growled Anustus. "Enough. Good spirit, but training swords only." He snatched away our gleaming weapons and threw *rudes*, wooden ones at us. "Titus, see that these dogs don't ever fight each other. Have Marcellus take a shot at Tristus. The man's begging for an out-and-out cat fight, and Marcellus here could use some practice in dirty moves. He fights like a jilted housewife, for Jupiter's sake. Icarus, you take on Septagerix—or Basta. You're too slow on the up-parry. One day your blood will run red in the arena. Mars' balls and Jupiter's whores! The gladius is your bane, but without a solid grounding in the Roman traditional weapon of choice, you're of little use. For now you're popular as a bizarre novelty, but you can't rely on some mad luck to pull you out of the jaws of death every time."

I took the dressing down in silence, knowing it was the lanista's way of giving me a compliment, while flinging barbs at every chance to drive us all to a more professional level of competence. I came to realize all good trainers have that skill. Not to undermine a trainee's confidence but to rouse us into pushing us to our edge. If only such skills would rub off on the thugs, Titus and Basta.

* * *

The next series of weeks passed like a hazy blur. Hard work, brutal training, in-fighting rivalries, cheap hits, jabs, aching muscles, brutal pummellings, black eyes, bruises. For a while I thought I wasn't going to last but instead perish like those wretches before me. But the tainted blood in my veins flowed strong. My mother's northern stock kept me alive and shored up my determination to live. I was a piece of meat, a throwaway. If I lived or died, the establishment did not care. But if I lived long enough to fight, I became an asset to them. The greedy management would extract every bit of flesh from their gladiator slaves as they could.

And so the fame of *The Clubs* grew, or rather my fame grew. The crowds came to chant my name at the gladiatorial games. *"Icarus the Terrible! Icarus, blood and fire, Icarus!"* I walked upon the scarlet-spotted sand like a Greek Olympian champion with my hand held high after each victory, feeling the euphoria of the crowd's adulation but the dread in my heart that I would disappoint them one day when I lay in a thick pool of my own blood. Worse, I'd fail my ruggies who numbered too few and who were one hair's breadth from death as each day passed. Oren's memory and the horrid manner of his mauling still burned in my brain.

Whenever the moment came that an opponent was to deliver a mortal blow, that old familiar itch would kindle my blood and I would duck, slash, dodge, leap, strike, bite, maim, anything to protect my vitals and save my sorry hide. Whatever demon lived inside me would not let me die. Two beings dwelt there—one benign, a human, and the other violent and sinister, a demon, and if I could go back to my regular self, just the Icarus I knew from my innocent boyhood dreams, I would, even though I'd be slain by the most innocent stroke. In moments like this I missed Mexor and Fortuna most.

"Icarus the Terrible!" The droning rumble of the crowd beat like a kettle drum in my brain as each game began and as I crouched to take my two-foot sword and thrust upward into men's guts, hear the leathers about my waist creak and my pig-like grunt, and watch steaming entrails spill upon the sand.

I thought it was a fine irony, considering the petty criminal I had become, but now a notable hero emerged after bringing the dogs to bay.

Many in that audience did not chant my name, the ones whom we had wronged and who plotted our demise. Pluvius Maxus for one, seemed none too pleased at our survival. I caught him looking down from the first tiers with baleful, piggy eyes, contemplating us with murderous contempt, eager to witness our sudden deaths, but I pledged to spite him in the end. Saddest of all, the desperate look of my father, whom I saw one day bobbing like a ship's prow among that feral mob. I wondered what passed through his mind, seeing what his son had become, reduced to a slave and murderer. Fortuna attended that day, seated on the highest tier with other women and slaves. She came to watch in the beginning, then she stopped coming. Likely she grew sick at heart to see me one day rent ear from ear by some monstrous brute.

* * *

Titus herded me off from the others later that day as we jogged our regular laps around the arena. "Me and Brolis have staged a little drama to win us some money," he said. He fingered his gladius, flashing a set of horse teeth. "You're to go along with it. Lose the fight."

"What do you mean 'lose' the fight?"

"What part of 'lose' don't you get, squib?" he sneered.

When I didn't reply, he grabbed my shoulder. "Listen, halfwit. How about some broken bones, a dagger in the groin some unexpected moment? Would that be something you'd remember?"

I grunted, seething.

"You'll be paired with Tabaxian. He's our gladiator stooge. You're to toss the fight, as I say. You'll be outfitted with a pig's bladder fitted under your breastplate near the ribs. It'll be full of blood. When Tab carves his gladius into you, you fall flat on your face and roll over, play dead like a possum. Got it?"

"What's the point of that?" I retorted, curiosity getting the better of me.

"What are you, a smart ass? Didn't you know some of the games are rigged? All a circus act. Gladiators are precious resources and not expendable, like everyone thinks. Takes years to train and we can up and die in the blink of an eye."

I scowled, pondering the implications.

"We get recycled. You will too some day, if you live long enough. Some who are injured come back a month later when everyone's forgotten them. New name, new technique, new fighting style. Others are rotated to other arenas about the province—Corinium, Isca, Durnovaria." He shook his head at my ignorance. "You're a dull sort, boy. I thought rich bastards like you had some education?"

Such news came as a surprise, but then again there were a lot of things

I didn't know about gladiators, battles, politics and religion. My tutor always said, 'what's a mystery for one man is common knowledge for another'. It seemed pointless to argue with Titus and I muttered something about Anustus cringing if he knew.

"He's as soft as an egg. Lets us lose fights and still live. We rarely ever fight to the death like back in the old days."

I didn't agree to or disagree with Titus's scheme. He strutted about as confident as a rooster. He assumed I was on board but I'd wait. The sneaky rogue I trusted less than a fly on shit. If I yielded now, how many more fights would I have to toss, each one more tasteless than the last? I had a feeling Titus'd already plotted my death in some devious manner. He and Pluvius Maxus conspired behind my back, I knew it. He had the mark of Pluvius Maxus written all over him.

The next day, blustery and cloud-wracked, Septagerix paired four sets of gladiators to face off in the public games. Always a public favorite of the dramas staged in the arena were the *retiarius* or 'net man' pitted against the gladius fighter. Roman audiences seemed to like the thrill of watching a perceived unfair fight and gravitated toward the underdog. The retiarius, with his heavy net, trident and dagger, hoped to outwit the *secutor,* 'follower', wielding a sword and wearing a helmet with a face mask that left only his eyes exposed. Me and my ruggies played the role of secutores. Regalis paired with Balariax, the bulldog. Feberiax pitted with sword and shield against Misor, a short, bald ballbasher; Marcellus oddly given club and dagger against Velarius, a heavily-armed Thracian. Me, fighting gladius on gladius against the bearded Tabaxian, master of the weapon I least preferred. None of *The Clubs* played the role of retiarius, us being ill-versed with the net.

I looked over to the portcullis before the matches began and saw Titus grinning back at me with a finger tapping his breastplate. A sure sign I was to use the bladder hidden under my leathers. My lip curled in a sneer. Perhaps the brawny sod needed a little reminder that I wouldn't be his stooge.

Upon Falco's signal the white flag fell. I used my shield to hammer Tabaxian back and sprang on the balls of my feet, protecting my flanks. With much dodging about and maneuvering around his strikes, I managed to evade his chops and stabs backed by seasoned muscle. It left me exposed for some brief instants, but by pure luck and reflex I managed to avoid all his hits. This whole scenario left a bitter taste in my mouth, the conniving Titus at the back of it, and the stubborn side of me refused to play his game. It felt wrong to give into his bullying.

The hard edge of Tabaxian's shield knocked me out my reverie, sending me sprawling sideways. He snuck in like a viper to jam his blade like a spear and I deflected it with a quick, crab-like movement. He hadn't expected that. One of Drace's signature moves. Twisting at my hips, I ducked under a cut and thrust out a foot to knock him off balance.

He came leaping up, a hiss in his throat. "Stay down, you grinning hound. Mars take you! How long do you want to prolong this ridiculous charade?"

"As long as need be. Let's play a little more, Tab."

He was getting rattled—just what I wanted. Easy to make a mistake. In a moment of frustration, he came blundering in, lips peppered with spittle.

When he leaned in to drive at the concealed bladder that would end the fight, he got a surprise. I turned and smashed him with the edge of my shield, catching a corner on his cheek, opening up a wide gash.

He stumbled and fell and I rolled on top of him, wrestling like an amateur. I pulled free the bladder from under my breastplate and jammed it under his own below the navel. I took an opportune moment to stab down and burst it, sending rivulets of dark pig's blood gushing across his groin and thigh.

"Stay down yourself, Tabass."

He jerked up, offering a brief spasm of rage as we jockeyed for position.

"Get up and you'll blow the whole scam," I jeered. "Falco'll have your head."

He fumed and rolled back over. I walked away, staggering for effect, one hand lifted in the air while the spectators roared their approval.

Titus gripped the bars, black with fury. Even Quintus Falco looked a little flustered at the outcome. So, he'd been in on it too, the bastard.

While the other fights ended, Feberiax emerged with a sweaty, sand-encrusted face, winning his round against the bald gladius gouger Misor who had yielded. Marcellus and Regalis lost their fights, but they'd live to fight another day. No deaths today, only sore losers.

Back in the training barracks, violent moods hovered over certain slimy fighters.

"You filthy, betraying dog," Titus growled at me.

Basta lay a hand on his shoulder and grinned. "He fought fair and square, Titus. Get over it. Pay up now, you peacock. Not all of us have the luck of nine lives."

Titus glared at me, shook off Basta's hand. He made a cutting gesture across his neck.

I shrugged. A favorite gesture of the lout's. Well, let him sulk all he wanted. I was already a dead man, should have died many times over. A careless recklessness washed over me—like a sleepwalker with hemlock in his veins. Slave to these violent masters, a part of me no longer cared whether I lived or died.

Titus uttered a surly growl. "You'll get your just desserts, scum-dog. Let's hope the games'll have a fine turnout on the emperor's visit three days from now. Think your luck'll hold?"

I didn't like the cruel sneer pasted on that villain's face. Titus offered no more as he turned on his heel and swept out of the barracks.

Chapter 16

Sure enough, Emperor Hadrian himself came to witness the games today on his tour of Britannia. The master of the games had rigged an interesting set of spectacles, along with gladiatorial pairings kept hidden from us until now—all to impress our renowned emperor.

Quintus Falco and Hadrian sat enclosed within a raised box in the choice first tiers of the amphitheater, front and center, a silk awning overhead. The emperor, a striking man of middle years with curly, fair-colored locks, small token beard and glowing eyes, wore full imperial regalia: the customary Tyrian purple toga, a *trabea* with draped under-tunic. The imperial guard, a dozen of the finest fighting men Rome could muster, held spears and gladii at their side.

A series of events marked the opening ceremonies, first, a colorful bloodbath, including bear-baiting and fat, muscled wild boar with upturned tusks, killing instruments to take down the unfortunate riffraff of Londinium. Wild dogs had become unpopular after the massacre at our inauguration into the arena. The prisoners, chained to their blocks in center stage, stood little chance against the beasts. And we, in our grisly curiosity, watched from behind the shelter of the iron grate, wincing and murmuring at each goring tusk and rending claw that hewed into flesh. I'd become habituated to the level of carnage that marked these events and the crimson bath of sacrifice and doom that stalked our lives every performance. But each groan, bawling shriek and spurt of blood still brought a new shudder of horror to my hackle-raised skin.

Arena slaves hauled the corpses off and the fierce bestiarii clutching spear, trident and net, forced the blood-soaked animals back with deft strokes. I grimaced, not immune to the desperate thrill that every gladiator experiences before each mortal combat. It was our turn now to do battle against lady fate and give the crowd the blood sport they came for.

We trotted out in pairs, Janus at my heels, the second last remaining rat-scum of The Painted Grouses. I did not miss the impish look on the lanista's face. This was his doing. The emperor, after all, deserved no less than the finest spectacle of barbaric combat. What better way than to pit together two street-gang cat-scrappers. Perhaps Anustus was saving Raicus for last.

Feberiax, paired with Tristus of the rangy physique, jogged out with fabricated indifference. Marcellus ignored his opponent Dastrinius, a seasoned Hispanian net fighter with dust-brown and sun-bleached hair. Both of Marcellus's and Feberiax's adversaries wielded trident, dagger and net while they fought with traditional shield and gladius. Titus strutted around making a big to-do of lifting his fancy oversized shield with which he planned to strike up battle with Basta—a joke really, considering they were our trainers. Who knew what staged trick they planned? Septagerix attended too, pitted against a junior member of our gladiator clan—likely an excuse for him to be present and oversee operations. Four other pairs joined the lineup, among them Utristes and Bellacollax clutching heavier weapons—the broadax and double-headed axe, barbaric weapons if ever I'd seen them, from Germania and regions further north. We stood before the emperor, gazing up to the high seats, saluting, then at our governor, awaiting their signal to drop the flag.

In the eyes of our public officials, I perceived stern appraisal. In the undulating waves of murmurs in the seats above that followed, I caught a flutter of colored cloth and glimpsed Fortuna, rising from her seat, waving a woolen stola above her lovely head. My father stood at her side, dressed in immaculate woolen toga. Hades' shades! Even from this distance, he looked twenty years older, his face grey and drawn.

Amidst a sudden trumpet blast, Hadrian stood up in the emperor's box and raised his voice to address the crowd. "Citizens and friends of the empire!" The spectators hushed as his words caught their attention, echoing across the sand. "Hadrianus Augustus, Emperor of this fabled realm, salutes you. In honor of your glorious province and to help you prosper, I have come from far off Rome. I see a people with fire in their bellies, a people proud of their city Londinium, which has much expanded in the years since the rebel Queen Boudicca burnt it to the ground. You have become known throughout the empire as the fierce defenders of a bountiful island. In Gallia, in Hispania, in Italia, and farther afield to the colonies of Macedonia and Thrace. People have heard of Britannia and your city whose forum is the largest north of the snow-covered mountains that girdle Italia."

"Euge! Hurrah! Vive Britannia! Vive Londinium! Vive Imperator Maximus Hadrian," shouted enthusiastic citizens.

"Thank you," responded Hadrian, nodding in approval. When the shouts abated, he cried out, "Let the action speak for itself. Quintus Falco—" he motioned a slim hand to the governor "—over to you. Let the games begin!"

Marcellus, in his most sardonic manner, uttered a shrill cry, *"Ave, Imperator. Nos morituri sumus, te salutamus—"*

And those, cognizant of the event in tribute to the famous speech given to Claudius nearly a hundred years ago, gave a laughing cheer. Dionos, my tutor, had quoted that phrase many times, *"We who are about to die, salute you."*

Hadrian acknowledged the declaration with a nod much more brisk than his last.

Falco's voice rose above the din, disturbing me from my reverie. "Citizens of Londinium and surrounding towns, our emperor has spoken. Let us welcome him to our humble capital. In addition to our fine stable of accomplished gladiators, I introduce you to…the Minotaur!"

All eyes swept to the sidelines as out from under the iron bars strutted a gigantic figure, wearing the bronze headdress of the famed minotaur, curled bull horns, ugly snout, with a face fully concealed under a heavy black mask.

"A guest gladiator to entertain you! Magnus Pugnax Batarus, champion of the games from far and wide. Trained at gladiatorial schools from Isca Augusta to Calleva. Fresh from victories in Cyrene and Crete." Pandemonium erupted in the stands as the monster sauntered about in a circle and his steel-tipped horns glinted in the sun's rays.

Arms, legs and torso of the massive gladiator lay tight-clad in blue-black leather. When his masked face with its eyes holes sighted on me, I knew a new level of fear. This lumbering giant's six and a half feet stature from toe to horn tip terrified me. He carried with him a mid-sized rounded shield edged with iron spikes for extra special skewering. A gladius six inches longer than our own hung in his belted scabbard. I figured this man had mastered its use beyond any of us here, owing to his enormous size and gigantic reach.

Pugnax. The name struck a chord. Some larger-than-life rising star up north by the sea at the arena in Deva Victrix whom other gladiators had whispered about in the barracks. A living legend. A bone-basher and killer from Crete, Malta, or some other hot place. Known to gore many of his fallen opponents with the razor-sharp tips of his bull horns.

Lo and behold his adversary: the infamous Raicus who with shrunken stature, padded out. I even pitied the poor rat, up against that brute, for I guessed he'd be easy prey for the Minotaur, that mass of muscled flesh. That giant'd go on to kill more of us over the course of the afternoon's battles.

Quintus droned on, his announcement peaking the interest of both gladiator and spectator alike. "An anonymous benefactor has brought this accomplished fighter to us today, in honor of our esteemed Emperor's coming to Londinium."

Wild applause rocked the seats. The stone foundations seemed to shake and the wooden seating to rattle.

Hadrian and Falco stood elbow to elbow, heads nodding at once, their hands upraised in acknowledgement of the obvious public enthusiasm.

"Let the games begin!" Falco's hand came down. A shrill trumpet blared as the white flag dropped from the lintel above the main entrance gate.

My attention wandered for an instant. A ball of nausea welled in the pit of my stomach. This hulking ape could only be bad news for us. I caught a glimpse of Pluvius Maxus, the fat, greasy clod wallowing beside Quintus Falco, a gloating grin mooning down on us. Suddenly I knew who our anonymous donor had to be. No less the significance of Titus's cryptic threat three days ago. A convenient way to dispose of me and *The Clubs* who had set Falco's ears burning in shame weeks ago. So much better for us all to disappear off the face of the earth in one fell swoop.

This flash of insight registered in my mind as a momentary blip. Already figures swept in, bronze weaponry came swinging at our heads. The clink of steel clashed from all directions at once. I gasped and jerked backward as Janus's blade arched near my head. The nearby black-armored Minotaur plowed forth like a bull, horns tipped to gouge. I'd barely had a chance to drive Janus back when a gut-wrenching cry smote the air from behind me. I risked a glance. There was Raicus already clutching his side, stumbling to his knees, one hand to his throat. I could see that his injuries were not trivial.

No preamble, no display of theatrics. The blue-black giant had beaten down Raicus in less than thirty seconds and loomed over his half crouched form like a predatory eagle.

No attempt to build up tension as was customary in our fights. I'd never seen a man fight like that before. He used his round, bronze-knobbed shield as a club to bash Raicus, assaulting shoulder, ribs, torso, helm, then led in with the tip of his elongated sword to skewer whatever part of the body lay vulnerable. And for Raicus that was the solar plexus.

Such was the strength of the barbaric colossus that he lifted Raicus up for Hadrian to see on the end of his sword. Raicus squirmed like a fish on a hook, his blood and guts spilling from his body.

Hadrian, in his emperor's purple, flexing gold-ringed fingers, acknowledged the token with a grim dip of head.

Falco called down, "Stop your posturing, Pugnax! We'll cede that as a victory. Get on with it."

The giant grunted and flung down Raicus's corpse, grinding his head beneath his heel then he came lumbering toward me. He flung Janus aside like a piece of balsam, nothing more than an inconvenient bug in his way.

I stared up into that monstrous face hovering before me. The mesmerizing eyes gleamed through his helm's slits and pinned me like a grasshopper in a collector's display case. *Icarus the Terrible*. What a joke. Not my fate to die this soon. I caught the swing of his murderous shield on my own, in time to counter the tide of blood before it was too late. I almost crumbled to my knees at the impact.

At the clash of armor, Feberiax and Marcellus turned their heads, appalled. Sensing treachery and the deepest, black acts in motion, they hurled growling curses and broke from their fights and scrambled to defend me.

Quintus Falco gave a shrieking command. At a signal of clenched fist, the retiarii led by Titus turned on them. A flexible, raspy net flew out and snagged Feberiax's legs, tripping him. Another slung out and caught Marcellus's sword arm and whipped him around like a top. Rough hands grappled the both of them, including Titus's and Basta's. They knocked Marcellus and Feberiax to the ground, subduing them with nets and boot heels.

For a moment, I stood stunned, barely evading Pugnax's next strike. So surprised was the audience at this sudden turn of events that only a shocked murmur rang through their restless masses. A mob smitten by awe, but not ready to see their hero spill his guts, despite the thrill of blood lust. With life and death hanging in balance, they roared, leaping from their seats while the gladiators turned in confusion, jarred out of their assigned pairs. It was too late. I felt all three hundred pounds of the monster lunging at me. Back I fell, swaying like a scarecrow in the wind, my face knocked soundly and blood pouring from my cheek. So hard was I put to parry his flurry of sword strikes that I was almost overwhelmed and bowled over by the sheer weight of him, trampled asunder like an ant on the paves. I backpedaled, slashing out, initiating that acrobatic dance taught me by Drace—feint, dodge, dive, somersault. But such was not enough.

With a choked cry, Regalis broke free of his opponent and came scrambling to assist me, sensing something rotten to the core. He angled in from the side hewing at the monster's ribcage.

The blue-black giant merely turned in a wide arc and shrugged off the blows. Only flea bites to him, so heavily padded and muscled was his upper body. His gore-crusted shield caught Regalis's last strike and swatted him aside like a tic and my ruggie lay on the sand, shaking his head in a blank daze.

The move had purchased me a moment of respite. Pugnax's next series of shield bashes sent me spinning back on my heels, oblivious of the crowd's deafening chants. *"Icarus the Terrible! Icarus the Terrible!"* Such fanatic roars now merged into the background as other forces took over.

Struggling to stave off the mounting vertigo, I tripped on the mutilated corpse of Raicus and fell hard to the sand. The shadow of the monster loomed over me, gimlet eyes blazing as if savoring a moment of triumph. Even before I could reach for my sword, I could see the emperor tilting his thumb for my death, as if for the moment I became but an ornamental sacrifice in this part of the spectacle.

Time slowed. As the tiny beads of the whites of his eyes showed through the Minotaur's mask, I watched the monster's naked steel drive down toward my gullet—until the green cloud of Xetriam's foul blood magic drifted out of my nostrils. Catching sight of such sorcery, the giant paused in his mid-swing, beefy hands clutching his weapon. Somehow he seemed puzzled by the supernatural impossibility of it.

I rolled, squirmed out of the way from Raicus's fly-buzzing corpse before Pugnax regained his senses and the heavy bronze could slam into my throat. The blade cleaved into the sand an inch from my head. Springing to my feet, I snatched up my fallen gladius and slashed him a withering blow across the right leg, opening leather and finding a fleshy place beneath. He lurched, bellowing out a roar, an inhuman sound projecting through his bull mask. Chest heaving, he advanced with a small limp.

I tossed my gladius aside, instinctively snatching up the broadax from the wounded Utristes five feet away; all the while my nostrils trailed the emerald green smoke. Hurling myself at the treacherous Titus, I smashed headlong into his shoulder, crushing collar bone. He had underestimated my speed and abnormal strength and toppled, slumped in a heap of broken bones. The giant limped after me, vocalizing bestial sounds from deep in his throat while I sprang toward the knot of retiarii a dozen feet away. I slashed at the spidery bonds of hemp netting that held my ruggies. They spilled out, tearing free with their gladii. Such was their fury that they joined me in a united front and we hewed those retiarii who stood before us. Septagerix did not oppose us; indeed, he blocked Basta's path, as if daring him to take another step forward. The crowd's howls rolled like breakers on a stormy sea. I could see the glint of hope in my father's eyes as I looked up in a fleeting instant and he clutched at Fortuna's arm.

I circled back in my blood-spattered craze to face the giant who limped after us and stood ready to hew a death stroke. The green smoke swirled from my nostrils and coalesced into a hideous goat's face, making my eyes sting. His body knotted in surprise, again caught off guard by this supernatural happening. Nursing his injured right leg, he roared a bull's cry and swung. Now *The Clubs* all turned on him, me swinging the heavy broadax, a weapon of vengeance.

Like a pack of wolves we circled him, harrying him like a cornered stag, now joined by Regalis who had regained his senses and charged our common enemy with equal zeal. Our rival bellowed like an ox, uttering monosyllables that sounded more like a dumb mute's than an intelligent, normal man. He abandoned his shield tactics and stabbed with his overlong blade. But we stayed out of its reach or parried. When one ruggie danced in from the side, another would sneak in and savage him from the back, leaving behind a dripping wound. Blood droplets seeped through the leather thongs.

He was starting to weaken, like the wounded bear that staggers as the hunting hounds circle closer and snap jaws ever nearer to vital organs.

Feberiax chopped him in the back of his leg. He fell hamstrung, half crouched on a knee, wheezing and shaking his massive head. The knobbed shield caught Marcellus's next blow and he pushed outward with enough muscle and strength to knock Marcellus backward. Regalis darted in to jam the hilt of his sword into his teeth, hoping to remove the mask.

At the same time Feberiax tore the blade from his hands and in a fit of bravado swung it into his skull, shearing off one of the horns. I did not wait for the emperor's signal. I could care less for that bearded stateman's imperial yea or nay, even as the incisors grew from my jaw and the misty beast grinned in triumph at the blood sacrifice in motion. With all my strength, I whirled the bronze axe head in a singing loop and chopped deep into leather, sinew, neck and down through to heaving chest. The mask shattered in a dozen pieces and the giant toppled headlong on the bloody sand.

We did not stop there. We stabbed and pommeled that evil giant into the sand, long after he was dead. Does such a creature ever die? Imitators would crop up almost the next day in today's arena where events turned on a moment's notice. And I could see now why he had not died easily; those leathers of his were threaded with iron plate to guard against blade thrusts. Mask and headdress disintegrated under the rain of our repeated blows. The mighty Pugnax fell revealed at last: an albino mutant, bald, hairless with cropped ears, snub nose, a man not meant for this world. A senseless sacrifice, commissioned to dispose of me, but now soaked in the blood of failure. Whether product of otherworldly spellcraft from Xetriam's arsenal or otherwise, I would never know.

As sustained applause grew to pandemonium, the shouts of *"The Clubs of Londinium. Icarus the Terrible!"* became a conchshell roar in my ear. A team of arena attendants burst from the sidelines and surrounded us, controlling us with iron and hook, net and barb. The demon of smoke had long vanished back into my nostrils, leaving me cold, empty and drained once more: and with a soiled feeling as if I'd committed shameful acts. I heard Quintus Falco calling for our deaths, but they stopped short on a crisp order from the emperor. We eased out of their huddle with our bloody weapons hoisted high. Hadrian himself gave us an ovation to the delight of the crowd who recognized us as champions, heroes who did not deserve to be hauled away in Falco's nets and chains. With stern face, Hadrian demanded Falco tell him who these young fighters were while warding off the red-faced governor's protests with a forbidding chop of hand. With a herculean effort Falco brought himself under control. To defy an emperor, as sure as rain meant death.

Hadrian called the arena to order. "*Pax!* This wooden arena is not becoming of the quality of its gladiators. Citizens of Londinium! I am moved to an impulse of quixotic generosity. Hadrian of Rome promises to erect another, vaster and more splendid arena of enduring stone. To rival that colossus in the greatest city of the gods!"

Wild cheers flew from the crowd. Up from their seats they leapt, clapping and peering down with wild abandon. Hadrian looked about with satisfaction. And I laughed, spitting blood at the irony of the emperor's proclamation—here was Icarus and his gang of ragtags giving rise to the next Colosseum of Londinium. Or perhaps Hadrian had planned the announcement all along, the clever politician he was, with an innate sense of timing to turn a situation to his advantage. Grandiose promises, possibly lies—who knew?

Hadrian raised his hands for order. Now a wider smile slowly spread over his Augustan features. "To these brave fighters, I bestow the ultimate honors. Rare is it I see such a blood-spirited display of bravery. Brothers-in-arms! Banding together as one to defeat a common enemy. If every soldier fought as hardily as them—we'd erase our problem in the north with the barbarians." He paused in thought. "They will go on to Rome—to compete in the capital's games."

Muted applause met this unexpected announcement, then a grumble of confusion. Sensing an awkward moment, Hadrian raised his arm once more with a sly tug at his beard. "Not long hence, people of Londinium, your heroes will return as masters of the craft to entertain the crowds here once more. Already I have sent scouts north to Coria. At this very moment engineers are planning construction of a great wall to stretch from sea to sea. To keep the barbaric hordes out, the enemies of Rome."

He spoke with more careful consideration then. "All the funds of Rome's treasury go back to the people to ensure prosperity and well-being for all."

The crowd seemed less put out at this proviso. I spit blood from my mashed lip. You sly dog, Hadrian. Repeat that to your sycophants like Pluvius Maxus always sneaking fingers into the coffers.

The fights continued until every gladiator had their turn, for better or worse. Only Varda, Titus and Utristes suffered notable wounds, the emperor showing mercy to Publius, the Dacian, who'd lost his fight against a spirited retiarius. In my mind the remaining combats had less impact than the one we'd fought against Pugnax, so Falco had the games cut short. No doubt he'd need to gird himself to face Pluvius Maxus's fury after his well-laid plans had gone awry. Hadrian's closing words rallied the people and pumped up more national sentiment.

I'd already tuned out such events. Amid a fanfare of trumpets, our emperor exited through the passage adjoining his box, separate from the general populace. From his oratory alone he'd proven his mettle by rising as high as any Hispano-Roman could.

With due honors the arena guards escorted us back to the vaulted antechamber behind the iron bars and from there to our training barracks. As the crowd poured out of the upper tiers in waves, exiting through the high arched gates, it was clear the spectacle had run its course. I caught glimpses of the flushed-faced mob dispersing to the city's taverns and thermopolia—the snack counters at every main street intersection. What I would give to be one of them, free to drink at leisure and merge into the background, just another anonymous face in the crowd.

* * *

Sometime later, Anustus drew me aside from the huddle of Marcellus, Feberiax and Regalis. He explained in a conspiratorial tone that I must be on my best behavior around the emperor, that I must keep this 'sickness' of mine involving the mysterious green smoke under wraps. We hashed over what being sent to Rome could mean.

"Will we be kept together?" demanded Regalis.

Anustus shrugged. "That all depends. There are no guarantees in this day and age."

"What does he expect from us?" growled Feberiax. "We're only mortal men. Those fighters in Rome are no doubt brutes."

"That'll be entirely up to you."

"Relax, Feb. Nothing we can't handle," Marcellus said with a swipe of hand. Though his tone seemed less assured than his words.

I frowned. Had Hadrian's intervention actually served to remove us from Pluvius's and Falco's dastardly reach?

"Your biggest challenge," said the lanista, "will be living up to your reputation and the one Hadrian's allotted you, and ensuring that it follows you to your graves. If you don't, you'll wish you died here in Londinium."

That seemed to be the least of our concerns. I'd prayed for death many times. Killing the monster Minotaur as a team had cemented our unbreakable bond. I could see a definite change in Marcellus. His conniving and arrogant leer seemed less marked now, perhaps trimmed down to size, knowing that his survival depended on his cooperation with us. Amid these musings, Anustus installed us in a private antechamber reserved for owners, selected staff and important investors to await the arrival of the Emperor. In a dazed shock we speculated what that might entail.

Not long after, sometime in the early evening, the Emperor graced us with his presence in our humble chamber, accompanied by several of his Praetorian Guard. Among his entourage stood Quintus Manius Aureus, an attendant, close to his side, a curled, oiled and scented man who seemed more the wife of a senator than a full-blooded Roman male. Poised on the alert, taking no chances after the slaughter of Pugnax, stood the five grim Praetorian bodyguards keeping diligent watch over their emperor and us.

After studying us with a mix of curiosity and frowning perplexity, Hadrian lifted his jeweled finger high and said in a sharp tone, "I hear you are a pack of vandals and murderers—petty Londinium street rabble sentenced to die in the arena to atone for your violent acts. What irony! But miraculously you have survived." He sighed. "To defeat a most savage gladiator—one of the Empire's most celebrated. A man lives and dies by his own sword, so I've heard, be it black, silver, bloody or clean. You—Icarus Veditio, Feberiax Duilius, Marcellus Aureus and Regalis Emilius—will come to Rome. Not to be pardoned for your execrable crimes which I consider heinous, but to display your mettle before a larger audience. Every drop of blood you stole from your innocent victims, will be paid back in an equivalent number of matches."

I lowered my eyes in sullen displeasure.

"In all my years I have never seen such a desperate, street-level interplay of offense and defense. If every legionnaire were to be so dauntless and bold…we'd tear out the hearts of all the barbarians. Bravo! Warms my heart to see it in this distant province." He turned to me with a curious look. "Icarus, it has come to my attention that you are infected with some wild disease—or some spurt of madness."

"'Tis neither, Emperor."

"Ah, so you do have a tongue." His eyes flashed with a hint of playfulness, and something else.

I shrugged. Even Marcellus was wise enough to keep his sarcastic mouth shut.

The emperor gave a short grunt. "No matter. You're not here for rhetoric or oratory. To fight, yes. Either to your death one day, or to earn your freedom as gladiators of exceptional standing."

He drew himself erect. "Quintus Aureus—see that these men are outfitted with the finest blades and armor Rome has to offer. They will be taken on the next galley to Rome. We'll not stint on expenses. Put them under the care of Gaius Lucius Camodus, the senior lanista at the Colosseum."

"As you wish, Emperor." The attendant bowed and gave a short nod to the lanista.

I caught another glance, one of lascivious curiosity, and it knotted my stomach. Hadrian gave a sly wink. "Perhaps when I'm next in Rome we'll have some wine together, you and I, under more…casual circumstances."

I licked my lips, resisting the urge to grab the knife from my lanista's belt and plunge it deep into the good emperor's ribs—but that would not be good for the empire, nor my own health, putting demon powers aside. The tingling sensation in my blood had subsided to a dull ache; now a sense of loathing of that beast that inhabited me burned ever brighter, the one that allowed me to crack skulls and survive atrocity more than ever in my young life.

The emperor stepped closer. The urge to strike him was almost overwhelming. "Look at me," Hadrian commanded, and he stared into my eyes, as if to read what kind of a man I was, and I swear that he shirked back under the otherworldly image he saw. It seemed he caught some startling glimpse into fathomless lunacy, of the thing that lurked in my body, that I had sheltered for weeks now and was slowly becoming. He gave an involuntary gasp, lurched back, reaching for the jeweled dagger at his hip.

The guards clacked forward, spears and swords leveled at my gut. I did not flinch. I expected death. For a brief instant tension crackled in the air, so thick it could be cut by a knife. But Hadrian collected his wits and brought his chin up in light embarrassment and slapped his thighs. He gave a small intake of breath.

Quintus Aureus spoke in a voice of high hauteur, "Emperor, it appears, this Icarus is the star of the ring show. Why take the others when—"

Hadrian gave a brisk flourish. "They'll all go, Quintus. This Septagerix will accompany them." He motioned to our lanista. "You've spoken highly of your assistant, Anustus. Seemed he has played a part in training these striplings."

"He has, Emperor. Though the loss of Septagerix will be a blow for me."

Hadrian waved a hand. "Certain sacrifices must be made for the greater good."

"Too true. Your wish will come to pass, Emperor."

"Then get them cleaned and ready for shipment at tomorrow's dawn. I go north to see about this wall at the end of the week. First, there will be special attention given to renovations in Londinium itself. I'm quite impressed by your run of gladiators. That play with the Minotaur added a special quality. You'll all be granted a new amphitheater, of such grandeur to rival those in Pompeii and Tarraco."

Anustus beamed. "Excellent, Emperor, excellent. The privilege is mine, a rare one to have an audience with you. Only the greatest of men rule empires with the magnanimity and support of the citizens you command."

Hadrian gave a perfunctory nod, as if accustomed to hearing such pat speeches by men in his company. "Keep on, lanista. You are running a fine school here. Now, Quintus," he said. "To dinner. Bring me wine!"

The procession made its way down the hall and I do not know how Hadrian's glimpse of the demon had not sparked violence of a more sinister nature resulting in all our deaths.

After the echoes of their sandals faded, the lanista closed the door and shook his head. "You're a lucky one, Icarus. Too lucky. Nine lives, I say."

Septagerix indulged in a low grunt. "Good news, boys. You get to die, in style—in Rome."

A messenger knocked at the door. "Enter," said Anustus.

The door opened and a thin slave approached. "Lanista, Pluvius Maxus to see you."

Anustus gave a grumbling curse. "Go!" he motioned to us. I felt a cold lump grow in my throat, followed by a heat of fire in my gut. "Take them back into the training area. Septagerix, shut the door."

We complied, following him for some time before I tugged at Regalis's arm at a shadowed T-junction. "Let's do some spying." We snuck back to the antechamber where Anustus conversed with the banker. Crouched in the grey shadows, our ears to the gap at the door's outer edge, we heard a muttered exchange.

"—Lanista, had a personal talk with me—"

A clop of boot and a clasp of hand piqued my attention.

"Anustus, you are looking good," a voice said having Pluvius's pig-tenor. "You should, after a display like the one today."

"I've seen better days," I heard the lanista mutter. "Hadrian's promise to build a better arena, of stone and high tiers like the one in Rome, excites me. But it also worries me. I wonder what is coming next. A complete revamping of our gladiatorial school? Me turfed out on the street? Hadrian says he's on board keeping me as an overseer, but I don't trust his imperial politics."

"Nor should you, Anustus. Our dear emperor has such a cosmopolitan vision. Sprinting from province to province, capital to capital, with his catamites in tow, seeing the world, and improving world order. Keeping up Pax Romana. I hear that after Britannia, he has Gallia and Mauretania next on his itinerary. His plan is a good one, building that wall to keep the wolves beyond the borders. But I suspect our naked, fang-toothed friends to the north won't cotton much to sitting on their heels and will see a way around that."

"I'm not one to say."

"No you're not, are you, Anustus? Always a yes man, the cautious type."

"Unlike certain others I know." Now it was the lanista's turn to jeer. "You'd better watch your back, Pluvius. Our shining boy-hero, Icarus, is now a favorite of your good Emperor Hadrian. He has many informers, *frumentarii*, who may not cotton to the tone of your talk, and if you go behind his back, murdering his poster boy, you'll be in for a rude awakening. Only takes one blabbing mouth to tip him off of your conspiracies and you're a dead man."

I could hear Pluvius's high-pitched bray. "You'd better watch yours too, Anustus. You think I'm some silly banker, who only powders his nose at night, perfumes his springy curls, puts grapes in his mouth at all hours of the day. My arm is longer than you think. This young hood who broke into my villa murdered my priest, a personal friend and agent. He stole my money and disgraced me. The act must be punished! The boy has had half his punishment, but the worst is yet to come."

I heard a snort. "Have it your way, Pluvius. But don't come bawling to me when your vengeful schemes backfire and your head's on a pike."

Pluvius gave a tittering laugh. "I assure you, they won't. Vagox, my spy, though he is two moons in the grave, has already seen to that."

I imagined my lanista's eyebrows raising at that, wondering what could be more cryptic than the tone of that remark. "If you think you're going to get away with murder, you're mad—"

"Your perceptions mean little to me, Anustus. Especially of my larger programs. There are secrets none will tell—not even you. And that swine Icarus will wish that Prosperina hadn't answered my prayers. The same prayer she will echo in her master's, dark Hades' ear before he visits an ever worse curse upon the young hood."

CHRIS TURNER

Chapter 17

Dawn came on the wings of a gentle wind. I awoke in the gladiator barracks to a nudge of a boot and rough hands pulling me up. Armed men escorted me and my ruggies with little ceremony to the wharf where the merchant galley *Argiseus* sat moored low in the water, laden with bolts of wool, sacks of grain, crates of clay bowls and salted fish, plus ingots of iron. Regalis raised an eyebrow. A significant look that I interpreted as 'well, Ick, there's our home for the next two weeks'. Feberiax and Marcellus stood stiff and sullen. Septagerix, our appointed trainer, seemed unmoved. We exchanged no words with one another. I watched the last of the cargo hauled aboard across the gangplank into the vessel's stern.

Our turn to board as 'guests' of Emperor Hadrian. Marcellus grinned from ear to ear, thinking it a smooth ride for us from here on in. How wrong he was.

A burly, rough-bearded man snapped down at us, "Here's our poster boys, is it?" He had the look of a captain, all leather and helm, weathered and salt-brined, with high-laced, black sandals, matching the color of his teeth.

The leader of our armed escort turned and muttered, "These men're special commodities. Wards of Hadrian—to be treated with care."

"Indeed, and Jupiter has tits," the seaman bawled. "They're prisoners, soldier—and by the blood of Neptune, they can row like the other galley slaves. Eighty five denarii is not enough for me to be playing housemaid."

A knowing grin broke out on our attendant's face. "No worry there. The emperor already anticipated as much. He said they'll season well with a fortnight of rowing, to consider it part of their gladiator conditioning."

The seaman grumbled, "Take them down below into the rowers' hold then. I'll have Iulio shackle them with the others. My ship, as I told your superiors, only goes as far as Gallia. We'll transfer them to a larger *corbita* bound for Rome when we get there." He thrust his attention back to lashing down the last crates of salted fish.

That was our introduction to captain Justanius Beranius Verogtri, a shrewd and loutish sort, middle-aged with a sea-lined face, crooked nose and a belt full of swords and daggers. Other knicknacks lurked there, such as spiked balls for whatever nefarious purposes we were yet to discover.

His ship, one of the lighter freighters with a single deck of oars, was to sail out of Londinium, bound for Gesoriacum, I guessed, on the coast of Gallia. Her two square rigged sails on pine masts, center and stern and a small triangular sail at the bow looked sleek enough. She was not a fast-running vessel like the military escort moored at her side: a liburnian bireme, long and fierce, with two decks of oars and a single-square rigged sail on a pine mast set dead center. Outriggers stabilized the ship—long wooden platforms to port and starboard—and the wales protected the hull from the protruding bows of enemy ships. While fast under oar, I knew from Dionos's teachings that this double-oared type of vessel capsized easily under too much sail.

The metal trapdoor to the oarsmen's hold clanged back and they hauled us down into the shadowy interior. Huddled under the main deck, we squatted helplessly as they chained our legs to iron rings in the third row, nailed into the solid oak hull at our feet. Regalis to my left, Marcellus to my right, Feberiax on the end while the rest of the motley crew of slaves gave us hollow-eyed stares. A hold of fifty sweating stinking hides, men resigned to a harsh fate, and urged on by a slavedriver with a cruel whip whose mentally-challenged crony beat an ox-hide drum with mallet.

"Full reverse!" came the captain's harsh voice down through the grate. We pulled those oars to the thudding beat of that bald, two-toothed crony drum-master at the fore. "Ahead strong!" bawled the captain. We sailed downriver. The slavemaster's iron-fletched whip would rake across our backs if we so much as missed a beat.

My hackles raised at this new bondage. My gut quivered at the sight of a black thumb-sized tic crawling out of the matted tangle of the slave's hair in front of me.

No time to dwell on it. We rowed and rowed. Through the small port-like window where our oar ran, I caught glimpses of the passing shore:

drooping willows, treacherous mudbanks, creeks and eddies. The haggard man in front looked ready to pass out. I signaled for more water. The slave attendant came by and I motioned to the fatigued figure, and the slave tipped a bowl of water to his lips. The man gratefully gave a moan and slurped away noisily.

He grunted his thanks back at me.

"How long you been here?" I asked, tossing him a grim look.

"Two years now," he answered. "Our captain, the cretin Beranius, is a harpy in fancy clothing. The wretch with the whip—another story altogether."

I grunted an involuntary acknowledgement.

"Shut up, you worms!" cried the rowmaster, hearing our dull murmurs. Stomping forward, he snapped his whip. "Row! You're not here to socialize." The leather snapped down hard on the shaggy-haired man's back. "Row as if your mother's life depended on it."

When the taskmaster'd turned his back to chew out another who'd sneezed and missed a beat, the haggard man shot me a fleeting look. "My name's Gerix. Here's to better days."

"To better days." I gave a gloomy sigh. "My name's Icarus."

Hard and long we rowed downriver. Finally we reached the wide, windy estuary of the Tamesis. Our ship left the coast on the ebb-tide with our bireme keeping close watch, protecting us from raiders. Two days it would take us to cross to Gesoriacum, the quickest crossing to Gallia, but on the second day, foul weather hit us hard. By the sounds of the creaking vessel and wind blasts on the furled sails, I'd gathered we'd swung far north of our designated route and lost our military escort—at least according to the panicked shouts rising from the decks above and the captain's raucous commands. The rough motions of the sea and the deep troughs pitching the ship up and down had my stomach heaving, but I fought the urge to upchuck. This freak storm escalating to a full gale would take us well off-course, away from the known trade routes.

The seething waters that I glimpsed out the tiny port square were only an affirmation that this journey to Rome was fraught with disaster. More testament still, the captain's brassy voice jarring me out of my midmorning daze. Mexor told me hair-raising tales of his journeys at sea fraught with dangerous storms, and it seemed I was living one. A pool of water swirled around our feet where the vessel had started to take on water. My hide oozed sweat and I cringed at the sound of the slavemaster's burning lashes. I heard the bump and grind of wood and the shouts of men above. Then the whoosh of arrows and sudden murderous clink of steel and men's dying cries.

The captain uttered hoarse curses. "Full speed ahead!" he rasped. "Get ahead of these swamp rats!" I couldn't see who these enemies of ours were, confined in this grubby dim box. Feberiax's and Regalis's eyes blazed with apprehension.

Through the overhead grate I heard angry words traded with the captain. I turned and saw Septagerix stumbling down the small stair, breastplate smeared with blood and the gladius at his hip stained crimson. He grabbed the battleaxe from the wall and staggered down the filthy aisle to crack it down hard on our iron rings, freeing me and Marcellus. Hope and panic spread like wildfire amongst the galley slaves. Dozens jerked up in wild-eyed terror from their benches, fouling the rhythm and three of the slavemasters joined to slash hard on their backs. The lead whipmaster scurried forward to snap leather on Septagerix's shoulders. Septagerix sneered and grabbed the whip's thongs and pulled the bearded ruffian close, half spitting in his eyes. "What the Minerva's on with you, you stupid dog? Strike me, will you?"

"Let go! We have to keep the pace. The scum are to row. Row, I say!"

"Shut up, you damn fool! These are fighting men. Without more of them on deck, we'll all die!" He jerked and smashed the whipmaster hard in the face with the flat of his blade. The slavemaster fell back, blood and broken teeth spilling from his maw. I snatched the axe from our gladiator-trainer's hand and chopped Feberiax and Regalis free. Gerix's chain and his mate's were soon to follow.

We scrambled up the stair and onto the heaving deck, leaving the other rowers behind. No sign of our military escort. We must have lost them during the storm. Marcellus clapped my shoulder and pointed. The dull grey of steel on the weapon's rack caught my attention. Tough wooden shields strapped to the gunwales too. We grabbed up short swords and spiked shields and stumbled on stiff legs midships to where our captain and crew fought off several dark figures climbing over the rails.

Two barbarian galleys rolled in the swells twenty feet away. They'd cornered us like scavenging sharks, their beastly prows shaped into those of monsters, one a weird sea worm with fangs and painted yellow eyes. The other like some monstrous griffin with wings. Already raiders had leaped across the gap on a close pass-by and were stabbing steel at our captain and crew. Our ship, laden heavy with cargo, lay low in the water, no match for the predators' speed. But Beranius and his men fought with deadly force, blades and shields a whirl of motion. The master barked frothing orders and pressed the invaders back toward the bow. One of the vessels rammed from behind. The force sent us lurching. Another slid along our starboard and sheared off several oars before the captain could bawl orders to retract them. We were doomed.

Men's cries died in their throats as spears and arrows flew. The boat tilted sideways. Grapples sang through the air and iron caught our rails; boarding planks fell and men in bronze caps with horns came roaring over the rail to smite us with steel. The captain fought two abreast with his last twenty men splashed in blood from knee to shoulder. We strove to help fend them off. If those killers got aboard, it would be the end of us.

Eight of the crew lay in pools of blood—trampled underfoot as dozens of savages streamed over their carcasses. I raised my gladius and smashed my shield into the faces of that horde of wild men with red and gold hair spilling from under their barbaric helms down their shoulders. My eyes burned like glowering coals.

Wolf furs draped over their leather armor and strange headdresses with horns and tusks; some sported black patches over their eyes—fierce caricatures of violence and rapine.

Marcellus surged in behind me, stabbing and parrying, a banshee of death who knew no fear. Feberiax's axe head swung. He pushed through the clot, with unfettered strength and grunting heaves, slashing deep through matted wolf fur and hide. Septagerix helped Regalis hurl a man over into the swells. My ruggies, seasoned by months of gladiatorial combat, did not flinch or fail in the face of that onslaught.

What turned the tide was the savage gusts of shifting winds and our jammed port rudder, crushed by the assault from the rear. The rowers couldn't keep us steady or outrun the remaining enemy with our sheared-off oars. The second ship smashed into our bow, cutting us off, and jerked us off our feet. A new wave of crazed, wolf-skinned savages leaped over the rail like rabid animals and stormed us from the back.

Now the green mist flowed from my nostrils in a pale stream. I saw green and red through my field of vision in a swath of chaotic color. The demon goat face I'd come to despise grew outward in the thick cloud, this time morphing into a perverted wolf shape. Its fanged muzzle bared itself to my foes.

The barbarians halted, then howling curses, cut at the apparition. I stormed through the cloud, my eyes scarlet like a devil's, my blade a saw-like mill of fury. I wielded that blade with the strength of ten. Even without armor, I chopped down foes like chaff, as the battle craze flooded over me. The demon fire burned, kindling my blood, and I smote men's hearts and pulled out raw flesh with the end of my blade, dripping wet and crimson, staining the bleached planks, twisting and roaring. I whacked my shield on sword arms and skulls, pushing forward like a ram to kick with my boots and send men flying off balance, parrying blades and slashing into more warm, living flesh.

Others of the ship's crew fell to the barbarian blades. But I fought madly on as did our small group of bravehearts, hacking and slashing, and by some miracle we kept them at bay.

Caught in a merciless vice between two sets of foes, I watched in dreadful awe as the chief, a black, wolf-furred, armored tower of power, broke through the knot of defenders and smashed his axe into the backs of the defending crew. They fell in washes of blood. With the lithe grace of a cat, but with the explosive power of a lion, the barbarian chief eased across the deck. Even our fierce Roman captain was no match for him. Arms clawing at air, he fell in a splash of crimson as the chief dragged him back by the hair and drove a dagger through his heart. I grimaced, sickened by the violence and gore. I gripped my hilt, ready to make a last stand. The chief pulled out an object and blew a horn that was ugly to the ear. Two notes—one shrill and one low that sounded like a dirge from Hades. The invader lumbered toward me, perceiving something odd and unearthly about my presence, someone not from this world. Barbarian faced timeless demon, this time in the guise of a smoke-wreathed wolf. Everything in his superstitious, barbaric heritage should have inspired enormous fear.

"Ak kergji!" he cried. "Ak Kerjgi!—Cadeergrum!"

What meant those words? A curse? A spell?

The green mist thickened around me. The chief clawed out with his hand but the green vapor bit deep and singed his fingers. Hissing a venomous curse, he swung his broad-axe blade through the swirling smoke, with his sky-blue eyes pinched shut. And yet nothing could disperse the formed perfection of evil incarnate. The cloud hovered there like some ghoul of yesteryear. In my grinning bestiality, my face curled in impish satisfaction, knowing that I had beaten that barbarian foe, though I be more animal than human. But the moment I thought this, the green smoke fled back into my nostrils. I was never in control of it, this dark demon power that welled within me. The last dying curse of the priest Xetriam still bound me to the mortal plane.

The chief blinked for a second as his invaders pounced on us, taking us down in thudding heaps. My blood-drenched ruggies lay backs to the planks, their speechless faces smothered by coarse hands, weapons wrested from their grips.

We had lost and we were taken.

A bunch of them tore open the grate to the rowers' deck and I heard hatchety sounds and dim meat-chopping. The howls of dying men drifted up from below and they returned, hauling the battered corpses of the three slavedrivers. They left them bleeding out on the blood-stained deck. I wasn't sorry to see those rogues dead, but I was sad that less of our numbers remained to stave off these northern savages. Wherever they were from, north Germania or farther, I could not guess, but they were a breed unknown to my eye, being taller and fairer and clad in hide, and crowned with curious helms I'd never heard of before, despite Dionos's wildest theories of the people beyond the mist. Why they spared us, I did not know. Perhaps for twisted sacrifices on the night of the full moon, judging from the carnage of their blood-smeared chief, and our lifeless captain, crew, and mangled whip-wielders. He reached down and tore the druid locket from my neck. With a grimace, he uttered some barbaric words and seeing it meant something to me, threw it down and crushed it under his boot heel. My last link to the druid severed. I stared up at him in hate. I watched them shear the heads off the corpses of the crew and rope the dripping heads to the gunnels, hurling the headless bodies overboard. In his deep, sky-blue eyes and the rough crags of his battle-lined face, I saw a rare savagery in him, not one witnessed even on the sands of Londinium's arena.

They forced open the hold and feasted their eyes on the bounty. Barking orders, the chief had several of them gather up materials from their mother ship. They caulked up the leaking hull, plugging it with cork and resins then boarded up the leaking areas with planks. Then with much painstaking labor they repaired the smashed rudder while more savages set our sail billowing in the diminishing winds. We were thrust below, shackled in our hard benches again, ordered to help row the ship.

The timbers creaked once more to the rhythm of our oar strokes and the power of the wind as the prow turned to the north.

Chapter 18

We did not head east for the coast of Gallia. Even handicapped by the loss of oars, we sailed north for several days against the biting wind and rain, where the coastline grew rugged and green, and tree-lined inlets merged with grey skies. Our three vessels approached their rocky shoals guarding a beach of shingle. This was not Germania that we sailed to, for I'd heard those lands were flat where the Rhine emptied. These were saw-edged with dark coves and soaring woodland, green and forbidding.

I feared we'd veered much farther north than that, to the land of my birth mother. After following the fabled shoreline for many miles, we slowed at last, having shot far west, I guessed, of our destination.

The tide rolled high up on the sand, and the barbaric chief moored our hijacked vessel at a place where a crude wooden wharf projected outward with logs pale as bone. Men in wolf furs piled out. Upon the sound of the chief's eerie horn, others emerged from the village and secured our ship with thick hempen ropes to sturdy timbers. The remaining barbarian vessels stayed at a distance and dropped their anchors, putting out longboats to bring the men ashore. In loud, raucous voices they greeted us and their captain-in-chief in a barbaric tongue. Clasping arms, they embraced and drank piss-colored ale from gourds thrust in eager hands. I could see the traces of a crude village somewhere back behind tall firs.

The chief displayed his prizes to his clan members—us first, then the new galley ship with her hefty hold of plunder being offloaded on the shore. He lifted a calloused hand in our direction, a signal that the villagers should herd us up to the communal grounds to a large palisade of sharpened stakes, set about two inches apart, housing other grim slaves like ourselves. They prodded us along, Septagerix, our gladiator trainer too and the rest of the captives, with thrusts hard enough to jar my teeth. I sent a snarl back in their faces. One slovenly brute jeered at me and sent me sprawling forward with a harsh whack from the butt end of his axe handle. I didn't fight back. It was suicide to fight these marauders. Too many others to back the hothead up. He reeked with confidence. If we were pitted one on one, he'd get his just desserts. Not days ago we'd been hailed as heroes by the masses in Londinium's big arena. Now we were shoved ankle-deep in the mud by lowly barbarians.

Stray dogs roved around the perimeter of the village, shaggy brutes that looked like wolves. I guessed they'd made half-tamed pets out of these mangy animals, foraging for scraps. Needless to say, my fear of dogs had not abated since Londinium. The mere sight of one of them made old wounds throb.

Women and children crept down from the houses of sod roofs to watch us with interest. The square, earthen and wood huts were set against a wind break of tall firs, arranged in curious and irregular orientations up the wild, wooded slopes. Some sported sod and earth extending from the roofs down the sides to the ground. I saw one large one set back from the others, which I reckoned the chief's hut.

As we hunched there in the muck with the pigs and the shaggy men huddled around us, we conversed little and could barely look at one another for shame. Among those wretches sentenced to the palisade I recognized Gerix who had survived the massacre and the hollow faces of other men once chained in the hold. I saw others of various sizes and breeds: Dacians, Gauls, Hispanians, Germanians. Slaves whom I recognized by their language and whom the reavers had recently captured and yet had not put to good use.

Regalis at last spoke, "They'll come looking for us. They must. The *Classis Britannica*. Hadrian sent us specifically, with an escort. As emperor, he's commander-in-chief of the fleets."

Septagerix, squatting on his haunches, grumbled out a weary sigh. "No one's going to come look for us, boy. We're as good as dead. We're much too far away."

"Yeah, think they're going to comb leagues of sea in barbarian territory for a few men?" I jeered.

"We're finished then," said Regalis. "Or slaves for life unless we can escape this pig sty."

"Escape?" breathed Marcellus. "Where are we going to run to, Reg? Those wild, wolf-haunted woods?"

Feberiax grumbled. "They'll clamber after us with steel and fire. Flush us out."

I couldn't accept such fatalism. "Brighten up, ruggies. We'll fight. Break loose! Find a way to commandeer a ship. One for all and all for one. Die by our own hands, if necessary."

Septagerix gave a grim smile. "You've good mettle, boy, for a stripling. I admire that. It's a wonder we're still alive. I'm guessing they've other plans for us, Icarus. Rituals we're better off not knowing. Maybe better to die than be fed to their foul gods and beasts."

I spat and Marcellus stirred. "I'll not feed a sacrificial fire or be victim to Taur or Gaur, whatever name they give their gods."

Septagerix grimaced. "I think they've much eviler deities than you've got in mind."

"Wheirl! Kerkul—Gakfe." A rough-bearded man thrust an arm up. Spear points prodded us through the cracks. I took that as the hint to back off and quiet down. Bastards. The northmen all laughed.

We clamped our jaws tight and stared out between the rough-hewn stakes at the men conversing on the shore beside our beleaguered ship and its confiscated cargo. I could hear the creaks of the strange, serpent-prowed vessels as they bobbed in the distance like toys of evil purpose. The surf surged and boomed. The air blew fresh off the water up to the open ground and the village. A chill wind bit into my hide, though the leather jerkin should cut it, for it was colder here in these northern lands.

The villagers opened the sacks of grain and crates of salted fish for the evening's feast while the chief ran his fingers through the chest of silver they'd hauled from the ship. I shuddered at the sight of the prows of their beastly vessels dressed with the grisly heads of the captain and his crew. I saw no shipyard, tools or building material outside of a few carpenters sent out to cut new oars for the *Argiseus*. So I guessed they were not shipbuilders then, and that they had stolen their boats.

The common grounds, I estimated, measured two hundred yards from end to end and from there to the woods perhaps another hundred. If we could cut ourselves loose at night…sneak past the sentries, we could make a break for the forest and take our chances in the night. A slim hope at best. I sank back in gloomy despair. Gripping one of the stakes, I felt solid beech beneath my fingers, three inches thick.

We spent a week in that sty, bearing the rain and the wind, and the reeks and discomforts with a slave's resignation. Our bodies stank and dried blood stained our ragged clothes while the chief forgot all about us and went hunting up in the hills with his henchmen, returning four days later with five antlered deer hauled by a dozen axemen and bowmen. Chunks of red meat became the staple of the evening stew. We devoured the leftovers, so ravenous we were—chopped bits of gristle and bone mixed with cabbage chunks and turnip tops that could have been set out for the hogs. How I hungered for the bountiful spreads of my father's table at that instant: fine fish and pheasant sprinkled with goat cheese and washed down with choice Italian wines poured with a generous hand. A wave of sorrow choked my throat. I remembered his gruff ways and his classic Roman features. Fortuna, with her doe-like eyes, her dove-pale skin and warm embrace, a thousand miles away. Her little nuances and mannerisms that I adored yet a lifetime ago seemed so dear to me now.

Squinting through the stakes on those rainy days, I stared at the mats of sod that grew upon their rooftops, their houses of wattle and daub, and wondered what it would be like to live in one of those earthy huts. Between the wild goats and swine they penned up in corrals, the forest animals and fowl they hunted and their plundered spoils, they enjoyed a respectable existence. These men carried axes not swords, favoring the heavier weapon like the most primitive of the Celts and the Picts. Their women carried themselves with a cold assurance—backs ramrod straight. Long blond-haired and untamed, they came to stare at us with the look of the north wind and snowflakes in their red-cheeked faces and their distant snow-maiden expressions. I could see my family resemblance in their flaxen locks and fine-cut features.

The dogs continued to roam the perimeter of the village. The beasts hunted for scraps and whined and barked, setting my nerves on edge.

At one point, a group of the village's rowdy teens became overly curious about us for they saw in me and the ruggies not the regular breed of cowed and broken prisoners, but ones more their age, with seasoned experience. Handsome with their long blond hair, but with giant chips-on-their shoulders, they looked lean and fit with strapping physiques, hale cheeks and a posturing arrogance that struck a chord in me.

They taunted us from a distance and I could not understand their spoken words, but the jeering tone of them suggested their contempt. We answered in Latin, some words which they may have understood. In response, they balled their fists and threw rotten vegetables and rocks at us through the gaps. Feberiax stomped up to the bars and dared them to come closer and try us, but the hooligans thrust spear tips through the gaps, pricking us if they could. Regalis arched back with a grunt, slower on his feet than Feberiax. I grinned, finding the interplay amusing. Marcellus went so far as to snatch up some of the rotten vegetables and hurl them back, clocking a few. Cries and jeers drifted back through the pales, then laughs from the elders who watched. But finally one of the village hunters got tired of the ruckus and threatened to put them in with us.

A brazen youth with topknot and swagger, seemed to think this just an idle threat and dared to challenge the hunter. A mistake. The man's jaw hardened and he picked him under the armpits and dragged him before the gate while another unwound the heavy ropes granting entrance to the slave pen. They tossed him into our midst, then retreated through the gate where they stood to watch how he fared. A slow relish grew in our eyes. Maybe it was the boy's father or uncle who decided on such a rash course. We circled the flummoxed youth. Wild-eyed, he drew back, his chest heaving. He made a swipe at Marcellus who was closest, snatching the dagger at his belt. The blade caught a slice of Marcellus's lower arm, drawing blood. But after years of training, Marcellus allowed no more than that cat scratch. He twisted left, ducked and jammed an elbow in the kid's teeth. Up came a hand, snatching the blade from his fist while he was momentarily blinded with the mud Marcellus had scooped up and slapped in his face. I admired Marcellus's craft. I grinned through my teeth and the layers of grime, seeing the handiwork of Drace's style in that move. Now it was fists and boots, with Marcellus getting the most punches in. He smashed his knuckles hard into the boy's ribs. A wild fist flailed out and caught Marcellus above the eye but this was the last of any significant hits and soon they were grappling and pommelling each other in the stinking mud. The two at the gate thought this punishment enough and stormed in to pull the pair apart. They hauled Marcellus off their young clansman while others warned us back with axe heads and spears and dared us to try anything more. They pulled the near senseless youth out on the grass.

Rubbing their chins, the elders stewed over the fight. They seemed to think it not very honorable that their kindred should have his nose wiped in the muck and not have won the contest, armed with a knife against a half-starved Roman. After a brief conference with others who had arrived and watched the whole shameful episode, the adults selected seven of their most talented youth and dressed them in war gear—square shield, leather breastplate, black-visored helm. They squared them off against those of their own age, me and my ruggies who were forced to fight. We got grossly inferior equipment: battered shields, dented helms and antiquated axes with dull edges.

A space was cleared on the common ground where many gathered around in a tight circle, heavily armed, should things get out of hand and we decide to cut and run. We sparred beside the roaring fire while Septagerix watched through the gate with an impassive gaze, Gerix at his side.

At this point I cared little. A thrill of empowerment coursed through my veins. My chance once more to wield a wild weapon while cold grey skies loomed over us and kept watch over our fights. Nothing felt more right than us with bronze in our hand and a chance at head bashing. War drums boomed to the soft thud of mallets to summon all to the event. Women, children, elders gathered to watch. Lurking at the heart of every culture was the compulsion to watch a tribal contest of strength and valor.

Under our ragged, filthy garb our hearts beat, our cheeks bared to the leaden skies. A fight worthy of a fight as they paired me with the blond-haired brother of the one vanquished earlier, a bruiser in his own right. He was my own height and weight. After witnessing his friend beaten down by Marcellus, his hackles bristled and he charged at me, hoping for a quick finish. Out of the corner of my eye I caught a glimpse of my ruggies pitted against opponents of similar character: Feberiax against a rugged teen with a dirty grin on his face, patting his axe; Regulis and Marcellus against brutes of equal confidence and size. As unfair as this totally rigged fight was, it didn't matter. Seven of them against four of us? After the arena in Londinium and suffering lowlifes like Titus and Pugnax, it became clear that a slave's life was never about fairness.

We hacked at each other like street thugs, blocking with shield, dancing around, trying to avoid a direct hit and stay alive. The clash and thud of axe on shield echoed throughout the communal grounds. Regalis followed through with a solid hit that knocked his opponent back and kept him panting for breath. Marcellus smote and parried amid the howling jeers of the onlookers. No different a mob than those screaming spectators at the arena, just on a less grand scale.

Feigning anxiety, I let my enemy come in, let him lead me back against the crackling fire. I backpedaled with sure steps, absorbing the impact of every wild swing of that vicious axe against my chipped and battered shield. A cheer went up among the gathering as I pretended to trip, but like a gymnast, I rolled out of the way before his axe came crunching down on my skull. At the same time I swatted out with the flat of my axe blade against the back of his calf, a dirty piece of fighting for sure. I'd gotten used to such tactics in the arena. I could have maimed the kid for life had I used the sharp edge of that axe, but an inner voice told me that would be a foolish move. Likely the worst mistake I could make. Fight well, but only wound these peacocks' pride.

The youth tripped and staggered, and walked around now with a gimping stride and a mounting sneer on his face. Boos and low groans spilled from the gathering. I beat him to the ground with my shield and let my weapon swing down a deadly inch from his throat where it should have pierced flesh and let dark blood warm the grass.

While the dark fever was on me, I could feel the green vapors swirling from my nose. It tore at me, itching my fingers to drive steel deep into the boy's flesh and let blood run. But I bit back the fire and raced to jam the axe pommel into one of Regalis's attacker's ribs. His competitor fell with a groan. My feet didn't stop; I charged head first into Marcellus' opponent, knocking him flat. Feberiax's foe was down, felled by a crashing fist during a close locking of steel. Now we were even, four on four, and the rest was just a mop up job. We could take them all down with our eyes closed. Within minutes they were on their knees, grunting for mercy. The crowd muttered and looked at us with a genuine hostility but glowering respect. We'd won, survived another one-sided battle. Lived another day to tell our tale in this world of chill air and grim uncertainty.

The chief lumbered over to assess us, his cold, pale eyes raking us in gruff scrutiny, neither pleased or displeased at our handiwork but not without admiration either. I could tell by his lip-chewing and plucking of beard with his index finger and thumb that it was his way of looking deeper and weighing options. I'd seen him demonstrate this habit on the ship.

He motioned for a bald, thin man with small ears and homely face who looked more like a cleric than a warrior. The chief spoke incomprehensible words aloud to the gathering while the man, a translator, I assumed, listened. He gave a hard slap on the bald man's back and a bitter laugh. The translator turned to us, expressionless, his clipped tongue speaking bastardized Latin, "Winter comes on swift feet, he says. Skürg needs good fighting men—like you—to man the ships. To forage for supplies. You will go with them!—stand alongside our chief, who is Lord of the Boats and Master of the Sea."

I said nothing, absorbing such words spoken in his barbarous accent. I didn't know whether to relish them or cringe. They gave us somewhat better food for our victory, for they were not without honor. Bits of half raw meat, deer, boar mixed with the usual slop of cabbage, turnips. All a nondescript mash served in troughs much as hounds are fed in the Londinium villas.

The translator approached and addressed us again, this short, young northman, scratching a pate balding too early. "New plans, slaves! He says you are to row and fight on the ships two days from now. A collar will be hammered around your neck—a symbol of your slavery—to Skürg."

I nodded, as if nothing could be more natural. "Better than being caged among the swine and muck," I muttered. "How did you learn the Roman tongue?"

He hesitated. "I picked it up from a slave captured from Gallia. That man did not live long."

I drew a grim breath, appreciative of the shortness and cheapness of life in these lands.

The village, we learned, was *Ozprei*, which meant *white eagle* in their barbaric tongue. This coast of rugged splendor did not please me, so ribbed with foggy bays enclosed by stark peaks. Too cold here with its hint of snow, which we rarely saw in Londinium.

Back to our sty they marched us but this time with no roughhousing and with eyes bearing some respect. None came to taunt us. The elders reserved judgment, as evidenced by their long and wary looks.

"What now?" Regalis asked nobody in particular.

"We go to sea. You heard," I said wretchedly. "That's certainly better than wallowing here in the mud."

"You think? Don't be too sure," Septagerix said, his face pinched in doubt. "The sea's a bigger threat than any land I know."

"We all have to die sometime, Septagerix."

Some time later three guards fetched me to the communal grounds before the ever-burning fire and the hated collar was fitted round my neck. They used metal tongs as a vise to close the thick ring about my throat. Not the others though, only me, no doubt for the beastly supernatural powers I'd demonstrated—as a last tribute to Skürg, a piece of property to him. A symbolic gesture. Back into the stinking dung of the sty, they flung me where I seethed with fury.

The old chief sent us no more messages that night. They drank like hounds from kegs long into the night, laughing raucously over their roaring fires, telling tall tales and sharing crude jests while the women cooked and danced and pleased the men in many ways. Occasionally I saw a heated fight break out when one man overstepped his bounds and laid sweaty hands upon another man's woman. But this behavior seemed natural among such rough men.

I pulled at the slave ring about my neck and could only look back in shame at my ruggies.

Chapter 19

As the rising sun crimsoned the swells, a dozen armed men hauled us from our pen and lined us up before *Argiseus* and the serpent boats. Two dozen more clustered around Skürg at the wharf, piling clay jugs of ale into the docked boats, along with salted pork and drinking water while others lashed shields and spears to the rails. Archers tested crude yew bows to the side. Before we boarded our native galley *Argiseus*, the tall blond youth I'd fought earlier stomped toward me. At first he thrust me a challenging look, his sour sweat clogging my nostrils, then he barked some guttural words.

The interpreter stepped forward, his face carved in a scowl. "Sven says that he will fight you again soon. No others of his age have ever bested him." He paused, stroking his chin. "Sven considers it an honorable deed you did, not running him through."

I absorbed the information, shrugging in surprise. "Tell him it was just a game of chance. A play of strength and speed. My object wasn't to kill him."

The man translated and the boy gave a short grunt and babbled more incomprehensible words. With the interpreter's help, I learned he was the son of one of the chief's brothers. Tough taskmasters, hard as nails on their youth, punishing one disobedient boy by thrusting him into the pen to prove himself. I shivered, tugging at the iron collar I wore about my neck like a dog, for it itched and chafed my skin. Ever did escape dog my mind, and being in the ship away from this dungpile, was one step closer to a chance at freedom.

Regalis and I plodded up the gangplank, spears pricked at our backs. Feberiax and Marcellus moved close behind, shouldered by axe-wielding northmen. Skürg slung us in the hold of the galley to row alongside the other slaves—Septagerix, Gerix and others. They put one of their own drummers on an elevated seat. If we thought our Roman whip-masters were bad, these animals were worse. My hide was soon red and sore from lashes of corded knout. So I pulled the oars with all my strength. For hours on end. But the muscles we built—oh, they were thick. Corded layer on layer—until our upper bodies were strong as oxen and we compared ourselves to Hercules on one of his labors. They fed us well, though they kept us in shackles: dried meat every morning, a mash of onions and turnips, building wads of muscles and stamina, keeping us warm, along with our mangy wolf furs in the gathering chill of coming winter, though they gave us no respect. Septagerix did not escape the cruel lashings either.

The old chief had a craftier reason for sparing the *Argiseus*. Our ship could be used as a decoy for fresh raids. Having the appearance of a Roman vessel, *Argiseus* legitimized their bold approaches: to the demise of the unsuspecting crew. And our slave hold flourished as captives replaced our own casualties rather than being tossed into the unforgiving sea.

South we rowed, attacking merchant vessels on the trade routes between Gallia and Londinium and between Gallia and Hispania. We struck mostly before dusk when our appearance became less suspicious. The *Argiseus* instilled confidence in passing ships and lured them to passivity while our own escort vessel, a fast warship, *Ubikrei*, now fortified with iron-tipped ram and a serpent-prow cleverly camouflaged, remained an instrument of terror.

Sometimes Skürg's warship rammed too hard and the merchantman sank along with its precious cargo. This loss generated some unease, but after heavy drinking, loud laughs would break out again among the northmen. If all went well, we'd take our few commandeered ships and booty back to *Ozprei* once we'd filled all three holds with plunder—wine, grain, weaponry, silk, wools. Yet storms kept us at bay, and the sight of a Roman fleet always sent us scurrying. Skürg was not bold or stupid enough to take on these vessels, though the spoils in military arms alone and the seizure of a new ship would be invaluable.

Whenever Skürg was in a good mood, he'd loosen our shackles and shove weapons in our hands. He'd let us join his boarding parties, shoving us up in front. He watched us fight, and he watched me carefully. Ever curious when the beastly green would billow and take over my body and I would slash and hew like no other. He knew in the thick of battle that I would be an asset and fight to the death to defend my hide rather than attack his own men. He was shrewd in that realization, knowing where my loyalties lay.

Marcellus had retreated into a shell and would seldom speak. I wondered what festered in his mind. Had he finally broken down? Feberiax and Regalis seemed resigned to their fate.

Through the thick of it all, I remained ever watchful for any means of escape. None came. Even if it did, to where could we flee? Too risky to appeal for mercy from the defending ship. The crew'd as easily slit our throats as these barbarians. I saw no working solution. Skürg smiled his wolf's smile, knowing we were powerless to defy him. Grinning through his mass of beard and weatherworn jowl, he let his nephew Sven fight in the boarding parties. It blooded the teen more and more. The odd time we fought together, Sven and I felt a kinship—and a rivalry. He envied the beastly power that drove my sword to demonic fury and I envied his status as a free man, fighting for the betterment of his tribe alongside his brethren.

The days passed and so did our grim, bloody pirating continue. From Gallia to the warmer waters of Hispania. My hair had grown long and tangled, a dull blond, matted like one of their savage selves. My face became a beastly mask, mossy with beard that most of us Romans hated. I became more and more feral like those savage northmen we served every day.

After one of my violent episodes and another of our heists, we stood about our amphorae of wine and fresh figs—ringed by the dead of the enemy ship and the green smoke swirling from my nose. The druid Derdimonix was right. This demon, Orcus or Gezilmüür, whatever he called it, used me as a vessel to glut its need for blood and slaughter. To clock up sacrifices and pave the halls of its dark dominion. With each new kill, the foul creature became stronger and more a part of my body. I could feel it, tingling in my veins, some dire creeping sensation. It left me alone mainly, only appearing when blood was to be spilled. But when blood was to flow, it flowed in rivers.

Skürg approached me, more curious than awed, a grim scowl carved across his face. He belted out several words. Only later did his fur-garbed translator, the messenger Osvwarr, translate in his bastardized tongue, "Boy, there's a devil in you. We call it the *Graandul. Werstag* in the old tongue, the ram-headed wolf-demon of old. But this thing inside you is something different, something worse, and more savage still."

His men shied away from me, their lips peeled back in contempt when the fever was upon me, as if I were some thing of filth and omen, a rabid beast ready to bite their heads off if given the chance. I opened my mouth and snarled back at them to heighten their fear, licking my lips and showing my teeth.

Old Skürg laughed. "You have a macabre sense of humor, boy. I like that in a man. From now on your name is *Wulfrin*—the beast of the wilds. Not that prissy *Ikrus*, your Roman playmates call you."

Sven lifted his dripping blade and pointed to me. "How came he by this power, uncle?"

Skürg gave a surly murmur. "That's not a question to be asked or answered."

Feberiax spoke, "He's cursed by a dark priest."

Osvwarr translated and Sven stirred. There came mutters of awe, but Skürg stabbed his axe in the deck planks. "It is as I say. Be still!"

I turned away, averse to any memory of the scourge that infected my blood.

That evening on the swaying decks, the northmen drank and roughhoused, swapped bawdy tales and slowly succumbed to the stupor of the plundered wine. They liked the tart fruity flavor better than their own sour ale.

As we sailed through the night I sat on the deck brooding over the heads of those slain garlanding the rails. The head-collecting was a ritual that Skürg brushed off, claiming that the souls of the dead would protect them from sea beasts and other perils that haunted the cold waters. They were a superstitious folk, these northmen—even more than we Romans. Perhaps a weakness I could capitalize on in the days ahead.

With boot heels outthrust, our ragged furs smeared with gore and our weapons freshly dripping of blood, I brooded more. Long ago in the Londinium arena, I'd become immune to death and carnage, even if it was by my own hand, even if it was Roman blood I spilled.

Skürg tipped his horn of ale to me and gave a grunt. "You're not Roman." His fur-garbed messenger translated for me. "You have the eyes and face of one of us, yet—" he sauntered over and reached a gnarled, dirty hand to touch my face. I could see the caked grit under his scored nails old with blood "—you're of some breed to the south too."

"My mother was Nordic—like you," I muttered.

"Was she now?"

He stared with suspicion at my nose. "Takes more than a priest's curse to cause that green smoke to ooze from your nostrils. That's black magic. You're chosen by the old spirits—the wolf gods. That's why I call you Wulfrin. And I name you one of my sons! Destined to pillage the seas." He gave a hearty roar and piked his axe in the air as raucous cheers broke out from his wolf-brothers.

Sven's face went blank. His eyes grew dark, seeing the pitched enthusiasm my presence had evoked among his kindred.

Picking up on his nephew's dismay, Skürg gave a harsh laugh. "Elkhorn's bane, boy!" he said in a rough voice, clapping him on the back. "Don't look so gloomy. You'd think you'd been asked to lick a sow's udders. There's plenty of honors and praise to go around. Fight well, Sven. Learn much and make me proud." He lifted his axe and they cheered again. Sven's eyes gleamed, basking in the recognition of his fierce uncle.

And so it became apparent why they spared us—the need for able warriors to fight and leap like savages from deck to deck alongside their bearded kin.

Skürg was a natural leader among the lot and there was no equal in his ranks. With those sky-blue eyes of his, he saw right through my ploys, pierced through my innermost desires and brooding thoughts, and that unsettled me most. The thing I hated most about him was that he used my demon power to his own ends. That we raided my father's own cargo—sickened me enough. My flesh crawled with shame, to think of Mexor's imported wine and grapes and figs falling into the greedy clutches of the barbarians as they tore into them like animals, cracking open our amphorae at will one night.

"Enjoy it, sprout," jeered the captain and our chieftain, his eyes mad with conquest and rapine.

Night passed to day and day to night and I grew more sullen and indifferent. To keep me in check during our raids, Skürg would order Regalis or Feberiax below with a knife at their necks and a promise to cut their throats if I betrayed them.

During those moments of lull when I was on deck, axe in hand, Sven would request I spar with him, eager to get the better of me. Perhaps he hoped to redeem some face after his last defeat. He never could. Drace had trained me too well, as had the lanista's and Septagerix's drills and their coaching. I could read Sven's body movements easily. I offered to teach him some of the defenses I knew, even the cheap bunt and chip technique with a shield I acquired from Titus. A growing camaraderie developed between us, as if we were both true 'sons' of Skürg. Some of the older slayers didn't like this and mumbled to Skürg about our mutual, growing bond. But he laughed and told them to mind their own business. "You're a bunch of cackling old hens. Sven's a big boy, a promising warrior. Let him associate with whoever he wants."

So the weeks passed and I picked up a smattering of their language, enough to get by on. I'd always grasped languages readily, Greek, in particular. Regalis could manage a few words here and there, like *udgurk* meaning water and *svasden* for blade. But Marcellus and Feberiax were hopeless. They could make no sense of this odd-sounding tongue and its varieties of inflections and singsong cadenzas. On one of the return trips to the village after a healthy plundering, I was given a barbarian woman, a tall and full-breasted maid, for my enjoyment. A prize for my feats and prowess in battle after the passing of winter. This rankled Marcellus to a great degree. Neither he nor the others were granted such recognition. Another thorn in the side that deepened the rift between us.

Often at night the chief would regale us with stories of the old legends, the fickle gods, the strong gods, the weak ones and the trials of blood and fire. Most famed was Ovvdein, the warrior-god of their people, the sea and sky lord of their kin born from the sticks and stones of mother earth. A god that decided the destiny of men and women and cast fates like the die carved from forgotten heroes' old bones.

Under the flickering torch and the low whine of the sea wind, his voice rose in shifts and starts as an otherworldly whisper, "Let me tell you the tale of Fafadel, the sorceress. Once a sea-nymph of such savage beauty as to tear the heart out of any man. She rode the swells in a large pink conch pulled by two giant white whales. One day she met the sea lord, Kiivrl, on the way to Waestrlys, after finishing his battle with his rival chief, Bael, which was a bloody one on the dark seas.

'Whence came you?' she asked, lifting a starfish-shaped ring on a bejeweled hand to the stark, deserted isles off the nameless coast. 'From those isles of dread?'

Kiivrl answered, a black brow lifted in mirth, 'My homeland, Nrvdvir, witch. Far to the north to see my rival lord Bael slain.'

'And you have done so, Kiivrl. Look, I see the stains on your leather and your axe drips with crimson. I see a ship burning and sinking 'neath the waves.'

'Aye, woman, so it does. And what of it?'

'I seek a man such as you.'

'As who?' he questioned.

'As you.'

'Then consider your search over.' He laughed.

She smiled a feline's smile, the depth of her devious smirk not penetrating Kiivrl's better sense. She took him as lover and husband but was ever suspicious of his many ventures ashore where he could take as many wives as he desired. Her magic lacked potency. It could not help her gain his loyalty.

One day in a jealous rage, she tore out his heart with her silver dagger of seashell and moon dust. But Kiivrl lived still as half a man, for his spirit was strong. Yet Ovvdein, lord of sea and sky, grew much incensed at this injustice for he'd had high plans for Kiivrl in the days ahead and he punished the witch by turning her into a white whale to pull her own conch forever across the seas."

The men laughed and tipped ox-horn of wine to their lips, well-pleased with such crude tales. They were as nothing compared to the Greek legends that Dionos had taught us late into the afternoon on those lazy days, yet I could personally relate to Kiivrl reduced to half a man at a sorcerer's cruel hand.

"A good one, lord," cried one blue-eyed, rat-bearded rogue. "And what are we to learn from such a tale?"

"To never trust a jealous wench, you stupid fool! Especially one too willing."

More laughter erupted. Rude jests followed rough talk and much wine drinking with it. There came tests and games of fortune, such as who could hold their hand over the brazier the longest. Aye, flesh burned and men howled. The winners always had the most ale in their bellies before committing to such insane ordeals. These barbarians were crazy, but then again, what of our own Roman rites? They'd surely laugh at them as much as we did theirs. Skürg encouraged such sport. It kept spirits high among the dog-brothers. Such antics kept up until the first rays of the dawn tinted the swells.

After a while the prospect of escape dimmed in my heart. I accepted my fate as an indentured slayer. I'd only passed from the smooth and oiled hands of Londinium's gladiatorial training school to the bearded brutes who plied the waters of the channel—one whom I was fast becoming.

Chapter 20

Early spring brought chill winds and with it scant cargo over the winter months. I guessed we sailed somewhere off the coast of Gallia now, judging from the pale, drab, windswept beaches and the flat treeline glimpsed occasionally from afar. Skürg, restless of spirit and ever with finger on his axe blade, grumbled an oath, eager for fresh spoils. "Get your sword arm ready, Wulfrin. To shore, you lugs!" he roared through the grate at the slaves. "Row south. South, I say!"

By this time the winter lull had left his sea wolves desperate for plunder.

An island loomed off the port bow. A shadowy hulk about four miles distant with high hill and a jumble of stones and boulders pushed up to chalk bluffs. A patch of green showed at its base. But this was soon obscured as a fine mist drifted in from the east.

As my gaze turned, I could tell from the sight of the twin blobs coming over the western horizon that something was amiss. I think Skürg did too, but he was too hungry to acknowledge such premonitions. He hadn't lost a sea battle yet, nor did he plan on losing one in the near future.

He ordered the convoy of three ships full sail ahead, to engage the unsuspecting prey.

The forms grew. A fat galley loomed out of the mist. Then another. They plied at half sail, their oars retracted. Skürg worked his lips, studying the scene with an enigmatic gaze, the gears working in his mind. What bounty nestled in her hold: furs, wines, exotic foods? Precious metals?

As the ships drew nearer and the glint of thickening spears appeared above the rails, it hit me in an instant that things weren't right. "Pull those oars, you slack dogs!" Skürg yelled down to the grunting slaves. "Turn us about. You're worse than a bunch of boils on my ass."

One of the slaves passed out and the slavemasters unclipped his iron anklet and dragged him up the stairs and threw him into the frigid swells. An auxiliary was shackled to his place. In the Roman fashion, a pair of slave drivers prowled about the aisle, ready to administer lashes should any rower lag or miss a beat which could throw off the ship's rhythm. Unlike their Roman counterparts, these cruel masters would wield killing clubs if he continued to slow.

"Too late to turn," one of Skürg's men rumbled. "Let's smash them while we can."

"Attack speed!" Skürg roared.

As we cut through the waves to ram the freighter, the escort suddenly surged to life, men bursting from the hold and swarming the decks. Her slender bow flashed toward us at improbable speed. Skürg's men bawled oaths; they gripped their weapons, eager to kill. Enemy oars dipped into the water. These men on the nearby ship seemed fresh and strong. I frowned. A liburnian bireme, double decked with oars, bristling with speartips and equipped with a heavy ram was gaining speed, as if welcoming collision to dispatch all our sorry hides.

"Pull in those oars!" thundered Skürg. The oarsmen dragged them in, just as the enemy whistled by us. Some oars were shorn from their fulcrums. I peered down through the grate. One unlucky sod was too slow and the ship's momentum drove the oar into his ribs, shattering bone. The long end of the blade clubbed his bench companions. Panic rippled through the slave deck, as the slave drivers tried to restore order with their falling clubs.

"Argyx, heel the boat to port! Steer us around, by Ovvdein! Roman tricksters are about!" Skürg gesticulated to his warriors. We were committed to a ramming tactic and couldn't reverse in time. Two lines of heavily-armed legionaries ranged the enemy rails, gripping swords, awaiting the centurion's order to board. Behind them a row of archers drew bows.

As the ship wheeled about, I knew with terrible certainty what had befallen us. Hadrian had sent scouts out to scour the channel and rid it of pirates, much like those who had waylaid *Argiseus* months ago. The ruse we'd played had been played on us. Thinking like true tacticians, the Classis Britannica, the provincial fleet, had set out to catch us in the early spring when our guard was down and we were desperate for spoils.

The two galleys encircled us. We rammed the closest one. The first vessel slewed to port, but the soldiers swarmed over the rails like lemmings and pushed us back.

Argiseus, manned only by a skeleton crew, came surging in, seeing we were in trouble.

We fought shoulder to shoulder with Skürg. But arrows flew like stinging wasps and peppered us, taking down the first members of our line. One flew by my ear, buried itself in the ribs of the man beside me. Carthgar, on my other side, fell in a groaning heap, his wound made gruesome by the violent power of the missile at close range. Skürg barked orders. His black beard bristled, flecked with blood, but his sky-blue eyes blazed, fierce with rage. Three warriors hurried from the cargo hold with buckets of pitch and upended them on the grapple-hooked craft at our stern, heedless of the arrows that flew by them. Skürg signaled for flame. A smoking brand flew out over the Roman heads and landed somewhere beyond, catching the edge of the thick black tar at their feet. A brief wall of destructive flame whooshed up, then crackling fire engulfed the foremost figures. Men screamed as their leathers caught and breastplates smoked. Skürg moved like a panther, howling a triumphant curse. Others, heartened by his battle cry, rushed to his side.

At first we strained muscles and hewed, but then seeing these well-disciplined soldiers regroup and hold their position, despite the flames, a wild hope grew in my heart. I turned blade on Skürg's men, slashing wildly. A sadistic relish burned in my heart, bridled for too long. Marcellus recognized the opportunity. He joined in; soon the rest of us, Septagerix , Regalis, Feberiax, turned in glee, envisioning our success.

"We're Romans!" cried Feberiax, waving a grimy hand. Roman ears perked up at the sound of Latin from a barbarian's mouth.

Skürg gave a roar of rage. He heaved through the masses, smiting through soldiers to get at us.

"Ick, behind you!" Marcellus's choked shout came too late as his blade licked out to stop Skürg's slash of axe head. But he overstepped, slipping in blood, or perhaps he was tripped by a body at his feet and Skürg's vicious blade swung and caught him high on the shoulder. I heard a hoarse shriek as Marcellus sagged with a look of horror.

I turned in dismay as Skürg bore down on him. I was not in time to save Marcellus from Skürg's next blow, but I caught the next cruel strike on my battered shield and the next as green smoke poured from my nose like a tidal pool. The face Skürg feared most swirled before him now, the restless demon. *"Wulfrin!"* he gasped. He stepped back, slipped in the blood and guts strewn on the deck, scrabbling back from that old, hated god of his. I surged in chopping and slashing. But by Jupiter's blood, the man's strength was enormous. He turned aside my gruesome blows. The man, protected by gods older than Rome's, saw his wicked blade catching every one of my vicious strokes, even while Marcellus rasped his tortured breaths, and Feberiax cried out in woe and Regalis and Septagerix arched steel in a whirlwind to keep back the multitude of foes, northmen and Roman alike.

I caught a look at Marcellus. The pale whites of his eyes rolled upward, his dark pupils glazed in agony. Blood spilled from gaping wounds to throat and shoulder. My heart was torn in two for this rogue whom I both hated and loved for so long. How the truth hits us in the most improbable of times!

Soldiers were all around us, stabbing, hacking amidst the clash of iron and the screams of the dying. Streamers of fog swirled off the water, a matter of some concern, but it purchased us escape. I could see *Argiseus* was almost alongside us, sliding by like a battering ram as horned-helmed men clambered over her rails to assist us. This was a last chance to save ourselves. I leaped forth, calling to my ruggies. "Jump, now! Board the other ship!"

The *Argiseus* was edging by. Men were shouting and clinging to the rail. She was pulling away.

I took a running leap and flew across that gap of water, sliding onto the deck. My blade flashed, ready to meet the few defenders left. Regalis, Feberiax and Septagerix vaulted after. The Romans raised perplexed shouts, astounded at this bizarre circus act but kept hacking at Skürg's men.

We smashed through *Argiseus's* skeleton crew, her first line of defense, her last six axe wielders.

All sounds dimmed to a droning hum. My mind flashed back to that massive figure of Skürg hewing soldiers with spear and axe on the nearby ship's deck. Were the last of the *Clubs* destined to remain slayers of our own kind? Was there any free will involved?

I could decide now to turn tail and jump in the sea. If I fought, I might live.

All this flowed through my mind as I drew my blood-crusted blade and hacked at human flesh, spraying blood, dismembering bodies. Emptying men of their precious resource of life. Demon fires burned in me—the ancient god invoked by Xetriam all too real. How else could such putrid smoke swirl in such sinister wrath and birth such a hideous wolf-goat head? In these moments, Orcus, the god-fiend, kept me and my ruggies alive and I gave myself over to his violence. How the fiend reveled in the slaughter, growing ever greener, larger and more powerful with each sacrifice.

Feberiax's blade joined mine, as did Regalis's. No less did the blood-drenched axe of Septagerix's. Before long the last six defenders lay in mangled heaps on the dripping deck. We crouched like gnomes, cut and battered, drenched in scarlet guts.

Feberiax's fist tapped soundly on my shoulder. "Up! Up, Ick. Snap out of it."

For a long second, I gaped in silence, my sightless gaze a million miles away. The green smoke had fled back up my nose into its deep tangle in my guts.

I pulled out of my dream. Through the thickening mist I saw flickers of crimson timbers and sails where those doomed ships had been. A louder, fiercer clash of arms echoed across the waters with the thump of arrows, wild yells as steel plunged into men's hides. Blood and destruction reigned high on the dark seas today, echoing in sorrowful unison across the swells.

"Row!" I yelled. I clanked my axe on the grate to the men below. "Row!" We stormed below, slew the slavemasters but forced the drummer to keep up his beat.

We stood as captains of this ship; a horde of white-eyed slave rowers huddled before us.

Regalis shook the blood from his hair. "We're our own masters now, Ick!" I could only vaguely register the truth thick in his throat. Thankfully, the slaves put their backs into it, sensing kinder masters in us than the northmen.

"Seize those oars!" I grunted. "Row for your lives. Your freedom!" Through the wreckage and blood the slaves rowed, like dream-haunted specters from a lost time.

The fog hid our movements. I knew the other boat, Skürg's, lurked out there, a feral threat. As for the Roman vessel? Who was to know? If we could make enough headway from the likes of Skürg's reavers...

The hope died as quickly as it had come. We pulled with savage force at the oars. To put as much distance between our ship and the others became my primary goal. One of them would win, Romans or northmen, and after seeing the greedy pitch fire and the stabbing fury of both enemies, I shuddered to be caught by any of them.

Chapter 21

As the slaves rowed, Regalis watchdogged the drummer with his axe at the ready. Feberiax returned topside, knowing something of navigating boats. He adjusted the sail and set the rudder.

I could not put the image of Marcellus out of my mind. My ruggie had died saving my skin. Why? In those cruel moments of fate I came to understand that a careful accounting is always demanded by the powers that be—of all our actions—be they gods, demigods, demiurges or something far stranger and more terrible still. No one is exempt from the accounting, as Marcellus learned in his final moments. I wondered what sins I'd have to atone for before it was all over.

Cries drifted up from behind me. I cursed and ran down the aisle of the rowers' deck. The hull had sprung a leak. Dark water was gushing from a hole in the starboard and pooled around the slaves' ankles. Septagerix peered over my shoulder with disgust.

"Saturn's testicles! Must have happened when the Romans scraped by her during that pass." He gave a rasping murmur. "We've got an hour, no more, before this ship becomes a tomb."

My heart sank. I saw another shape through the port hole. "There's the island."

"Where?" said Regalis, rushing up behind us, breathless. The smell of fear is a tangible thing and the slaves' sweat oozed out that very same pungent reek. We'd been so twisted around during that skirmish, it was hard to know which direction was which in the thickening mist.

I thought hard. The wind—it blew from the northwest. Almost at the same time, Septagerix gripped my arm. "Row. Row with the wind! The island's toward shore, east of us."

I scrambled topside to alert Feberiax. He worked with speed to adjust the rudder on a heading in line with the gentle swells. Regalis ensured the drummer pounded a steady beat. Thankfully I could see no more crimson fire across the water.

As the ship sank lower, so did my hope. An hour—an overinflated estimate. We had less than an hour; no way to repair that leak. Seawater was surging in faster than ever. The slaves quailed. We were not ship builders; what chance did we have in the open water?

A dim shadow loomed out of the thinning mist. "To starboard," I yelled hoarsely. "There! Adjust course!" I gesticulated at Feberiax.

He saw the vague blur, then pulled hard on the rudder. I hollered down to Regalis. He halted the rowers on the starboard side so that the others could swing us about a full thirty degrees. I'd seen the captain do it many times.

In a maddeningly slow arc the ship turned, slewing across the slate-grey morning swells.

"We're in line. Hold!"

The ship wallowed. I rushed down again and seized the reserve battleaxe off the wall and we hacked at the rowers' shackles. Septagerix smote at others' leg irons with his own axe. The slaves gibbered in panic. Some I'd loosed, others jerked at their chains.

"Row, damn you, row!" I cried. This was exactly what I feared. Panicking rowers and us drowning at sea.

The drummer seized the moment to spring for the stair until Regalis's axe sank deep into his spine. His body floated gruesomely among the gibbering slaves.

Water gurgled up to our knees, soon to our waists. I freed as many as I could before it was too late. Jupiter's wrath! Half naked bodies trampled others in a mad scramble up the stairs to the upper deck. Ducking down in the frigid water, I struck at rusty iron while grasping hands grabbed at my shins in terror, struggling to pull me down. I wrested myself away from those doomed grasps. I couldn't save them all. I felt sick to my stomach, but what else could I do? I paddled my way along to the stair and pulled myself out of that briny tomb. I flashed a last glance back at those drowning men, fingers clawing at the cold water and their shrieking gurgles dying before water slicked over their heads.

The bottom hit. We had ground ashore. The deck tipped at a crazy angle and loud cries erupted from the men on deck. Some jumped overboard to scrabble to shore.

The island's bulk loomed out of the mist, a dim hump of rock and bush. A small stretch of foreshore rose about five hundred yards away. More of the slaves I'd managed to free jumped into the water to wade to safety, a longer distance now at low tide. Feberiax, Regalis and I struggled to lower the spare rowboat, our feet laboring to purchase hold on the slanted deck. The back end of the boat was jammed against the rail between broken, containing supports. It took all our efforts to jar it loose. The ship continued to cant, her timbers creaking, her decks slicked with blood. The rowboat was broad, of solid beech, large enough to hold eight people and selected cargo. We needed to get our weapons to shore. On Septagerix's orders, I threw in what shields and spears I could, still hooked and fastened to the rails.

We rowed ashore with four others, Gerix and his friend Leros among them, pulling in the oars as our craft beached on loose shingle.

Some of the slaves, the original *Argiseus* rowers, rowed the boat back to salvage more weapons from the crippled ship. She listed on a sickening angle, her mast teetering. Her heavy white sail rippled in the breeze like a martyr's flag. Others of the teeth-chattering swimmers detected a distant blot of a ship approaching from the west and took to their heels like frightened goats. They scrambled up the stunted scrub extending to the island's south end.

"Fools! Where are they running to?" Septagerix rasped. "If that's Skürg, we're sunk. This island's not that big."

"Let them go," I said. "Each man must choose his fate and look to his own safety." I hunched, shivering in the wind, my slashed leathers, goose-pimpled skin and reedy hair dripping wet. Every ache, cut and bruise assaulted me at once.

"Stupid jackasses. We have more chance in numbers," grumbled Feberiax.

"With so few weapons to spread around?" muttered Regalis. "They'd be cut down like wheat. As will we, if we don't come up with a plan."

"They could keep using the boat to transport weapons from the ship."

"You're talking about panic-stricken men, and a ship that could roll over at any moment. They're not going to risk—"

"Shut up. We have to think fast," I cried. "The ship's gaining on us every moment. They'll be taking no prisoners."

We scrambled up the shore to higher ground, Feberiax limping and me favoring my throbbing shield arm. The mist had burned off and the pale sunlight shone through a hazy gap in the fleeting grey.

Feberiax grumbled sourly, "What luck, marooned on this slagheap, and in plain view."

Sure enough, the northmen's ship grew larger.

Regalis exhaled, his hand covering his eyes. "There! Over to your right." I turned to see the dark blip coming faster on the water than ever. My heart dipped.

"Hope you haven't lost the urge for fighting?" Septagerix's nostrils flared.

Feberiax gripped his axe with a grim smile. "We live or die here."

I saw no Roman ship closing in on that approaching hulk, so I assumed it must have burned along with the other vessel. A greyness washed over my spirit. Had I set out to become a remorseless pirate, or a ruthless gladiator, or was I a victim of my own actions? Did I ask to be cast out on this wretched sea—cold and grey, slipping on a bloodstained deck amidst sword and blade, fire and ruin, and dying men's cries? Or was all that misfortune a result of growing up in a rough-and-tough environment, born and raised on the heels of my brother who had an affinity to violence? I muttered under my breath, "If we survive, Feb, sure as Hades I don't want to be marooned on this barren piece of rock forever."

What foul gods had favored Skürg, I couldn't know—only that his gods waxed stronger than ours. Yet I still didn't believe in any of them.

We all clasped arms, Septagerix growling a curse. "Let's not look upon death too soon. There's fire in our bellies and strength in our arms yet."

"You'll lead the charge, old man." Feberiax said with a laugh.

"Medusa's snaky tits to that."

"Up there," Regalis grunted. "Let's take to the high ground. It's harder for them to fight us from below."

Septagerix muttered, "It'll be a brief deterrent."

We scrambled up the hill with the eight remaining slaves, Gerix one of them who had equipped himself with full weaponry. Four carried shield and axe; the rest only axes. I tripped along a series of goat paths, cursing as I stumbled. The trail, goat-trampled sod amidst loose rock and a few boulders, proved treacherous terrain. At the summit we stared—before us loomed a plateau of jumbled stone and grass-covered mounds.

Old standing stones teetered in ruin, set in a wide circle like those at Caerdyg. A place of pilgrimage, long abandoned. Only old ghosts wandered about these mysterious ruins. Whatever gods the druids worshiped I hoped they'd cast in their lot with us today on this forsaken isle.

Below, Skürg's men had anchored nearby and looked with glee upon our foundered galley. No mistaking their brazen movements and fur-draped hides. We gathered rocks in a frenzy and whatever other projectiles we could to defend ourselves. The northmen would be upon us before long. When a heaping pile of stones stood before us, I caught a glimpse of the enemy clambering out of the longboat and sloshing ashore in the shallows. From the sight of his black-horned helm, I could spot Skürg among those wolf-skinned slayers. Sven too with his silver-colored one.

I looked among the forlorn druid stones, standing proud in their defiance, survivors of a timeless age. Many such isles, deserted scrubs of rock, windswept by sea, peppered these waters. Nonetheless, a lonely place to die.

The wolf of the north had survived…returning from the grave with his sea dogs to kill.

A score of them loped up the hill as a wolf pack would, haggard, battle-hardy, blood-soaked men with crimson-stained locks under their battered helms. Itchy fingers clutched battleaxes and blades and square shields with spiked edges.

On my signal, we chucked the first stones down on them. Two of them fell clutching their heads.

They formed up into a line, shields locked, so our hurled missiles only clattered off their armor. We'd only managed to brain two so far. Carrion birds, sensing slaughter, had begun to circle, smelling the blood on our ragged cloaks.

Septagerix called for our help. We all put our shoulders into a mid-size boulder and set it rolling down the hillside. Gathering momentum, it tore through their ranks, crushing three more unable to dodge its advance before hurtling toward the water.

Skürg roared an oath. Stabbing his axe in the crusty soil, he spewed a spate of words I had no trouble recognizing, his foul tongue promising death to us all.

In seconds they were upon us in a flash of steel, howling in rage, their armor glinting in the fleeting sunlight. Amid the standing stones we fought, those silent markers of an earlier time. Using the stones as shields, we dodged behind them as necessary and let the enemy dull their blades on them in their savage lust for revenge.

They outnumbered us by four men and that was a significant advantage with axe slayers as fierce as black-hearted Skürg. He sighted me out and came shambling toward me like a bear, his heavy axe lifted.

We fought as we'd never fought before. My crimson blade matched Skürg's fury and the demon smoke swirled from my nostrils. Yet this time with the stark memory of Marcellus's pale corpse back on the dying ship and a patchwork glimpse of our horrible deaths, with heads tacked to the rails of Skürg's serpent-prowed ships.

His blood-grimed face came close to mine on an intimate parry. I could see the seamed ridges of skin edged in a rictus of hate, the spittle dripping from his cracked lips. The feral gleam in the whites of those calculating, sky-blue eyes blazed. We circled each other like animals, our blades locked, then we thrust apart in a vicious heave driven by his massive strength. His eyes remained ever lit in its madman's gleam.

"You puny demon shit. Let's see what you're made of now. I should have killed you long ago." His axe fell like a mortared block on my shield. "Devil boy with the green smoke swirling from his nose. What can it do for you now?"

I said nothing. Conserved my strength. His weakness was excessive vanity and sureness in himself. Let me goad him into a mistake. Up till now I'd never had a chance to jab at him and I had no doubt he was the better axe man. Again we faced off and the thud of axe on shield reverberated like giants' hammer blows, trumping the hollow clash of the other fighters in those close quarters.

"I let you fight at my side!" he sneered "—you betray me, slay my men and steal my ship! I made you part of my clan—then what do you do? You throw it all away!"

"You gave me slavery, Skürg!" I yelled back at him, over the clash of striking axes. "You gave us no choice. Rule by blood, slaughter, the iron fist. You're no father to me. You're a swine and murderer of lowest cast."

"Your father is dead! Everything you know is dead, devil boy. Die now. Haven't you heard? Londinium's been overrun by fire. Charred to a crisp. Half its people dead."

I choked at the news. A lie? I couldn't know if the old sea wolf was bluffing. It'd be a perfect taunt to throw me off guard. His men pressed us in a tighter circle despite our attempt at using the massive weathered stones to protect us. I caught his axe on my shield, shuddered and faltered under the force of it. Beside us Feberiax smashed an axe on an unprotected arm, cutting into bone. A long-haired brute bashed him back with his shield. Stumbling back at the blow, Feberiax turned to parry an axe aimed at his spine while Regalis fought back to back with Septagerix. Gerix and the others hacked and jabbed, dripping blood in a tight-knit huddle.

Skürg rushed at me and sent me reeling back again, raining blows too fast for me to parry. I staggered, fell, saw his axe raised, rolled aside but was too late. Septagerix gave a roar and leaned in to defend, deflecting Skürg's axe a whisper-breath from my ear. The crimson blade would have sheared through iron helm and mutilated my face.

Skürg wheeled in anger, kicked Septagerix back. Fast as a snake, the chief struck the edge of the older man's shield, spiked at its edge into Septagerix's ribs. With a wounded cry, Septagerix hunched, groaning in anguish, lifting a shield grown heavy to parry the axe of another of Skürg's murderers. I watched as Septagerix nearly crumpled, his eyes widening in shock.

Skürg came in at me with such speed and fury that I could barely keep up with his strokes. His axe battered my shield, chipping off chunks and nearly broke my arm as the impact slammed me back. The last stroke had nicked my ribs, shredding leather and biting into my flesh. For a moment, a pulse of white fire burned in my side. The demon fire relit my veins. It kept the shock down, leaving the pain throbbing below a tolerable threshold. I could feel the dream-like haze of death's shroud drawing near.

The demon in me went berserk. Was it a demon? Was it me?

I hewed from far beyond the place that living flesh considered sane. From shoulder to forearm the demon power surged, sending the axe splintering off the end of Skürg's shield to bite deep into his right shoulder. I saw surprise etched in the cold blue eyes, a face gushing with anger and disbelief that a mere boy could have penetrated the defenses of one far more experienced. His face knew fear at that moment when the swirling green mist in the guise of a wolf-goat swarmed before him.

I scrambled to my feet, sick with apprehension at seeing Septagerix and my allies harried by steel from all sides. Without warning, the demon did something unexpected. It wisped out in glee from my inner being, untethered at last from my nostrils, ripping amongst the enemy in its glory, knocking them down and heaving others six feet away. Those in proximity witnessed their eyes and teeth tinted a sinister green, a raw energy surging through their bodies.

The madness of possession was still upon me. While this shadow of death capered about and a sea lord still lived, I knew I could help no one, not even myself. In ultimate desperation I threw myself into Skürg, axe ripping and tearing at his upraised shield. Some of those strokes shredded his wooden guard and bit deep into the leather beyond. The demon, its job done, struggled to escape back into the living reservoir that was me. But I did not want that reeking thing back. I pinched my nostrils with one hand, my lungs near bursting. I held my breath, resisting the demon as it pushed full in my face, nose and mouth. I saw Skürg's grin widen. With his one arm hanging limp from the shoulder, he hunched, gasping for breath where my blade had cut deep.

"You can't escape it, Wulfrin, can you?" Triumph lit his face. He took another rasping breath. In his delirium, he looked at me with ghastly fervor and sputtered, "I know you. You're the war demon in the sky, the one who drives men to madness, to slaughter and rapine. We call you Ovvdein."

In senseless fury the green demon flitted amongst us, looking for someone to inhabit. With the head of a wolf with foot-long fangs and upthrust horns of a goat, it whirled about, knocking men down like pegs, snarling otherworldly growls, howls, beastly sounds. I gasped, unable to hold my breath any longer. I stumbled forward, my dripping blade questing for that hateful, smirking chief. "No, Skürg," I shrieked. "I am Icarus. A man who can fly close to the sun and not get burned. For Marcellus!"

And I sank the blade deep into his chest. He gurgled on his own blood and lay there, his eyes glazing over.

A cry of soul-shattering agony smote the air over my shoulder. One of Skürg's men stabbed his blade right through the green swirls. It pierced the mist but the ethereal wolf fangs encircled his head and ripped it off at the neck and ground it in its teeth. The headless corpse flopped around and crumpled in a twitching heap. The wolf-demon snapped and clawed at both us and the ragged, howling northmen, killing Gerix, tearing him apart from inside out. Every instinct told me we had no chance against that supernatural force of vileness. But its powers began to fade, fangs passed through torsos and limbs, though they remained unscathed. Without a body to contain it, it could not survive.

It came at me again, pushing to get back through my nose. But I shook it off with all my strength and turned and staggered away even while axes rained on my upraised shield. Pinching my nostrils for one last time, my face growing red with the effort of holding my breath, I saw Skürg's grin widen in his final death throes. I sucked in a long, wheezing rasp. I dreaded that demon flying back into my body like a burst of flame, but it didn't.

The demon fled to the nearest vulnerable soul, the sea lord, lying in his pooling blood and squeezed itself through his bloody nostrils. From the chief's lips came a shriek of agony never before heard on this earth. Raising itself from the turf like Vulcan's bronze automaton Talus, his corpse tottered, clutching axe in a dead fist, the twisted face coming alive and gleaming.

His men reared back in stark terror. My ruggies backed away in silent dread. What was it we were seeing? Some ghoul from the grave, animated by something putrid? Or a mass group hallucination, orchestrated by an ancient Druidic magic?

One of Skürg's closest warriors sucked in a horrified breath and roared, "You're not Skürg. Foul spawn of Ovvdein, be gone!" In a violent rage, he flew at it, his axe upraised to lay a felling stroke upon the ghoul that had been his chief. But the animated corpse parried with impossible dexterity, jamming its wedge-headed blade up into that charging man's ribs. Staring into his chief's hollow eyes, the warrior hung off the axe head for a second, then slid to the turf with cold sightless eyes turned on us.

Skürg's remaining warriors fled in superstitious panic down the slope, gibbering like lunatics. We chased them, our blades slashing at their backs, like scythes on wheat. Such was our battle fury. We hewed them down—all save Sven who stood like a puppet in shock, his blade slipping from his nerveless fingers. I fled down the incline with a curse in my throat, yelling at the others to spare him.

The creature that was Skürg staggered down the hill like some stygian horror. His dead legs propelled him by necromancy, bloody axe lifted. I suspected the man's soul had not properly passed the river Styx, nor could it.

Sven at last took hold of his senses and came running after us with the monster dogging his heels.

I rallied what was left of our company, ignoring the ache in my side. We fled to the barbarians' boat as huge vultures swooped down to tear at dead men's brains. We scuttled onto the shingle beach.

Septagerix held his ribs, sweating and wheezing.

"What about the others who fled?" Regalis demanded.

"Cowards. No time," he gasped. "They'll be fodder for Skürg, or whatever's left of him."

The water lapped at the longboat's flanks. We pulled it along the sand and sloshed into the water. Taking to the shallows, we rowed like fiends to Skürg's warship. None ranged the decks. Only Sven and one of the eight slaves had survived. We passed the listing *Argiseus*, and through the gentle waves, bumped aside the galley's hull and scrambled up the rope ladder. Regalis and I helped the struggling Septagerix. They'd left the ship unmanned.

The mist had almost completely lifted, leaving a golden haze blanketing the low swells. Gulls circled and cried into the sea winds, looking for dead fish, crablegs and flotsam washed ashore.

We found the rowers, all two score of them, shackled at their benches, moaning and pleading for release. From the stern we looked back and saw a figure staggering drunkenly down to the shore, garbed in black breastplate, helmless, hair askew, dragging a shield in its useless arm—the monster-demon Skürg, stranded there to walk as an undead on that island. Even possessed with such bewildering sorcery, he stumbled into the water and quickly rose up to his head, before he sank from sight. At first I felt relief that the ghoul would drown himself and that would be the end of him, but then I saw a bedraggled form beach itself on that bleak scrap of shore—and I shuddered to think of the others we'd left behind, or what unfortunate landing party would come to that ill-fated island.

"Row, if you want to live!" I called down to the slaves in the lower deck. "Full reverse!"

Regalis and Feberiax struggled to hoist the anchor. The last surviving slave of our company helped us ready the sail. The white canvas billowed in what little wind blew. The oars tilted down into the water and brought us wheeling around, backing with maddening slowness out of the natural harbor.

Sven stood mute on the midships deck, a tall statue, staring back at the shore.

"What do we do with him?" Feberiax jerked a thumb at him.

"He can row with the others," grunted Regalis. "That or throw him overboard. One less mouth to feed."

Sven spoke some words and I translated, "He said he'll row. As like as not there'll be none of his clan coming to that cursed island."

"Good choice," said Septagerix, rasping a breath.

"You're in a bad way, soldier." I gripped his arm and steadied him.

He gave a grim laugh. "I'll survive—though I won't be as fast on my right side ever again."

Cut and battered, we hunched on deck in the wan sunlight, drenched in blood spatter, nursing our wounds.

"What do you think happened to the blackheart Skürg?" I ventured.

"Who cares?" grunted Feberiax.

"I think he got his reward for sending too many men to Hades." I motioned to Regalis to fetch a pail of seawater for Septagerix while I bent to untie his breastplate and pull up his tunic. I winced. The wound, a dark welt below on the right side looked red and raw. The cut was not deep but oozed pus, and the old man stirred with every touch. While Regalis dabbed the wound clean, I wrapped a strip of leather around it. We cleansed and treated our own wounds, throwing buckets of sea water over our heads to wash away the grime and gore. The grievous wound in my side had dried and knitted over, as if well advanced on the path to healing. The demon's last gift?

"We can sail this ship on our own," I said in defiance. My eyes flashed with challenge, daring any to disagree. "This boat I christen, *Superstes,* like ourselves—survivors." I instinctively clutched the miserable slave ring around my neck, knowing first priority would be to remove the cursed thing.

Our ship's sides were battered, half her rails ripped down and her decks bloodied, but her hull was intact and her holds held rations of meat, amphorae of wine, water, and sacks of grain.

"It'll be a long haul and hard dogging it all the way," said Septagerix.

"Since when has it been otherwise?" I said with a wry smile.

We all broke into hoarse laughs. Partly from camaraderie, partly from realizing we were still alive when we should all have been dead. We set a general course south for Hispania, following the coast of Gallia.

"Too bad Marcy isn't here," sighed Feberiax.

The first pangs of crushing sadness hit me. My lip quivered. I needed to look away. As much as I'd held Marcellus in contempt, we were blood brothers, ruggies joined in a mutual pact from long ago, and now there was one less of us to continue the tradition.

I struggled to shrug it off and many moments passed. We were free— all of us! That illusive pot of gold more sacred than anything else in the world. I reveled in the feeling.

Septagerix slumped in a weary heap, his axe thudding on the bloody planks. "So, what now?"

I shrugged, grinning through my teeth. "I'm sick of this pirate hell."

"Let's dump this boat then and forge our own futures," croaked Regalis.

"Where? Back to Londinium?" snorted Feberiax.

"We're slaves, remember? With a price on our heads."

"I wasn't being serious."

"Even if you were, I'm sick of Londinium," I said. "The corruption, the rain, the soldiers. Plus you heard, it's been burned."

"Could have been a lie," grumbled Septagerix.

"Maybe. But my father, Fortuna, and your families could also be dead. Mexor always talked of exotic lands that he'd seen and explored. I'm thinking we should take to the open road, leave the sea behind."

"Well, what do we have?" said Feberiax. "Skills as fighters. Rome's as best a place as any to make our mark. We sell our swords to the highest bidders. Hades' fires! We could even open our own gladiator school."

"Are you forgetting Hadrian?" I growled. "The man's reach is long. We'd have to assume different identities. I say Macedonia, or Thrace."

"Not a bad idea, Ick. Septagerix, what do you think?" Feberiax fixed him a questioning glance. "You could be lead trainer."

"You've got some adventurous ideas in those heads of yours. What about the rowers?"

"They can join us."

"This school, how—?"

"We sell the ship. The proceeds'll be enough to get us off to a good start."

"And what if we don't have enough denarii to start a school and acquire gladiators?" Regalis complained.

"We steal it—from sleazy scumbags like Pluvius," I said.

"What about Gallia? We could—"

"Forget Gallia," I murmured. "Too close."

I looked to the sky, clearing of its clouds, while a freshening wind caressed my battle-wearied face. I felt the thrill of adventure beckoning as my ruggies looked over the ship, examining it for supplies, contemplating the possibilities and wondering where fate would lead us next. I felt a weight lifted from my shoulders with the beast out of my body, gone for now at least. Whether it would ever return was another question. Hopefully not. There lurked a secret dread that the ghoul would fly back to possess me again.

I turned my eyes out to the open sea, letting its tranquility ease my nerves. The waves danced under golden sparkles. Life was too short to burden myself with hopeless unknowns. Live today, die tomorrow.

The only thing is, things never go to plan.

Historical Note

Roman civilization reached its peak during the mid-second century, around the same time that Londinium was being established as a major merchant city. Emperor Hadrian (117-138) came to Londinium in AD 122 and initiated construction of the 73 mile wall from the River Tyne to Solway Firth in northern England, a significant milestone during *Pax Romana* and which remains the largest construction in Roman history. Eighty years prior, Queen Boudicca had sacked and burned Londinium and put all its citizens to death, shortly after Emperor Claudius's conquest and his setting up Londinium as a port to serve Roman trading interests in the province of Britannia. The cause, allegedly, was Boudicca's resistance to Roman rule after her husband passed away and the Romans plundered Celtic lands, voiding the historic Iceni-Romana pact. Boudicca was whipped and her daughters raped. According to Tacitus, seventy to eighty thousand Romans and Roman sympathizers were slaughtered during this uprising, an unprecedented loss for such a power as Rome.

Although not much is known about British history during this period, there is no doubt that it was a savage era. Many religions and cults proliferated: of Roman gods, pre-Roman gods, Celtic deities and imported deities from Egypt, Mesopotamia and further east.

Most historic fiction focuses on the significant events of Romano-British formation: Caesar's landing in 55 BC, Claudius's conquest in 43 AD, and Boudicca's rebellion in 61 AD. Not so many authors tackle the relatively golden period afterward (100-180AD), if such years could be considered 'golden' in any phase of Rome's history after the Republic. This story was written with this in mind, adding the magical element. I wondered what it would be like for the rebellious half Roman teen, Icarus, to live in those times, what his destiny would be, how the forces of the time would shape his life. Like Boudicca he is disenchanted with status quo, Roman society, the soldiers who had brought about the death of his brother, Drace, and the moneylenders like Pluvius Maxus who almost broke his back and his father's. But in this case, Icarus is a Roman, not a Celt, and his impact and vision is clearly not epic like Boudicca's, though he is as scarred as she and tormented by the time he gets to the arena. Basic primal drives, such as survival of the fittest and live and die by the sword, would have ever been the same. The difference was *Pax Romana*, Augustus Caesar's vision that Rome's central government not expand her borders but focus on good governance. Britannia was notably the exception to this rule. Nonetheless, this general principle was largely successful for Rome, as it did keep peace at the borders, though this later evolved into a propagandistic scheme to portray Rome as a 'protector nation'.

While Pompey dealt with Spartacus and cleared out piracy in the Mediterranean circa 67 BC, no doubt other sea raiders were rising a century or two later when Rome drank deep of the spoils of Gallia and Britannia. Few historical records exist for this period. Vikings didn't come on the scene until 650 years later. However, logic dictates that barbarians from Germania and those farther north in modern day Denmark, Sweden and Norway would use Roman galleys as models to build their own warships to search out plunder and raid the coasts in the names of Odin and Thor—or whatever gods these gods derived from, be they *Ovvdein* or something else. When this actually birthed is anybody's guess. I venture that it started around the time of Icarus's journey at sea, possibly through bouts of minor piracy given the strength of *Classis Britannica* at the time. And this forms a basis for the bulk of the last part of the story.

An ancient Roman god called Orcus guarded the entrance to Hell. Romans likely borrowed Orcus from the Etruscans who depicted him in their tombs as a hairy, bearded god. Orcus had no official standing in the cities; mainly worshiped in rural areas. Long after the fall of the Roman empire, the cult of Orcus continued in medieval times when the other prevalent gods had ceased to be worshipped. As for the cults and priests and magicians that would worship such an entity and perpetuate the mysticism surrounding it, there is no doubt there were many.

Curse tablets were long used in ancient times to lay hexes on enemies.

Tacitus describes such used against Germanicus in AD 19. Similar to the curse texts, voodoo dolls were also used in spells against enemies. Some dolls were wrapped in lead sheets inscribed with the curse victim's name; the dolls themselves could even be made of lead. Other dolls have been discovered made of bronze, clay, wax or terracotta. Ancient finds include voodoo dolls representing the victim bound, either with visible binding or by the positioning of the arms and legs. Often the neck and legs were twisted violently which did not represent an intended injury to the victim, but a distortion to confuse the design, as some fourth century AD Greco-Roman voodoo dolls suggest.

Sacrificial animals were common for the times and used in conjunction with offering blood sacrifice to gods for favors. Musical instruments, possibly flute, pipes, and drum, accompanied the rite and the priest kept his head covered to prevent the sound of ill-omens. If no disturbances occurred, the animal's blood was poured on the altar and its entrails were examined. Normal entrails signified the god's acceptance of the sacrifice, but any abnormalities demanded the sacrifice be repeated. The entrails were frequently used for divination as well.

There is archaeological evidence of a fire striking Londinium sometime in the ten years following the visit of Hadrian, wiping the city out. Whether it occurred shortly after Hadrian's visit is not known. Perhaps such a fire spurred Hadrian's renovations of the city, improving fortifications around the city, and ultimately the amphitheater. Such facts likely we will never know. But it makes a great springboard for historical fiction writers...

ABOUT THE AUTHOR

Chris is a prolific author of fantasy, adventure, and science fiction. His writing spans many genres: heroic fantasy, sword and sorcery and speculative fiction.

Browse Chris's books at:

https://www.innersky.ca/books

www.ingramcontent.com/pod-product-compliance
Lightning Source LLC
Chambersburg PA
CBHW050732180626
46814CB00002B/715